JEW SÜSS

"Undoubtedly one of the most remarkable historical novels of recent years. The centre of its setting is the Duchy of Württemberg in the middle of the eighteenth century; but the vast canvas of the novel gives us an extraordinarily composite and animated picture of the whole of Germany, of the politics of the German States and of the Empire and the Papacy, of the Courts and the life of the common people throughout Central Europe, during the undefined period of Karl Alexander's rule in Swabia. There can be no two opinions of the immense knowledge and learning which have gone to the making of this long novel. The author moves with ease among the complicated political issues of the period; he knows the precise historical circumstances, and he has no need to trouble us with dates and familiar landmarks in the telling of his story. The result is that one reads his book with an unusual confidence in his accuracy and historical insight.

"Impressive as the author's grip of his historical material is, however, what counts to an even greater extent in the reader's enjoyment is the art of the personal narrative. The figure who dominates the story, Josef Süss Oppenheimer, is a magnificent study of character. The slow uprooting and spiritual integration of the man is recorded with unfailing justice and understanding. . . .

"It is difficult to give an adequate idea of the range and beauty, the colour and depth of ' Jew Süss.' Nor is it possible to do justice to its unerring psychology and spiritual illumination. . . . Every portrait is firm and of human vitality. . . . There is an unmistakable quality of greatness in the novel. It has been beautifully translated."—*The Times Literary Supplement*.

"This book is remarkable, full of food for vigorous minds. . . . ' Jew Süss ' is a splendid story, but it is also a complete picture of a complex social organism from top to bottom. It entertains, it enthrals, and simultaneously it teaches; it enlarges the field of knowledge. To the ordinary reader it brings home, far better than any history could do, the realities of the eighteenth century, and enables him—nay, compels him—by partly unconscious comparison with the realities of to-day, to perceive the strange rapidity of the evolution of mankind."—ARNOLD BENNETT in the *Evening Standard*.

JEW SÜSS

by

LION FEUCHTWANGER

Translated by

WILLA AND EDWIN MUIR

TWENTYSIXTH EDITION

LONDON

MARTIN SECKER

MCMXXVI

COPYRIGHT, 1926, BY MARTIN SECKER LTD.
NUMBER FIVE JOHN STREET, ADELPHI

FIRST PUBLISHED IN ENGLAND NOVEMBER 1926
REPRINTED JANUARY 1927
REPRINTED JANUARY 1927
REPRINTED FEBRUARY 1927
REPRINTED FEBRUARY 1927
REPRINTED MARCH 1927
REPRINTED MARCH 1927
REPRINTED APRIL 1927
REPRINTED APRIL 1927
REPRINTED MAY 1927
REPRINTED MAY 1927
REPRINTED JUNE 1927
REPRINTED JUNE 1927
REPRINTED JULY 1927
REPRINTED AUGUST 1927
REPRINTED SEPTEMBER 1927
REPRINTED SEPTEMBER 1927
REPRINTED OCTOBER 1927
REPRINTED OCTOBER 1927
REPRINTED DECEMBER 1927
REPRINTED DECEMBER 1927
REPRINTED JANUARY 1928
REPRINTED JANUARY 1928
REPRINTED FEBRUARY 1928
REPRINTED MARCH 1928
REPRINTED APRIL 1928

CONTENTS

BOOK		PAGE
I	THE PRINCES	3
II	THE PEOPLE	81
III	THE JEWS	163
IV	THE DUKE	247
V	THE OTHERS	349

Book One

THE PRINCES

Book One

THE PRINCES

A network of roads, like veins, was strung over the land inter-lacing, branching, dwindling to nothing. They were neglected, full of stones and holes, torn up, overgrown, bottomless swamp in wet weather, and besides everywhere impeded by toll-gates. In the south, among the mountains, they narrowed into bridle-paths and disappeared. All the blood of the land flowed through these veins. The bumpy roads, gaping with dusty cracks in the sun, heavy with mud in the rain, were the moving life of the land its bread and pulse.

Upon them travelled the regular stage-coaches, open carts without cushions or backs to the seats, jolting clumsily, patched and patched again, and the quicker post-chaises with four seats and five horses, which could do as much as twenty miles a day. There travelled the express couriers of courts and embassies, on good horses with frequent relays, carrying sealed despatches, and the more leisurely messengers of the Thurn and Taxis Post. There travelled journeymen with their knapsacks, honest and dangerous, and students as lean and meek as the others were stout and saucy, and monks with discreet eyes, sweating in their cowls. There travelled the till-carts of the great merchants and the hand-barrows of peddling Jews. There travelled in six mild and some-what shabby coaches the King of Prussia, who had been visiting the Stadtholder, and his retinue. There travelled in an endless toil of men and cattle and coaches the Protestants whom the Prince-Archbishop of Salzburg had driven with insults from his country. There travelled gaily-decked soldiers and polerky-clad devotees, sunk in themselves, and in a magnificent coach with outriders and a large escort the lean and amorous Venetian fema[...]

Book One

THE PRINCES

A NETWORK of roads, like veins, was strung over the land, interlacing, branching, dwindling to nothing. They were neglected, full of stones and holes, torn up, overgrown, bottomless swamp in wet weather, and besides everywhere impeded by toll-gates. In the south, among the mountains, they narrowed into bridle-paths and disappeared. All the blood of the land flowed through these veins. The bumpy roads, gaping with dusty cracks in the sun, heavy with mud in the rain, were the moving life of the land, its breath and pulse.

Upon them travelled the regular stage-coaches, open carts without cushions or backs to the seats, jolting clumsily, patched and patched again, and the quicker post-chaises with four seats and five horses, which could do as much as twenty miles a day. There travelled the express couriers of courts and embassies, on good horses with frequent relays, carrying sealed despatches, and the more leisurely messengers of the Thurn and Taxis Post. There travelled journeymen with their knapsacks, honest and dangerous, and students as lean and meek as the others were stout and saucy, and monks with discreet eyes, sweating in their cowls There travelled the tilt-carts of the great merchants, and the hand-barrows of peddling Jews. There travelled in six solid and somewhat shabby coaches the King of Prussia, who had been visiting the South German courts, and his retinue. There travelled in an endless tail of men and cattle and coaches the Protestants whom the Prince-Archbishop of Salzburg had driven with insults from his country. There travelled gaily-decked actors and soberly-clad devotees, sunk in themselves; and in a magnificent calèche with outriders and a large escort the lean and arrogant Venetian Am-

3

bassador to the Court of Saxony. There travelled in disorder, on laboriously constructed vehicles, Jews deported from a middle-German city of the Empire, making for Frankfurt. There travelled schoolmasters and noblemen, silken harlots and woollen clerks of the Supreme Court. There travelled comfortably with several coaches the plump, sly, and jolly-looking Prince Bishop of Würzburg, and on foot and out-at-elbows a Professor Landshut from the University of Bavaria, who had been dismissed for seditious and heretical opinions. There travelled with the agent of an English shipping company a party of Swabian emigrants, wives, dogs, children and all, who wanted to go to Pennsylvania; and pious, violent and bawling pilgrims from lower Bavaria on the way to Rome; there travelled, with a rapacious, sharp, observant eye on everything, the requisitioners of silver, cattle, and grain for the Viennese War Treasury, and discharged Imperial soldiers from the Turkish wars, and charlatans and alchemists and beggars and young gentlemen with their tutors journeying from Flanders to Venice.

They all swept forwards, backwards, and across, came to a standstill, spurred on, stumbled, trotted easily, cursed the bad roads, laughed bitterly or with good-natured mockery at the slowness of the stage, growled at the worn-out hacks, the ramshackle vehicles. They all poured on, ebbed back, gossiped, prayed, whored, blasphemed, shrank in fear, exulted, and lived.

THE Duke stopped his magnificent carriage, dismounted, and sent his chamberlains, secretary, and retinue on ahead. To the surprised looks of his gentlemen he returned only a snort of impatience. The carriages stood and waited where the road climbed a soft green rise. The chamberlains and the secretary shrank into the inner corners of the coach to escape the fine continuous rain, the chasseurs, servants and bodyguard spoke in low tones to each other, whispered, jested, and burst out laughing.

Duke Eberhard Ludwig, a stout, heavy man of five and fifty with full cheeks and thick lips, lingered behind. He paced moodily, his velvet hat in his hand, so that the fine warm rain bedewed his peruke, and he gave no heed to the puddles which splashed his shining boots and his magnificent long-skirted coat embroidered

4

with silver. He walked slowly, absorbed, often stopping short, snorting with nervous ill-humour through his big fleshy nose.

He had gone to Wildbad to break with the Countess. Had he managed to do it? Not really. He had not said anything. The Countess had met his hints only with veiled glances; she had made no answer. But yet she must have understood; she was so clever, she must, she must have understood what he wanted to do.

It was really a piece of luck that it had gone off without scenes or hysterics. It was nearly thirty years now since he had begun to live with her. How the Duchess had lamented, cried, shrieked aloud, whimpered and intrigued since then to separate him from the woman! What had not his Privy Councillors tried to do, and the Emperor, the prelates and the accursed rabble of Parliament and the Ambassadors of the Electorate of Brunswick and Cassel. For nearly thirty years the woman had been bound up with all that the country and he had experienced. She was himself, she was Württemberg. If one thought of Württemberg one thought "the woman," or, "the harlot," or, "the Countess," or, "the Maintenon of Swabia." Indifferent or full of hate, whatever the interest, every thought about the Duchy was a thought about her.

He alone (and he smiled) could think of the woman by herself, apart from politics and from the Duchy. Only he could think "Christl" without thinking of soldiers, money, privileges, quarrels with Parliament, mortgaged castles and estates, thinking of the woman only, alone, smiling, reaching out her arms to him.

And so it was all over; he would be reconciled again to the Duchess, and the Estates would exult and make him a grand present, and the Emperor would wobble his head with satisfaction, and the uncouth, ill-clad King of Prussia would send him congratulations, and the Courts of Europe would be deprived of the scandal which had given food for gossip to two generations. And then he would have a son by the Duchess, and the country would have a second legitimate heir, and there would be joy on earth and in heaven.

He trumpeted loudly through his nose. A sullen anger surged in him when he thought of the joy with which the Duchy and the whole of Germany would celebrate the woman's fall. He listened and heard the country drawing a breath of relief; he saw the greasy bourgeois canaille of his Parliament grunting in triumph, with gaping mouths and slapping their thighs; he saw the sober, stiffly-starched, correct kinsmen of the Duchess and their thin, sour, supercilious satisfaction. The whole lousy pack would fall on the woman as on a carcass. All his life he had kept her in spite of the rabble; if he let her go now that he was fifty-five the rabble would attribute it to senile weakness. He had issued innumerable edicts to punish every disrespectful word against the Countess; for her he had embroiled himself with the Emperor; he had hounded the bosom friend of his youth, his chief minister, out of the country because of a single insolent remark concerning her; he had wrangled with his Council, his Parliament, with the whole land, about taxes, more and more taxes, about money, money, money for her. He had kept her in the teeth of his people, the Empire, the whole world, for nearly thirty years.

What a storm had swept through the whole of Europe when in the very beginning he had summarily attempted to set up the Countess, beside the Duchess, as a second wife! He was snowed under with imperial appeals, entreaties and threats; the Estates raged like mad dogs; the Duchess's kinsmen from Baden-Durlach went green and blue with wrath and contempt; thunders from the pulpit were launched at him, and he was refused the Sacrament; the whole country was a seething whirlpool. Well and good, he had bowed to the storm, he had dissolved his marriage-contract with the Countess and again made his peace with the Duchess. In so far, certainly, as his personal affections were concerned, and the consequent fulfilment of conjugal rites (he smiled as he remembered the fine phrase with which he had put off the Emperor,—a phrase rounded for him by the Countess's brother), his personal affections, then, and the consequent fulfilment of conjugal rites were a matter between himself and his Maker, in which no compulsion could be exercised by outsiders upon a reigning prince. And then, at the renewed and stern command of the Emperor, he had really sent Christl away out of the country, and accepted in return a large gift of money from his thankful Parliament, and the whole land had rejoiced. But thereupon—he smirked, for that was the best trick he had ever played—

6

through his agents in Vienna he had hunted up a doddering old fool of a count and married him to Christl and made him his Lord High Steward, and so she had come back as the Lord High Steward's lady, to the frenzy of cheated Württemberg, while the Emperor shrugged his shoulders in helpless regret; for who could forbid a reigning prince to have his chief minister's wife at his court? And how Christl had laughed when he spent the money voted him by Parliament in return for the separation in buying her the estates of Höpfigheim and Gomaringen!

The storm had died down now. True, the Countess was still lampooned now and then, but his connection with her had been an accepted fact in German and European politics for nearly thirty years. The Estates grumbled, but they had given their consent to the appropriation of certain lands for the Countess. The Duchess, bleak, sour and resigned, had taken up her residence in Stuttgart Castle, and her kinsmen, the stiffly-starched Margraves, had withdrawn into haughty and resentful silence. Everybody found the situation deplorable, but they had been doing that for thirty years now, and had become accustomed to it, and adapted themselves.

And now, really without any special reason, all connections with the woman were to be severed, dropped, annihilated.

Were they? He had not spoken out. If he chose, the situation was unaltered.

The Duke stood still on the muddy highway, alone and bareheaded in the fine, drizzling rain. He drew off his right gauntlet glove, and slapped it mechanically against his thigh. Or had there been a reason? Was there a reason? The hectoring King of Prussia on his recent visit to Ludwigsburg had made suggestions to him. He really ought to be reconciled to the Duchess; he should give the country and himself a second heir and not trust the stability of his house to the Crown Prince alone; especially as the Catholics were preening themselves on the probable extinction of the Protestant line in Swabia. But that was not it. No, that wasn't it. Let the old Prussian clear off home to his sand and pines, with his dull prosiness and his barren moral discourses where every third sentence was a sermon on death. He, Eberhard Ludwig, although he was fifty-five, was still in his prime, thank God. When he was

7

dead anyone who liked could shoulder the land and its debts, and quarrel with the lousy pack in Parliament. Dismiss Christl for a reason like that! He was not such a fool. He stepped out more quickly, whistling loudly and out-of-tune an air from the latest ballet. What else had the Prussian brought forward? That the Countess was a worse affliction for the Duchy than all the French invasions or the most grievous wars of the Empire. That all the misery, discontent and disorder in Württemberg could be laid at her door. That she bled and squeezed the people mercilessly, and all the sweat of the land ran into her pockets. Well, confound it, he knew that! That was the burden of a hundred lampoons; that was the sauce his Estates served up to him every week. Was it not her fault too when there were droughts or hailstorms? They should be glad, the malcontents, the greedy grumbling grocers, to have their dirty nickels so gorgeously transmuted into pomp and splendour. She needed money, of course she did; she needed it all the time; in the whole Holy Roman Empire there was not as much money as she needed; she coaxed for it, begged for it, whimpered, threatened, raged, sulked and defied him for it; he had often been in the depths of grief and despair when he did not know where to turn for more and more again. But which was better, the mean, shabby housekeeping of the Duchess who never expended a penny too much, or the full blaze of his mistress's splendour in which castles and forests and all the revenues of the Treasury went up like gailycoloured sparks?

No, arguments of that kind would never make him sick of her. And he had sent the Brandenburger home with a fine flea in his ear, and he would have snapped the brute's head off in a still more Swabian fashion if he had only had that thousand or two more soldiers which his Estates would never grant him. No, all that had made no impression on him at all; and though, after all, it was the rough old curmudgeon who had pushed him into breaking with her, he had done it with something else, a much more casual remark to which he himself apparently attached little importance. They had climbed together, the King and he, up to a hill with a view, and as the Brandenburger looked at the soft and undulating landscape, the green enchanted hills with

8

their corn and fruit and wine and forests, he had sighed to himself. "How lovely! How lovely! And to think that an old woman lies over it like a blight and a plague!"

Eberhard Ludwig cared little for that "blight and plague." But, "an old woman." That touched him on the raw. He, Eberhard Ludwig, tied to an old woman? All the curses, threats and abuse of her had flowed off him like water from a duck's back. But, "an old woman?"

The Duke recollected some inveterate rumours about her. Despite his stern edicts the scandal had always started up afresh that she had bewitched him with black magic. He remembered one affair in particular down to the smallest detail. One of the Countess's waiting women, he could still recall even her name, Lampert, it was, had rushed to Urlsperger the Court Chaplain and retailed to him the godless and abominable practices reeking of witchcraft with which the Countess sought to bind the Duke to her. The Court Chaplain had drawn up a statement, signed by the Lampert woman, sealed it and kept it secretly in his desk. The Duke had got wind of it, and Urlsperger was removed from office by a Commission of Enquiry, and the Lampert woman was birched and driven from the country. But the Duke was convinced that not only his people, but the Commission itself believed the infamous and filthy abominations which were sworn to in the statement. It attested that in Geneva the Countess had cut up one of the Duke's shirts into small square pieces, dipped them in a preparation of fine bismuth and brandy, and used them afterwards for her toilette in the most impudent and shameless manner. In Urach she had procured the newly-dropped calf of a black cow and cut off its head with her own hands, and then she treated three black doves in the same way; worse still, she had cut off the genitals of a he-goat, and carried out other abominable and immoral practices, not to be thought of. By these means, it was averred, she had brought him to such a pass that he could not endure his wife, and was unable to live without the Countess herself, since as soon as he was away from her he had palpitation of the heart.

Donkeys that they were, dried-up and bloodless donkeys! Drivelling about black magic—could they not put two and two

9

together and comprehend that any healthy man's blood can be driven into his heart and loins in the most natural manner without the help of sorcery? When he thought of Geneva, how the laughing image of Christl rose before him, as she lay in voluptuous beauty upon the wide bed in the pale-blue room at the Cerf d'Or! God knows, she needed to kill no calves or doves then in order to fire his blood. But now? An old woman? At any rate, he had not lost the use of his hands and eyes. She had grown somewhat stout, yes, she even suffered from asthma; but was it the exercise of diabolical and abominable sorceries that kept him still bound to her? Her grey eyes in moments of tenderness were still as large and compelling as they were twenty years ago, her chestnut hair had not changed its colour, and all the bells in her voice still rang as on the first day. True, the little scars on her face which used to enrapture him beyond measure—the scandalmongers averred they were the traces of a vile disease—these she now concealed behind paint and powder. An old woman? She had been so melancholy this time, so mournful. She had not laughed at him, she had made no scenes, she had not even asked for money. Did she suspect something? But let her be as meek as a day-old lamb, he was not going to love an old woman. Not he, Eberhard Ludwig. So he could go straight back to his sour Duchess and give the land a second heir and live at peace with God and the Emperor and the Empire and his Parliament.

But still, she had called him "Lux," "Eberhard Lux," and the bells had rung as on the first day. And then she had ridiculed the Estates, who were demanding the expulsion of the Jews from her estates and villages—her Jews, each of whom had more brains in his little finger than all the Estates put together had in their heads. And what fun she had made of the stupid, malicious, boorish petition of the Estates; so brilliant and clever and gay as she was, he had never seen another woman like her, young or old, in the whole of Europe, from Turkey to Paris or from Sweden to Naples. It was a good thing after all that he had said nothing final to her.

He held up his hand, and his carriages drew up in front of him. He gave orders to turn back; he had changed his mind

10

about going to Stuttgart, he did not want to go to Ludwigsburg either. To Nesslach, the small and solitary hunting-lodge. He wanted to be quiet, to have room to breathe. He sent an express to fetch Privy Councillor Schütz; he would talk the whole affair over again with him in peace and quietness.

An old woman?

While he was still on the way to Nesslach he sent out a second messenger. The new Hungarian dancer, a fresh young creature who had appeared in Ludwigsburg a week ago, should come immediately to the hunting lodge. Dash it all, he must wash the taste of the Prussian's visit from his mouth.

ISAAC SIMON LANDAUER, Court Treasurer to the Duchy of Württemberg, had been in Rotterdam arranging credits with the Dutch East India Company in settlement of accounts with the Palatinate. From Rotterdam he was urgently summoned by an express messenger to come to the Countess Würben at Wildbad. On the way thither he had encountered a business colleague, Josef Süss Oppenheimer, Chief Minister of Finance and War for the Palatinate, and also Treasury Agent for the spiritual princes of Cologne. Josef Süss had just completed a succession of interesting and exhausting business deals, and was anxious to recuperate in some spa or other, so he was easily persuaded to accompany Isaac Landauer to Wildbad.

They travelled together in Süss's elegant private carriage. "Costs you at least two hundred rix-dollars a year, this carriage," announced Isaac Landauer, with good-humoured and slightly mocking disapproval. In the dickey sat Süss's valet and secretary, Nicklas Pfäffle, once a notary's assistant, a pale, stout, phlegmatic fellow whom he had encountered in Mannheim when he was working in Advocate Lanz's office, a man who could turn his hand to anything and who had accompanied him since on all his journeys as his personal attendant.

Isaac Landauer wore Jewish dress, with a curl on each temple, a caftan and a straggling goatee of reddish yellow turning to grey. He even wore the Jewish badge, in obedience to a custom introduced a hundred years ago into the duchy, a hunting-horn with the letter S on it, although no magistrate would ever have dreamed of

11

exacting compliance from such a distinguished and powerful man, who was high in favour both with the Duke and the Countess. Isaac Landauer was the cleverest financier in the West of Germany. He had connections extending from the Viennese Oppenheimers, the Emperor's bankers, to the capitalists of Provence, from the rich traders of the Levant to the Jewish financiers in Holland and the Hanseatic cities which financed deep-sea voyages. He leaned back awkwardly and stiffly on the cushions, a dirty insignificant-looking man, and buried his cold and bloodless hands in his caftan. Somewhat sleepy with travelling, his small eyes half closed, he studied his companion with a slight smile, good-natured but a little mocking. Josef Süss, handsome, clean shaven, and fashionable, almost dandified, in his dress, sat upright, and took in with his quick keen restless glance every detail of the landscape which was still veiled by a fine rain.

Isaac Landauer looked his colleague up and down with amicable amusement. The elegantly-cut brown coat, bordered with silver, made of the finest cloth, the powdered peruke with its fastidious formal curls and the delicately-pleated lace ruffles, these alone must have cost forty gulden. He had always had a weakness for this Süss Oppenheimer, whose eager and adventurous spirit flamed so fiercely in his great, restless, round eyes. So this was the younger generation. He, Isaac Landauer, had seen enough and to spare of life, the kennels of the Jews' quarter and the pleasure-houses of the great. Confinement, dirt, persecution, arson, death, oppression, utter helplessness—and pomp, spaciousness, despotism, lordliness and beauty. He knew the machinery of diplomacy as only three or four others at most within the Empire knew it, and his eye could examine down to the smallest detail the whole apparatus of war and peace, of the government of men. His countless business interests had given him a keen eye for the connections between things, and he was aware, with a good-humoured and mocking awareness, of the absurd and subtle limitations of the great. He knew that there was only one reality in this world—money. War and peace, life and death, the virtue of women, the Pope's power to bind or to loose, the Estates' enthusiasm for liberty, the purity of the Augsburg Confession, the ships on the sea, the coercive power of princes, the Christianizing

12

of the New World, love, piety, cowardice, wantonness, blasphemy and virtue, they were all derived from money and they would all turn into money, and they could all be expressed in plain figures. He, Isaac Landauer, knew that; he was among those who sat at the source and could divert the stream to bring barrenness or plenty. But he was not so simple as to cry his power aloud; he kept it secret, and an infrequent amused little smile was all that witnessed to his knowledge and his power. And one thing more. Perhaps the rabbis and scholars of the Ghetto were right when they expounded in detail, as if they were realities, God, and the Talmud, and the Garden of Eden, and the Valley of Destruction; for his part he had little time for such theories, and was more inclined to believe certain Frenchmen who dismissed things of that kind with elegant scorn. Nor did he bother much about them in practice: he ate what he liked and worked on the Sabbath as on a week-day. But in his dress and appearance he clung obstinately to the traditions of his race. He wore his caftan as he wore his skin. In it he entered the closets of princes and of the Emperor. That was the other secret and more profound symbol of his power. He disdained gloves and perukes. He was indispensable, and this was his triumph, even in his caftan and his ritual curls.

But now there was this Josef Süss Oppenheimer, the younger generation. There he sat, in proud magnificence, with his buckled shoes and his lace ruffles, and puffed himself up. It was not subtle, this younger generation. It did not understand the refined pleasure of keeping power secret, of possessing it without betraying it, and the still more refined pleasure of relishing its flavour quietly and exclusively by oneself. Knick-knacks and silk stockings, and an elegant travelling carriage with attendants up behind, and the trumpery external signs of possession, these were of more account to it than a jealously-guarded chest containing a bond on the City of Frankfurt or on the Margrave of Baden's Treasury. A generation without fineness, without taste.

And yet he liked Süss. How he sat there, tense in every fibre, eager to cut himself an enormous slice of that cake, the world. He, Isaac Landauer, had given the young man's ship a push out into the open when in spite of all its efforts and its wild tacking it was unable to get away from the shore. Well, now the little ship was sailing bravely in the middle of the stream, and Isaac Landauer observed with quiet curiosity its course and direction.

A post-chaise approached them. A large portly man with a strong, resolute face was inside, and beside him a fat, round, stupid woman. They were perhaps a married couple on the way to a family festivity. While the two carriages were trying to pass each other with much fuss and a noisy cross-fire of greetings, jests and curses from the coachmen, the man set himself to exchange a few friendly words with Süss. But when he saw Isaac Landauer in his Jewish dress, he drew back ostentatiously and spat forcibly and far. The woman, too, tried to impose a severe and contemptuous expression on her stupid good-humoured face. "Councillor Etterlin from Ravensburg," said Isaac Landauer, who knew everybody, with a little chuckling laugh. "They can't stand Jews, the Ravensburgers. Since they had that infanticide case, and murdered, burned and pillaged their Jews, they have hated us more than all the rest of Swabia. That was three hundred years ago. To-day there are humaner and more complicated ways of stealing money from the Jews. But when such injustice has once been done, of course the victims continue to be hated, even three hundred years later. Well, we'll survive it."

Süss hated the old man at that moment. He hated the filthy side-curls, the greasy caftan, the chuckling laugh. One was compromised by his idiotic, old-fashioned Jewish rig-out. He couldn't understand the man, with his senile follies. He had stacks of money, endless credit, dealings with all the courts and the confidence of all the princes—he, Süss, sat in front of him like a lizard before a crocodile; and the man went about in a dirty gaberdine, inviting people to hoot and spit at him, and was satisfied with amassing wealth which got no further than his bank account. What was money unless it was transformed into prestige, magnificence, houses, horses, gorgeous clothes and women? Did the old man have no desire to spit upon others, as he was spat upon, to go on still further? Why did one seize power, if not to display it? The Ravensburg ritual murder case! That was the kind of trash he brooded on! Long forgotten, out of date, buried. The modern world, thank God, was better, more polished, more civilized. A Jew to-day, if he only set about it in a politic manner, could sit

14

down to table with great noblemen. Was not his grand-uncle, the Viennese Oppenheimer, in a position to boast in the Emperor's presence that the victory of the Imperial arms against the Turks was in great part due to this Jew's assistance? And the Imperial War Office and Field-Marshal Prince Eugene had acknowledged the truth of this statement with the best grace, and had formally delivered their thanks under seal. One only needed not to stick obstinately to idiotic notions such as running round in a gaberdine and side-curls. Then even Councillor Etterlin of Ravensburg would exchange compliments and be at one's service.

Isaac Landauer still sat in the same uncomfortable, irritating and inelegant position. He easily fathomed Süss's thoughts from his expression, but he held his peace, half shut his keen eyes, and muffled himself up.

Süss really intended to rest and recuperate in Wildbad. He had just completed two risky and strenuous undertakings. The first was the introduction of a stamp-tax into the Palatinate. The Elector had farmed it out to him at a terribly high price. The people had turned against the new tax like surly dogs. All the same, he had not been intimidated; fortified by the seal and hand-writing of the Elector against all abuse, threats, lampoons and riots before his offices, he had not bated one jot from his bond; and that had paid him, too, for he had sold the contract again at a profit of twelve thousand gulden. And he had allowed himself no rest even then; no, his twelve thousand gulden must multiply themselves immediately. With his mind made up, coolly and quickly—they had only allowed him two days to think it over—he had plunged into the minting agreement with Hesse-Darmstadt. A risky business. His brother, the Baron, who had turned Christian, although he lived in Darmstadt and knew all the ins and outs of the affair, had not dared to take it up; even Isaac Landauer had shaken his head and stopped smiling. The exchequers of Baden-Durlach, Ansbach, Waldeck, Fulda, Hechingen, and Mont-fort were his bitter rivals and coined all they could. To coin still baser money a man would need extraordinarily cold blood and a front of iron, even to desperation. Süss had them. And here too he knew when to let go with profit in the nick of time. His suc-cessor could be involved in the thousand and one complications

15

now arising. He himself was covered by a degree of the Landgrave; he had resigned from his service with profit and in high favour. Now he had a magnificent house in Frankfurt, and one in Mannheim, both freehold, and certain interests besides, which no one suspected, in the eastern parts of the Holy Roman Empire. Capital, connections, a handle to his name, and credit. A reputation for a resourceful mind and a lucky hand. Surely to goodness he could now allow himself leisure and enjoy life to the full. He wanted to show the world who the Palatinate's Minister for War and Finance was. The very luxury of his leisure hours would be good for business, and recommend him to great noblemen.

Determined as he was to devote his sojourn in Wildbad to recreation, and false as he thought Isaac Landauer's fundamental principles—his own method of dealing with princes and noblemen by courting their favour was certainly the only right one and more befitting the times—it would be madness all the same not to profit on the journey from this genius of the older generation, this most cunning of all financiers in men and affairs. So he began to ask direct questions about the Countess, her prospects, hopes, difficulties, and her financial credit.

As soon as the conversation turned to business matters Isaac Landauer shook off his heaviness and fixed his clever, alert, searching eyes upon his companion. It was a business maxim of his to stick to the truth whenever possible. It was precisely by his deliberate and disconcerting candour that he had brought off his greatest coups. He knew that Süss was inclined to detest the Countess; her lust for money seemed to him ignoble and vulgar. Why should he not tease his colleague a little by revealing in the strongest light the certainty and the profitable opportunities in her investments? He gave a brief, clear, and business-like outline.

"A clever woman the Countess. A good eye for property. She has made the Duke pay in estates and privileges for every increase of his passion, and if his love died down a little he had to make up for it in cash and jewels when he came again. What was her capital to begin with? A pretty face, an insignificant rank, a scrap of hypothetical virginity. She had not even clothes when she first came to court. And what has she made out of it? She is the Countess of Würben, the Countess of Urach, Her Excel-

16

lency the Lord High Steward's Lady, and wife of the President of the Council. She supervises the ducal Privy Purse. Has an allowance of eighteen thousand gulden. All the lesser heirlooms and jewels of the house. All the honours, emoluments and privileges of an independent princess of the Empire. Cash and bills of exchange in Prague, Venice, Geneva and Hamburg. In her private purse, her secretary Pfau tells me, three hundred thousand gulden. Suppose it is only two hundred thousand, that is not to be sneezed at. The baronetcies of Freudenthal and Boihingen, the villages of Stetten and Höpfigheim, the estates of Wilzheim, Brenz with Oggenhausen and Marschalkenzimmern. A clever woman, a pleasant woman, a woman who knows what's what. She ought to have been a Jewess."

"She is said to be in disgrace," hinted Süss. "She has quarrelled with her brother. It is whispered among the Estates that her own brother has advised the Duke to get rid of her. The King of Prussia too has advised him to do that. She is getting old, peevish, and difficult to manage. And so fat. The Duke has recently lost his taste for so much fat."

"She knows what she's about," returned Isaac Landauer. "She knows that the Bank of England is safer than the sworn love of a rakish Duke. She is insured, she is in a better position than many a reigning prince. Believe me, Reb Josef Süss."

Süss made a wry face. Why did he say "Reb Josef Süss?" Why not "my honourable friend" or "colleague" or something like that? It was difficult to associate with the old man. He compromised one. "If the Duke drops her," he said after a while, "she will not be able to save much from the wreck. In the Duchy she is regarded as a pest and a blight. She has the hate of the whole country to contend with."

"The hate of the country!" said Isaac Landauer, in contemptuous amusement, shaking his head, and running his fingers with a smile through his red, greying goat's beard. And Süss felt that he was right. "Is there anyone who is worth while who hasn't the hate of the country to contend with? Anyone who is different from the others gets the hate of the country. The hate of the country is good for one's credit."

Süss was annoyed by the other's calm, superior tone. "A

17

harlot," he shrugged. "Greedy and vulgar in her manners, and fat and old besides."

"Quite so, Reb Josef Süss," said Isaac Landauer tranquilly. "Harlot! Only a word. A comfort to the virtuous old spinster ladies who are jealous of her. And Queen Esther herself could not have known at first whether she was not going to be Ahasuerus's concubine. I tell you, Reb Josef Süss, the woman is good for five hundred thousand gulden. She is shrewd, she knows what she wants. Has she not admitted Jews into her villages and estates? Not for sentimental reasons, far from it. But she is clever; she has a flair for those who are clever, with whom one can talk and have dealings clearly and profitably. Five hundred thousand! She is good for seven hundred and fifty thousand!"

Meanwhile the carriage drew up before the Star Hotel in Wildbad. The landlord rushed out and doffed his bonnet. But when he saw Isaac Landauer's caftan, he turned on his heel, with an insolent "No Jews wanted here." Still, the pale secretary climbed down from the dickey. "These gentlemen are the Ministers Oppenheimer and Landauer," he said coolly over his shoulder, as he assisted them to descend. And the landlord in a trice was bowing them profoundly to their rooms.

Josef Süss had grown dark with fury at the rudeness of the fellow, but he followed Isaac Landauer in silence. "Well," smiled the latter, "he could not have scraped his foot further back even for a gold-braided Privy Councillor!" And he smiled, and combed his fingers through his lank, greyish, wagging beard.

THE Countess had escorted the Duke to his carriage; and while the bulky man climbed into it ceremoniously she stood with the gracious assurance of a woman accustomed to admiration, made light and friendly remarks, and then smiled and waved to him. Her step and bearing were still light and elastic as she turned and climbed the steps to her blue boudoir. She did not relax until she was there, but then her shoulders sank, her arms and hands hung limp, her mouth fell half open, her face sagged suddenly and alarmingly.

All over, it was all over. She had manœuvred skilfully; he had not dared to speak; but it was clear, it was obvious that he had

18

come with the intention of breaking it off; and even though the final word had stuck in his throat, his embarrassed courtesy spoke plainly, and was a hundred times worse than the occasional sparrings, bursts of rage, or sulky silences of earlier days.

She sat huddled together; she was so tired and worn out; the composed and gracious bearing, with its faint air of melancholy, while her heart was pounding, while she was cursing and foaming with rage inwardly—this composure had been so trying. Now she sat on the broad, low couch stunned and so terribly exhausted that she could not move. The powder and paint cracked on her face; the gay light which she had kindled in her large eyes was quenched; the majestic embroidery of her silken skirt lay in dead folds; and beneath the beautifully-wrought sbernia, set with small rubies—a fashion which she had introduced and which was copied in Versailles itself—beneath the beautifully-wrought sbernia even her exuberant nut-brown hair had lost its careless freshness.

So it was all over. And why? The King of Prussia had been nagging, the dirty hound, with his stale harping on duty and rubbish of that kind. Her brother had been urgent, the intriguer, the malicious, cold-blooded villain. She was of no more use to him; his position at court was firmly enough established; it was cleverer to shake her off than to be involved in her downfall. She was an obstacle, she caused complications in his political dealings with the Emperor. She cost money, much money, which could be more comfortably and plentifully diverted into his own pockets if she were out of the way. Oh, how she could see through him, the calculating scoundrel! Faugh! But she would pay him back. She was still alive and in power. The Duke had not yet spoken; she, she, she was still the ruler of the country. But none of these things could have influenced the Duke. She had weathered much worse storms. She had had the Emperor, the whole Empire, the people, the Estates and the clergy against her, and she had still breathed and stood her ground. Her brother! The King of Prussia! Bah, they counted for nothing. And she saw the real explanation come creeping upon her, slimily insinuating itself among her thoughts, acknowledged and yet unacknowledged; and, like a worm on a pin, she twisted to keep it from leaving the obscurity of her feelings and emerging into consciousness. Her

19

eye sought the looking-glass, and avoided it. Helpless still, she collapsed more completely, the ponderous woman, a flabby mass upon the gorgeous coverlets.

> Upon thy brow is throned
> Minerva proud and mighty,
> Zeus lightens from thine eye
> And in thy hair is Aphrodite.

That had been sung by the court poet, thirty years ago. She needed no looking-glass; she knew the explanation.

She groaned, doubled up, her eyes shut, her hand on her heart. Air, air! Her asthma choked her. When she recovered, she pulled herself together and raged through the house, ordering, countermanding, boxing the waiting-women's ears, screaming and sending off couriers in all directions.

She was still to be reckoned with. They should see that she was still to be reckoned with. He had not spoken. She had fortunately hindered him from that. She had curbed herself. The restraint she had put on herself was superhuman. But she had achieved it. And for the present he had not spoken; aye, and for the present they must still hold back their foul rejoicings, and for the present she was still to be reckoned with, and would show them how.

She had reliable information of the Duke's movements. Eberhard Ludwig was still in Nesslach, in his hunting-box. That was good, very good. She got news daily. Daily her courier rode from Nesslach to Wildbad. She knew his most trivial occupations, what he ate and drank, when he went to bed, to the chase, to table, or for a walk. His sole visitor was the Hungarian· girl, and she came only for half an hour a day. Nobody else was admitted, not even his Councillors. Good, good. He was certainly ashamed of his failure to speak out, and he was determined not to be pressed further. Government documents waiting for his signature were piling up. The difficult negotiations with Baden-Durlach regarding their share of the expense in fortifying Kehl were on the point of being successfully settled, the Margravine's man of business chafed, but the Duke was not accessible. The arrangement, too, with Heilbronn and Esslingen about the regulation of the

Neckar urgently demanded completion; and there was no Duke, no Duke. All good, all good. Instead of attending to business he summoned his Knights of the Order of Hubertus and caroused with them. He never laid aside the badge of that Order, the golden cross with its ruby-red enamel work, its golden eagles and the hunting-horn with the device *Amicitiæ virtutisque fœdus*. The Hungarian dancer was also detained in Nesslach, a silly young thing with a lovely figure. All good, all good. Let him booze with his boon companions, let him whore with the silly creature, but no Councils, no instigators, no intrigues.

Meanwhile she gives herself no rest. Her agents and stewards get sharply-worded instructions to squeeze the last cent out of her farms and estates. She creates twenty new posts in the Civil Service, completely unnecessary, and sets her touts to sell them from day to day, paying the purchase price and securities into her private account. The Ducal Treasury, although it already provides all her wood, wine and fruit, receives an enormous bill for her expenses incurred during the last visits of Eberhard Ludwig. She gnaws at all the revenues of the Duchy, like a starving dog gnawing at a bone, with snarling greed, and sends huge sums of money daily out of the country to her bankers in Geneva, Hamburg and Venice.

And the Duke is still in Nesslach. He has sent to the stables for his three great eight-in-hand carriage teams and is now putting them through all their paces. The Hungarian girl screams, and the Knights of Hubertus applaud in honest admiration.

At last, yearned for with wishes and curses, anxiously awaited, Isaac Landauer came to Wildbad. In his greasy caftan he sat in the Countess's study, surrounded by mirrors and delicate ornaments, lapis lazuli and gold. The Countess was magnificently ensconced opposite him at her writing table, and between them lay enormous piles of documents, deeds and bills. He examined and checked them; the Countess gave him unlimited information; here and there he discovered still existing loopholes, and suggested ways and means of further extortion. The Countess, her too plump neck bare like her flawless arms, listened with attention, brought up objections, and took notes. Finally she demanded an enormous loan on the security of three of her villages.

21

Isaac Landauer looked at her, shook his head, and said reproachfully "Have I deserved this, your Excellency?" "Deserved what?" "That you should take me for an utter fool." She flew into a passion. "What does the man want? What are you driving at? Did you not lend me the money two years ago? Am I less prosperous now?" The Jew answered cautiously: "Why does your Excellency need the money? To send it out of the country. But why to send it out of the country? Only because you fear certain contingencies. But if contingencies are to be feared, your property is no security. Do you want me to lose money by it?" The Countess gazed blankly into vacancy, then at him, and her eyes said that much more than the money was at stake, her eyes told him all her anxieties, hopes and doubts. "You are clever, Jew," she said after a while. "Do you think that I dare to risk"— the words stuck in her throat—"not mortgaging my property?"

He would have liked to reassure her with a friendly word. But she was a shrewd and steadfast woman; she needed, she wanted no reassurance or palliation; it would be positively indecent to hand her out anything like that. He looked her up and down; she was an incredibly open book to him; he saw her strained face, her obese, flabby body, and to her urgently questioning glance he could return no other answer than a silent shrug. At that she broke down completely. She burst into loud and uncontrollable sobs like a little child. Then she began foully to abuse the ministers, her brother, her nephews, and all the others, who were her creatures, who allowed her to fall without moving a finger and even helped to push her down. The filthy canaille! She had raised them to their offices, she had been their ladder. For every penny they owned, for every button on their uniforms they had her to thank. More than that, they had drawn up a formal contract with her—she had the paper there in the drawer—engaging to stand by each other for better or for worse to the utmost of their resources. The scoundrels! Hell and the hangman were too good for them! For even utter rascals, thieves and devils kept faith among themselves.

The Jew quietly watched her in her rage and left her alone to exhaust her frenzy. At last she began to cough. Her face grew red, she blew her nose, wheezed, and finished up by weeping unceas-

22

ingly and quietly to herself. "Oh Jew!" she wailed, "Oh Jew!"
—shaken, broken and abandoned, the big handsome woman, her
paint and powder slaked with tears, her magnificent gown hanging
dead about her.

Isaac Landauer combed his straggling beard with his fingers,
and shook his head. Then he cautiously took her large warm
hand in his, and while he stroked it murmured soothing words.

FROM some unknown source rumours of the Countess's imminent
downfall were sent flying about the country, here, there and in
every corner. Nobody dared to mention them above a whisper,
but there was whispering everywhere. There was a deep and
secret breath of relief. In certain villages bells were already
rung and services of thanksgiving held, no specific reason being
assigned for them; they were offered up "for a merciful deliverance."

For the present, however, there was no further sign of it;
on the contrary the yoke became harder to bear and more grievous.
Elderly civil servants were dismissed from office because new can-
didates offered higher prices for their posts. The general inspec-
torate let loose on communities and private individuals a hail of
writs and summonses which could be settled only by the payment
of enormous fines; all the government departments, even the
Ecclesiastical Commission and the Widows' and Orphans' Funds
were compelled to lend large sums on uncertain security free of
interest to the Countess's Treasury; and the Countess's agents
ruled the roost more haughtily and tyrannically than ever before.
And on the appearance of a stern Ducal edict which renewed and
recapitulated the severest punishments for all slanders against the
Countess, the newly-fledged hopes fluttered lamely to the ground.

The smaller offshoot of Parliament, the Estates, had a sitting
every three days. They were deliberating about the possibility of
lodging a new complaint with the Emperor and the Empire and
about a new petition to the Duke against the recent excesses of
the Countess's people. There was much blustering and wild
denunciation of the Countess; the creature should be whipped with
rods from the country; and Johann Friedrich Bellon, Mayor of
Weinsberg, smote the table as he declared that if it came to that

23

he would take his children with him into the streets and set them to spit in her face, the hussy, the pock-marked disease-ridden baggage. The chamber resounded with noble sentiments: was there in Europe another land with such a heritage of freedom? Only in Württemberg and in England had so much parliamentary security been won. The atmosphere reeked of bourgeois pride, sweat, and democracy. But the resulting conclusions were timidly worded, and since Eberhard Ludwig could not be got at, and the Privy Councillors gave only courteously non-committal replies, these resolutions too fell flat, and in three weeks were yellowing in their pigeon-holes.

The Duchess Johanna Elisabetha, who sat and waited in the deserted castle at Stuttgart, had also heard of the Countess's approaching disgrace. The representatives of the Estates visited her constantly, the Emperor sent her a special courier, the King of Prussia had waited upon her with unusual ceremony. How they laughed in the Countess's circles over this ceremonious visit of the shabby King to the threadbare Duchess! The Duchess listened attentively to all of them, and carefully noted every vacillation of Eberhard Ludwig's, but her hopes were never high, and her disappointment was not profound when the expected change in her fortunes was postponed. She had waited so long. For thirty years she had sat in her bleak castle, stripped by the Duke of everything but the barest household necessities; despondent, neglected, obstinate, and sour, she had sat and waited. True, she was respectfully visited by the foreign ambassadors, but she knew that they found it a wearisome duty, and that she was only so distinguished when they were on bad terms with the Duke and wished to annoy him. Life passed her by for Ludwigsburg, the town which Eberhard Ludwig had built for her rival, while she, the Duchess, sat stubbornly in Stuttgart, ignoring threats and humiliations. Life passed her by and went to Ludwigsburg, whither the Sovereign had transferred his seat, compelling the reluctant government departments, the colleges, the Consistory and the Ecclesiastical Court to follow him. There he had built a magnificent castle for that other, the Mecklenburg woman, his mistress, and had filled it with all the treasures and the state furniture taken from the Stuttgart palace.

24

Johanna Elisabetha could remember the Mecklenburg person—even in her thoughts she would not give the accursed woman her name—from the day of her first appearance. She had loved and honoured her husband; she was proud of her war-hero, her cavalier; and she knew also that she was not pretty enough for him, and did not blame him for amusing himself with her ladies-in-waiting. Even when she bore him a son and a daughter, and learned that their feebleness was the consequence of the Duke's wild life, she was not resentful. When the Mecklenburger came to Court—her brother brought her, the intriguing pander, to make his career for him—she certainly did not see much in the woman; but if Eberhard Ludwig wanted her, she did not grudge her to him; she had shut her eyes already to so much. Besides, the Duke thought nothing of her at first; it was only later when they played together in an amateur performance that his passion was kindled. She could still see the shamelessly naked bosom which the woman had flaunted before him in her frivolous shepherdess costume. And since then not a day had passed on which she did not hate the woman. It was clear that she had seduced the Duke by witchcraft; she had also tried to poison her, the Duchess; for it was the Mecklenburger's poison that had made her feel so ill on that occasion after her chocolate, and it was only a gracious providence which had preserved her from worse and kept her from touching the cakes. Anyone who had eyes could see that the woman was an accursed witch, a poisoner, hand in glove with the devil. Was she not prematurely delivered of a hairy, shrivelled, black-and-blue monster?

But she, the Duchess, had allowed no outrage, mortification, or witchcraft to drive her from her rights. She had long since ceased to feel a full-blooded hate within her; there was only a withered, dusty waiting for the downfall of the other woman. So she sat in the gaunt and empty castle, dejected, bleak and sour, and the news which penetrated to her lost its savour and became insipid and cobweb-grey like herself.

DURING these weeks the Wandering Jew had been seen in the Swabian districts, now in one place, now in another. In Tübingen it was reported by some that he had driven through the town in a

25

private carriage; others would have it that they had seen him on foot on the highway, or in the stage-coach; the gatekeeper at Weinsberg told a tale of a queer stranger who gave a curious name and had an extraordinary appearance; and when he pressed him for identification papers the uncanny visitant pierced him through and through with such a malevolent look that he was completely dazed and had to let him go, and he could still feel the effects of that diabolical look as a shooting pain in all his limbs. The rumours spread everywhere; children were warned to beware the stranger's eye; and Weil, the town where he had been last seen, gave its gatekeeper the strictest instructions.

A little later he appeared in Hall. At the town gate he declared boldly that he was Ahasuerus, the Wandering Jew. The Magistrate was sent for at once, and ordained that for the present he should be allowed into the suburbs. Anxious and curious crowds gathered. He looked like any peddling Jew, with a caftan and side-curls. He spoke freely, in a gurgling voice, often unintelligibly. Before the Crucifix he prostrated himself wailing and beating his breast. For the rest, he sold small-wares, and disposed of many amulets and souvenirs. Finally he was brought before the magistrate and proved to be a swindler, and was flogged.

But those who had seen him pointed out that he was certainly not the right one. The other had had nothing remarkable in his garb: he was clad in a respectable Dutch coat like other people, a little old-fashioned in cut; he looked like a superior official or a comfortable citizen. It was only his face, and his general atmosphere, above all, his eye; in short, one felt immediately that he was the Wandering Jew. This was the story in which the most diverse people concurred, in all corners of the land.

The Countess asked Isaac Landauer what he thought of the rumours. He got round it by saying he was no Leibnitz. He did not like to discuss things of that kind; one could not see clearly into them; he was inclined to believe nothing; but his scepticism had no certainty. Besides, anyone who meddled with these matters was likely to fall into the hands of the police and the Church authorities. The Countess was a firm believer in magic and the occult arts. As a child in Gustrow she had often visited old Johanne, the shepherdess, who was afterwards beaten to death

26

for invoking bad weather. She had often openly watched the old woman preparing her salves and potions, and still oftener had spied on her after being turned out; and in her own heart she was convinced that she owed her rise to power entirely to the fact that after Johanne's death she had privily smeared her body with the blood of a he-goat which was the last thing the old woman had touched. With the alchemists and astrologers who came to the Court at Ludwigsburg she associated gladly, excited by eagerness and dread; and although she posed in society as a philosopher and free-thinker, she distilled in secret, holding her breath with suspense, many a recipe for preserving youth and winning power over men. That the Jews owed to magical practices their incredible success and happy inspirations in financial affairs she was not so stupid as to be unaware. They had inherited their occult arts from Moses and the prophets; and it was because Jesus wanted to betray them to all the nations of the world, and thus to render them valueless, that he had been crucified. And now when Isaac Landauer twisted and turned before her, and left her in the lurch when she had shown him so much confidence, it was a mean-spirited fear of competition on his part and a bitter injustice.

The rumours of the Wandering Jew had confirmed her anew in the project to win the Duke back by magic means, if everything else should fail. She begged Isaac Landauer impetuously to bring her face to face with the Wandering Jew. And if he were not available—he was not to make any excuses, of course he could do it with a little good will—at least let some other cabbalist be procured, one who was authentic and in whom she could believe.

Isaac Landauer shivered a little as he rubbed his pallid hands. Her demands and her impetuosity were embarrassing. Heavens, he was a trustworthy man of business, he could procure whatever he was asked for, money, estates, a title, even a little independent earldom if necessary, exotic spices, negroes, brown slave-women, talking parrots; but where in all the world could he procure the Wandering Jew or a genuine cabbalist who could make an effective appearance? Of course he glanced for a moment at the possibility of bringing a clever swindler to the Countess; but he was unwilling after all to make a fool of this good client, who trusted him so absolutely. He had always been honest. And besides it was too

27

risky. As it was, he was well hated by all classes in the country, and it would give them the greatest pleasure to hale him to judgment, or even, which God forbid, to the stake. He took leave of the Countess with unusual ill-grace, having committed himself reluctantly to a half-promise.

He went straight to Josef Süss Oppenheimer.

The latter had meanwhile made strenuous efforts to be idle, but he had not the knack for that kind of recuperation. He was miserable with nothing to do; he felt himself ill at ease and indisposed if he was not hatching projects, doing business with great men, setting affairs in motion and being involved in their activities.

His temperament had driven him on from childhood and given him no rest. When he was still quite young he had insisted on not being left behind in Frankfurt with his grandfather, the pious and meditative Reb Salomon, leader of the synagogue. His father was the director of a Jewish theatrical company, and he made his parents take him with them on their tours. So when he was only six he had been at the ducal court of Wolfenbüttel and made the acquaintance of grand people. The Duke was partial to his father and still more to his mother, the lovely Michaele Süss, and the Duchess doted on the handsome, passionate, quaint, fascinating little fellow. How different he was from the flaxen stolidity of the other children at the court of Wolfenbüttel! His eager desire to associate with gentlefolk dated from that time. He needed variety; he must have many faces thronging his path; he had a thirst for people, a raging desire to cram more and more faces into his life, and he never forgot any of them. It was a blank day for him on which he did not see at least four new people; he was proud of knowing personally a third of all the German noblemen and half of all the great ladies.

The school at Heidelberg could hardly hold him. Three times in four years he ran away after the players. And when his father died, all the entreaties, tears, threats and curses of his mother could not control him. The handsome, precocious boy, pampered by the whole town, admired as a youthful prodigy in arithmetic and proud of his princely looks, played the maddest pranks. The Jewish neighbors clapped their hands, the Christians laughed in benevolent amusement, and his mother, weeping, wailing and scolding, was

28

torn between pride and indignation. In Tübingen, too, where he was supposed to be studying law, he was not to be detained in the lecture-rooms. Mathematics and languages were child's play to him, and he had at his finger ends the pettifogging details of jurisprudence which cost the professors much theoretical labour to compile. He thought it of more importance to associate with the aristocratic students, and he gladly made himself their butt and lackey for a week if it procured his acceptance as a comrade and a gentleman for an hour. More and more he recognized that this was his vocation, to manage great gentlemen, to be their associate, their parasite. Who understood as he did how to insinuate himself into the caprices and pleasures of princes, how to lie low at the right time, and at the right time to sink the seed of his will into them as an insect sinks its eggs into ripening fruit? And who could so dexterously as he address himself to the ladies, and bend even the most disdainful to his will with sure and gentle hand? It burned in him like a flame; more lands, more people, more women, more elegance, more money, more faces. Movement, action, ferment. He could not bear to stay in Vienna, where his sister was well married and spent money royally, nor in the counting-houses of his cousins the Oppenheimers, the imperial bankers and army contractors, nor in the office of Lanz, the Mannheim advocate, nor in the bureaux of his brother, agent for the Darmstadt Cabinet, who had now become a Christian and was called Baron Tauffenberger. He was driven, he was hounded on. New women, new speculations, new magnificence, new customs. Amsterdam, Paris, Venice, Prague. Life and excitement.

And with it all he was swimming in a shallow backwater and could not get out properly into the full stream. Isaac Landauer helped him to his first serious transactions, the Palatine Stamp Tax and the Darmstadt Minting Contract: and it was only the dexterous courage he showed in undertaking these risky affairs and in dropping them at the right moment which had for the first time given his name its real weight. He would have been quite justified in stretching his arms out at Wildbad and taking his ease.

But this was a gift he did not possess; leisure tormented him; and he contrived hundreds of small amours, projects and transactions, merely for the pleasure of watching his energies at play.

29

Nicklas Pfäffle, his body servant and secretary, whom he had detached from the Mannheim advocate Lanz, a stout, placid, unaggressive, indefatigable, pale man, had to be on the trot the whole day procuring him novelties and unearthing the addresses, occupations and past careers of the other visitors.

Süss looked very young, and he was proud of being commonly taken for about thirty, nearly ten years younger than he really was. He liked to feel women's glances on his back and to have heads turning after him when he rode on the promenade. He tended with a hundred essences the ivory skin he inherited from his mother; he liked to be told that he had a Greek nose; and he made the hairdresser wave his rich dark-brown hair every day, to keep it from being spoilt by his peruke; often, too, he wore it without a peruke, although that was not really fitting for a gentleman of his standing. He took pains to keep his small mouth with its overripe red lips from being contorted by much laughter, and anxiously looked in the mirror to see that he had a smooth and untroubled brow, which he considered the mark of a gentleman. He knew that he was charming; he needed continually fresh proofs of his charm; and a woman whom he had dismissed after one night was dear to him all his life because she had called his quick sparkling dark-brown eyes under their arched brows "fly-away eyes."

The dictates of fashion and of his temperament demanded a succession of new dishes, new wines, new crystal and porcelain for his table, and, in the same way, of new women for his bed. He used them and used them up. His memory, an enormous museum, which kept everything in good preservation, retained faithful reproductions of their faces, bodies, perfumes and attitudes; but none of them moved him further. One solitary woman had touched something more deep in him than his senses, and the year she had spent with him, the year in Holland, was apart and very lonely in his life; but he had sealed up the memory of it, he never spoke of it, his thoughts shyly skirted round this year and its hidden sorrow; only very rarely it opened great eyes upon him and looked at him terrifyingly and bewilderingly.

There was another reason why he had been so easily persuaded to accompany Isaac Landauer; a course of the waters at Wildbad had been for some years a necessary recreation for anyone who wished to pass for a man of the world in the west of Germany. Visitors came here even from France; here the most fashionable carriages were to be seen and the most elegant conversation to be heard; and with the manners of Versailles for a model one could rub off the little corners and roughnesses which were to be found even in the most fashionable German courts. Here was the great world, here one could most clearly perceive slight variations in the prestige of individuals and of whole classes as they ascended or sank; the living model was a hundred times more instructive than the *Mercure galant*. It was the only place in Germany where one could be quite certain which ankle an *à la mode* gallant must advance in selecting the lady of his heart if he wished to be considered up to date.

Süss, since he was engaged in no more important matters, flung himself completely into this life, and paddled around with dexterous strokes among the elegant triflers. Empty and hungry for events, he drained the life of others. He conversed with the landlord, and drew up plans for improving the turnover of the hotel in which he lodged; he slept with the young chambermaid; he ordered new and more elegant faro-tables for the proprietor of the Casino, and earned a hundred gulden for doing so; he was the most popular guest at the Princess of Courland's levée; he disentangled the bathing attendants' love affairs; through the adroitness of Nicklas Pfäffle he procured orange-blossoms from the Ludwigsburg hot-houses for the daughter of the Ambassador from the Netherlands, and when she sat in the bath conversing with her attendant cavaliers he was allowed to sit next to her on its wooden cover which left only her head free, and many declared that he had other privileges as well. He made a profitable deal with a jewel merchant in Amsterdam over the cutting of certain stones; in a quarrel with Count Tratzberg, a brusque and insolent Bavarian gentleman, he came off so well that the Bavarian had to clear out of Wildbad on the next day; he arranged credit for the gardener for the laying out of new grounds by the pump rooms, and made a hundred and ten thaler off the transaction. He was the only one who stood up to the young Lord Suffolk at the gaming table, when all the German gentlemen hung back in dismay, and lost four thousand gulden, with smiling courtesy. He boxed a tradesman's ears

31

who had tried to cheat him of four pennies in the sale of a garter. He waited daily in the antechamber of the Saxon minister—the Saxon Court was trying to arrange a loan—and stood bare-headed and bowing low as the minister passed him without a greeting, his formal nose in the air. He was consumed with envy of Isaac Landauer, who was mocked at by the street arabs, cursed by the people, and despised by Society, but who went into the Countess's house, cast up accounts, transferred lands and money, threw men out of work and loaded them with chains.

In this mood Isaac Landauer found him. He began cautiously to speak of the extraordinary whimsies with which God, praised be His Name, had seen fit to punish the Christians. Then he touched circumspectly on the gossip about the Wandering Jew, and ended with the casual information that the Countess had taken the freakish notion of consulting the Wandering Jew, or any other magus or astrologer, preferably an authentic cabbalist. Then he paused and waited.

Süss had remarked at once that the other wanted something from him. He pulled himself together, and lay low. But when Isaac Landauer brought up the Wandering Jew he was thrown quite out of his reckoning. This raised a question which had nothing to do with business, and could not be translated into figures. It touched on his own hidden secret. Naturally, he too had heard the rumours; but his inborn talent for cutting himself off from anything which could disturb his security had enabled him to glide rapidly and easily over his presentiments and alarms. He must keep clear of that hidden secret. But now, when Landauer raised the topic, the uneasy feeling crept inevitably upon him. He saw Landauer's proposal advancing like a distant wave; he feared it, and wished it were over; and now that Landauer paused he sat in a torment of agonizing suspense.

But the other resumed the subject. Hesitatingly, concealing his eagerness under a matter-of-fact tone, he remarked: "I have been thinking. Reb Süss, perhaps Rabbi Gabriel."

There it was. So this man who sat there before him, slyly and comfortably nodding his head, was aiming with sure deliberation at the thing which he had shaken from him, the presentiment he had refused to acknowledge. He was compelling him to look it in the face.

"I think," probed the other, the enticer, the envied man, "I think, the Wandering Jew of whom they gossip can be nobody but he."

Yes, yes, of course Süss had thought so too when he first heard of these rumours. But that was precisely what he had wanted to cut himself off from, that such a suspicion should become certainty. Rabbi Gabriel, his uncle, the Cabbalist, the uncanny man, shrouded for everybody in a queer and terrifying cloud, the only man about whom he could come to no clear conclusion, the man who simply by his presence took the colour out of his coloured world, took the life out of his realities, made his clear round figures ambiguous and illegible—he should keep to himself, far away. It was assuredly not good to let him be mixed up with business. He would raise the hidden secret. Confusion would arise from it, hesitation, things which evaded all reckoning and calculation. No; no; business was here, and the other thing was there, guarded, far away; and it was good that it should be so, and it should remain so.

"Of course I do not expect you to do it for nothing, Reb Josef Süss," ventured the other further. "I would take you on as my partner in the affairs of the Countess."

Josef Süss had set a-going all the wheels of his calculating machine. He sat in great temptation. He worked quickly and smoothly within him, with terrific energy and precision. With rapid objectivity he weighed all the advantages of such a proposal, polished them up, counted them and examined the result. A connection with the Countess, that was much, that was more than the offer of a large sum of money. A partner in her affairs, he had his way open to the Duke, and from that to Prince Eugene was only a step. He saw a hundred possibilities, dizzy perspectives came within his reach.

But it would not do. One could sacrifice everything in the world for a business deal. Women, happiness, life. But not that. To bring Rabbi Gabriel into business, to stake him, not that. He believed neither in good nor in evil. But that would be to plunge into things where all balance and reckoning would be at an end;

33

that would be to plunge into a whirlpool where courage would be as irrelevant as the power to swim would be unavailing.

He breathed heavily, oppressed; lifted his shoulders with a movement of aversion, and a violent shiver. It seemed to him suddenly that someone was looking over his shoulder, a man with his own face, but shadowy and quite obscure.

"You need not commit him to anything," continued Isaac Landauer circumspectly. "You do not need to make any proposal to him. All that I require, Reb Josef Süss, is that you shall get him to come here to Wildbad. You only need to send out your young man, Pfäffle; he would certainly run him to earth. I would give you a very advantageous share in handling the Countess's affairs."

Süss shook off his stupefaction, and rallied his faculties. The world took an again its wonted colour, outline, clearness and comprehensibility. The shadowy face behind his shoulder disappeared. His scruples were nonsensical. He was no hot-brained foolish boy. On that other occasion, when it was suggested at the Palatine Court that he should be baptized, his hesitatio nto take that step was only natural. True, he did not even yet understand why he had not followed his brother's example and procured by such simple means prestige, position, and a barony. Still, he did not do it then, and he would not do it now, or at any time, for any consideration in the world. But there was nothing much in what this crafty, clever and experienced man was asking him to do now. Nobody demanded that he should use the uncanny Rabbi, that threatening and disconcerting figure, as a pawn. His imagination had run away with him again, and confused his thoughts. All he had to do was to get the old man to come to Wildbad. And in return there was the connection with the Countess, the Duke, and Prince Eugene. He would be a fool not to accept because of a little (he looked for the right word) a little uneasiness.

Hesitatingly, in an unfinished sentence, he said that merely to send for the Rabbi was of course possible. Isaac Landauer immediately followed this up. But now Süss demanded in the Countess's business a share which the other could not possibly grant. Minutely, with keen thrust and parry, they discussed the details. Süss gave away only step by step, fighting fiercely.

34

When they had finally come to an agreement, Süss lived and thought only for these negotiations. Rabbi Gabriel sank into oblivion as soon as the valet was sent away.

NICKLAS PFÄFFLE travelled by post-chaise. This taciturn person attracted no attention. He looked calm, bored and faintly weary, concealing his industry behind the phlegmatic melancholy of his pale and puffy face. Once he had undertaken a duty he stuck to it tenaciously and placidly.

The tracks of the stranger led to and fro in Swabia, apparently purposeless and capricious. They disappeared from sight and then came to light again in Switzerland. The stout pallid man followed them conscientiously in every twist and turn, inevitably and serenely.

It was a curious journey that the stranger took, and very unlike any other. He seldom chose the nearest way, but plunged into by-paths; the more difficult a road, the more he seemed to welcome it. What in the world could a man be looking for in desert tracts of stone and ice which God had smitten with his anger?

The few peasants, hunters, and woodcutters of this region were obtuse and sparing of speech. If the stranger climbed higher than their highest meadows they certainly turned to look at him, but slowly and indifferently like their cattle, and slowly and indifferently they turned away again when he had passed. The stranger wore unremarkable heavy clothes, of a nondescript colour, fairly old-fashioned, which might have been new in Holland twenty years ago. Small, broad and thick-set, stooping slightly, he wandered on steadily with heavy step. Here in the mountains where no other strangers came, it was easy for Nicklas Pfäffle not to lose him. On the other hand, it had been difficult to follow the unobtrusive man in the more thickly populated plains. It was something very queer and difficult to define which had made it possible to trace him in spite of the absence of external evidence. People could not put it into words; it eluded their grasp; and yet it was unique and not to be mistaken; and they always spoke of it in the same frightened whisper. His path was discernible by the impression he left behind him; those who saw him caught their breath;

35

laughter failed in his presence, which made itself felt like an oppressive constriction round the head.

Nicklas Pfäffle, pale, stout and placid, did not inquire the reason. The directions were enough for him.

*　*　*

Three peasant crofts lay quite high with a small wooden chapel beside them. Further up cattle were grazing. Beyond that was nothing but rocks and ice.

The stranger clambered up the ravine. Beneath him ran the mountain stream, small and noisy; one could see clearly where it welled up among glacier ice and boulders. On the other side stone-pines crawled up the hillside, stunted and tough, choked by rocks. Peaks shining white, so that the snow-glare hurt the eye, cut sharp and bizarre notches in the shimmering blue, and shut in the high valley with their rigid circle. The stranger climbed circumspectly, carefully, not very skilfully, but steadily. He crossed torrents, slippery ice, and sliding slopes. At last he stood on a spur facing the enclosing arch of icy walls. Below him a glacier stretched its naked broad creviced tongue, and another opened beside him; everything ended in rubble and desolation; a wild confusion of granite boulders lay in mysterious, rigid, and shattered lines. High over all, sunny and unattainable, glittered mockingly the noble and delicate sweep of the snowy summit.

The stranger crouched and gazed, cupping his large pale cleanshaven face in his hand. Above the small flat nose troubled grey eyes looked out, which were much too big for the short, massive head; they were full of a suffocating and hopeless sadness. The forehead, broad, heavy and not high, pressed upon thick eyebrows. His elbow on his knee, his cheek on his hand, he crouched and gazed.

Was it here, what he sought? One thing flowed into another from the upper world to the lower; every human face must have its correspondence with some part of the earth. He sought a part of the earth which would look at him with a human face but bigger, more legible, more significant, the face of that man in whom he was imprisoned. He sought the stream which united that man, and therefore himself, with his star, the Word, and infinity.

He crouched lower, and declaimed, in an obscure, unpleasantly broken and rumbling voice, half chanting, verses from the secret revelations. Skin, flesh, bones, and blood vessels are a garment, a shell and not the man himself. But the mysteries of the highest wisdom are in the organization of the human body. As in the firmament enclosing the earth there are stars and constellations which interpret deep and hidden mysteries, so there are on the skin of our bodies lines and wrinkles and symbols and signs, and they are the stars and constellations of the body, and they have their mystery, and the wise read and interpret them.

Come and behold! The spirit chisels the countenance, and the wise man recognizes it. When the spirits and souls of the upper world take shape, they have their form and their certain outline, which later mirrors itself in the faces of men.

He fell silent. One should not think. These things cannot be thought of; thought only destroys them. They must be contemplated or left alone. Was this the countenance that he sought? Waste land, ice and boulders, the mocking blue glitter above it, and a small rill trickling out of it with difficulty? Blocks of granite, or icy crevasses, falling into meaningless and gloomy patterns, was this the countenance that he sought?

He sank more profoundly into himself. He annihilated every activity which was remote from what he sought. Three furrows, sharp, deep, short and almost vertical above his nose cleft his forehead; and they formed the sacred letter Shin, the first letter of God's name, Shaddai.

The shadow of a great cloud obscured the glaciers; the peaks in their unending and delicate line of shimmering snow glittered unattainably in light mockery. A vulture floated in the blue haze, circling peacefully above the petrified chaos of this upper valley.

The man crouching on the projecting ledge, a tiny speck in the immense landscape, absorbed its configuration, the rock, the waste land, the creviced ice; the delicate mocking glitter, the cloud, the bird's flight, the gloomy meaningless caprice of the boulders, the hint of human beings lower down and of grazing cattle. He scarcely breathed; he looked, seized and comprehended.

At last, nearly staggering after such tense immobility, he rose up exhausted, smoothing the furrowed symbol from his brow, in deep and composed sorrow. Then he descended to the valley toilsomely, still half disabled.

Below, from the first of the three crofts, there came to meet him a stout pale man, a stranger, who looked enquiringly at him with a placid face, and made as if to speak, a letter in his hand. Rabbi Gabriel interrupted him. "From Josef Süss," he said, as casually as if he had known for a long time about the man and his message, as if he were confirming what he had expected. Nicklas, unastonished by this recognition, bowed. "I am coming," said Rabbi Gabriel.

AFTER ten days of frenzied activity the Countess had relapsed into apathetic waiting. She sat among lapis lazuli and gold, in a state of gloomy enervation, fat, her energetic cheeks sagging, her arms relaxed. Vacantly she let her chamberwoman massage her, deck her with jewels, envelop her in magnificent robes, she who was wont to supervise and control the smallest detail. She sent for Kaspara Becherin one night, who was a reputed witch and seer; but the filthy old woman, overwhelmed with fear in the midst of so much magnificence, only stammered unintelligible nonsense. And the magician, the cabbalist whom Isaac Landauer had promised her, did not come, and did not come.

The couriers from the Nesslach hunting-lodge at first brought always the same news. The Duke hunted, caroused, and slept with the little Hungarian. But then, with a precipitate change, surprising messages overtook each other from one day to the next. Privy Councillor Schütz, courteous and indefatigable, had finally forced his way in to the Duke. On the next day the elegant prelate Weissensee appeared, the cosmopolitan diplomat from the parliamentary Committee of Eleven. The Duke conferred with Schütz for two hours, and on that same afternoon the Hungarian was sent back to Ludwigsburg; and on that very evening Eberhard Ludwig received the prelate Osiander, that obstinate bully, the Duchess's most fanatical adherent.

Once this news came to Wildbad the Countess could not contain herself longer. Osiander with the Duke! Osiander! She

38

raved. When she had demanded to be included in the prayers of the Church Service, the rude pigheaded villain had had the audacity to say that she was already mentioned there in "Deliver us from evil," and his broad smirk had been backed up by the laughter of all Germany. The Duke had not dared to dismiss the most popular man in Württemberg, but he had refused to receive him. And now he was in Nesslach, blustering against her with his coarse and vulgar jests. No, no. Go on waiting? Nonsense. She would suffocate if she held off longer. She had not even the patience to wait for her carriage. Her orders showered in frenzied haste; her steward, secretary, waiting-women and lackeys should follow. She herself with a single groom in attendance flew on horseback to Nesslach, giving herself not even time to eat; she rode like one of Satan's dragoons.

She encountered the Duke amid the halloos of his Knights of Hubertus, showing off his skill in coaching, shouting lustily. Taken helplessly at advantage, among his gentlemen who, suddenly struck dumb, bowed in profound courtesy while secretly grinning, Eberhard Ludwig, red as a lobster, uneasy and embarrassed, snorted through his fleshy nose, led the Countess into the lodge and ordered a bath and refreshments. That woman was the very devil! Such a ride! That Christl! A devil of a woman.

The Countess, still in her riding habit, hot from her exertions, covered with dust, forced him to an explanation. No panicking. Steady. The fumbling, twisting, elusive fluttering uncertain thing there must be pounced on, and grasped firmly again in the hand. Grasp it now when it is taken unawares and cannot escape, when there is nobody to interpose with words, to whisper shrewd, shameless, restraining advice. Be still, ye twitching nerves. O palpitating heart, be still.

She made light remarks, taking little sips of lemonade, and teased him for being so unassuming; Knights of Hubertus and a little dancer—he was easily pleased with his company. Then gentle reproaches. He should not have received Osiander. She understood quite well that he wanted to have some fun out of the old blockhead and his vulgar jests, but it would be misconstrued. Eberhard Ludwig, bulky and embarrassed, could find no loophole of escape from the grey brilliance of her eyes, and wriggled and

39

sweated in his heavy coat, blowing his nose. What a woman! That Christl! What a devil of a ride! Came down simply like a flash before one could tell what was up, illuminating his twilight state of being neither on nor off. Then she asked him directly; all that with the Duchess, reconciliation and so on, that was surely foolish gossip? Or was it not? He cleared his throat noisily; yes, of course, it was only talk. They dined together pleasantly in the evening, and drank wine alone without the Knights of Hubertus. No Schütz, and no Osiander. The Countess filled the room with her spontaneous ringing gaiety, and wrapped the rescued Eberhard Ludwig completely in it. The devil! What a ride! What a woman! A devil of a woman!

The Countess slept dreamlessly all night, deep, happily, and long. When she awoke, the Duke was gone. With the utmost secrecy he had slipped away in the grey dawn. She boxed the ears of the devoted caretaker, shrugging his shoulders and inwardly sneering, and set off madly after the Duke on whipped-up horses. In Ludwigsburg the castle was deserted. No Duke. The Duke had gone to Berlin to return the visit of the King. He was awaiting his usual magnificent escort beyond the frontier.

With contorted face, swishing her riding-whip, she raged through the empty salons between the rows of lackeys flattened against the walls. Finally in the last chamber, at the Duke's desk, between the busts of Augustus and Marcus Aurelius, in front of the picture by the Italian master which represented her in the robes of the Duchess, a man in the wig of a superior official, infinitely courteous, bowing profoundly, smiling sweetly: Schütz. Andreas Heinrich Schütz, her creature, her Schütz, whom she had ennobled and made a Privy Councillor.

The diplomat, his uniform cut carefully in the latest style with only semi-precious stones on his shoes, a fashion from Paris not more than three weeks old, bowed his great hook-nose again and again with the profoundest compliments, scraped his foot out behind him, and assured her in fluent nasal French, full of courteous flourishes, that some god had breathed a hint of Her Excellency's coming to His Serene Highness, but unfortunately His Serene Highness could not wait, and had honoured his most obedient servant with the commission to entertain Her Excellency

40

for lunch and to make a communication to her at table. The Countess, flaming red and panting with rage, snapped him up and ordered him not to be a fool, but to tell her plainly and straightly what was wrong, or else—and she made a gesture with the riding-whip. But the Privy Councillor, with impeccable courtesy, was not to be shaken; he was distressed that in this matter he could not be of service to his noble patroness, but he was bound by strict orders.

At last, when they were at table, he passed on to her with a hundred tags and compliments the Duke's command that she should leave the Residence and retire to her estates. She burst into loud and ringing laughter. "You wag, Schütz!" she cried. "You wag!" laughing helplessly. The old diplomat sat quiet and courteous, with the sharp bright eyes of the climber who watches people going up and down. Secretly he admired her; how natural her laughter sounded, and not at all shrill; how well she played her part!

The Countess stayed on. Ah, she had no intention of quitting Ludwigsburg. She had senseless fits of rage, abused the servants, and smashed the china. Schütz, shrugging his shoulders, for he simply had orders to communicate His Serene Highness's commands to her, with many finely-turned phrases expressed his delight in the pleasure and the honour of her further company, but added that she remained at her own risk and with the certain prospect of being visited by wrath and black disgrace·from on high. They took their meals together. The old double-dyed intriguer, who kept himself in favour under every regime, had genuine sympathy for the Countess and her audacious rise to power; and he was full of professional admiration for the complicated financial sleight-of-hand with which her Jews were quietly spiriting her plundered treasure out of the country. The dry, hardened cavalier would not have believed that he could pay court with such honesty and assiduity to a fat and ageing woman. Their conversation at table was witty, spiced with a hundred pert allusions; and he waited in suspense to see how far she would push her disregard of Eberhard Ludwig's strict command.

The Duke did not stay long in Berlin. Schütz was able to inform the Countess that the Duchess had been requested to go to Teinach Castle. A deputation from Parliament was also summoned thither, as well as the ambassadors from Baden-Durlach,

41

and the Electorate of Brandenburg, and Cassel. The Duke wished to be reconciled to his wife in the presence of his people and of the Empire. Long and quietly the Countess stared at the Privy Councillor, who looked at her earnestly and attentively. Then with a small stifled cry she made as if to rise, and fell unconscious. He exerted himself to help her, and called her women. In the evening he paid her another visit, and inquired what her arrangements were. With quiet hauteur she announced that she was going to her castle of Freudenthal, to her mother, whom she had installed there five years ago. Schütz asked if he could provide her with an escort, for he feared an outburst of popular fury. She declined his offer, her head high and her lips pressed together.

On the next day she departed from Ludwigsburg—in six carriages. The Privy Councillor stood bowing profoundly in the approach to the castle as her horses were being yoked. Behind the curtains of the tall windows peeped the grinning ducal lackeys. The citizens looked on stolidly, without saluting; they did not dare to jeer. But the shrill mockery of the street boys followed her coaches.

She had sent on in advance a whole convoy of waggons with furniture and bric-a-brac. The Castle was bare after her departure. Even the Duke's magnificent inkstand was missing, and the busts of Augustus and Marcus Aurelius stood very nakedly before the splendid picture by the Italian master, which represented the Countess wearing the insignia of the ducal house.

Schütz had smilingly left her to do as she pleased.

Süss had to give up two of the four rooms he occupied in the Star Hotel at Wildbad. Prince Karl Alexander of Württemberg, Imperial Field Marshal and Governor of Belgrade, had arrived earlier than was expected and needed the rooms. The Prince detested the Countess profoundly. He had no prejudices. "An out-and-out harlot," he used to say, "bring her along! But a stingy harlot, that is the most abominable invention of the devil!" And the Countess in his eyes was a stingy harlot. So he wanted to wait for her departure, in order to avoid seeing her. And as she had gone away sooner, he was able to cut short his stay in Würzburg.

The visitors to Wildbad stared curiously at the carriage of the newly-arrived Prince: Karl Alexander, the victor of Peterwardein, Prince Eugene's right hand and the Emperor's Field Marshal high in favour at Vienna. Everywhere in Germany and especially in Swabia hung a picture of him storming the heights of Belgrade at the head of seven hundred halberdiers under a hail of Turkish bullets. An exciting picture. A hero. A great general. Bravo! Hurrah! For the rest, politically insignificant. A princeling from a collateral branch. Quite harmless. A gallant gentleman besides, a pleasant comrade and a fine fellow. The general good-will flew to welcome him; the ladies above all were interested in the war-hero, and the daughter of the Ambassador from the Netherlands threw a sprig of laurel into his carriage.

His array was hardly magnificent. A roomy, solid, and some-what shabby travelling-carriage. The Prince himself certainly very elegant, his open, merry face framed in its beautiful, long, fair hair, since he wore no peruke while travelling, and his tall powerful frame imposing in the rich uniform. But his following was very small. An orderly, a footman, the coachman; that was all. Only one touch of pomp and luxury; in the dickey sat a dark brown, silent, grave figure, a mameluke or something like that, whom the Prince may have captured in some campaign.

Süss and Isaac Landauer were standing in front of the hotel among the gaping and cheering crowd as the Prince drove up. Süss gazed enviously at the gigantic and elegant man. Mille tonnerre! That was indeed a Prince and a great man. The other people drifting about Wildbad did not reach to his shoulder. The dusky servant also made an impression on him. But Isaac Landauer appraised the coach and liveries contemptuously and with good-humoured pity. "A poor devil, the Field Marshal. I tell you, Reb Josef Süss, he is not good for two thousand dollars."

The Prince was in his gayest humour. It was three years since he had been in the west of Germany, and he had been living for some time among the heather and savages under his government in Serbia, laying about him with tongue and sword. So the mature man, now five and forty, breathed the air of his own country with delight.

After the long journey he took a bath, had his lame foot rubbed with embrocation by his orderly, Neuffer (it was a reminder of the battle of Cassano), and sat comfortably at the window in his dressing-gown gossipping with his attendant, while the dusky servant squatted on the floor.

He had been valiantly tossed from pillar to post. From his twelfth year onwards he had been a soldier, and had fought in Germany, in Italy, the Netherlands, Hungary and Serbia. Next to Prince Eugene, whom he heartily honoured, he was the first general of the Empire. He had finished his training as a cavalier in high society at Venice and Vienna, and his stately bearing, his jolly and somewhat boisterous humour, were beloved in drawing-rooms, among boon companions, and on the hunting-field. All that a German princeling from a collateral branch could achieve he had achieved. An intimate friend of Prince Eugene, an actual Privy Councillor, an Imperial Field Marshal, Commander-in-Chief of Belgrade and the Kingdom of Serbia, Commander of two imperial regiments and Knight of the Golden Fleece.

In Belgrade he was surrounded by a perpetual whirl of officers and women. He greatly enjoyed his irregular life. If the cheerful, forceful soldier ever had a care, it came always from the same thing, money. His pay was small, his princely allowance ridiculous. And he could not economize. There he sat as Imperial Governor among bloated Hungarian barons and pashas of the Sultan, who were bursting with all the riches of the Queen of Sheba. He was not exacting, he could live like the meanest soldier, and had eaten filth until his stomach heaved, and had slept on icebound mud. But he could not set his friends down to empty tables, he could not let his women run about in rags, and he could not fill his stables with worn-out hacks.

At the Viennese Court they had only half an ear for such complaints and lamentations. Heavens above, if the Prince didn't like the job there were gentlemen and rich men enough in the Empire who would be glad to have the proud post of Serbian Governor and would jump at paying all its expenses out of their own pockets. The Viennese bankers had helped the Prince out from time to time with small sums of money, but now they were difficult, almost shameless, in their conditions.

He found serious support first in Würzburg with the Prince-

44

Bishop. He had known the thick-set jolly man for a long time, ever since his early years in Venice. There the prince, the present Prince Bishop, and Johann Eusebius, now Lord-Abbot of a monastery in Switzerland, had cemented a good friendship. The three young men, all of them cadets of noble families, were in Venice to study life and politics. The ageing republic, long on the downgrade, still displayed the airs and graces of a Great Power, like a coquette who cannot abdicate her throne, and had ambassadors at all the courts; the Signoria spread a net of intrigues over Europe and the New World, clinging convulsively to the appearance of a great and important political life. The machine functioned all the better precisely because it ran empty, and all the young nobility of Europe studied the routine of high diplomacy in the political circles of the republic.

Both the young priests had a professional admiration for this perfect mechanism, and being trained in Jesuit schools, threw themselves into the study of it with wild enthusiasm. But the Swabian prince stood with a helpless laugh in the middle of the vortex; whatever he grasped eluded him; so he took refuge in the shimmering rustling life of society, in the routs, clubs, theatres, gaming saloons and brothels. The young Jesuits were heartily amused by his naïve soldierly candour, became honestly fond of him as of a large clumsy good-natured dog, and made it a point of honour to steer the simple and amiable fellow unharmed through the wild and hazardous whirlpool of Venetian life. With a subtle smile the young diplomats of the Church wondered at so much noisy harmlessness, so much jolly, confiding, aimless dabbling. So that kind of thing actually existed. Here was a man going round making visits, dancing, playing and making love in diplomatic circles, and all without any ulterior motive; patently he was not thinking at all about a career. And they conceived a frank and slightly supercilious liking for him.

Such was the basis on which was grounded the friendship of the Prince with the two Jesuits. These had now become prelates, they were feared and consulted in all matters of high politics. He, the Prince, sat on the eastern outskirts of the Empire, a brave and renowned general, gently and benevolently smiled at by the gentlemen who decided the destiny of Germany. He was not aware of this smile; he went his way comfortably and directly; and the only thing that vexed him was his lack of money.

In Würzburg, where the Lord Abbot was also a guest, he spoke openly at table with his two friends about his necessities. No money, insolent creditors, it was a perpetual calamity. They had eaten piquantly and drunk themselves hot; the prelates fanned themselves, the Prince unbuttoned his uniform.

The Bishop on principle never gave an answer on the spot. He promised to give the matter his consideration.

The prelates, when the Prince had withdrawn, sat in the park, overlooking the town and vineyards from a shady seat. They would help the Prince, of course; it would be very easy to help him. Perhaps they could help him and at the same time further the good cause? They looked at each other and smiled; they had each the same idea. In Venice, in Vienna, and now in Würzburg they had often shown the Prince Catholic masses, and rejoiced over his naïve enjoyment of pomp and incense. A princeling from a collateral branch, it was no great catch; but still, if one member of the stubbornly Protestant House of Württemberg were to be won over to Rome, the General of the Order would make a note of the success, without over-estimating it. It must not be clumsily done, of course. Artistically, with the finest threads. Everything must happen as if of its own accord. The two experienced gentlemen understood each other with half a word. One would first recommend Karl Alexander to apply to Protestant sources, to his cousin the Duke, perhaps, who was already involved with the Countess, or to the Estates, who were small-minded and greedy; in any case one could arrange matters so that they would definitely refuse. The Prince-Bishop had a gentleman at his court, Privy Councillor Fichtel, who was a specialist in Swabian affairs; and he would certainly be able to manage it. Then when the Prince was left high and dry, naïvely resentful of this evangelical stinginess, one would produce a Catholic princess, perhaps the rich Princess Thurn and Taxis from Regensburg, and the Church would receive the convert with gold and incense and chanting.

Quietly and benevolently, with half-spoken lazy words, the two prelates span the project; from the shady seat in the park, eating ices, they looked down on the lovely town and the sunny vineyards.

46

The Prince-Bishop accordingly helped Karl Alexander with a small sum, and the Prince, in order to get out of his worst difficulties for two or three years, applied to the Württemberg Estates for an increase in his allowance, or at least for a large advance on it. The petition was cleverly and circumstantially drawn up by Privy Councillor Fichtel, so that the Prince thought success was as good as assured.

And so now he sat in Wildbad, with the certain prospect of money, in his gayest humour. An undulating landscape, comfortably wooded, looked in at the windows of his room. He felt himself well refreshed by the bath and the massage of his lame foot; after the dirt and disorder of Serbian and Hungarian villages the place seemed to him doubly neat and clean, and he expected to have a good time. While he sat looking so happily out of the window and being shaved by Neuffer, a footman arrived from the Princess of Courland with a courteous invitation to a fancy dress ball, which she was to give on the next day. Karl Alexander had no fancy dress. Neuffer consulted the landlord, who thought that the Court Steward Josef Süss Oppenheimer would perhaps be able to assist. Oppenheimer? The Prince had no objection to Jews, however wry a face his attendant made. But Oppenheimer was the name of the Viennese bankers who had treated him so badly. Meanwhile, however, the assiduous landlord had already been to Süss, and now he brought a very becoming Hungarian peasant costume, which Neuffer could easily alter so as to fit the Prince. Karl Alexander gave Süss a ducat by the hand of Neuffer, which Süss gave to Neuffer as a tip. The Prince did not know whether to beat the Jew or to laugh. Since he was in a good humour he decided to laugh.

At the dance he was the centre of curiosity and admiration. He floated merrily around, buoyed up by the respect of the men, and the coquettish favours of the women. Then a small procession of couples was marshalled, and a professor from Tübingen, who was also a poet, dressed as a knife-grinder, saluted each couple with spicy verses, the comical freedom of which was hailed with shouts of acclamation. Even the haughty Saxon Minister had mud slung at him, which he took with a sour smile: only young Lord Suffolk, in a magnificent Roman costume, wanted to protest, but he too had to submit. The Prince's partner was his hostess, the Princess of Courland. The poetaster greeted him with more seriousness, hailing him among the applause of the guests as the Alexander of Württemberg, the Swabian Skanderbeg, the German Achilles.

It struck Karl Alexander that all the guests received their couplets except one. This gentleman was young-looking and well set up, and like one or two others wore a half-mask. He did not seem to be astonished at his exclusion from the line of couples passing the rhymester, and took this manifest snub with a good grace, leaning modestly in a window to watch the others. The Prince asked who he was, and was told with a shrug that it was the Jew, Josef Süss Oppenheimer, the Frankfurt Steward.

Ah, that was the fellow who lived in the same hotel and had lent him the handsome costume, the hero of the incident with the ducat. The Prince has drunk well, and is in a good humour. One can surely spare the Jew a friendly word, he is so modest and isolated in his corner. Perhaps too one can pull his leg and have a little fun with him. The Prince advances to Süss with many eyes upon him. "Do you know, Jew, that I very nearly gave you a beating because of your ducat?" Süss takes off his mask at once, bows, smiles, and looks up at the Prince with a kind of ingratiating frankness. "Then I should not have been in bad company. If I am not mistaken the Padishah's Grand Vizier got a beating from Your Highness, and the Marshal of France." The Prince laughs loudly. "You can trim your words as well as if you had learned the art in Versailles!" The Florentine girl beside him pressed forward eagerly. "He has been in Versailles, your Highness." And Süss, boasting demurely, "Yes, I know the Marshal who was beaten. He speaks of your Highness with the greatest respect. I know other friends of your Highness. The noble Prince of Savoy."

"Ah, you are one of the Viennese Oppenheimers?" enquired Karl Alexander, with interest. "Only a third cousin," replied the Jew. "But I do not care for them; they have not the right kind of feeling towards great gentlemen. They think of nothing but their figures." "I like you, Jew," and the Prince clapped him on the shoulder and nodded to him before rejoining the surround-

48

ing circle of guests, the most of whom he overtopped by a head. Karl Alexander drank, danced, and made clumsy compliments to the ladies. Later he sat down at the gaming-table, making loud comments, as was the custom, on every gain or loss. Young Lord Suffolk held the bank, stiff, ceremonious, taciturn and sparing of gesture. The Prince won; all round the table others were losing. At last he was left as the Englishman's sole adversary, hot and somewhat confused in his head. He lost suddenly in a few throws all that he had, and came to himself with a start, laughing somewhat constrainedly, on every side a row of eager spectators. They thought that the Englishman would offer him credit. But the Englishman, courteous and correct, sat silently opposite the heated and embarrassed Prince, waiting. Suddenly, Süss stood almost behind him, ingratiating, adroit, low-voiced. "If His Highness would vouchsafe him the honour." The Prince accepted, and won.

Before he went he told the Jew that Neuffer had orders to admit him to the levées.

Süss bowed, with heaving breast, and kissed the Prince's hand.

ISAAC LANDAUER laboured with Süss at the Countess's business. He appreciated fully and sympathetically her energy, her tenacity in the struggle for the Duke, and he bestirred himself to wind up her affairs as cunningly and skilfully as possible. With a shrewdness which compelled amazed respect from Süss, he knew how to involve the bitterest of the Countess's opponents in her great lending transactions so that it was precisely her enemies who were financially interested in the upkeep of her possessions. But greatly as Süss admired Landauer's genius for business, he none the less restricted their intercourse together as much as possible. He found that the old man compromised him with the Prince. The latter laughed loudly over the gaberdine and the side-curls, and occasionally asked Süss if he should not send Neuffer over one day to comb his friend's wig. Landauer, on the other hand, shook his head, and smiled: "You are usually able to count, Reb Josef Süss. Why are you wasting time and money on a poor devil who is not worth two thousand dollars?"

Süss would have been sore put to it to find an answer. True,

49

in the Prince he saw his ideal of an aristocrat. The poise and assurance with which he met other people, the noisy lordliness of his good humour, the princely grandeur which compensated the scantiness of his means, all that impressed Süss. But that was no reason at all for throwing money away on such an uncertain client. It was something else, something more profound which drew him to the Prince. Süss in general was no gambler. But he was aware that luck was an attribute. The man who did not possess that mysterious knowledge, that gift of knowing instantaneously, infallibly and unshakably that this or the other undertaking, that this cast of the die or that man was lucky, might just as well leave business alone and give up all idea of success in life. And an infallible presentiment bound him to Karl Alexander. The Prince was his ship. The ship might look somewhat dismantled for the time being, somewhat ill-found and uninviting, and clever financiers like Isaac Landauer might turn up their noses at it. But Süss knew that this was his ship, and he trusted himself to this insignificant vessel, unconditionally and completely, with all that he was and all that he had.

Karl Alexander treated him more confidentially than any great man had ever done, only to spurn him with ridicule the more brutal whenever the mood took him. Süss attended the Prince's levée without missing a morning. Once when Neuffer had shown him straight in, a startled girl dived under the blankets. The Field Marshal, while his dusky servant poured pails of water over him, snorted with laughter, protesting that she should not feel shy before a circumcised man; and embarrassed but happy there peeped from the pillows the young chambermaid with whom Süss had also slept.

Süss accepted the Field Marshal's confidences with gratitude, and took no offence at his outbursts. If the Prince had cancelled an invitation to lunch by sending Neuffer to say that he did not want a Hebrew stink in his nostrils that day, Süss turned up in the evening all the same with his usual smiling and obsequious assiduity. No man had ever captivated him like Karl Alexander: he studied his smallest gesture with absorbed attention; his confidences made him happy; his brutality impressed him; whatever the Prince did or permitted served only to bind the Jew more closely to him.

50

Meanwhile Nicklas Pfäffle came back and reported that Rabbi Gabriel was coming.

The Countess was gone, and Süss needed the cabbalist no longer for business purposes; his connection with the Countess and his partnership with Isaac Landauer were established. Süss, happy in the present, had forgotten his motive for summoning the Rabbi, and remembered only that he had given him no other reason for coming but his urgent wish to see him and to speak with him. He felt himself very noble and courageous for daring to meddle with the hidden secret, and had blotted out every recollection of having sent for the disconcerting and uncanny man for very different reasons.

But when Rabbi Gabriel stood before him, his fine and elegantly-poised assurance was suddenly and inexplicably destroyed. He was able to think "He is still as old-fashioned as ever." But he thought that only casually, as it were, and without conviction. That uneasy feeling of depression settled on him which as inevitably as the air one breathed shrouded everything wherever Rabbi Gabriel appeared.

"You sent for me because of the child?" began the rasping, discordant voice. The other wanted to reply passionately, to defend himself; he had prepared several adroit, well-turned phrases; but the infinite and hopeless sadness emanating from those troubled grey eyes tied him up as in a noose. "Or is it not because of the child?" And although the voice sounded weary and toneless, it was cuttingly contemptuous, and Süss with his elegant bearing and fine clothes looked remarkably small and crushed before the thick-set insignificant man, who might have been taken for a superior official or for a respectable citizen.

And yet at other times he could speak with such sureness and conviction. How dexterously his words could spring from his lips, seizing his listener and storming him, insinuating themselves into all his deficiencies and weak points! Why was it that what he now said sounded so flat and unconvincing that he could hardly bring himself to finish his sentence? He admitted that he had promised to take the child. But to do it just then would not be good. Not good for him and not good for the child. He had a thousand things to settle, and he was pushed and driven to and

51

fro. And Rabbi Gabriel could shelter Naemi much better, and even though he, Süss, was interested in culture and in intellectual matters, still that kind of breeding was less important for the girl than the things which his uncle understood better than he did.

He put these arguments together hastily, flimsily, and ineffectually; then relapsed into silence. He saw the troubled grey eyes in front of him, the small nose in the pale massive face, the broad and weighty brow cleft above the nose by three vertical furrows, sharp, deep and short, and he saw that these furrows made the sacred letter Shin, the first letter of God's name, Shaddai.

Rabbi Gabriel did not take the trouble to answer the other's objections. He merely looked at him for some time with his clouded, stony, wise eyes, and was silent.

And during this silence, suddenly and painfully the hidden secret sprang into the light, and that year lay open before him, that strange and incomprehensible part of his life, that year in the little Dutch town which Süss diligently and yet with secret pride hid from himself and from all the world as something disturbing and out of place. He saw again the white inscrutable face of his wife, full of devotion and yet so unspeakably strange, he saw her pathetically relaxed limbs, he saw her dead, as suddenly extinguished as she had been kindled, when the new candle had only just been lit. He saw the child and himself in a state of helplessness that was at once blissful and unendurably oppressive. He saw his uncle, the disconcerting and uncanny man, who had suddenly appeared as if it were the most natural thing in the world, and as naturally vanished again with the child into obscurity, emerging only for a day at a time after intervals of years.

"The child is now fourteen," said Rabbi Gabriel at last. "She is making herself an imaginary father out of my descriptions of you. It is not good that there should be such a discrepancy between her imagination and the reality. I am like Balaam the heathen prophet," continued the cabbalist with a gloomy smile. "I ought to curse when I speak of you and I find myself blessing you. So I will bring her into the country," he concluded, "to see you."

Süss quaked with profound terror. The child! There sat this man in front of him, absolutely indifferent, and said to him simply, "I am going to destroy your life. In the middle of your life so full of pomp and women and varied interests I am going to set your child, your daughter, Naemi. I am going to unhinge your life, I am going to tear your heart from its hinges."

"I shall stay here a while," said the cabbalist, "to study you at close quarters. When, whither and how I shall bring her, I shall let you know later."

When Rabbi Gabriel had gone, the other sat on in rage and confusion. Even as a small boy he had never let himself be so browbeaten and stupefied. But he would tell the old man what he thought, he would be able to find the right words, he would serve him out, the old sorcerer in his shabby old-fashioned coat!

But deep down within himself he knew that the next time he would sit there feeling just as small and stupid as he did then.

BEFORE the Countess in the castle of Freudenthal stood her mother, an enormous mountain of flesh, who could move about only with difficulty. Her peasant face rugged and earthen under her snowy hair, the ancient woman supervised the castle and the estate with hard rapacious eyes, scraping money together slowly, greedily, and insatiably. With the abandonment of frenzy the Countess wailed: "All over, Mother, it's all over! Cast off. Expelled from the Court. He is kissing the withered old goose in Stuttgart with all the world looking on. He is going to give her a child. Cast off. After thirty years cast off like a harlot who is worthless for his bed!" "Squeeze him dry, my daughter," cried the old woman in a deep hoarse wheezing voice. "Make him bleed. If it cost him money when he was hot, let it cost him more now that he is cold. Squeeze him dry! Wring him out till there is not a penny left."

"And Friedrich advised him to do it!" raged the Countess. Friedrich Wilhelm was her brother. "Give it to him, Mother! Let him see! Bring him low! Strike him!" "I will have him come here, I will listen to him, and I will show him," promised the old woman. "But that is not important," she concluded, and sat there billowing with fat, colossal as an Oriental idol, her earth-coloured face distended beneath her snowy hair. "You have sent waggon-loads of things here. That is good, daughter. Send more. Send them out of the country. Possession, that's the thing. To own. To possess money and goods. The other thing is not important."

The Countess waited and fretted. Isaac Landauer came with reports and papers. All his financial affairs were running smoothly and well. She asked about the cabbalist. Yes, he was on his way to Wildbad. It was difficult to command him. Her Excellency could have patience, he would be in Freudenthal in two or three weeks.

Hardly was he gone when the news came of the ducal pair's meeting in Teinach. It had been conducted grandly and ceremoniously like a nuptial celebration. The faded Johanna Elisabetha had dressed herself and her ladies-in-waiting—"that museum collection of scarecrows," sneered the Countess—in new and costly gowns. The Ambassador to the Court, who deserved well of the Duchess, had proceeded thither, and the whole Cabinet, the smaller Sub-Committee of Parliament; and her brother, the Countess's brother, the scoundrel, with his oily and poisonous tongue, had made a speech at the banquet.

On the first evening there was a ballet, *The Return of Odysseus*. Ah, how they must all have simpered when the wicked Circe threw herself into the crater of the volcano, and how all the stringy old Court hags must have wiped their bleary eyes when the virtuous Penelope sat at her spinning-wheel. But they could wait, they could wait a long time before she would throw herself into a volcano! Then the ducal pair had withdrawn, and the Italian quartette had played at the door of their bedroom while they went to bed. On the second day there were fireworks, and shimmering rockets wrote the Duchess's initials flaming on the sky; the people, their bellies crammed with ducally-bestowed sausages, their bladders full of ducally-bestowed wine—in the absence of her watchful eye, the cellarer would cheat the Duke of about 180 gulden—snuffled piously as they gazed and roared "Long Live the Duchess!"

When the Countess received this news she shut herself in and wrote. She sent the letter by a courier to Stuttgart. It went to the Duke's groom of the chambers, and contained a note of hand for three hundred gulden and the promise of a further eight hundred, if he would procure for her a sample of the Duke's blood.

This letter was rash and foolish, and only a few hours after her courier had gone, the Countess regretted it. She had never before committed anything of that kind to writing. It was the first time that she had not held her hand until her frenzied rage was exhausted. It was also Isaac Landauer's fault, with his cursed procrastinating cabbalist. When Eberhard Ludwig's groom of the chambers received the missive he made a calculation. Before the festival in Teinach he would very likely have done what the Countess wanted. But now after the Teinach celebration it was obvious that the Countess had nothing more to hope for. So he delivered the letter to the Duke.

Eberhard Ludwig, bulky and full-blooded, stood for a minute stock still with amazement before this incredible thing. Then he waved his attendant violently away, choked, gasped, stamped up and down and snorted through his nose. Black anger seethed in every vein. So he had been deceived. He, himself, the Duke, had been for thirty years deceived by an accursed witch, a jade. The others, the filthy bourgeoisie, the grumbling grocers of the Estates, the dull dry priests preaching in the Consistory, the shabby King of Prussia, the perpetually reproachful and sour Johanna Elisabetha, they had all been right, they had put him, the Duke, in the wrong for thirty whole years!

Death and damnation! He had had women of all kinds, fair, dark, and auburn. He had fallen in love with small pointed breasts, and with flowing ample ones, with massive hips and with hips that were taut and boyish, with fine long shining brown thighs and with soft rosy dimpled ones. He had had languid, indolent, indifferent women, and tempestuous women who drew the very marrow from his bones. They had clung to him with their hearts and bosoms and all their passions, and had cried out with rapture in his embrace. Powers above! They were better at it than Christl. But he had lost his head about none of them. He had them, and he laughed, and that was all there was to it.

That it was just Christl who had so got into his blood, that he was so stupidly tied to her, and uneasy about her and powerless to get away from her, that was naturally the result of something far from right. And he had never noticed it, and had sat there with poison and abominable witchcraft infecting his body. Oh, the harlot! The accursed evil woman! The details of that protocol crept

55

upon him, and changed into disjointed and disgusting pictures. The black cow with its head cut off, the he-goat without its genitals. Perhaps she had even made an image of him, a teraph, in order to bewitch his heart and his living blood into the figure, and Satan of the nine tails alone knew what accursed and abominable practices she may have contrived with forbidden things.

But now he had unearthed her handiwork. Now he was done with magic and horrible witchcraft. He would show her that he had sweated out of his system the last drop of her hellish poison and satanic potions. He wrote a letter, sealed it, and summoned councillors and officers. A hasty, secret and important bustle began. On the very next day early in the morning a detachment of hussars appeared in the village of Freudenthal. The soldiers drew up in front of the castle and occupied all the exits. Their leader, Colonel Streithorst, followed by his adjutant, pushed past the trembling castellan into the hall. Here he was met by the major-domo, while excited, anxious and curious servants peeped out of all the doors. Her Excellency could not receive visitors, said the major-domo quickly. Her Excellency was still in bed. The officer answered calmly that he would wait for a few minutes, and sat down. Then the major-domo urged with undue eagerness that the Countess was indisposed, and regretted extremely that she could not receive visitors on any account. If the Colonel brought commands from His Highness, would he be so good as to deliver them to the Secretary. The Colonel, very correct and calm, replied that he was sorry, but he had orders to speak personally with the Countess in any circumstances whatever. Upon that the Countess's mother appeared. Like a colossus the earth-coloured aged woman stood in the doorway which led to her daughter's chambers. The Colonel saluted, and repeated his message in a cool and matter-of-fact tone. The old woman railed at him in her deep, wheezing voice; he should clear out, he knew as well as his master that her daughter was an independant Countess of the Holy Roman Empire, and answered only to the Emperor. The officer shrugged his shoulders; he was no lawyer, he had to do his duty, and he would give the Countess half an hour to put on her clothes and then he would break in her door. The old woman planted her bulk in the doorway, raging; that would be a breach of the peace, and he would get into difficulties with the Swabian chivalry of the Empire, and his master would have to pay dearly for it, and he himself would be cashiered in disgrace. "There are only twenty-six minutes left," responded the Colonel.

The Countess meanwhile in frenzied haste swept round her rooms, burning papers, pigeon-holing, sealing, and delivering them to her secretary. When the officer forced his way in she was lying in bed in a gorgeous nightgown, and raised herself up, a picture of outraged innocence. In a weak voice she asked what he wanted of her. Herr von Streithorst excused himself, saying he had strict orders from the Duke himself to take her away under escort. Screams from the chambermaids, indignant and hoarse vituperation from the old woman. The officer remained inexorable. When she came to herself again, while the old woman branded the Colonel as a murderer, she said in a broken voice like that of a little girl that she was in his power, she knew that he could take her away before the cavaliers of the Empire could bring up an armed force to oppose him. That she was very seriously ill, and that this invasion had aggravated her condition, and if he insisted on removing her in such a state it would be her death. She spoke with difficulty, struggling for breath, while the chambermaids wailed around her. It took the Colonel four hours to get her into the coach and take her away into the rain in the middle of his cavalry. Her mother and two of her women accompanied her. By the road her peasants stood stupidly staring. But the Freudenthal Jews gathered in their synagogue in great anxiety for their lives and property, and prayed for their patroness.

The Countess was conducted to Urach, and there treated with all the respect due to a person of rank, but was confined to the castle and the park. She bore herself haughtily, bullying the servants and dumbfounding them by enormous gratuities. She refused to give any information to the Duke's commissaries, declaring that as a sovereign Countess in her independent barony of Freudenthal she was answerable only to the Emperor. When the Swabian chivalry took up the affair and lodged a complaint of breach of privilege in the arrest of a Countess in her independent barony, she was triumphant, and her steward in Vienna upheld her complaint in a speech against the House of Württemberg such as had never before been heard. Everywhere in the Empire her agents started sinister rumours, pointing out the insecurity of law and order in the Duchy since not even the rights of the nobility were respected. Isaac Landauer, shaking his head cautiously, explained to the Ambassador from the Netherlands that in these circumstances it would be undesirable to sink capital in Württemberg, and his words were retailed in the bureaux of great financiers and had dangerous consequences.

Meanwhile the mother went to see her eldest son. The slippery, cold-hearted, arrogant minister crumpled up like a wet rag before the old woman's abuse. He declared that the insolence and political ambition of his sister would have ruined them all forever, and so he had had to step in. Now that she was politically out of the game he would do his best to secure her safe departure. He had no intention of confiscating her properties.

The arrangement that was proposed to the Countess after that was favourable to her from the start. It became clear how subtly and widely Isaac Landauer had thrown his net. It was to everyone's interest to leave the Countess undisturbed in possession of her investments in Württemberg. So although she had to give up Breuz, Gochsheim, Stetten, and Freudenthal and to put up with the condition that she should not set foot again in the Duchy, Isaac Landauer had squeezed out a final sum for her so enormous that even her Jews dared only to whisper the amount.

A strong military escort accompanied her out of the country. Her road was thronged with people, whooping and flinging mud. Before and behind her in an endless row trailed waggons of clothes, household gear and valuables.

Only when the last load was over the frontier was she followed in a coach by the old woman, earth-coloured, colossal and immovable.

THE Prelate of Hirsau, Philip Heinrich Weissensee, Consistorial Councillor and member of the Sub-Committee of Parliament, had just welcomed a guest, Privy Councillor Fichtel from the Court of the Lord Bishop of Würzburg. The two gentlemen had been friends for years, the slim polished Protestant and the insignificant

58

diplomat with his small shrewd face. Both of them were passionately fond of pulling strings, and although to their neighbours they were impenetrable they disclosed to each other the inner workings of their art, taking a professional delight in the fine machinery which spun the countless threads of the Protestant parliamentary policy of Württemberg and the diplomacy of the Catholic Court.

In the Duchy Weissensee was valued, but disliked by most people. His amiable indifference and the light, sceptical superiority arising from his many-sided culture, kept at arm's length the countless acquaintances who thronged his large and comfortable rooms. He was a distinguished mathematician, and was a close friend of the two best theologians in the west of Germany, the quiet, earnest, and sincerely pious Johann Albrecht Bengel, and the downright, stubborn Georg Bernhard Bilfinger. His critical edition of the New Testament, of which as yet only a small part had appeared, was renowned far beyond Württemberg, and his word was decisive in the Sub-Committee of the Estates.

But in his manifold interests he lacked warmth. True, he accomplished everything to which he set his hand with thoroughness, industry and expert skill. But whether it was the New Testament, or a report in Parliament or the cultivation of a new kind of fruit in his garden, he took it all as a game; there was nothing which went past his nerves and touched his heart.

In the wide rooms with the enormous white curtains his tall slim daughter Magdalen Sibylle moved to and fro, nineteen years old, dark-skinned with a keen, masculine face, and large full blue eyes, very remarkable and disturbing under her dusky hair. Her mother had died young and she had never been able to pierce the lukewarm amiable indifference of her father. Her intercourse with Beata Sturmin, the daughter of the Stuttgart Estates Advocate, and her reading of Swedenborg, had drawn the lonely girl into pietistic circles.

For conventicles and Bible circles flourished in the land. In spite of interdicts and punishments the needs of the time bred believers and initiates all·over the Duchy. Of course there was no one in tiny Hirsau to compare with Magdalen Sibylle's Stuttgart guide and friend, the blind Beata Sturmin, who wrestled with God in prayer, dunned Him with His own promises which He was bound to fulfil, and compelled Him to oracular utterances obtained by opening the Bible at random.   But in the quiet little place there dwelt a certain Master Jaakob Polykarp Schober, who had read all the writings of De Poiret, Boehme, Bourignon, Leade, and Arnold, as well as the forbidden books of the Perpetual Evangel and of the Philadelphians, a good-natured simple man who went his way gently and loved to take long meditative walks.   He held a Bible study circle in Hirsau, and Magdalen Sibylle, the Prelate's daughter, attended it.   Her large blue eyes lost in some far-off dream, she used to sit, tall and beautiful, with her dark, keen, masculine face, among the pious, wretched, harassed, pallid and misshapen students of the Bible class.

She profoundly detested the Privy Councillor from Würzburg, and she grieved to see her father in the company of such a worldly heathen.   The Catholic had brought with him some of the new-fangled stuff called coffee which the cannibals had discovered, and he had to be served with a black strong-smelling liquor prepared from it.   Magdalen Sibylle observed with frightened and hostile eyes that her father joined him in drinking the Satanic brew, and she prayed passionately that God would not let it poison him.

There they sat, the two men, over this drink or over their wine, and discussed endlessly the vanities of the Empire and of that utterly wicked Babylon, the Catholic Church.   The Privy Councillor quite naturally spoke also of Karl Alexander, who had recently been a guest of the Lord Bishop.   Weissensee knew the Prince too.   A charming man.   His fame spread from the lower Danube to the Neckar.   A noble leaf on the cedar-tree of Württemberg.   The Privy Councillor spoke of the Prince's financial difficulties; he had even applied to the Estates, as he knew, for an increase of his allowance.   Yes, Weissensee had read the application, and had an idea that he knew the style of it.   It had certainly not originated in the Prince's study; and now that he came to think of it, he seemed to recognize in certain turns of expression the manner of his honourable friend, he concluded with a smile.

The gentlemen sat at their ease in the warm evening, and drank. But since the conversation had veered round to this affair, questions and answers came at longer intervals, with more friendliness, and eagerness lay behind their masks of indifference.   "As things stand now," ventured Weissensee, cautiously trying to draw his friend out, "it would be worth considering to grant the deserving Prince this small increase."

"Humanly speaking, of course that would delight the Bishop," answered Privy Councillor Fichtel, very slowly, and one could read in his small clever face how carefully he formed the words so that they would say nothing but mean everything. "The Bishop is a close friend of the Prince's. But the see, as such, has no interest—my honoured friend will understand me well—no interest at all in the question whether the Estates are to help the Prince or not." The Privy Councillor relapsed into silence and sipped his coffee.

Weissensee observed him attentively, and said gently: "If I understand you rightly, dear sir, it matters little to the Bishop whether we give him the money or not?"

They looked at each other, guardedly, and with friendliness. Then the Catholic said: "If I were a member of the Sub-Committee, I should vote against it. Especially now, after the fall of the Countess, no concession should be made to the reigning House." And the two diplomats smiled on each other courteously, understandingly, affectionately, with their thin, fine lips.

When the Prince's petition came up in the Sub-Committee of the Estates, there was a general inclination to grant it. The disgrace of the Countess had put the Eleven into a good and generous humour. It fell to the downright blustering mayor of Brackenheim, Johann Friedrich Jäger, to introduce it. He pointed out that Prince Karl Alexander was a great man and a Field Marshal, that he had carried the glory of Württemberg all over the world and spread a respect for Swabian courage and fists among Moors, Turks and other heathen; also that the Duke had now dismissed the pock-marked harlot. So they could show themselves noble, and grant the few thousand gulden they were asked for. The others were all of the same mind. Then Weissensee arose, and with his fine, courteous, flexible voice, said as if casually that the generosity and noble gestures of his praiseworthy colleagues were much to be commended, and he too would like to bestow the money on the deserving hero. But it was questionable whether it was a practical policy to show complaisance to the ducal House at that very moment. The Duke had at last given up the Countess, well and good. But, after all, it was only his confounded duty to do so, and if they were to thank him for it by a special gesture of complaisance, a mere matter of duty would be stamped as an act of grace, and they would be giving a retrospective sanction to the stiff-necked obstinacy which the Duke had shown for thirty years.

The members of the Sub-Committee shook their clumsy heads, hesitated, and were completely convinced. Weissensee had touched them on the weakest spot. Yes, that was the thing! To show the Duke that they would not yield an inch. Their privileges existed not merely on paper; they were exercised. That was something.

The petition of His Highness Prince Karl Alexander, Field Marshal of the Empire, was refused.

RABBI GABRIEL lived a withdrawn and quiet life in Wildbad. Towards evening he was wont to take walks in the surrounding country. Rainy weather had set in. He walked in the warm, damp air, his step awkward, his back slightly stooped, his head raised, and his eye resting on nobody. But insignificant as he was, wherever he went he struck people dumb with amazement, and they stared after him. Whispering arose in his wake; the rumour of the Wandering Jew sprang up again. Three times the authorities went through the papers of this composed and surly man; but they were in perfect order. He was a valid citizen of the Netherlands under the name of Mynheer Gabriel Oppenheimer van Straaten, and he had the grand passport which requested all magistrates to afford him every assistance.

Prince Karl Alexander also had naturally heard of the strange visitor, and that he was much in the company of Süss, his own pet Jew. The Prince was gradually becoming somewhat impatient of waiting so long for the money from the Estates, and he was beginning to feel bored. In Venice and elsewhere, like so many other noblemen, he had dabbled in astrology and other magical arts, and besides his great friend the Lord Abbot was deeply versed in such matters. Recently in Würzburg he had spoken of a magician whom he maintained in his palace and in whom he had great confidence. So the Prince immediately desired Süss to bring the cabbalist and introduce him. Süss twisted and tried to evade the point. He knew that Rabbi Gabriel would never lend himself to such an exhibition. At last he found a way out of the difficulty. When the Rabbi came to see him he would send a message to the Prince. If the Prince would then call on him, he would naturally encounter the Rabbi. Karl Alexander agreed with a smile to this proposal.

The cabbalist said to Süss: "I will bring the child, then, into Swabia. Near Hirsau I have found a small country house, quite secluded. Let the house be bought. It is in the middle of a forest, far from men. Nothing evil can reach her there."

Süss nodded mutely. "It would be good," continued Rabbi Gabriel in his rasping voice, "if you were to remove yourself from your present life and occupations. But it is foolish of me to talk to you," he concluded morosely. He saw Süss's face, he saw only flesh and blood and bones in it and no light, and he was annoyed at the deep, mysterious bond which tied him to this very man, and brought him repeatedly to defeat.

As he was making to go, the door was flung open, and past the lackeys standing at attention the Prince came into the room, limping a little and crying, "Ah, you have a visitor, Süss?" before he threw himself into an arm-chair. Rabbi Gabriel bowed slightly, without haste, and observed the Prince coolly and attentively while Süss made a profound obeisance. Before the quiet, troubled, grey eyes of the cabbalist the Prince lost his blustering assurance and a painful silence fell on the three until Süss broke it by saying, "This is His Highness, Uncle, the Prince of Württemberg, my noble patron." As Rabbi Gabriel was still silent, the Prince said with a laugh which sounded embarrassed, "This is surely the mysterious stranger of whom everyone is talking. An alchemist, hey? You can make gold?"

"No," said Rabbi Gabriel unmoved. "I cannot make gold."

The Prince had taken off his glove, and slapped it against his thigh. From the large clean-shaven face with the small flat nose there stared at him uncomfortably the disproportionately large grey eyes with their troubled and melancholy fire. He had imagined the magician to be quite different; he remembered the amusing thrills which other seances of magic had given him. This one was as depressing as if all the air were slowly leaving the room. "I am very interested in alchemistic experiments," he said after a while.

"If you care to come to see me at Belgrade,"—he was speaking now much more courteously—"I am not rich, your nephew knows that apparently better than I do, but I could assure you a reasonable income."

"I am no maker of gold," repeated the cabbalist.

There was silence once more, flowing in a melancholy stream until it filled the chamber and surrounded the men, banishing their assurance and their thoughtfulness. Suddenly, with a precipitate movement, as if he were rending fetters asunder, the Prince flung his left hand high before the eyes of the cabbalist. "But you cannot refuse me that, Magus," he cried with a strained smile. "Tell me what you read in it!" and he thrust his palm into the other's face. It was a remarkable hand. While it seemed to be slim, long, bony and hairy on the back, in front it was fleshy, plump, and short.

Rabbi Gabriel had not been able to avoid a glance at the hand. With a barely suppressed movement of horror he recoiled a step. Anxious depression more and more grey, constricting and oppressive settled down like a cloud. "Speak, then!" urged the Prince. "I beg you to excuse me!" replied the cabbalist, hardly yet master of himself.

"If you have a prophecy of evil to make me, do you think I am likely to go into hysterics like an anæmic schoolgirl? I have stood in a hundred battles, I have fought a duel over a pocket-handkerchief. I have escaped death by a hair's breadth." He tried to laugh. "Do you think I cannot bear to hear it, if an old Jew foretells trouble for me?"

"I beg you to excuse me," said the cabbalist. He did not raise his voice, but his eyes like frozen pools looked at the Prince in such a way that for a moment he could find no words. Sharp, deep and short the three furrows cleft the broad brow of the Rabbi like a strange, uncanny letter. But just then the Prince caught sight of Süss, tense and anxious, backed into a corner, and it brought him up short that he should look so small and ridiculous before the old man; and thrusting out his hand again he cried masterfully, "Say on."

Rabbi Gabriel spoke, and his surly matter-of-fact tone fell on the Prince's excited mood with a more uncanny effect than any grand gesture or magical apparatus could have done: "I see a first and a second event. The first I will not tell you. The second is a ducal crown."

The Prince, amazed, laughed through his nose. "Mille tonnerre! You lay it on thick, sir Magus. Not so vague and superficial as other chiromants and astrologers, who say 'great fame and glory' or the like. But roundly and clearly, 'a ducal crown.' By jove! My cousin can draw comfort from that!"

Rabbi Gabriel did not answer. "I am going away to-night," he turned to Süss. "What I told you still holds good." He bowed to the Prince, and went out.

"Your uncle is not very courteous," said Karl Alexander to Süss, trying to laugh off his embarrassment. "You must excuse him, your Highness," the Jew hastened to reply, also trying to master his emotion. "He is morose and peculiar. And even if his manners are lamentable and faulty," he concluded, once more at ease and in his old form, "what he had to tell is all the more gratifying."

"Yes," said the Prince thoughtfully, with an abstracted eye, tracing the lines on the floor with his dagger; "but what he refused to tell?"

"He has his own queer ideas," Süss assured him. "What he sets down as important and as great misfortune is the kind of thing that men like us laugh at who see life as it really is. A ducal crown is something real. But the evil which he did not want to divulge is certainly something which to us is visionary and chimerical."

"The ducal crown!" laughed the Prince. "Your uncle is wonderfully far-sighted. For the present, my cousin is still alive, and his grown-up son too, and neither of them is thinking of kicking the bucket. In fact he has made peace with his spouse the Duchess, so that he will have more children." The Prince stood up and stretched himself. "Well, Jew! Will you raise me a mortgage on the throne of Württemberg?" And clapped him with a loud laugh on the shoulder. Süss looked him respectfully in the eye. "I am at your Highness's disposal with all that I possess. With all that I possess," he repeated. The Prince stopped laughing, and looked at the financier, who stood before him very serious and with more than his usual respect. "Enough of this joke," said Karl Alexander suddenly, shrugging his shoulders as if he were shaking off something alien and burdensome, and drawing himself up. "Little Kosel has begged me for Turkish slippers," he went on in his old tone, "with small blue stones. Get them for her, Jew! The best that there are!" And as he went out, limping slightly, "But see that you don't run me in for more than three ducats!" And he burst into a roar of laughter.

RABBI GABRIEL left Wildbad in the ordinary mail-coach. In his respectable coat, cut in the old Frankish fashion which was worn in Holland twenty years before, thick-set and slightly round in the back, he looked like a disagreeable bourgeois or a surly superior official. Before he entered there had been a gay exchange of chaff in the mail-coach, but after his arrival the passengers sat dumb and ill at ease, and Rabbi Gabriel's neighbour imperceptibly drew away from him.

They had scarcely left the town when the mail-coach encountered a magnificent travelling equipage. It was Prince Anselm Franz of Thurn and Taxis, from Regensburg, who with great pomp and a large retinue was proceeding to the little Château Eremitage, in the forest, which he had rented. The Prince, a fine elderly man with a long and very aristocratic head rather like a greyhound's, was a widower, and was accompanied by his only daughter, Marie Auguste. The Princess, renowned far over Germany for her beauty, drawing the admiration of the world in countless pictures and pastels, sat beside her father with the customary detachment of a beautiful woman who knows that many eyes follow her every movement. With languid curiosity she glanced into the crowded mail-coach, and her slight, rather mocking, haughty and lovable smile did not falter before the gaze of the cabbalist. Her father in his gentle way had hinted to her that in Wildbad she would be faced with important, and, he hoped, pleasant decisions. So she travelled now in the glittering coach, more ready to accept than to refuse any experience, young, indolent and yet avid. Under her shining black hair there peeped out a small, delicate, lizard-like face, of the mellow tint of fine old marble,

66

with a pointed chin, long eyes, a clear open forehead, a finely-chiselled nose, and a small, pouting, mocking mouth.

The ladies in Wildbad were bitter over the new visitor. The Princess of Courland, and the daughter of the Ambassador from the Netherlands, who found themselves wallflowers, sneered arrogantly and called the Thurn and Taxis girl a coquette and a man-hunter. But she, her small delicate head held high, and an indolent enigmatic smile on her lips, went on her way, which was thronged with admirers.

The first evening on which Princess Marie Auguste appeared in society was a successful one for Josef Süss. In marked contradiction to the other gentlemen he made not the slightest attempt to be introduced to the Regensburg royalties. While even young Lord Suffolk made himself ridiculous by his staring, round-eyed, stricken love-sickness, Süss remained beside the two neglected ladies, by whom he had always been prized, and in whose favour he now stood doubly high. Only rarely, and when his companions could not observe it, did his large brown eyes fly to the Princess, but then his pale face radiated such boundless and devoted admiration that Marie Auguste kept looking at the stately and elegant gentleman with unembarrassed curiosity. Otherwise she moved with her slight, provocative smile delicately and a little mockingly through the adulation of the evening.

The man who was usually the crown of these festive evenings and the focus of attention, Karl Alexander, Prince of Württemberg, Field Marshal of the Empire, hero of Belgrade, Peterwardein and many other battles, was disappointingly absent. He sat grimly alone in his room at the Star, with a single candle on the table. He sat in a dressing-gown, his wounded and gouty foot, which pained him more than usual that day, rolled up in bandages, with a row of bottles and carafes in front of him. Neuffer, his valet, emerged from time to time out of the dusk to fill up his glass, and in the shadows squatted the dark brown slave. The Prince sat drinking and cursing. In the afternoon with the usual post he had received a missive from the Parliamentary Sub-Committee which starkly and unceremoniously refused his petition for an advance.

Karl Alexander foamed with rage. He knew that he was popular in the Duchy; his picture hung in countless kitchens; the people cheered his name. And now this canaille of Parliament, the moth-eaten snivelling louts, this rabble with its nose in the air, had sent him a filthy scrawl like that.

He tore off the furs which Neuffer had wrapped round his foot and stamped up and down. And the old Jew prophesied him a crown! The charlatan! A fine crown! A vagabond and a wandering beggar was more like it, since that gang dared to send him such an insult. He roared so terribly and blasphemously that Süss coming home from the festival was profoundly alarmed, and although the hour was late asked the valet what was the matter. But Neuffer, who detested the Jew, evaded the question.

On the next day, towards noon, after he had twice presented himself in vain, Süss paid his respects to the Prince. He came circumspectly into the room wearing stockings of a special design which he wished to show the Prince; His Highness was always very interested in new fashions. Also he wanted to tell him of yesterday's festival. But he had never found him so forbidding. Naked and towering he stood there, while Neuffer and the dusky slave poured pails of water over him and rubbed him down. He flung the Sub-Committee's letter over, and while Süss with bent head skimmed it with a quick eye, sneezing and dripping he boomed at him: "A fine Magus, your uncle! You've cheated me nicely with him! It looks hopeful, my crown!"

Süss honestly resented the churlish refusal of the Estates, and began in dexterous phrases to assure the Prince of his angry contempt for such insolence and of his devoted readiness to take any action. But when he saw Süss standing there so elegantly with the abominable letter in his hand, the Prince, irritated with every one, cried suddenly: "Neuffer! Otman! Baptize the Jew! Let him learn to swim!" And the valet and the dusky slave immediately slung the bath-water over Süss with an enormous splash, while the Prince's dog sprang yelping upon him; and the Jew escaped in startled haste, his breeches and new stockings soaking wet, and his shoes ruined, with the loud laughter of the Prince and his servants echoing behind him.

Süss bore the Field Marshal no grudge. Great men had their

moods, that was simply to be accepted. And while he changed his wet clothes he decided to present himself next time as courteously as ever, even more respectfully than usual, with the probability of a better reception.

On the same day Privy Councillor Fichtel arrived from Würzburg. The unobtrusive man with the small shrewd face visited the Prince that very afternoon. Yes, the Court at Würzburg was already aware of the unexpected and extraordinary insolence of the Estates. The Lord Bishop was deeply incensed, and filled with contempt for such miserable and shameless meanness. But his master in his wisdom had already thought of another remedy, which would aid the Prince in his need and would teach the arrogant populace a bitter lesson.

But before he explained himself further he begged for the Prince's gracious permission to prepare himself the coffee to which he was accustomed. Then as he sat over the hot, black liquor, looking doubly insignificant beside the stately Prince, he opened out to him smoothly and objectively a plan of marriage with the Princess Thurn and Taxis, who was the loveliest princess in the Roman Empire and immensely wealthy. Then, too, it would rouse the choler of the insolent and rebellious Estates if the Prince were to become a Catholic. The Lord Bishop of course was ready to assist the Prince, even if he were to reject the proposed marriage. But he thought that this solution was the best, and with all his heart would like to see His Highness in possession of a lovely wife and untold wealth, and the Estates in a fine and bilious rage. And the Privy Councillor drank his coffee in comfortable little sips.

When he was alone, Karl Alexander paced to and fro, his head still confused from his solitary carouse during the night, drawing deep breaths and ruffling his thick yellow hair. What foxes they were! They wanted him to turn Catholic. Schönborn, Friedrich Karl, his good jolly friendly comrade; what a fox he was!

He laughed. Confound it, an excellent jest! By far the greater number of officers in the higher ranks were Catholics, and Catholics made the best soldiers. For his own part, ever since he was at Venice he had been very broad-minded in religious matters, and he had always liked the Catholic mass, and for soldiers the Catholic religion with its incense and holy images and scapularies was really the more suitable. And if it were to do his friends in Würzburg and Vienna a good turn, so much the better. It would do himself no harm at any rate. A lovely, rich Princess. There would be an end of this perpetual stupid lamentation and worry over money. And what a glorious trick he would be playing the refractory Estates! Damn it all, he would at least have a look at the Regensburg girl.

When Süss came in the next day he met him with a merry shout: "Are you dry yet, Jew? Did the baptism do you good?" "Yes," replied Süss, "since your Highness enjoyed it." "If I were to ask you for thirty thousand gulden, would you give me them?" "Only ask me!" "And then you would squeeze me till the blood started! Ho! I have someone who will give me the money without a cent of interest!" "Have you chosen another man of business?" enquired the Jew in alarm. "No," laughed the Prince reassuringly. "For the present I need you more than ever. I am going to stay for at least two more weeks; but I would like to get out of this hole of a hotel. Take the Villa Monbijou for me! Furnish and staff it in such a style that no one in Versailles could carp at it. I appoint you to be my High Steward and Keeper of the Privy Purse." Süss kissed the Prince's hand and thanked him effusively.

Karl Alexander sent his brown slave to the Château Eremitage to ask when he could pay a call. Thereafter, although the way was short, he drove thither in his respectable coach, which still looked terribly old-fashioned in spite of its new varnish; but Neuffer and the coachman had already been rigged out by Süss in new liveries.

At Eremitage the Field Marshal was received with great distinction. Besides the Prince and Marie Auguste, he found also the Thurn and Taxis Chief Steward and Privy Councillor Fichtel. Franz Anselm of Thurn and Taxis was an old and experienced gentleman. Benevolent, gay, inquisitive, with ceremonies and excellent manners, he loved society, enjoyed scandal, and believed in nothing and in no one. They had a host of mutual acquaintances at the Viennese Court in Würzburg, in the army, and among the European nobility. The old Prince made little malicious comments; Karl Alexander spoke freely and vivaciously, agreeing with some of them and deprecating others. His host courteously inclined his fine, long head that was like a greyhound's and listened attentively. He approved of Karl Alexander. To be sure, he was a little blunt, and got excited, which one should not do; nor had he much judgment. But he had temperament, and, mon Dieu, he was a Field Marshal and a hero; one expected victories from him and not intelligence.

Marie Auguste spoke little at first. She sat there, very regal in her dove-grey silk gown, with delicate affectation holding the upper folds of her enormous spreading skirt in her small, plump, well-manicured hands as fashion prescribed. Under their lace, her slim well-poised neck and her bosom and shoulders gleamed with the mellow softness of fine old marble. Small, lizard-like and delicate in its pastel colours, her face looked out from under her shining black hair. With unembarrassed and friendly curiosity she examined the Prince, who looked enormously broad and manly, planted beside her slender father.

Privy Councillor Fichtel described a brave deed of Karl Alexander's. Marie Auguste, glancing at the Prince, mentioned a French Opera in Vienna which she had seen, *Achilles the Hero,* where Achilles, after dragging Hector's body around, had sung some noble sentiments. "Yes," commented her father, "in ancient times people were generally noble." Karl Alexander was of the opinion that he acted on the impulse of the moment, and did not think that he had much aptitude for noble sentiments. Whereupon the Princess, fixing him with her eye till he blushed, smilingly remarked that they had not been speaking of him at all. And everybody laughed.

Iced drinks were brought in, and coffee for the little Würzburg Privy Councillor.

The flaxen-headed Württemberger liked the dusky Princess amazingly. Mille tonnerre! If she were to preside at a ball in the huge castle of Belgrade, what eyes they would make, all the Turks and Hungarians and other wild folk down there! That was a Governor's lady with whom one could hold high state in Vienna and everywhere. Especially since she would bring the ducats with her to renovate the bleak Belgrade castle. What a fox Schönborn of Würzburg was, and what a friend, confound it, what a

true friend and comrade, to smuggle him into such a good thing!
And she was not only a show-piece. A sly rogue, he was sure
of it. Those eyes, and that mouth! That was something for one's
bed! He beamed all over his face, and had to remember not to
smack his lips. She was different from the sour Durlach woman,
his cousin the Duke's wife. It would not need the authority of
the Emperor and the Empire to force one to give children to her.
And how cleverly she could chatter! How her tongue wagged, the
rogue, how she teased him and let her eyes play! They would
make a good picture, he and she. Eberhard Ludwig would open
his eyes wide. He, Karl Alexander, would not need to keep an
expensive harlot. His legitimate wife would be lovelier and better
ornament for his bed than the costliest French mistress, and she
would fill his purse instead of emptying it.

And the Parliament! That accursed rabble of citizens! His
chest expanded with rising satisfaction. They would be sick and
yellow with rage. It would be worth it to turn Catholic.

He looked at Marie Auguste, while her father was speaking to
the other two gentlemen; he looked at her with the appraising,
masterful, slightly barbaric look of the soldier who is accustomed
to throw a woman on the bed without many preliminaries, and the
Princess with her small imperceptible smile let it envelop her.

When he took his leave Karl Alexander was firmly determined
to turn Catholic.

JOSEF SÜSS had fitted up Villa Monbijou very sumptuously, and
he was especially proud of the small gallery and the adjacent yellow salon. The latter was really Nicklas Pfäffle's achievement;
the stout and phlegmatic man had impressed all the merchants
and handworkers for miles around in a promiscuous whirl of
activity.

So the Field Marshal's new hotel spread itself in great magnificence, and the Prince clapped Süss on the shoulder. "You are
a wizard, Süss. And how much are you going to stick me for
this affair?" The brown slave fitted excellently into this setting,
the Prince beamed with satisfaction, and even Neuffer, who had
a pick against the Jew, had to admit that he could not have done
it better.

72

Privy Councillor Fichtel also, to whom Karl Alexander showed his new abode before he gave his first fête in it, extolled it lavishly. Secretly, however, he found it all a little too overloaded, too parvenu-like, and he instigated the Prince to have some things taken away here and there. He informed his master, the Lord Bishop, that the Prince had let himself be fitted out by a Hebrew; and so it was no wonder if his establishment were somewhat oriental, and his Wildbad château reeked more of Jerusalem than of Versailles.

The old Prince Franz Anselm had a similar impression on the evening when Karl Alexander gave his entertainment. The old Prince, who set great store by a good appearance, was certainly annoyed also because he had chosen a pale yellow suit which did not look well in the pale yellow salon of Monbijou. Karl Alexander had invited his guests to a grand operatic performance, *Zerbinetta's Revenge,* because he knew that Marie Auguste enjoyed comedy, music and ballet-dancing. Süss had had to procure the little troupe from Heidelberg in great haste, through his mother, who lived in Frankfurt and still had many connections with the theatrical profession.

The company was small and elegant. The Prince wanted at first to exclude Süss, but his good nature had not been able to withstand the hungry and devoted dog-like eyes of his Steward, and to the great annoyance of Neuffer the Jew was invited. In a chestnut-brown coat embroidered with silver he glided among the guests, adroit and happy.

But how Marie Auguste queened it in wine-red silk and brocade! The sash of the order of the house of Thurn and Taxis was proudly displayed on her bosom, and on her puffed sleeves she wore in diamonds the distinctive star which the Emperor had conferred upon her for her services in connection with a patronage. She spoke little. But the Princess of Courland and the daughter of the Ambassador from the Netherlands—she had deferred to both of them with the most gracious courtesy as her elders—thought that they could hear her indolent childish voice in every corner. They vowed to each other never to appear in the Regensburg girl's company again, and in any case they were going to leave Wildbad in a few days. Quite independently of each other they

73

came to this conclusion, and Süss assured each of them in the same words that he was inconsolable.

The prevailing topic was the latest news from Stuttgart; the Duchess thought that she was pregnant again. The doctors and midwives strengthened her in this belief, the Consistory had already ordered prayers on her behalf, and curious people went to look at the hawthorn which Eberhard of the Beard had once planted in a hermitage after his return from Palestine and which now unexpectedly was putting forth new shoots. A fortunate omen!

Privy Councillor Fichtel cracked a few shrewd and smutty jokes at the expense of Eberhard Ludwig and the doubtful joys of his bed prescribed by the Emperor. He made drastic comparisons between the Duchess and the deposed Countess. The gentlemen in the corner round the Privy Councillor roared with laughter, the old Prince's face was seamed with mirthful wrinkles. The ladies enquired the reason of this merry fit. Süss enlightened them, giggling. The Jew was chaffed about the growth of the hawthorn from Palestine. Resounding laughter. Even the almost imperceptible smile on Marie Auguste's pastel-like face dissolved into a hearty and ringing laugh.

Karl Alexander jeered: "A fine prophet, your uncle! The Crown Prince happily married, and the old Duke bringing a second heir into the world. You have swindled me finely with your magical uncle."

Marie Auguste had never seen a living Jew at such close quarters before. With fearful curiosity she enquired: "Does he murder children?" "Only now and then," Privy Councillor Fichtel assured her; "usually he prefers to hang on to great men."

Süss's tactics were clever; he obtruded himself on her as little as possible, contenting himself with admiring her at a respectful distance with his warm, arched eyes. After the opera she allowed him to be introduced to her. His boundless devotion flattered her. "He is quite like a human being," she said wonderingly to her father. Karl Alexander scored a point with her because of his elegant, gallant, confidential Court Jew. Yes, even in the rapture of his first kiss, while he was still intoxicated by the warmth of her small voluptuous mouth, she said with a smile,

74

setting her dress to rights: "No, what an amusing Court Jew you have got!" And therewith they returned into the salon from the little chamber adjoining.

Moreover, the Prince, without being really aware of it, had the obscure feeling that this wild and experienced kiss had not been her first.

In the Parliamentary Sub-Committee of Eleven bad temper reigned. The pregnancy of the Duchess had turned out to be a false alarm, and then on top of that came the report of Prince Karl Alexander's forthcoming marriage to a Catholic, and of his conversion—his reversion the Jesuits impudently called it—to the Roman Church. Simple honesty compelled the Eleven to recognize that they were not quite guiltless of this extremely annoying change of religion on the part of the most popular man in the Duchy.

They first abused the Prince, roundly, virulently and stupidly. At last Johann Heinrich Sturm, the President and Chief Secretary, an earnest, thoughtful, tranquil man, put an end to the purposeless and irrelevant abuse, by asking for positive suggestions. The rough Mayor of Brackenheim declared outright that it was really all Weissensee's fault, and that it was his damned duty to put the matter right again.

Weissensee, smiling and casual, found that things were not so very far wrong. Since the Prince was ready to be converted at a moment's notice, the true faith had not lost much in him.

But the uncivil Brackenheimer stuck to his guns; even though the Ducal pair, thank God, were still robust, and had not lost the prospect of further successors, even though the Crown Prince was there and in sound health, yet since Rome plotted so far-sightedly it was necessary to lay counter-plots in good time.

"Why not?" was Weissensee's airy rejoinder. They could get into touch with Friedrich Heinrich, the Prince's brother, secretly of course, and without committing themselves. Only as a precaution, academic rather than real. Not the slightest threat of danger to evangelical or to Parliamentary freedom would be likely from that mild and pious gentleman.

The eleven sat embarrassed, silent, and thoughtful. Did not

that smack a little of high treason? Only academically of course, only as a precaution, without prejudice. After all——

The insinuating Weissensee, still mild and casual, explained the matter further. Belgrade was far away; it was only a theoretic proceeding, only security for contingencies that were problematical. Of course they would not let any written document out of their hands. And the Corpus Evangelicorum would be on their side.

The thick heads stared, heavily and uneasily. Even the most remote possibility of a Catholic Duke seemed incredible, unendurable; it gave them a sense of nausea. A Catholic sovereign was unthinkable except as a despot, a tyrant. And this one above all, who had connections with the Court at Vienna, the arch-enemy of all religious freedom, all parliamentary independence. Their glorious liberties! And they, the eleven who sat there and took counsel and had daily sessions, they represented those liberties. They were personally threatened, they themselves, by a Catholic sovereign.

They decided that Weissensee should open negotiations with the Field Marshal's brother, the mild, Protestant, harmless Prince Friedrich Heinrich. But quite privately and quite non-committally, and in utter, utter secrecy.

THE Cathedral of Regensburg was filled with music, incense, and a company of brilliant guests at Karl Alexander's wedding. The Emperor had sent an Ambassador, and the Papal Nuncio Passionei was there with a personal letter from the Holy Father, and the Lord Bishop of Würzburg, and the highest representatives of the Imperial Army, among whom was Karl Alexander's most intimate friend, General Franz Josef Remchingen, who had been educated by the Jesuits, with his swollen, brutal face glittering vinously under the white peruke.

There was no handsomer couple in the Empire. The Prince, tall as a cedar, gorgeous with the Order of the Golden Fleece and his Field Marshal's staff. Marie Auguste, her small delicate face gleaming with the radiance of fine old marble above white satin and brocade, across her bosom the scarf of the Order of the House of Thurn and Taxis, the Emperor's star in pale gold on

76

her puffed sleeves, and the cross of the Papal Order at her neck. Her step light and elastic under the bridal crown, a marvel of the jewellers' art for which Süss had hunted out single stones all over Europe, she bore into the Cathedral her young, ambiguous smile.

She was completely unembarrassed, and rather inclined to find a touch of comedy in all this solemnity and ceremoniousness. With indolent curiosity her roving eyes swept over the guests, and while the Bishop extolled her for having won back to the Catholic faith that great conqueror of the Turks, that lion in the fight, she was telling herself that Privy Councillor Fichtel all through the banquet would certainly be thinking only of his coffee. And how comic it was to see the Jew standing solemnly in the Cathedral. Anyhow he was quite pleasant and amusing, and not at all like a werewolf, as she had originally imagined all Jews to be. In fact his wrist-ruffles were much more à la mode than her husband's.

And the festive candles flickered, the organ blared, the incense mounted in a cloud, and blissful boyish voices soared up to heaven.

On the very next day, while silver trumpets heralded the banquet, the newly-wedded pair went on board the yacht, a gift from the bride's father, which was to take them down the Danube. They travelled in courtly state with chasseurs, servants, footmen and chambermaids. At the prow squatted cross-legged the dusky slave Otman, and stared down the Danube with the ancient fathomless eyes of an animal.

On the bank stood the old Prince, the Bishop of Würzburg, Privy Councillor Fichtel, and further back between them and their attendants, Josef Süss. A light breeze blew, the air was clear and exhilarating, everybody was merry. Jests flew back and forth between the yacht and the bank while the anchor was being weighed. Marie Auguste stood in a brightly-coloured travelling dress and shaded her eyes to look at the receding quay. The Prince and the Privy Councillor had already turned away and the last things that she saw were the sly, satisfied face of the Jesuit, and the Jew, displaying his elegance in an attitude of boundless devotion.

"I never should have believed," she smiled to Karl Alexander, "that anybody could be at once so elegant and so humble as your good Jew." "The good Jew!" boomed the laughing Prince. "One could buy whole towns and villages with the money he has done us out of." And when she looked astounded he explained bluntly: "That is his right. That's why he is a Jew. But he is very useful," he added with appreciation; "he provides everything, jewels, furniture, villages, men. Even alchemy and black magic." He told her merrily the tale of Rabbi Gabriel. "He did me in nicely there, your good Jew. A crown! There are still two between me and that. The Crown Prince is as sound as a bell. He was hunting when he sent me his congratulations. And the Duke, sour as his Duchess is, he can still breed children from her like rabbits, if the devil will." And he laughed loudly and caressed her hand, while the ship in a light breeze glided down the blue-green waters between smiling banks.

In front the dusky slave squatted motionless, and stared over the prow to the east. The last pictures of her home lingered in the eyes of the Princess, the sly, jolly face of the Jesuit and the servile, elegant one of the Jew.

* * *

Even before they had reached the Serbian frontier an express from Süss overtook them. "He has important news, that Jew of yours," smiled Marie Auguste. "What is he so anxious to sell?"

Karl Alexander tore open the dispatch. The Crown Prince had died unexpectedly while the Court at Stuttgart attended a ball.

He handed the paper to the Princess. The blood flew to his head, he heard a surly, rasping voice, and through his dancing pulses he saw above troubled, sad, stony eyes three short, sharp furrows, threatening and mysterious, like a strange illegible letter.

Book Two

THE PEOPLE

Book Two

THE PEOPLE

SEVENTY-TWO towns the Duchy of Württemberg counted in its possession, and four hundred villages. Wheat and fruit and wine abounded. It lay like a magnificent garden in the midst of the Holy Roman Empire. The burghers and farmers were cheerful, sociable, obliging, vivacious. Patiently they put up with the government of their princes. Had they a good prince, they rejoiced; a bad prince, it was the decree of Heaven, a punishment from the Lord. Every Württemberger, man, woman and child, had to pay ten golden gulden to the Ducal revenue.

Good Duke, bad Duke, sun came and rain came, wheat grew, wine grew, the land was blessed.

But threads were being spun from all sides; hands coveted, eyes lusted; from every point a web was being woven over the land.

In Paris sat Louis XV and his ministers. A fragment of Württemberg, the earldom of Mömpelgard, was encircled by his lands; he waited only the opportunity to swallow it up. In Berlin sat the Countess, intriguing with the Knights of the Empire, seeking assiduously to extort the last penny; from Frankfurt and Heidelberg lowered Isaac Landauer and Josef Süss, waiting to put the screws on the Duchy; the Pope's Secretary of State span webs from Rome to the Prince Bishop of Würzburg for the destruction of the land of Mithra; in Vienna the Imperial Council was wheedling out of the Crown Prince, the Catholic Field Marshal of the Emperor, new treaties, alliances between Stuttgart and Vienna; in Regensburg the old Prince Thurn and Taxis blinked across, and in Belgrade the Field Marshal Karl Alexander, and Remchingen, his friend and general, wove great plans.

81

They all sat waiting in a circle, filled with mistrust of each other, and cast across the land their great, mute shadow.

And sun came, rain came, wheat and fruit and wine. The land was blessed.

On the first day of November died, as precipitately as he had worked and lived, Eberhard Ludwig, by the grace of God Duke of Württemberg and Teck, and by the grace of his Imperial Majesty, Field Marshal of the Holy Roman Empire and of the important province of Swabia; also commander of three horse and foot regiments.

He lay now on a gigantic catafalque, his face a bluish yellow from bronchial catarrh, in a great uniform with many orders, among which shone out the Danish Order of the Elephant and the Prussian black eagle, many lights round him, at his head and feet two lieutenants standing at watch. The sour, faded Johanna Elisabetha, the Duchess, crouched miserably in the great, silent room. Her triumph had been so short; and that her husband, won with such indomitable waiting and with sweat and blood, now lay there, after a few months, blue and choked and dead, this had been brought about by the evil arts of the other, the Mecklenburger, the witch, the trull. But it was she who sat there, she alone, and not the other! Who ruled henceforward in Württemberg was a matter of indifference to her. The Catholic, probably, with his proud-stomached, wanton, decked-up wife. But she felt annulled, all this did not interest her. She had only one more task in the world; to brew till it was ready the potion of her fixed revenge. Still the relatives of that slut sat at the Ducal table; still the hussy shone in great splendour and magnificence; still she drew through a thousand little channels, through the stewards of her estates, through her accursed Jews, the sap of the land to herself. But now that Eberhard Ludwig was dead she had no protector left, her adroitness would avail her nothing. She, the Duchess, would impeach her anew and more bitterly before the new Duke, before Emperor and Empire. The hussy had sought her life, had brought death upon the Crown Prince and upon the Duke by witchcraft. She would not expend all her strength in the first battle. She would not let her enemy escape; though there was no use in raising a hubbub, her accusing voice would not cease until the other stood ragged and naked in all her shame. So the Duchess sat by the proud catafalque, grey and sorrowful, and twisted in her hands the poor remnant of her life, and the heavy blossoms out of the hothouse exhaled their perfumes, and the great candles burned slowly, and the lieutenants stood with naked swords and held the watch of the dead.

When the heralds announced the Duke's death the burghers bared their heads; they were moved. Now that the Duke was dead they saw only his magnificence, affability, soldier-like devotion to duty, elegance, splendour, and they were inclined to attribute all the miseries of his reign solely and exclusively to the Countess and her witchcraft. The money she had extorted from the country was added to the total of her guilt; and not only that: damnation and pestilence were called down upon her because through her the ancient, well-established position of the princely house had been shaken and many advantageous opportunities of gaining new rights and prerogatives lost; for the Imperial Court was difficult to deal with, one had always to act circumspectly, and alas, exactly at the right moment, the necessary money had usually been wanting. And ever deeper in the mud sank the image of the Countess, and ever more radiant rose that of the Duke, and the women wiped their eyes: "So grand he was, and so friendly he spoke with everybody! Such a good prince! Such a handsome prince!"

And the couriers ran, drove, rode. One to Frankfurt, where Isaac Landauer wagged his poll, rubbed his chilly hands, and said: "Eh, now Reb Josef Süss will be an important man and have great dealings!" One to Berlin, where the Countess had a heart attack and fell unconscious on the floor. One to Würzburg, where the stout, jovial Prince Bishop smiled and called for his Privy Councillor Fichtel; and one to Belgrade, where lived Prince Karl Alexander, now Duke. Now Duke! and as if from a height he saw himself carry the war deep into France, and beheld his hands pressing on the spokes of the world. But through all this and at the same time he saw two troubled grey eyes and heard a morose and grating voice: "I see a first event and a second. The first I will not tell you." And he regarded thoughtfully his hand, a remarkable hand; the palm was fleshy, fat, short, while the back seemed long, slim, bony and covered with hair.

But Marie Auguste stood before her mirror. There she stood often, naked, and smiled. With the long eyes beneath her clear, slender brows she contemplated her body which was soft and slim and of the colour of an old and noble marble. She stretched herself voluptuously; the small lizard-like head with the very red lips smiled more deeply. It would be lovely to journey to Stuttgart through a loyal populace, in a golden coach, as Duchess. It had been lovely here, too, in Belgrade, queening it over the wild, jealous, reverential, barbarous people. Yet it would be very welcome to watch homage rising to her like clouds of incense at the Imperial Court and the other German courts. She would wear the crown without a peruke; it was against the mode, but she would do it, and the crown would sit high and tiny and very proud on her magnificent black hair. With half-hieratic, half-obscene bearing, the naked lady lifted both arms stiffly to her head so that the black tufts under her armpits were visible, and warmly breathing, smiling, she moved with lithe steps, dancing almost, through the chamber. Many noblemen would be at her court, German, Italian, French, not half-savages as they were here; yes, one would almost think one was at Versailles. And many who had regarded the Princess half-impudently, half-admiringly—how would they regard the Duchess now! The courtier Jew, he too would be once more on the outer fringe of her circle; the irrepressible gallant—her lips half smiled with amusement. Ah, it was good to be beautiful, it was good to be rich, it was good to be Duchess. How lovely to think that there existed men and beautiful clothes and crowns and lights and festivals! It was a beautiful world, it was beautiful to be alive.

In Castle Winnenthal, only four hours from Stuttgart, Karl Alexander's brother, the feeble Prince Heinrich Friedrich, fell into a profound fit of agitation when he heard of his cousin's death. He lived in the beautiful, tiny castle, and read and played music. In the past few years he had taken to himself a mistress, a calm, golden-brown creature, daughter of a small landed nobleman, with soft movements, beautiful, profoundly calm eyes, and a little dull in the understanding. When the prelate Weissensee had come to him with the project of putting him forward for the throne in place of his Catholic brother, the bemused man had laid hold of the idea with both hands. But the acute prelate was soon forced to recognize that the Prince in his vacillating, unreliable way regarded political things as if they were fantasies and lost himself in a rosy cloud. No, with this pretender one could accomplish nothing against the energetic, impetuous Karl Alexander. After the death of the Crown Prince, when the question of the succession emerged from idle speculation into credible reality, there came in from Belgrade—Heaven knows how the Field Marshal had come to know the news—an urgent letter wherein Karl Alexander earnestly admonished his brother to keep out of machinations and despicable intrigues. Terrified and shaken, the weak Prince drew back from the undertaking; he even avoided with the greatest care all intercourse with Weissensee. Now when he learned of the Duke's death, all his coloured, fantastic dreams rose up again. Pouring with sweat, his limbs trembling, terribly excited, the weakling wandering around in the wan morning light building fantasies to himself of what might be if he had only a little more initiative; how he might seize possession of power, write to the Emperor, appoint ministers, dismiss them, close treaties with France, make burning speeches to the people. Sighing deeply he returned at last to his bed-chamber again. He did not wish to awaken his beloved darling. Softly and heedfully he undressed, stretched himself, miserable and impotent, by her side, put his arm fumblingly round her great, warm breast, making her open her beautiful, stupid eyes, solaced himself in her fresh youth, and at last fell asleep again, sighing, pensive and soothed.

On the news of the Duke's death the prelate Weissensee roamed, exasperated to the point of desperation, through his spacious rooms with the white curtains. How many problems, complications, conflicts! A Catholic Prince in the native state of Protestantism—a new, unanticipated, never-precedented constellation in western Germany. He, Weissensee, had taken his position in good time; there were many possibilities; he could be dislodged by none of them. He had never exposed himself, he had always

85

pulled wires. He went to and fro, conceived plans, cast them away, enjoyed the pleasant tension and excitement, the pleasure of the great master of intrigues and maker of projects.

But his daughter Magdalen Sibylle sat, and the blue eyes in the brown, keen face worked and changed from grave to gay. A Catholic, a heathen, on the throne! Now confusion and dire need break over the land. Help, Lord God of Sabaoth, that the land remain firm against the temptation with which the idolater seeks to seduce it, and against the threats whereby he would make the true gospel a pariah. The heathenish Prince would come hither in splendour and great glory; he had won battles, stood in the favour of the Emperor; his consort bore herself arrogantly, frivolously. Help, Lord God of Sabaoth, that the people might stand firm amid all temptation and need! And her father, her father stood in the forefront of the battle; on him it devolved to become the shield and buckler of the threatened evangel. Oh, she did not wish to sin against the fifth commandment; but she greatly feared whether even he had true steadfastness before God and men. As ever in such need, she sought refuge in God; she flung open the Bible and implored a sign. But she found only the injunction: "Every clean bird you may eat. These, however, are those which you may not eat: the eagle, and the ostrich, and the hawk, and the pelican." She considered long, but by none of the resources of divination could she find any connection between the need of the country, her zeal for the pure, firm faith of her fathers, and the ostrich and the pelican, which the Israelites might not eat. She decided to lay the oracle before her friend Beata Sturmin, the seer, the blind saint in Stuttgart Bible Class. But first, anxiety and heavy thought on her keen, masculine face, she regarded her father who, not at all overcast but highly stimulated, his fine, vivacious countenance working, walked in pleasant excitement to and fro.

A HALF-HOUR already before the sitting should begin the eleven members of the Estates had found themselves in the Chamber. Only trivialities stood on the order of the day, but all was so confused, they sat as if in thick darkness; they wished at least to feel a neighbourly form beside them, to hear some answer out of the night.

86

Oh, if only at the time they had granted the Prince his loan! Oh that they had not intrigued with his younger brother! Now they sat in the dust, in dire need. The Prince would have to be a saint if, now that he had the power, he did not make them suffer for that. And he was certainly no saint. A soldier, a Field Marshal, accustomed to mute, blind subordination. They had heard that in Belgrade he had treated his councillors with anything but gentleness, that ever and anon he had rushed into wild, raging disputes with his colleagues, cursed filthily and raged, endured no opposition and smashed crockery and anything breakable on his councillors' heads. In short, that he was a despot as only Pagan Cæsars had been. They would have their real test, their devil's sabbath, with this Leviathan.

For none of them was willing to give up, even if it were a tittle, of his rights and liberties. Ah, power was sweet! The Eleven licked the first pure honey of the Constitution. The rest of Parliament was only there to ratify what they decided. They kinged it over the land, spent their days behind closed doors, like the Venetian Signoria, span, trafficked, higgled among themselves, and bound the hands of the Duke and his ministers. Goodly it was and sweet to feel oneself so mighty and so clothed with power. No one would be allowed to come in and disturb it. They would plant themselves broad and immovable and shield the land from tyranny and Catholic servitude. In truth they had their firm protection and goodly shield. For firm and good was the law whereby the Duke must swear to protect their rights and those of the Protestant Church. From this law Rome with all her wiles of misinterpretation could whittle away nothing. This decree not even the subtlest Jesuit could have improved on. Only let him try to bite, the heathen, the raging tyrant! On this iron he would soon crunch his teeth out. O clear law! O blessed reciprocal bond of religion! O good, firm constitution and Tübingen treaty! O wise, wholesome, ever praiseworthy, ancestral prescience to provide such a muzzle for a biting Duke!

Punctually at ten o'clock Johann Heinrich Sturm, the president, opened the sitting. But before they had begun the order of the day, there appeared before the dumbfounded gentlemen Councillor of State Philip Jaakob Neuffer, brother of the advocate. He

87

produced documents by virtue of which Karl Alexander took over the throne of Württemberg as natural heir, and until his arrival in the Duchy delegated to Councillor von Forstner, and Neuffer as responsible minister, the conduct of state affairs.

Smiling and courteous, the Councillor declared further to the startled assembly that it was known to the Duke that in Parliament certain apprehensions were entertained concerning religion and existing liberties. He was happy to be able to deliver to the gentlemen present in the name of the Duke the most reassuring news. While still a Prince the Duke had occasion to gauge the feeling of some of the members of the Estates over the possibility which was now realized, and the gentlemen had considered the above-mentioned assurances as highly desirable for the establishment of confidence between the Duke and the nobility.

Dumb and deeply confounded, nine out of the eleven listened to this speech. Even the serene, self-possessed President Sturm could only with constraint force himself to pronounce a few sentences in which he recognized the full powers of the Councillor, now minister, gave thanks for the papers confided to them, and declared they would examine them at their leisure.

The Minister gone, the gentlemen remained dismayed, perplexed, suspicious, deeply angry. There were men among them, then, who intrigued for their own hand? The neighbours of Weissensee and Neuffer drew almost imperceptibly a little away from them. Meanwhile the other Neuffer, now minister, presented himself at the War Commissariat, and in the name of the powers delegated to him by the Duke, requested a detachment of soldiers, and held on to them in spite of a protest from the Estates. He burst (still the old Duke was not under the sod) into the Ministers' Council, arrested in the name of Karl Alexander the heads of the Countess's party and consigned them, gnashing their teeth, protesting, threatening all the curses of heaven and hell, to Hohentwiel. In captivity was Friedrich Wilhelm, the brother of the Countess, the icy man who had pushed his sister out of political life to seat himself more firmly as High Court Marshal and Minister President; in captivity were both his sons, the Head Groom of the Chambers and the Conference Minister. Their petty supporters and creatures were also apprehended, Pfeil of the Ecclesiastical Court, the State Councillors Vollmann and Scheid, and the innumerable underlings in their retinue. How they had preened themselves once! How haughtily they had walked, their noses in the air, hardly acknowledging salutations! Now they sat in their cells in thick darkness, and no one cared a brass farthing for them.

Then Neuffer waited on the Duchess and imparted to her, she who had passed from affliction to brilliance and triumph, what had happened. He had it announced by heralds and posters that Karl Alexander had assumed supreme power, would in a short time arrive from Belgrade, had already proceeded against certain unfaithful servants who for their own advantage had oppressed the people, and with princely and true words had ratified in advance all their liberties, especially those of religion.

Rejoicing among the people. That was a prince! He impressed you even before you saw him. Just as he is shown in the picture where he storms Belgrade. Bring out ribbons and greenery to garland his picture! A prince and hero. They would get on well with him.

In the vicinity of Hirsau a cart track branched off from the main road. From the cart track, again, ran a footpath which was lost in the forest and ceased altogether before a strong, very lofty wooden fence. Trees shut off the farther prospect. Of the neighbours only a gardener had access, and an aged day labourer who went errands, both of them surly men who made no reply to the inquisitive. All that was known was that a Dutchman had acquired the declining house from the heirs of an earlier proprietor. With the authorities he was registered as Mynheer Gabriel Oppenheimer van Straaten; he had letters of safety from the General States. The purchase was in all respects regular; all the demands of the police and revenue officials were met with scrupulous conscientiousness. The Dutchman stayed there with a young girl, a servant-maid, and a man-servant. A remarkable story was related of a vagabond who had tried to break into the lonely house. He had been seized and overpowered. The Dutchman had done nothing to him, only locking the insensible and jeering ruffian all night in a room with books. Tottering and deeply confounded the tramp had staggered next day through the forest, and had left the vicinity forever.

Rumours began and were silent again to the effect that the Dutchman was the Wandering Jew. He kept himself out of the way, took lonely walks, usually in the forest; very few had succeeded in seeing him. Finally people became accustomed to him. There was a mighty wooden fence and behind it dwelt the Dutchman, and if he wrought forbidden things at least he did it very quietly, and without molesting anybody.

Now there lived at Hirsau a certain Master Jaakob Polykarp Schober who taught in the Bible Class of which Magdalen Sibylle was also a member. The young man, rather fat and chubby, given to quiet meditation, and loving long, pensive walks, arrived in the course of one of these (half-involuntarily following a bird which lured him on from tree to tree) at the high fence, clambered over it without much thought or great trouble, traversed the belt of lofty trees, stood suddenly on the verge of a glade, and saw in the midst of tulips and rising terraces of flowers of a kind unknown to him, but fastidiously cared for, the Dutchman's house. It glittered uncannily, a blinding white, tiny square in the laughing sun. But before the house a primitive tent was pitched, and in it lay, relaxed and dreaming, a girl dressed after some foreign fashion, her face a smooth white under her blue-black hair. The Master stood still, stared round-eyed, full of diffidence, and tiptoed away. But after that there crept into his imaginings of the Heavenly Jerusalem the picture of the girl in the tent before the very white house with the tulips.

RABBI GABRIEL allowed the girl every freedom. Naemi bloomed peaceful and gentle and without many desires. She had the broken old serving-man and her Dutch maid Jantje, who for many years already, good-natured, devoted, garrulous and anxious, had done all her little commissions for her. Often she would have been glad to see people, but since her uncle kept them away it was no doubt for the best.

She threw herself with delight into the books which her uncle read with her. They were mostly Hebraic books, among them the mysterious Cabbala so rich and various in its interpretations.

She did not so much think of it as see it. The Cabbalistic Tree, the Divine Man, were to her actual, comprehensible entities. The lettered characters of God's name danced a sacred dance; they had gay, shimmering banners; the symbols of the sacred science moved in all their files, the triangle climbed, the square sank, from peak to peak leapt the five-pointed star. But the heptagon and the nonagon could be reckoned in regiments; they lanced themselves menacingly at her, or clustered round her in love. And all was intertwined in an endlessly winding, orderly dance.

She read in the Song of Songs: "My beloved spake, and said unto me, Rise up, my love, my fair one, and come away. For, lo, the winter is past, the rain is over and gone. The flowers appear on the earth; the time of the singing of birds is come, and the voice of the turtle is heard in our land. . . .

"Arise, my love, my fair one, and come away. O my dove, that art in the clefts of the rock, in the secret places of the stairs, let me see thy countenance, let me hear thy voice; for sweet is thy voice, and thy countenance is comely." She sat, soft and attentive, her practised eyes gliding over the great, unwieldy Hebrew characters.

Rabbi Gabriel declared that what she had read signified the creation of the world; that the flowers were the All Father, the voice that of the youth who, learning the mysteries of the written word, labours that the world might be preserved and the Father manifest Himself. And he interpreted it this way and that, with much profundity and subtlety; and finally, absorbed and lost, he was silent. She listened piously, but hardly had he ended ere the flowers were once more flowers, and she heard the sweet and simple melody: "For, lo, the winter is past, the rain is over and gone. The flowers appear on the earth; the time of the singing of birds is come, and the voice of the turtle is heard in our land." And she closed her eyes and listened to the seductive voice, and she lurked behind the trees and held her breath: now, immediately, in the very next instant, the Shepherd would become visible, he whose words chimed with a silvery ringing. But no one came.

The heroes and saints of the Bible, too, signified certainly what Rabbi Gabriel said. But when he was not there Naemi regarded them with her own eyes. She herself was Tamar, loved by Haman,

91

she was Rachel who fled with Jacob, she was Rebecca at the well. She was Miriam, too, who danced the dance of victory over the Egyptians drowned by the Lord. But she was not Jael, who drove the nail into Sisera's temple, nor was she Deborah, who judged in Israel. With the few people of her acquaintance she filled the histories of the Bible. Hagar bore the lineaments of the garrulous maid, Jantje; the prophets had the melancholy, grey, stony-sad eyes of her uncle and his flat nose, and they spoke with his rasping, ill-tempered voice.

But the heroes had the mien of her father, his face, his eyes, the sonorous flow of his flexible, eloquent, persuasive voice. Oh, her father! How radiant he was, how splendid! But oh, how seldom he came! To hang upon his neck, that was life, and all that was left over was the anticipation that he would come again. All the heroes of the Scriptures she saw in his image. Samson, who slew the Philistines, wore her father's olive-green coat, and stamped, swift, splendid and dangerous, in his jingling riding boots. David, when he overcame Goliath, moved daintily in the red, elegantly-cut tail-coat in which her father had arrived last time, and the lifted arm with the sling threw back from the wrist the exquisitely-frilled cuffs. But with secret, lascivious horror she saw one thing more, that the hair by which Absalom was caught to the tree was the rich, chestnut hair of her father; and when David lamented, O Absalom, my son!—then he groaned with the rasping voice of her uncle, and it was the glowing, beloved eyes of her father that he closed.

FESTIVELY the new Duke sailed up the Danube in the yacht which his father-in-law had given him. Motionless at the stern huddled the dark-haired Duchess with fathomless eyes. Near her, massive, sat General Remchingen, his vinous face scarlet under the white peruke; puffing and blowing and modish he paid his court to the beautiful lady in his singing Austrian German. He sparkled, a hundred foolhardy and vain plans blossomed now into ripeness. One of the first measures of the Duke had been to appoint his friend to the presidency of the Ministry of War and the highest command in Württemberg.

There was a brilliant reception in Vienna:—their majesties

extremely gracious; high mass; banquet at the Castle; opera. The old Prince Thurn and Taxis had come to Vienna to meet his son-in-law; nor had his two spiritual friends foregone the privilege of meeting him at Vienna to tender him their congratulations. When the yacht was brought alongside, the Prince Bishop of Würzburg with his Privy Councillors Raab and Fichtel, and the Lord Abbot stood on the quay, kissed the Duke, pleased and cordial, and twinkling, pressed Marie Auguste's hand.

After the opera—their majesties and the Duchess have already withdrawn—Karl Alexander, the Prince of Thurn and Taxis, and both prelates still remain sitting. Dusky yellow Tokay smoothly gleams; the Duke has grown used to it in Belgrade, and drinks it in great gulps, while the Jesuits content themselves with sips. The air is heavy with candle-smoke and wine.

Before these friends and tried comrades Karl Alexander laid bare his heart. Oh, he had not a mind to rust away among his possessions as a petty princeling! His ambition went beyond seeing that his subjects cultivated their wine properly, wove their linen, and kept their children's noses and the tails of their shirts clean. He would let his councillors manage, but he would rule. He had not been so long in camps for nothing. He was a soldier, a soldier-duke. If he had fought and conquered so long for another, if friendly house, how much better he could fight and conquer for himself. Louis XIV had conquered; little Venice had bitten off a good part of Greece; starting from Sweden the twelfth Charles had borne his banners through half Europe; in Potsdam they were preparing for a campaign of conquest. He felt it; he was the man to make out of his little state a greater one; perhaps, if God willed, a great one. In any case he would not let his land remain as it was now. In it one knocked oneself blue and silly against all sorts of corners, whichever direction one turned, and could stretch neither arm nor leg. He was enough of a strategist, however, and understood enough of the art of warfare, to know that his little state by virtue of its geographical position was the nucleus of a greater. If only one drove straight forward from the Württemberg dependencies beyond the Rhine, from the earldom of Mömpelgard which lay right in the midst of the French ones, and from there went on: for a strategist that was an excellent basis of action. Then the host of tin-pot towns in the middle of the Duchy and round the frontiers, the free burghs, Reutlingen, Ulm, Heilbronn, Gmund, Weil die Stadt; he could not understand how his predecessors had allowed these to flourish and luxuriate so rankly. He would take good care that they should not lie any longer on his stomach like stones, but should be nourishing provender.

"Your Highness is very keen," smiled old Thurn and Taxis, and sniffed with his greyhound nose at his Tokay. Well pleased he listened to the temperamental projects of his son-in-law. He held all that to be mere Utopia; but, God knew, the Duke was a soldier; one did not demand political insight from him. Two months in his Residence, and the fire would peter out.

The two Princes of the Church listened attentively to the emphatic words of Karl Alexander. They had prosecuted his conversion to Catholicism with great zeal, for one thing because one should always help an erring soul towards the light, for another because he was a great propaganda weapon for bringing over the Württembergers; but most of all for pure sport. They had not followed their victory, indeed, with great political plans. But now that God had disposed things so happily and had set the newly-won convert in such a high place, one could pocket with a smirk the innumerable compliments one got for one's wise prescience. But it was urgently important to utilize with all one's power the unanticipated opportunity. Fire such as burned in the Duke was always useful. Many a concoction might be warmed at it.

Cautiously the stout Prince Bishop of Würzburg began. His brother the Duke was occupied with great projects in which every Christian Catholic prince must wish him luck. But he forgot that God had chosen him out to rule a rebellious and wholly impenitent Babylon. Like rats these accursed Evangelicals had nibbled the divine rights of German princes, so that now, ruined and pitiable, they hung in tatters.

The Duke said that the Württemberger was not wicked; he was a loyal subject and faithful to his princes. It was only that accursed party in Parliament, that obstinate company of stingy donkeys who once had refused him his appanage, that unwieldy, treasonable herd of muttons, who had intrigued with his brother.

But he had been on the *qui vive*, he had not let himself be cheated out of his throne, and now, in power, he would pay them back and give them such a blowing up that they would sweat blood.

The Abbot smiled: that was not quite so simple. In the first place his promises were there. That was paper, paper! cried the Duke, reckless and inflamed with wine. "Certainly," quietly answered the Jesuit, "but provisionally binding. After all, the Bible, too, is only paper, and yet upon it stand Rome and the world."

The Würzburger interposed smoothly: Karl Alexander's strength and wisdom, the help and craft of his friends, his soldiers and the justice of his cause, would at last shred away the scrap of paper. The Catholicizing of the Duchy, the foundation and corner-stone of all those projects, was difficult, but not impossible. One had that model of adroitness and success, the Catholicization of Pfalz-Neuburg. First of all only Catholic officers and soldiers. No parliament could oppose that. Then all the court charges filled gradually with Catholics exclusively, and finally all the official posts in the country. The Protestants would be dismissed without distinction, all of them. Oh, how many souls skipped into the true Church in the Pfalz at that time! First of all the public officials, who had families and were chiefly concerned to save their skins. Oh, how lustily they adjured the Protestant heresy. Oh, how they leapt and hurried breathless, the good, valiant souls, into the bosom of the Church!

They laughed, drank. Many ways were opening. The Prince Bishop promised that he would work out with the help of his sagacious Privy Councillor Fichtel main lines of action specifically designed for Württemberg. They parted full of enthusiasm and hope.

Next day three Imperial Councillors appeared before the Duke, to take counsel with him over the French War into which the Emperor had imprudently been drawn. Karl Alexander, who hitherto had had relations with the Imperial Councillors only as a suppliant, a nuisance, a salaried general, swaggered now that he was courted at last, and carelessly, with a grand gesture, flung to the ministers his subsidy of twelve thousand men, for which they had anxiously begged him. With many diplomatic clauses and in veiled terms an imperial secret treaty promised him in return protection and augmentation of his sovereignty against the eventual encroachments of his Estates.

When the Duke left Vienna, his Roman Majesty kissed him on both cheeks before court and people.

When he heard of Eberhard Ludwig's death, Josef Süss stood for a moment holding his breath, his ripe red mouth half open, his left hand raised as if to ward something off, and all his blood flew to his heart. Arrived! He had arrived. Quite suddenly he was at the top. He had drawn the winning number among a hundred thousand blanks, his intuition had been right, he stood like a proud genius before the shrewd Isaac Landauer, who had smiled and shaken his head over his belief in the insignificant Prince, and had rubbed his chilly hands.

Ah, now he would walk with high and mighty tread. A hundred brilliant salons would be thrown open to him. He had sprung high with one bound. Now he would sit at magnificent tables, an equal among equals, with the great of this world. Those who had kept him waiting in their antechambers would now wait before his door until he admitted them. And women, fair, shining and elegant, who had graciously accepted his love, would now come begging him to take their proud bodies. He would repay with interest the kicks which he had had to accept. He would show the great men that a Jew could carry his head ten times as high as any of them.

He sold his houses in Heidelberg and Mannheim and published a haughty announcement that whoever had claims on him in the Palatinate should present them at once. Meanwhile he bought secretly through intermediaries the palace of a decayed noble family in Stuttgart, in the Seegasse, had it magnificently done up, and enlarged his staff of servants, his wardrobe and his table.

Isaac Landauer found him in the middle of these preparations. Mean and dirty-looking the great financier sat in an awkward, angular posture in a large arm-chair and warmed his wasted bloodless hands, irritating Süss profoundly by his side-curls, caftan and shabby Jewish garb. Vexed and disappointed, Süss had to admit that Laudauer was manifestly neither impressed nor envious. "You have been lucky, Reb Josef Süss," he said, shaking his head, good humoured and a trifle mocking. "But it might well have turned out badly, and then all your money would have been thrown away on the sponger." "At any rate he's not a sponger now," said Süss sharply. "That's just what I am saying," agreed the other with great readiness. And confidentially, authoritatively: "Why all this fuss and feathers and foolishness? Be advised by an old business man; it is not practicable, it will only do you harm. Why puff yourself up and take a place in the sun? It is not good for a Jew to set himself where everybody can see him. Be advised by an old business man; a Jew is much better off in the shadow." And with a small chuckling laugh, "An I. O. U. in the strong-box is better than gold lace on the coat." And good-humoured, with gentle mockery, he fingered the embroidery on Süss's sleeves, while the latter almost with disgust sought to pull them away.

"So that's what these youngsters are," thought Isaac Landauer, when he had taken leave of Süss. "They sink and sink to the level of the Goim. They need noise and glitter and embroidered coats. They have to feel that they are acknowledged by others. Of the subtle secret triumph in caftan and side-curls they have not a notion, these superficial creatures."

Süss sneered to himself: "What a coward he is! Always hiding himself. What is the good of power if it is not seen? These stupid, timid, old-fashioned prejudices! Oh, yes, only keep the Christians from noticing you! Only cower in the shadow! In the broad light of day I will set myself up, and I will look every man straight in the eye."

He travelled to Frankfurt with a magnificent equipage, visited his mother to show himself to her in all his glory. The beautiful old lady, from whom he had inherited his white skin and his arched lively eyes, lived in great comfort an empty life. Ah, how full her days had once been! Michaele the actress had scoured Germany behind galloping horses, and all the streets were full of men, of adventures, of lusts, triumphs, sorrows and excitement. Now her destiny was only faintly tinged from outside by the hues of experience; she filled her hours with beauty-culture, kept up a manifold and voluble correspondence, and crept into the lives of

97

her innumerable acquaintances. Süss inflated himself and postured before her; she feasted on his glory and with large foolish eyes absorbed his loud and windy boasts.

Into the rainbow froth of their chatter fell Rabbi Gabriel. Süss had just been bragging with gleeful triumph of the women who thrust themselves into his chambers, and Michaele had been listening greedily. But now the broad stony surly face of the old man obliterated all these gay light faces like an enormous boulder. Yes, he was aware that the new Duke had already left Vienna and would soon make his entry. Süss was naturally on his way to meet him. He spoke with such cold, weary mockery that all Süss's achievements seemed bare and equivocal. Then he asked casually when Süss was coming to Hirsau, if at all; for the child needed to see his face. When Süss evaded the question and excused himself, he did not push it farther, only the three furrows deepened in his brow. He looked from the mother to the son, from the son to the mother. Soon he went away.

Süss's pride and glory had been scattered to the winds, and it was only with difficulty that he picked up the pieces again. Slowly and not quite securely he balanced himself again atop of his old magnificence, and cautiously made fun of the old man. But his mother did not chime in with him, and his departure was not quite so radiant and satisfactory as his arrival.

The journey to Regensburg was rapid; loudly and in the gayest of humours the Duke received him. Remchingen, excessively red under his white peruke, fell upon him with malicious jests; he could not stand Jews, and this one with his too courteous and insinuating address was doubly repugnant to him. The old Prince Thurn and Taxis also met him with reserve; he had not forgotten that the Jew had killed the effect of his pale yellow coat by his pale yellow salon in Monbijou.

But the Duchess smiled to him with great favour, very amused. Graciously she extended her small plump well-cared-for hand for the Jew to kiss, while in the other, as fashion prescribed, she held with delicate affectation the upper folds of her skirt. Oh, what dark and wicked thoughts might he not have kissed into her hand! And how fashionably he was got up, to the last hair. It was amusing to have a Jew like that about one, who looked like the most

98

gallant gentleman from Versailles, and who hid behind such a fine maroon coat his evil Jewish heart which was certainly full of every kind of wickedness and slimy poison.

Later, when they were alone together, the Duke asked him about the temper of the country. Süss at once perceived how much importance was attached to his judgment, and became immediately business-like, objective, concentrated, and skilfully on the alert. He sat as the clever financier, with his nerves tense and all his assurance at work; drew more out of the Duke than the Duke out of him; arranged his answers cleverly so that they all went to confirm Karl Alexander's expectations.

Of his own accord the latter clapped him on the shoulder. "You have not swindled me after all with your Magus, you devil of a Jew!" Süss shrank, and contrary to his habit gave a forced, constrained, hesitating answer; he had himself staked something on these cabbalistic prophecies; it was no wonder that they should be dependable and true. Watching him, the Duke, also in a slightly false manner, replied that the Rabbi had prophesied a bad end. If the prophecies were so dependable why did Süss link his fortunes with his? And Süss, after a pause, said that what the Rabbi held to be good or bad lay in another sphere, and men like His Highness and himself who were not fantastic did not need to scratch their heads over such subtle and metaphysical matters.

He was suddenly stricken dumb, struggling for breath, his head turned aside. It seemed to him that a man was looking over his shoulder, a man with his own face, but quite shadowy and vague. The Duke too was silent. The things around him lost their colour, the Jew before him faded out of sight. He saw himself treading a strange unreal measure; ahead of him moved the uncanny Magus, Rabbi Gabriel, holding one of his hands, while Süss behind held the other.

The Jew wrested the Duke out of his vision, switched him on to other matters. The Duke had spoken with contempt and bitterness of his brother, Prince Heinrich Friedrich, and of his intrigues with the Estates. Here Süss made an opening with some discreet jests at the expense of the mild and incompetent conspirator, and then spoke of his mistress, the quiet, golden-brown, stupid creature. The Duke listened with interest, amusement and malice. What the deuce! The mild Heinrich must be poor fare for her, a lean dish without any sauce! He laughed without stopping, and in his eyes there kindled a wicked, calculating glitter. The Jew knew the girl, of course; he must describe her. Süss described her carefully, and dissected her skilfully, the daughter of a small country squire, mild, big and bulky, her fairness, her warm and sluggish youth. The Duke listened maliciously, greedily, and with satisfaction: obviously his plan was ripe. "You are a connoisseur, Jew," he laughed. "You are an expert in Christian flesh and blood, you swindler."

Süss, left to himself, smiled profoundly and triumphantly, and considered the line he was to take. It was clear. To flatter the Duke unhesitatingly, without any fear of exaggeration. To procure money for him, and, through money, women, soldiers, and glory. More, and still more. Not to pocket too much for himself, but to procure so much money that he would be rich if only a little of it stuck to him. To pay no attention to the Estates. To treat them *en canaille*. His sole aim to be money for the Duke's treasury.

He had taken Karl Alexander the right way. He had also done well to purchase the palace in Stuttgart. When he left Regensburg in advance of the Duke he was Privy Financial Councillor to the Duchy of Württemberg. To his letters of appointment was attached a decree of the Duchess, nominating him as the keeper of her Privy Purse.

In Stuttgart there were enormous preparations for the reception of the new ruler. Three triumphal arches with proud Latin inscriptions and many allegorical figures, countless banners and garlands. The streets packed with people rosy with the cold and exhilarated by the bright and joyous clearness of the December day. Hawkers everywhere with the Duke's picture for sale, the famous picture of him at the head of seven hundred halberdiers martially storming the fortress of Belgrade amid a hail of bullets. Süss had caused several thousand copies of it to be printed, as a pleasure for the Duke and his people, and as a source of profit for himself, and now citizens and peasants struggled to obtain this cheap, patriotic and heart-warming decoration for their walls. The whole town resounded with music, cheering, and the firing of small mortars. At last came the procession two miles long: officials, officers, soldiers both horse and foot, couriers and pages. Sixteen horses drew the Duke's gala-coach. So he made his entry through streets glittering with snow under a radiant and clear blue December sky, and a thousand gay banners waved in the lusty wind.

Open-hearted and open-mouthed the Stuttgarters gaped with delight at their imposing sovereign, who sat with lordly mien and leonine head, his fur cloak thrown back from his broad chest covered with stars; and still more perhaps at their amazingly lovely Duchess, smothered in white furs, whose small, strange, lizard-like face under the diadem peeped delicately and smilingly at them with indolent curiosity. But how she inwardly laughed at the Swabians who were cheering her! How much that was ridiculous did she find in the orator from the University of Tübingen, the fat, self-conscious, perspiring professor who used up all his energy in declaiming with a Swabian accent the stirring verses with which he greeted the princely couple! She listened earnestly and attentively while he spoke of the people whom the Duke was called to rule with his sceptre, and announced with pathos that Karl Alexander's renown combined all the fame of Charlemagne and of the other Karls in history with all that was renowned in the Grecian Alexander, all that God's chosen people had prized in Samson together with all that Hercules had ever possessed, finishing by comparing him with the Cæsars of Rome. And she did not even show her amusement when he glorified the Duke as being already famous for all time since he was like the Prince of Ithaca whose soul yearned for a Mentor. But inwardly she questioned who this mentor might be, the small cautious Privy Councillor Fichtel, with his black coffee, or the elegant Jew with his sly foxiness and gallantry?

Meanwhile the latter was standing modestly and with great respect quite in the background, in a corner among the attendants. He had thought it wise to enter Stuttgart quietly and without much outward show: he had taken possession of his magnificent house and was not as yet very much remarked. Nothing could be got out of his confidential attendant, the quiet, phlegmatic Nicklas Pfäffle; it was just some great man or other from the

101

Court of the new Duke. Only gradually did it become known that the Privy Financial Councillor, although he looked and carried himself like any other great man, was merely an ordinary unbaptized Jew. Now Jews were actually forbidden to reside in the Duchy. Still, people admitted that considering the involved state of the Treasury's finances, and the slyness of the Jews in charge of the Countess's affairs, the Duke must be allowed to keep a Court Jew of his own. Moreover, they had to concede that for the present the new Jew bore himself honestly and quietly, and now, while the Duke was being celebrated, he kept himself modestly in a corner for all his grand title and magnificent uniform.

But three days later, at the reception given to the Estates, he was quite different. Proud, cold, and keen he stood among the Ministers and cast a distant, unfriendly eye on the swarming members of Parliament. The little group of Cabinet Ministers, among them the Jew, stood in gay and brilliant uniforms arrogantly aloof from the thickly-packed black-coated Parliamentarians. Fourteen Prelates were in the House, and seventy representatives of the towns and government departments. Only a few like the subtle, clever Weissensee and the hard-worked advocate, Veit Ludwig Neuffer, were equal to the occasion; the majority had anxious, embarrassed, perspiring faces, and were sulky and ill at ease under the cold and haughty glances of the ministerial group. Among the Ministers were Forstner, the President of the Council, and the ambiguous, insinuating Neuffer, who had both been supporters of Karl Alexander even while the old Duke was alive, and had quashed the intrigues of the Estates with Prince Heinrich Friedrich. Then there was Andreas Heinrich von Schütz, with his enormous hooknose, originally a creature of the Countess, who kept his place under every government. These three boded no good to the Estates; the Jew also boded no good, whose behaviour at the welcoming ceremony had been obviously a provocation. The Estates had confidence in only one of the Ministers, and the fact that the Duke had summoned him into the Cabinet balanced the presence of Neuffer and the Jew. That was Georg Bernhard Bilfinger, the philosopher and physical scientist. Karl Alexander had become acquainted with this comfortable man, with the open, plump, energetic face, when he had to go over with him certain of his calcula-

102

tions and plans for fortresses. And however much he mistrusted all philosophy, he had not been able to resist the temptation of putting into his Cabinet this reliable mathematician and designer of fortifications instead of a lawyer.

Both groups, the small group of Ministers and the large group of Parliamentary representatives, confronted each other like two hostile animals, the one large, clumsy, black-coated and helpless, the other small, brilliant, gay, quick and dangerous.

They waited; they waited very long, nearly an hour beyond the appointed time. And still there was no triumphal march, no presentation of arms by the guards in the antechamber, still the door remained shut which led from the Duke's private suite. Perspiring in the over-heated room, with black and surly looks, the representatives of the people shifted from one foot to the other, even the Ministers began to be uneasy. That from the very first moment the Duke should treat his Parliament in such an off-hand manner was quite unexpected. Was it intentional? Or, was it a whim or an accident, or absence of mind?

Only one person knew. The Jew stood smiling, sharing with understanding and enjoyment the relish of this extraordinary triumph which Karl Alexander had planned. Had the Estates intrigued with his brother? Good, then let them prop their bellies on their legs and wait until he had indulged himself with his brother's mistress, the gentle, golden-brown, tranquil creature.

PRIVY Councillor Andreas Heinrich von Schütz read out the Constitution to which the Duke had to swear allegiance. It was all set down with terrible caution, circumlocution, and long-windedness.

Not very loudly, in a level, well-trained voice, Herr von Schütz read the endless document through his enormous hook-nose with a slight French accent; the chamber was over-heated, a winter fly buzzed, and from the crowd of men in heavy clothes arose an exhalation of steam and stertorous breathing. With surly irritation Karl Alexander surveyed the rows of dull workaday faces which tried to assume an air of pathos, with surly irritation he listened to the declamation of these stiff and solemn periods, every word of which meant obligations, shameless, unlimited, subversive

103

compulsions laid upon him. And it droned on, unendingly. He had to keep himself from interrupting, from venting suddenly a loud and peevish yawn. He was newly out of an embrace, he could still hear her unrestrained, low, tearful sobbing which had wetted his face, arms, and breast; he was filled with loose and brutal mirth.

The members of Parliament were scandalized by the way in which he repeated the solemn oath in a hoarse, husky voice—a consequence of the dalliance from which he came—asthmatically, with maddening indifference, and with his thoughts obviously far away.

"This I confirm and swear to on my true and princely word, after mature consideration and of my own free will." And it sounded as though he were telling his valet that the shaving water was not warm enough.

Dejected and full of anxiety the members withdrew. If he had abused them like the late Duke, Eberhard Ludwig, if he had fallen upon them roundly with vituperation, they could have made against that a better stand than against this uncivil, contemptuous, and astonishingly nonchalant treatment. O lovely freedom! O pleasant power of the leading families! You will have to be fought for strenuously now.

Karl Alexander stretched himself when the members had gone, threw himself into an arm-chair, and was complacent. He had given them it. How they had slunk out with their tails between their legs! He gave a snort of intense gratification. A good beginning; a good day. First one in the eye for the soft Heinrich Friedrich, the interfering sneak, and then the impudent, greedy, sweating rabble sent home well basted, choking with the rage they had had to swallow.

He dismissed the Ministers also, and as they took their leave he chuckled in Süss's ear: "I have still something in there to comfort, golden-haired and sobbing. The sneak has taste, more taste than I credited him with." He roared with laughter and clapped Süss flatteringly on the shoulder.

"I WANT to rule personally," he had said to a deputation from Stuttgart. "I will myself hearken to and help my people." He let it be known all through the country that he would not shrink from any labour or difficulty conducing to the true welfare and prosperity of the Duchy, and would make it his care to see that in every part of it justice should be dealt out with the good old Württemberg honesty and uprightness, without any evasions, intrigues or complications. Whoever had a complaint against any official, or any request to make, should set it down circumstantially on paper and put it into the Duke's own hands.

For three consecutive Sundays this ordinance of the new Duke was read out from all the pulpits in the country; it was printed and affixed to the Town Hall of every parish. The people shouted delightedly, "This is a real Duke; he does not let his bureaucrats rule, he rules in person." Like snow in May the Countess's party melted away. The sour Dowager Duchess flourished on their downfall. And the picture of Karl Alexander storming Belgrade with his halberdiers went like wildfire, and when an edict actually forbade petitioners to kneel before the Duke, on the ground that such an honour was due only to God, Süss had to print an enormous new edition of it, and there was no town or country house in the Duchy which had not that picture in a place of honour.

The Duke supported with all his influence the prosecution of the former Lord Marshal and of his sister, the Countess, but without any real success. True, a specially-constituted Court of Justice was set up to deal with the Countess, and the first lawyer in the country, the Tübingen Professor Moritz David Harpprecht, respected throughout Germany for his strict impartiality, presented capital charges against her for bigamy, for repeated and long-continued adultery, for three attempts to murder Eberhard Ludwig's wife, for lese-majesty, for abortion, for forgery, treachery, and embezzlement, and the Court of Justice found her guilty and condemned her to death. A special agent from Württemberg, Baron Zech, was sent to Vienna to assure the ratification and execution of this decree, and he spent money to the extent of 143,000 gulden in trying to win the imperial counsellors. But whether it was that Isaac Landauer had spent more, or whether he was simply cleverer, the process dragged on wearisomely and relapsed finally into a complicated and formal transaction for monetary compensation.

This affair, and all the business of government from the Cabinet downwards, soon became a weariness of the flesh to the Duke. He had published fine manifestoes, and won the love of his people; and his advisers, Remchingen the blustering general, Schütz the smooth diplomat, and Süss the wily financier, assured him from day to day that now all abuses were swept away and that the golden age of Württemberg had dawned. Where could one find in Germany another ruler with such a sense of duty? Carrying himself proudly before God and men and in his own esteem, inflated by the feeling that he well deserved the title bestowed on him in an address from the University of Tübingen, the title "truest shepherd and blessing of mankind," he left the fulfilment of his promises to his advisers, and betook himself with his hunger for new glory to the army, pleased and happy to go back to a soldier's life.

Süss conferred with Privy Councillor Bilfinger and Professor Harpprecht about the prosecution of the Countess and her brother. The gentlemen sat in Süss's magnificent study, the Jew slim and elegant, the two Württembergers broad and bulky. The case was not going well. Vienna was not inclined to ratify the death penalty on the Countess, and suggested instead a financial compromise. This compromise seemed a poor one to the Württembergers, and hardly consonant with the Ducal dignity. Süss, on the other hand, considered that the most palpable form of success was a large sum of money. If they would leave the financial settlement in his hands he would certainly carry it out to the Duke's satisfaction. Both earnest and upright men found this attitude frivolous and Jewish. But after all the agent from Württemberg had come back from Vienna without anything to show, there was no way out except by financial compensation, the Jew would certainly arrange that better than any one else, and the Duke had unlimited confidence in his luck and skill. Reluctantly they consented.

When this had been settled, Süss asked the lawyer further for his opinion about some disputed powers of the Estates. This was a question which moved both Württembergers to the bottom of their hearts. Harpprecht, the jurist, slow, thoughtful and circumspect, accustomed to turn things round and to look at them closely from all sides, and Bilfinger, the trusted friend of Wolf the famous philosopher, inclined to regard things seriously and from a lofty point of view, both of them thorough patriots and quiet, practical men, did not blink at the fact that a few leading citizen families encroached on the Constitution as if it were their private inheritance and portioned out the seats of the people's representatives among themselves; they both knew that the flag of liberty is always liable to abuse by individuals who cut pieces out of it for their own private purposes. But in spite of that they were profoundly convinced with all their hearts that the statutes and parliamentary liberties of the land were the pillars of the state, and they interpreted all controversial questions arising between the people and their rulers with the responsible seriousness and love of liberty which had inspired the first Duke of Württemberg, a really great ruler in his small country, to bequeath them the Constitution.

The matters under discussion were certain proposals made by Süss for taxes and monopolies which undoubtedly violated the spirit of the Constitution; the letter of the law, however, was not so impervious but what an inventive and unscrupulous quibbler could make breaches in it. Harpprecht, seconded by Bilfinger, spoke till he was warm, and Süss listened with attention and courtesy. But suddenly the scholar noticed the financier's eyes, the large, malignant, clever, lurking, conscienceless eyes of a beast of prey. To eyes like that what were liberty, constitution, conscience or people? Before the gaze of the Jew, rapacious, and purified by no ideal, all these great things faded into silly dreams of youth, and became discredited and ridiculous. He felt that he was an idiot to speak to this man of business about the spirit of the laws and their fine and earnest intention. Of course the other was only culling from his words what would be useful to himself in his unctuous and self-seeking projects. Harpprecht broke off rather suddenly; even the slower Bilfinger had guessed what hampered his friend. The two Württembergers withdrew immediately, icy and out of temper, and were escorted respectfully to the door by the immovably courteous Süss.

At the door they encountered Isaac Landauer in his caftan and side-curls. Süss had invited him to come and settle the Countess's affairs with him. They both understood each other without having to hint at their common purpose. This was to draw up a balance-sheet which would apparently be favourable to the Duke, but in reality to the Countess. Bargaining sharply they put all their forces into play against each other. Each had his own special interests as well, for each of them had claims on both the Duke and the Countess. Finally Süss reckoned up an apparent gain of 323,000 gulden for the Duke, but in fact the Duke had to pay the Countess 158,000 gulden. In handing over this sum Süss to be sure kept back for himself 30,000 gulden against alleged loans and advances, and he charged the Duke for his services a further 5,000 gulden.

So the love-affairs of the Countess, which had plunged the Duchy into rage and confusion for so many years, ended with a considerable profit for Privy Financial Councillor Josef Süss Oppenheimer. The Countess protracted in Berlin a brilliant and restless existence. The sour Dowager Duchess had fallen ill of an incurable disease, which gained upon her until her doctors wondered that she did not succumb. But she, full of bleak, grey, dusty hate, stared fixedly at her enemy in Berlin, the hussy, and did not die until three weeks after her.

KARL ALEXANDER was in the fortresses, among the redoubts, at the camps; he rode, travelled around, gave orders, and was enormously active. He gave a hearty celebration in honour of meeting Prince Eugene again, the old, clever, somewhat formal and dry Commander-in-Chief. The prudent Prince had retreated before the superior forces of the French, and entrenched himself strongly near Heilbronn. The French were in the Duchy again already, and were ravaging and confiscating everything. But the strengthening of the Imperial Army, for which Karl Alexander was mainly responsible, forced them back over the Rhine. With wild impetuosity the Duke now devoted himself to making the frontier secure. The fortresses were enlarged, and redoubts were added, and all the time he was conferring with Bilfinger. A very far-sighted project of real strategic genius was seriously and skilfully undertaken. From Rottweil to Rottenburg escarpments were made at certain points in the mountains, and in the Black Forest from Schiltach to Oberndorf lines of defence were drawn right up to the Neckar, and the Heuberg was secured with barricades. Five battalions and ten or twelve squadrons were enough to hold these fortifications. And with such relatively small means a Swabian Thermopylæ was fashioned, against which every French Xerxes would have to break his head.

The Estates at first did not oppose Karl Alexander's plans. In Eberhard Ludwig's time the Duchy had suffered too much from the incursions, pillaging, forays, violence and swords of the French not to appreciate from the bottom of its heart the strong, professional and soldierly protection provided by its new ruler. Once the French were driven back over the Rhine, however, and the immediate danger dissipated, the Estates became difficult. They annoyed the Duke by raising countless formal and pedantic objections. At every minute deputations appeared with complaints about his methods of recruiting and of raising war material, and irritated him by their thick, stockish, shopkeeping faces, by their stupid self-conscious clumsiness. Difficulties arose everywhere. The reserve of troops came trickling in slowly and reluctantly; horses, material, and provisions were provided without any enthusiasm and never to the required extent; the war taxes fell off obstinately, supplies stopped, and the treasury was exhausted. Naturally inclined to be mistrustful, the Duke began to suspect his advisers of being secretly in alliance with the Estates. He summoned his Jew into the field.

The latter had already noted with the keenest attention even the most insignificant details of Württemberg politics, and had long been waiting avidly for this moment. In his sharp, clear, alert way he had marked out his goal, and every inch of his province lay before him like a map drawn up with mathematical precision. So he betook himself to the camp with pride and decision. Karl Alexander received him immediately. It was night, candles were burning, and in a corner squatted the dusky brown slave. The Duke was sitting with Bilfinger over geometrical tables. In a sudden fit of rage he vented all his pent-up ill-humour and vexation; before these two he let himself go. His suspicion of his ministers had increased. They were hand in glove with the rebellious and malicious Estates. Bilfinger was shocked and ill at ease as he listened to this unwarranted and senseless outburst, and tried to convince the Duke of his error by objective considerations. Süss restricted himself to listening closely; his pale, tranquil face with its significant smile contrasted strongly in the flicker of the candles with the red excited faces of the Duke and his fortress-builder. Suddenly Karl Alexander turned to him: "And you, Jew?" Süss, shrugging his shoulders, remarked that it was certainly striking how badly and incompletely the clear and wise commands of the Duke had been carried out. It might well be possible that the Privy Councillors had secret dealings with discontented members of Parliament, but whether that were true or not, in any case they must be incompetent, cavilling, and underhand in their methods, for the results to be so unsatisfactory. "What do you then propose?" inquired the Duke. Süss replied that, judging from his experiences in the Austrian war levies, they would have to punish every case of passive resistance with high fines. Fines would be the most efficient spur. Both citizens and peasants hung on to their possessions; they would sacrifice their lives sooner than their money. The Duke said he would think it over and Süss should work out the special applications. The Jew explained that he had already done so, and laid down a bundle of documents and calculations. Bilfinger began afresh to muster soberly all the arguments against the suspicions of the Duke and to recommend milder and slower measures. Karl Alexander cut him short with a nasty glance.

On the very next day he gave Remchingen orders to put Süss's proposals strictly into practice. Both men now worked in unison, the General the fist, the Jew the brain.

Remchingen jeered at the Jew with brutal, vulgar witticisms. Süss hated and despised him, but did not let himself be enticed into hostility, and received the jeers and abuse of the soldier with a smooth, insensitive and courteous smile. The two men had in common their unlimited ambition to serve the Duke, to procure money and soldiers for him; common to both also was the profound and unquestioning conviction that the people were chattels of their sovereign like his dogs and his horses.

As if by magic everything was now on the spot which neither force nor persuasion had formerly availed to secure. Where the

110

recruiting drum with its rattling had hitherto brought in only a few thousand volunteers on not very sound legs, many of them broken-down cripples, the depots were now bursting with recruits. In the remount lines the horses were crowded thick, the store-rooms were piled with uniforms, the strong-boxes swollen with money and securities, the barns and magazines had no more room for the grain that came pouring in, and the provisions were heaped up to the roof. Everywhere reserves and reinforcements. Karl Alexander swelled with triumph, and boasted to all the world of the genius and dexterity of his Privy Financial Councillor.

But on the people all this weighed like lead, choking the breath out of them. Formerly there had certainly been a kind of con-scription, but only for wanderers and vagabonds, for work-shy young fellows who were a burden to the parishes. But now the recruiting was extended to include all the young unmarried men in the country. Those who wished to buy themselves off had an enormous sum to pay. Married men were exempted; but any one who wanted to marry before he was twenty-five had to give up the fifth of his possessions as a tax. The horses were inspected and all the fit ones requisitioned, and the State paid for them with bills which could be presented only after long intervals. Trade and commerce were burdened with heavy war-duties, and the taxes were sternly enforced.

Ah, how the wreaths and ribbons vanished from the pictures of the Duke! The flower of the young men were forced cursing into uniforms. Mothers, wives, and brides sobbed, went to pieces in the absence of their men. Through the ban on marriage the number of illegitimate children increased; abortion and in-fanticide became common. The fields were badly worked for lack of hands, the best horses were seized and carried off. High prices threatened; food and wares were not to be had. Loud was the cursing and the rage. Sharp decrees forbade on pain of imprison-ment or death any disrespectful comment on the ducal ordinances, any rioting and breach of the peace. A few grumblers and mal-contents were arrested and prosecuted. The shouts of rage died away, but the curses rolled on wherever there was no fear of eavesdroppers.

111

This frame of mind did not disturb Süss by so much as a hair. In the Palatinate, when he had introduced the Stamp-tax, he had grown accustomed to demonstrations before his house, abuse and lampoons; all that flowed off him like water from a tarpaulin. Who could touch him? He sat throned in power, he was the nearest adviser of the ruler, nobody could manage the Duke as he did. Nobody understood as he did how to bend with abject humility before the raging storms of the violent man who was accustomed to military discipline, and to present himself again, an hour after he had been kicked out, as if nothing had happened. The Duke's officials were informed that they must follow unquestioningly his advice in all monetary affairs, and no financial arrangement was made without his knowledge and consent.

With dilated nostrils, complacently, Süss savoured the atmosphere of power in which he now lived. Since his successful measures for replenishing the army, he had been the real ruler of the Duchy. He was very high, he was nearly at the top, it made a pleasant shiver run over his back to look down and see the swarming crowd struggling to climb up. Indeed many a time when his anteroom was full of waiting, anxious petitioners he paced alone in his study, to and fro, his ripe red lips open and smiling in his pale face, listening to the barely audible hum which penetrated to him, his breast expanded, and breathing deeply he smiled to himself and sent the whole of them packing without having seen them. It was sweet, sweet and glorious, to have power among men.

An epigram was reported to him which was going round the country, coined by Benz the small, fat, pig-eyed confectioner who was in the habit of talking politics with other small tradesmen in the Blue Boar: "Under the last Duke it was a harlot who reigned, under this one it's a Jew." Süss had the confectioner brought up before him, and the small fat man, sweating with fear, his eyes shifting and furtive, denied everything. Süss assembled all his domestics, and in front of the tittering nudging pack, who all knew that he had coined the saying, the short-necked wheezing man had to swear on his honour and his conscience and by his Saviour that he knew nothing of it and had never permitted himself a single disrespectful word about His Excellency. Then after kissing the smiling Jew's hand he was allowed to back himself out. But Süss piously notified the Duke that he was falling into bad odour among the people because of his true and loyal services.

He ran his house in princely style. For the internal decorations he had called in a Sicilian, Ubaldo Raineri, who was famous and fashionable chiefly because of the commissions he had executed for great French nobles. His rooms teemed with gorgeous carpets and Gobelin tapestries, with scrolled and carved furniture, with stucco, lapis lazuli and gold, with vases and busts. Beside Homer, Solon, and Aristotle, the architect—whether from innocence or malice—had set up the busts of Moses and Solomon. On the painted ceiling of the dining-hall sprawled the Triumph of Mercury in a many-figured fresco. But on the bedroom ceiling Leda played with her swan, her eyes veiled, her limbs relaxed: and the citizens in their public-houses gossipped with broad lewd grins about the magnificent bed, which stood enormous, bare and shameless between countless mirrors, while the young girls whispered its temptations. He was proud of being the first man in the west of Germany to adopt this erotic fashion then in vogue in Paris. Chinese figures and small tinkling pagodas stood in strange contrast between Moses and Solon, beside Homer, Solomon and Aristotle. But the admiration and delight of the ladies was the parrot Akiba in his gilded cage, who could cry *"Bonjour, madame"* and "Has your Highness condescended to sleep well?" and *"Ma vie pour mon souverain."* His table was the choicest in the land, it was a wonder where he got all the strange kinds of meat, shellfish and fruit; and with an evil eye Benz the confectioner observed the masterpieces of ice and fruit which the French chef of the Jew constructed in ever new and delicate shapes.

The Jew's wine-red livery with silver buttons was soon well-known everywhere. He kept a secretary, a librarian, couriers, footmen, a cook and a cellarer. Among the domestic staff moved Nicklas Pfäffle with his pale, fat, phlegmatic indifferent face, ever seeing, arranging, and completing everything. Süss's valet did not have an easy time. He had to know the *Mercure galant* by heart. The Privy Financial Councillor attached great importance to his reputation for being the most elegant gentleman in the Duchy and his wardrobe was replenished every two or three

113

weeks. He had a wild passion for jewels. The solitaire which he wore on his finger was famous, and the buckles of his shoes and of his gloves were set with stones which changed with the fashion. In his boudoir, as in his magnificent bedroom, there were glass cabinets of jewels, which were always filled with new and charming things acquired through his connection with the Amsterdam merchants and with certain Italian jewellers. It was his custom to make gifts from these cabinets to his feminine visitors, alike to ladies of high nobility and girls from the people. He was jeered at and sardonically abused on this account, and laughed at to his face for needing to employ such inducements; but he smiled, knowing that nobody could withstand his methods; the greedy recipient was bound to him for ever. Among men, however, and this was his dearest occupation, he was wont to trade jewels, driving sharp bargains. It was glorious to let the small precious toys trickle through his fingers, so many of them, to exchange a small stone for a heap of gold, and again a heap of gold for a small stone, sensitive to the great power that lay in that small stone.

His stable was not large but choice. He was glad to deal in horses with great men as far away as Holland. For his own use, too, he kept a white Arabian mare, Assjadah, which meant Daughter of the Morning. The Levantine merchant Daniele Foa had sold her to him; she was bred from the stables of the Caliph. He did not really love the mare, but he looked well after her; he knew how princely he looked on the slender, nervous, delicate animal. Even the blustering Remchingen had to admit of Süss: "On horseback he looks almost like one of us."

It was more difficult to be admitted into Süss's presence than into the Duke's. It cost one many letters, much running to and fro and importunity, to obtain an appointment for audience, and even then he often sent the waiting people away. He was the Duke's banker and had the title of Privy Financial Councillor. Nothing else; his signature was never affixed to a political document. Jews were forbidden by the Constitution to hold office in the State, and Süss was clever enough to appear content with the possession of power without its title. He knew that it was not the Duke, who was nearly always with the army, nor any minister, who was Regent of the Duchy; it was himself. Already there was the nucleus of a party which was openly attached to him and surrounded him like a court. The Tübingen lawyer Johann Theodor von Scheffer, Government Counsel, an expert in State Law, was one of the first to become his open adherent; the Councillors Bühler and Mez from the Ducal Treasury followed, the Orphan Superintendent Hallwachs, Knab, the Master of the Rolls, and Councillors Crantz, Thill and von Grumweiler. Von Lamprechts, President of the Demesnes, even sent his two young sons into the Financial Councillor's service, so that as pages in his house they might learn etiquette and courtly observances. People christened this Court of his the Hebrew Guard, and made themselves merry with many cheap witticisms at the expense of the Yiddishers. But it soon became clear that these Yiddishers had trimmed their sails to the right wind; for more and more openly the house in the Seegasse became the real seat of government in the Duchy.

The women who passed by the palace in the Seegasse peeped curiously and with thrilled interest through the huge folding doors into the vestibule, where the huissier towered, huge, in his wine-red livery with the silver buttons. Wild, uncanny and obscene stories were whispered about Süss, how he wallowed and raged in women's flesh, how he burned himself into women's blood by black magic, and delivered them to the devil. The Duke thought that his Jew had better taste than any of his other intimates, and Süss had to provide the insatiable man under all sorts of pretexts with relays of women for his camp. When Remchingen made fun of the circumcised's orgies, and enviously hinted that he did not understand how any self-respecting Christian woman could creep into a Hebrew's bed, unless he used wicked black arts, the Duke roared with laughter, saying that a well-made face and good legs were the best magic of all. He also entrusted Süss with the task of choosing the women for his opera and ballet, and often he laughed, saying that the Jew was a sweettooth and had nibbled many of his titbits before him.

Through the mirrored bedroom, too, under the wanton Leda painted on the ceiling, there passed a long train of women, young and mature, fair and dark, Swabian and French. But the Jew, who bragged loudly enough of other matters, kept his mouth stubbornly shut and betrayed none of his successes, neither the difficult ones which flattered his vanity nor the innumerable easy ones. Among the noisy and boasting cavaliers he was the only one silent, and neither Karl Alexander's jovial persistence nor Weissensee's courteous and flattering curiosity, nor Remchingen's gross and mocking attempts to pump him, succeeded in drawing the slightest hint from his evasive amiability. If, all the same, at court, in the bars, and among the soldiers, many juicy, uncommon, and certainly not invented stories from Süss's bed were grinned at, rolled under the tongue, and obscenely retailed, it was the fault of these women who were proud of their connection with this dangerous and unusual man (the object of so much feminine curiosity) and who felt compelled to whisper their uncanny secrets with tears or giggles into the bosom of a friend, under repeated oaths of confidence.

When the Jew had finished doing up his palace, the Duchess, accompanied by Remchingen, came on his urgent invitation to inspect it. Affectedly she carried her small delicate head of the colour of fine old marble through the brilliant rooms, glanced out of her long, roving, lizard-like eyes at the Chinese ornaments, smiled at Akiba the parrot who cried *"Ma vie pour mon souverain,"* tinkled with her small and well-kept fingers at the miniature pagodas, accepted from Süss a poison-ring of remarkable shape and not much value, glided with small steps past the bowing wine-red lackeys into the stables and gave the noble white mare Assjadah a piece of sugar. She drank in with satisfaction Süss's unlimited devotion.

But when she was in her carriage between rows of gaping and bareheaded spectators, she said in her indolent, provocative voice, above the head of the Financial Councillor as he bowed profoundly over her hand: "All very fine, Jew, and very beautiful. But all the same you have not shown me the room where the little Christian children are butchered!" And she laughed her little, bell-like, amused laugh, and drove off.

But Süss stood bareheaded before his house, and the people gaped and nudged each other, and he paid no attention to them

116

but stared after her carriage with his arched, restless, eloquent eyes, his ripe red lips slightly parted in his pale face.

WITH the advancing spring Rabbi Gabriel, suddenly, as his habit was, forsook the little white house with the blossoming terraces. He travelled unobtrusively, without servants, his massive, heavy face appearing first in one place and then in another; he was never in a hurry, and had no special business anywhere; but he travelled continuously without stopping, and however intricate his movements were, followed what seemed to be a previously thought-out plan.

He turned up among the mountains. He sat for two whole days in a peasant cabin beside a small bridge over a mountain stream, watching the floating logs carried down by the seething water, jamming, interlacing, stranding, and then whirling on again with the rising water. He listened for several nights to the endless tinkling of the bells on the cattle which were being driven to the high pastures. He drove up the winding pass which led to the South. Wind blew from the Midi; it had been raining; the air was damp and heavy, the mountains were veiled in dusky blue. He alighted, and paced on ahead of the cumbrous and creaking carriage. Over the damp shining road a huge snail dragged its shell; at the last moment he avoided it carefully. Fifteen minutes later his carriage crushed it to pieces.

He crossed the summit of the pass, wading deep in snow. The wind blew more freely, striking warm and pleasantly upon him. The land lay steeped in bliss; it was in full blossom. He came to a large wide lake; paused beside it; squatted for long hours by the shore, immovable, massive, like a block of stone in the sun. Dark green around him stood orange-trees in thick leaf; further below olives, silvery and light, climbed up the bank.

Meanwhile Süss journeyed to Hirsau. Since his uncle had brought the child into the country, since his silent and contemptuous threats, Süss had not been able to keep the hidden secret so closely sealed as before. A breath of it crept over his papers in the middle of his calculations, glided into his nights, whispered behind his ear as he rode brilliant and hated through the streets

117

on his white mare Assjadah, so that the beast became uneasy and curvetted and neighed. It sometimes happened that he, the matter-of-fact calculator, who saw things sharply, soberly and nakedly in their proper contours, and called a spade a spade, shrank with sudden terror in the broad light of day, and breathed deeply, his shoulders lifted as if to parry a blow. A face looked over his shoulder, obscure and shadowy, and it was his own face.

He had been long eager to journey to Hirsau, to the white house with the gay and festive terraces of flowers. What had prevented him, time and again, although he did not admit it, was the presence of Rabbi Gabriel, the suffocating, uneasy, oppression of his unavoidable, weary, insistent, grey eyes.

He did not even now admit to himself that it was the absence of the old man which had made him so rapidly decide upon the journey. He was on the way to Naemi, he was accompanied only by Nicklas Pfäffle, he was more light-hearted and free than he had ever been. He was going to see his child, and he was already in spirit with his child, and all his accounts and politics and power and vanity lay broken and dusty behind him. He saw the young field and he savoured its fragrance, and he did not calculate how much this field would bring and how new taxes could be squeezed out of the price of the grain; he saw only the soft colour of the young corn and sniffed the fragrant breeze blowing over the field. He was going to his child, and his heart was already with her. When would he see at last the small sunny white cube of the house, with the flower terraces in front and his child inside? There, branching from the highroad, was the cart-track. He left the carriage, and turned aside into the footpath, with ever increasing strides. Here is the fence; he opens the locked gate; now the tall trees, now the flower-beds, and now breathing deeply, clinging to him, the child hangs round his neck, swooning.

She does not say a word. For a long never-ending time she does not say a word. She clings to him, weeping, clasps him, drinks him in with her large streaming eyes.

How lovely his child is! She is quite perfect. There is not a feature, not a hair, not the slightest of her movements, nor any vibration in her voice, which he would have altered. She is lovely above all women; tender she is, and pure; she is purifying like a

118

soft flame; she purifies even himself. He shares complaisantly her pleasure in the old, waddling, devoted waiting-woman Jantje; he, to whom all plants and animals are cold, insentient things, learns to comprehend every single flower as if it spoke to him; she imbues these things with her soft breath and he feels her life in them.

But then he stood with Naemi in the library. There were scrolls there with magic figures, and astrological tables, and suddenly it came over him that the eyes of the old man were somewhere in the room, as if they were staring at him, grey and troubled, morose and enervatingly sad. But then Naemi spoke. She spoke of the heroes in the Holy Scriptures. Her eyes, devoted and tearful, were set on her father, and with bold tread David entered the room, proudly, with his sling, Samson rushed forward, felling the Philistines to right and left, and Judas Maccabæus, full of holy wrath, hunted the idolators out of the Temple. And they were all her father, they flowed into his image and borrowed from him their strength and beauty, their zeal and fire.

For three days he lived in this way, light-hearted and freed from the cares of his daily life. Suddenly on the third day when he was alone in the room, with Nicklas Pfäffle standing fat and composed in front of him, the external world which he had left behind fell on him again. He saw his documents waiting in a pile for his signature, he saw the vortex of the world going round without him. Officials and merchants were all pushing, striving, swarming their way up to the point where he stood, threatening him with peril, and he had not his hand at the wheel; he sat here far away and attended to nothing. It was incomprehensible that he had thought of nothing during these days. The flowers sank again into insentience, he felt no more the breath and life of things, the ciphers and letters of the Holy Scriptures became stupid nonsense. Before him stood calculations of profit, ducal edicts, intrigues of the Estates, complicated business, life and power. Half abstractedly now he looked at his daughter, who lay sobbing in his arms. He tore himself free, and then the girl, the white house, the gay and festive terraces of flowers, lay insubstantially behind him and the lid fell down on them.

As he went quickly through the forest with Nicklas Pfäffle

towards the cart-track, he saw suddenly under a tree at the border of a clearing a girl, with a brown keen face and large eyes oddly contrasting with her dusky hair, staring obliquely through the tree-trunks, her hands clasped behind her head. But she was not lying in repose, her attitude was tense and constrained. He made straight towards her; she was lovely, not like a country girl; over her brown keen face there flitted strange thoughts far removed from the workaday Swabian world. He was on the soft grass quite near her before she saw him. She sprang to her feet, stared at him with dilated pupils, and screamed: "The devil! The devil is walking in the wood!" and ran away. Nicklas Pfäffle, indifferent and all-knowing, explained to the astonished Süss: "That is Magdalen Sibylle Weissensee. Daughter of the Prelate. A pietist."

In the carriage Süss reflected that it would be more sensible, now that he was already on the way, to go to Frankfurt and personally arrange some affairs with his agents there. But this was an excuse with which he cheated himself. What he needed was not personal attendance to his affairs in Frankfurt; what he really needed, what he yearned for after the perplexing and uncertain oscillation of his feelings in the house with the flower terraces, was the restoration of his self-confidence, the re-echo and assurance of his power and his success. He sent for his secretary and his attendants, and entered Frankfurt in brilliant state.

The Jews of Frankfurt assembled in wonder and excitement, gathered in gesticulating groups, clicked their tongues in astonished admiration, and waved their lifted and eloquent arms. Eh, Josef Süss Oppenheimer! Eh, the High Steward and Privy Financial Councillor of Württemberg! Eh, how he has got on in the world! His father was an actor, his mother, the singer, was lovely and elegant, yes, yes, but a frivolous woman, no honour to the Jewish community; his grandfather, Reb Selmele, an upright man of blessed memory, an honest man, cantor in the Synagogue, a pious and respected man, but still a poor and humble man. And now Josef Süss, so high, so brilliant, so powerful, much higher up than his brother in Darmstadt, the renegade, who turned Christian to be a baron. Eh, how visibly the Lord has exalted him! Although he is a Jew, the Goim doff their bonnets to him and

120

bow down to the earth before him, and when he whistles, the Councillors and Ministers come running as if he were the Duke himself.

Süss greedily licked up this admiration. He contributed a sum of money so huge as to be stupendous, to the funds of the Synagogue and to the poor. The leading elder and the Rabbi, Jaakob Joshua Falk, a small, serious, reflective man, with a withered skin, large veins, and deeply-set eyes, came to thank him, and the Rabbi gave him his blessing for the journey.

And he stood before his mother, and the lovely, silly old woman spread her vain admiration under his feet like a soft carpet. He wallowed in these warm and endless waves of homage, his success was reflected intoxicatingly from a hundred shining mirrors; and from the hidden corners of his soul he brought forth his most secret dreams for this most willing of hearers, who caressed his hand with a blissful smile. His mind firmly made up, disturbed by no after-effects of the white house, he returned to Stuttgart filled to the brim with bold and unheard-of projects.

THE war was over, and Karl Alexander was coming back to his capital. He was in an evil humour. True, he had shown that he was of some account, that he had to be reckoned with both as a general and as the possessor of a considerable army. But in reality these were but meagre results, and far removed from the glory of which he had dreamed. He sat morosely in his carriage; his wounded foot was worse than ever, and his asthma bothered him.

A stage-coach coming from the opposite direction swerved respectfully aside and stopped to let the ducal carriage pass. Among the countenances effacing themselves in humility Karl Alexander recognized one that greeted him with surly composure—broad and pale, with an insignificant nose under the enormous brow, and troubled grey eyes. He shrank slightly; he seemed to hear the rasping voice saying: "The first I will not tell you." An uncanny constraint fell upon him like a noose. He suddenly saw himself treading in a silent and shadowy dance; the Rabbi in front held his right hand, Süss behind him his left. Was not the Bishop of Würzburg there too, the fat and jolly Friedrich Karl Schönborn, ahead of him in the chain, linked to him by many hands? How ridiculous he looked. And everything was opaque, misty and colourless. He drove on more dejectedly than ever.

In Stuttgart annoyances cropped up on every side. The Duchess had greeted him joyously; but in the night, as she lay in his arms, she had asked him in her light, gently-mocking voice where were all the lovely things he had looted from Versailles; as a bride she had dreamed that he would pull off the French Louis's wig and bring it to her as a trophy. It was certainly only innocent teasing on her part, but it had rankled considerably.

Then the Parliamentary Sub-Committee had appeared with its boring, persistent, harassing grumbles and complaints. And in a second audience it demanded urgently and plainly that the army should be disbanded, now that peace was secured. The Duke went purple in the face, and struggled for breath. With great difficulty he forced himself to listen to the deputation instead of cuffing them soundly, arresting them, and putting them in the stocks. Half-strangled with coughing at last, with boorish ill-humour and a flood of raucous abuse and curses, he drove them out in a state of distress and terror, and summoned Süss.

He, as usual, had a ready-made project in his pocket. Karl Alexander received him in his dressing-gown, for he had just had a bath, and Neuffer was massaging his wounded foot while the brown slave ran to and fro with towels, combs and brushes. With smiling courtesy Süss unfolded his subtle and poisonous plan. In a matter of such importance His Highness should not be content to deal only with the eleven gentlemen of the Parliamentary Sub-Committee. The Sub-Committee must be strengthened by the addition of other members from the House.

"What would be the advantage in that?" asked the Duke, his choleric blue eyes fixed unswervingly on the smooth, smiling and mobile lips of the Jew.

"In enlarging the committee," continued Süss with airy fluency, "naturally only those deputies would be considered whose loyal attachment to the Duke is beyond question."

Karl Alexander looked at the Jew's lips attentively, considered his words keenly and turned them round and round. He perceived

122

all at once that in this way the opposition in Parliament could be wiped out and the Estates turned into a parcel of powerless puppets. He sprang up, overturning his valet Neuffer who was rubbing his wounded foot. "You are a genius, Süss!" he shouted gleefully, and strode excitedly about the room with one foot bare. The brown slave, cowering in his corner, followed his master's movements with slow eyes.

On that very evening Süss had a conference with Weissensee. He informed him that the Duke thought it necessary to strengthen the Sub-Committee for the decision of such an important matter; and asked which of the members in the prelate's opinion had an understanding of great problems and a sufficient awareness of Karl Alexander's position in Europe to make it an advantage both for the ruler and for his people that they should be chosen to fill up the number. The other was wary, praised the circumspection and conscientiousness of the Duke, and only after a long digression cautiously and hesitatingly mentioned two or three names. Then he immediately went off at a tangent and spoke courteously of irrelevant matters. Süss politely followed his lead, and then with a casual reference to the President of the ducal Ecclesiastical Court whom the Duke considered old and worn-out, he asked whether Weissensee wanted to spend all his days in Hirsau, saying that an adviser of his diplomatic ability, with his experience and learning, would be greatly appreciated in Stuttgart. Covetous and strongly tempted by this bait, the prelate sniffed at it and then swallowed it with a smile and a pang over his own weakness and treachery, and when Süss touched again upon the members to be selected he gave with a sigh the names required, betraying in those he withheld the Constitution and its supporters. Ah, it was not at all the best of all possible worlds, as sundry fashionable philosophers were insisting; it was a badly arranged and vexatious world. Only single-minded people could keep themselves pure; one who was clever and complex and wanted to be not quite remote from the currents of life had perforce to become a dirty traitor.

The election day was appointed. All members of the opposition according to Weissensee's list were excluded from the poll and their protests disregarded. Ducal commissaries appeared in the individual towns and polling offices with strong military escorts, and forcibly edited the wishes, mandates, and binding commissions laid on the deputies by the electorate.

Under these auspices assembled the Parliament which had to decide the most important question for decades in Swabian politics, the maintenance of a considerable standing army. Nor did this Rump Parliament hold its sessions in the Chamber of Deputies in Stuttgart; the Duke had decreed that to facilitate personal communication with him the sittings should take place under his own eye in the castle at Ludwigsburg. The little town overflowed with soldiers, the deputies in their daily sessions were policed by a strong military levy, and were in constant danger of being arrested by their protectors at the slightest hint of opposition. The Duke after a nonchalant opening speech absented himself completely; he held parades and military exercises in the neighbourhood while his ministers with gracious indifference gave vague and arrogant answers to the timid questions of the deputies.

In this way the monstrous military requirements of the Duke were granted, and in addition the yearly tax was doubled and a thirtieth of all produce confiscated. This scheme of taxation was to remain in force so long as the times were critical and the land was able to bear it. Under the muskets of the soldiers the members, usually so deliberate, such cautious hagglers over every iota, did not dare to press for a more precise definition of this decisive clause, and when in an unofficial conference they modestly brought up the question who was to be the judge of the critical nature of the times and the land's capacity to pay, Süss and Remchingen browbeat them with such insolence that the broken-spirited and terrified deputies did not insist on a more definite clearing-up of this extremely important point. Never since the Constitution had been established had a Duke of Württemberg obtained such latitude from Parliament as did Karl Alexander and his Jew.

Two weeks after the convocation the Prelate of Hirsau, Philip Heinrich Weissensee, was appointed President of the Ecclesiastical Court in Stuttgart.

SHORTLY after this victory of Süss's over Parliament the Duke's brother, Prince Heinrich Friedrich, died at the family seat of

Winnenthal. Since Karl Alexander had taken his mistress, and then with an insolent grin had returned her dissolved in tears, the weakly man had eaten out his heart in helplessness and savage phantasies of revenge. He often turned his tormented and distorted glances towards the mild, golden-brown creature, whose life was now a single and sorrowful plea for forgiveness. Once he put his feeble sweaty hands round her full, robust, beautiful neck, and slowly compressed them, strangling her, then desisted in alarm, and caressed her, murmuring: "You could not help it, you could not help it." He imagined wild and fantastic scenes of revenge in which he stabbed his sweetheart, threw her body over his horse, and tore through the country calling the people heroically to revenge. Or he captured his brother, and compelled him to kiss her feet, and then killed them both, and had her buried with all the pomp befitting an Empress, and his brother thrown into a hole like a dog. And he himself sat enthroned on high like a dramatic God of Vengeance. But none of all this could he carry into execution; he could only fret himself to death about it.

As soon as he heard of his brother's death, Karl Alexander sent his minister, Forstner, and Dilldey, his Councillor for War, to Winnenthal Castle to seal up the dead man's possessions, and especially to confiscate all his correspondence. Just while the Rump Parliament was sitting he had heard that his brother was renewing his intrigues with the Estates, and he burned to get hold of evidence in black and white against certain members of the Opposition. Oh, how he would seize them and torment them, and crush the hydra's head!

His ambassadors found a few dazed servants slinking about the quiet castle, and the golden-brown creature sunk in apathy beside the corpse. They brought nothing back to the Duke but irrelevant scribblings.

The Duke foamed with rage against his messengers, who had procured only rubbish for him. They had spirited away the incriminating documents, they had burned them. They had bungled, they had deliberately botched and ruined this splendid opportunity of exposing the intrigue.

Süss stirred him up and egged him on. Such a chance of undoing those he hated would never recur. Was not Karl Alexander tired of governing with this double-faced cabinet, packed as it was with men who, if they were not high traitors, were in any case obstinate tricksters, pedants, white-livered curs, compromisers and clumsy fools? He achieved his purpose; the ministers Forstner, Neuffer, Negendank and Hardenberg were dismissed from office in disgrace. Only Bilfinger was left. Süss was too clever to attack this firm and scholarly man, who was renowned far beyond Württemberg, and besides the Duke prized his intercourse with such an expert builder of fortifications too highly for Süss to have had any chance of success.

Then the Civil Service was overhauled. Hitherto the higher offices had been filled by respectable, good-humoured, slow and honest Swabians; but now smooth and adroit men were moved in, many of them foreigners, cunning and voluble, versed in all kinds of complicated business, adherents of Süss, men like Scheffer, Thill, Lautz, Bühler, Mez and Hallwachs. They occupied all the strategic positions, and barred every avenue of access to the Duke. Süss himself still refrained from holding any office; he had only the title of Privy Financial Councillor and Chief Director of Finance to the Court, besides being Keeper of the Privy Purse to Her Highness the Duchess; but he was the real regent of the country, and all the courts in Europe knew it; his hand lay, even without a seal-ring, over the whole Duchy.

THE land drew a breath of relaxation, and stretched itself in joyous expectancy. The war was over. Life would flow smoothly and securely now, and not in spasmodic fits and starts, with gaps here and stoppages there and chicanery everywhere. The sturdy young men would come back to work which had suffered from their absence, the heads of families would return to their homes and beds. Business would be properly distributed again, and things would no longer be left to chance. The horses would come back, the beloved and powerful beasts; they would be worn to skeletons, but they would soon be fat and glossy again. All the fields would be ploughed as before, and the vineyards would not be neglected any longer, nor the houses go to rack and ruin. The small tradesmen in the towns would make both ends meet as they did before the war; they would have wares for their shops, and plenty of provisions and wine. All eyes were turned to the west towards the returning troops, the men, the horses, the tents, carts, baggage, and forage trains, to all that was coming back and had been sorely missed and yearned for, the sap and life-blood of the land.

Corroding disappointment when Parliament miserably resigned and the army was not disbanded. Into the fire and onto the dung-heap flew the pictures of the Duke, Belgrade and the seven hundred halberdiers. Despair set in, and demagogues more threatening than at the beginning of the war arose, but were still more quickly and effectively suppressed. All the vassals of the Duchy had troops quartered on them, for there were not enough barracks, one soldier to every two families; all over the land they were billeted among townsmen and peasants. Spies were rife, and whoever grumbled or fell under suspicion was burdened with a double load.

On every side the other countries and the free towns blossomed with the prosperity of peace; but in the Duchy the peace was more terrible than the war had been. For then Karl Alexander had needed money only for his army, but now he needed it for the troops and for the maintenance of his Court, which shone more brilliantly day by day.

Süss—it was a miracle, it was sheer magic—procured him the money. As if he had had a divining-rod he dug up into the light of day every hidden coin. He had first put on the screws during the war, and now with uncanny sureness he slowly turned them tighter. Throttled by the pressure of the soldiers, the tortured land did not cry out, but groaned in torment, and bled to death amid strangling sighs.

Under Eberhard Ludwig and the Countess, office and position had already been bartered. Süss refined on their system, and set up a special office, the Patronage Bureau, to auction to the highest bidder every post that fell vacant, and to create new posts and titles for this purpose. Every appointment had to be bought, from that of Transport Minister to that of village mayor or magistrate, even down to the superintendent of baths and of State knackeries. Neither traditional usage nor obvious capacity gave the children of the land any claim upon a post; those who had no money could

127

look out for themselves and prosper in another country or in some other way. The penniless Friedrich Christoph Koppenhöfer could not be helped to a professorship in Tübingen even by the warm recommendation of Bilfinger; and the famous Swabian physicist had to win respect and honour for himself in Saint Petersburg among the hyperboreans. Instead, adroit men of business from all corners of the world sat in the ducal bureaux.

But the most lucrative business of all, mills which never failed to grind, were the Courts of Justice. Süss's method had the simplicity of genius. Justice was dispensed like any other commodity and on the same principles.

A Fiscal Bureau was set up, and spies ranged round the country looking for rich and well-endowed people without any protection from friends at Court or in Parliament. They were then impeached for having gained their wealth by illegal means, and a course of threats, distraints, and false evidence reduced even the most voluble to such a feeble state that they were glad to get rid of the lawsuit by paying the required sum. This Bureau of Justice squeezed six and a half tons of gold into the ducal Treasury within twelve months.

In Stuttgart, although Süss was still without an official position, it had long been known that the country was ruled from the house in the Seegasse and not from the Castle. Fists were clenched before that house; it was execrated and spat upon; once a daring hand pasted a lampoon upon it, but only secretly by night, with furtive glances to right and left. For the Jew had his spies and hussars everywhere, and any one who came up against him would find himself sitting behind the bars of Neuffen or Hohenasperg, shackled to the stocks in perpetual darkness.

The small shopkeepers, however, plotted and whispered in the Blue Boar, Benz the confectioner among them. He took good care not to burn his fingers a second time. But it was comparatively simple; he had only to say: "Yes, yes, under the last Duke it was a harlot who reigned——" and everyone completed the sentence for himself, "and under this one it's a Jew."

The land groaned and writhed under the strangling pressure. Corn grew, wine grew, industry wrought and produced goods. The Duke lay upon it with his Court and his soldiers, the land supported him. Two hundred towns and twelve hundred villages sighed and gave of their blood. The Duke sucked it from them through the Jew; and the land bore both of them on its back.

INTO the conventicles and Bible circles of the pietists gathered the weary and heavy-laden. They crept to God like whipped curs and licked His feet. All over the Duchy, in spite of interdicts and severe penalties, there arose initiates and converts. In Bietigheim the preacher Ludwig Bronnquell extolled Süss as a welcome scourge. "If a dog is beaten all day," he preached, "he runs away and seeks another master. The common people are just like a dog. The Duke beats them, the soldiers beat them, the officers and officials beat them, but the best rod of all is Süss, the Jew. Him they cannot endure, and so they run away and seek another master, Christ."

Mademoiselle Magdalen Sibylle Weissensee had stayed behind in Hirsau when her father moved to Stuttgart. Since she had seen the devil in the wood she could not banish his apparition. She felt herself called to wrestle with the devil and to win him to God. She was driven to the wood again and again by a desire to see him, a desire compounded of fascination and horror, but she did not meet the devil a second time.

It was strange that she could not speak of her encounter to the brethren and sisters of the Bible Circle. Even from Beata Sturmin, her spiritual guide, the wise and holy blind woman, she concealed her vision. It was reserved for her, it was her task, her vocation, to wrestle with the devil. Lucifer was beautiful, that was his strongest power and temptation. To take him by the hand, not to let him go, to bring him to God, that must be a triumph to make one die with bliss.

Master Jaakob Polykarp Schober, too, had his secret. Even the brethren and sisters of the Bible Circle, who were simple, self-absorbed, unobservant people, noticed the holy radiance which beamed from the young man's mild and chubby face, when the pious hymns about the Heavenly Jerusalem were sung. At those times he saw the white house with the flowery terraces, and in front of it the maiden in her tent, relaxed and dreaming, dressed in a strange fashion, her face like ivory under her blue-black hair.

It happened once that the Stuttgart Brethren urged him to apply for the post of Ducal librarian, but it had come to nothing, because he did not have the money demanded for the post by the Patronage Bureau. And he was really very glad of it, for so he could remain in Hirsau and wander dreaming around the wood and the white house.

But between him and Magdalen Sibylle there arose an extraordinary bond of affinity. The brethren and sisters sighed humbly and gratefully over the difficult but blessed times of hardship and awakening, over the terrible Jew whom the Lord had sent to chastise the Duchy; and the Master saw the heavenly maiden, and Magdalen Sibylle saw Lucifer, and their dreams floated above and played through their simple hymns and bound everything together, and filled the bare, bleak and lowly room.

THE white mare Assjadah, which means Daughter of the Morning, became rapidly acclimatized to the mild Swabian air, but she did not like the Swabians; she did not like their hands nor their narrow, sulky obtuseness. She had been born in Yemen, had been sent as tribute to the stables of the Caliph, sold by an under-treasurer to Daniele Foa, the Levantine merchant, who had again sold her to his business friend Süss. Süss took great care of her, for she was his and he looked well on her. But he did not love her. He was not yet aware that in every living creature there was something of himself; he suspected it uneasily while Rabbi Gabriel spoke to him; and the feeling ran deliciously through his veins while he was with Naemi. But once these brief hours were past it sank beneath the surface and he did not know it.

But the white mare Assjadah knew it. She knew her master's step, his hand, his thighs, and his odour. While she paced lightly and delicately beneath him she thought: "He does not like me. But he is glorious to carry. One hardly feels him. He is like a piece of myself. He rises and sinks with my breath and my muscles. When the others look at me I feel suffocated, and I do not belong to them. But he is a bit of myself. His eye is free, and I feel like running and flying when he looks at me. When he claps me I am surer of myself, full of quietness and strength. I belong to him, and I am in my own country when I am with

130

him." And she arched her head high and whickered loudly and triumphantly to the listening citizens: "Look out! He is coming!"

For Süss now wore his power openly in the light of the sun, and displayed with coquettish ostentation his skill in the arts of court life and society. He made a point of being the pivot of all the court functions. No foreigner of rank came to Stuttgart without waiting upon the all-powerful favourite. He increased his domestic staff so that his footmen in their wine-red livery became a small regiment. The ministers and upper officials he kept in slavish subjection. They feared him nearly as much as the Duke; they ran in frantic haste when he whistled. At the slightest contradiction he threatened them with the stocks, the cat o' nine tails, and a grave beneath the gallows.

Süss had the Duke completely in his power. Karl Alexander felt himself mysteriously bound to this man who had been the first to believe in his fortunes, and on that tottering basis had established his whole life. With genuine admiration and a slight touch of horror he watched this Jew conjuring out of nothing everything he was asked for; money, women and soldiers. And he followed blindly every suggestion of his Director of Finance.

Süss had had unlimited confidence in himself from his earliest youth. But yet he had moments of sheer paralysed astonishment at the task he had taken upon himself and the ease with which he was mastering it. He, the Jew, stood alone before the whole of Europe on his dangerous pinnacle and smiled and was elegant and took it all as a matter of course, and betrayed not a tremor for the most observant eye to pounce on.

To maintain his house in such princely magnificence and to keep the Duke in the hollow of his hand he needed money, money poured out at his feet in fantastic profusion. In Vienna, among his relatives the Oppenheimers, the Imperial bankers, he had learned to handle large sums. But now the revenue of the whole Duchy ran through his fingers; he could dispose of the income of two hundred towns and twelve hundred villages. With feverish industry he cast it here and there, and let it roll in mad gyration. He had dealings with all the financiers in Europe, and through his innumerable and mostly Jewish agents the money of Swabia flowed through the most complicated channels, founded plantations in the Dutch East Indies, bought horses in Barbary, and sent trains of elephants and black slaves down to the coast of Africa. His fundamental principle, and his deliberate goal, was a fevered and whirling exchange of commodities. Not large profits on single transactions, but a huge total profit through making a little on everything.

His private income was enormous. All those who wanted anything at the Court of Württemberg took pains to bestow *douceurs* and presents upon him. The Duke, when Remchingen drew his attention to this, said with a laugh: "Let the rogue make his profits. Every cent that he makes means two for me!" He had dealings far and wide in pedigree horses, but above all his traffic in precious stones greatly increased. He had always been a fanatical lover of jewels; but hitherto he had been crossed in every big deal by a certain Dom Bartelemi Pancorbo, a Portuguese, a tall, quiet, uncanny fellow, with a compressed, fleshless, bony face, who, wherever really priceless jewels were to be waylaid, turned up suddenly on the spot as if he had an occult informant, always in the same old-fashioned, badly-fitting and slovenly Portuguese court dress. He had high titles and powers at the Palatinate Court; through his diplomatic connections he dominated the market in Amsterdam, and through that the whole of Germany's trade in jewels. Süss now employed his political influence to break this hated rival. The Jew carried on the battle wildly and with passion; the other, the haggard, uncanny Portuguese, gave way coldly, obstinately, warily, and one step at a time. He could not be completely destroyed, his shadow still fell over Süss's transactions, but it had already come to the point that the best and rarest stones were brought first to the Jew and that certain very choice pieces could only be procured through him.

He had also taken over the Mint. But he disdained to make a profit from coining base money. A manœuvre so obvious and inferior had been his only recourse when he was still small and unknown, at the time of the Darmstadt Minting Contract, when he could do nothing else. But now he could profit on a grander scale from the higher exchange value of a good coinage. So the money which he minted was the best of all the current coin in

Germany, the most marketable and the most sought after. Above all, it tickled him to put such a stopper on the slanders of his enemies as the unimpeachable solidity of his coinage presented. He knew that here the first attack of his opponents was to be expected, and the slightest slip would bring about his downfall; but if on the other hand he was proved sterling here his credit would be enormously increased. He waited anxiously for some complaint, and tried to provoke one. The coarse-grained Remchingen, abetted by others who were just as primitive as himself in their understanding of finance, could not account for the growing wealth of Süss except on the conventional hypothesis that the Jew coined base money. He egged the Duke on until a Commission was finally appointed to investigate. And Süss, smiling with modest pride, proved by his agent's papers that his money was over-weight, and brought in too little profit, and sunned himself in his inviolability.

He span over the land a web of enterprises, with complicated ramifications. He spread himself and luxuriated in his power. But it seemed to him at times as if it were not he who set the whole brilliant vortex in motion. Then a shiver would run down his back and he would lift his shoulders as if to ward something off. He would feel suddenly caught in an uncanny snare. The objects around him would fade; he saw himself treading in a dumb and shadowy quadrille. Rabbi Gabriel held his right hand and the Duke his left. They wove in and out, set to each other, and bowed. Was not that Isaac Landauer moving ahead of him, bound to him by a chain of many hands? How gruesome and ridiculous he looked with his caftan and his side-curls in the earnest, silent, circling measure, with its bowing and winding figures!

But the obscure and cloudy picture tormented him only for brief moments. Then it was dissipated by the broad light of day and faded into nothing and vanished. And there was still left gold that could be weighed and counted, and women whose bodies could be touched, caressed, seized and enjoyed. They were there and they remained—brilliance, power, movement, life.

IN Urach there was a linen company belonging to the Schertlin family. The Schertlins had made a small beginning under Duke Eberhard Ludwig; now they had branches all over the country. Their business prospered, they had an establishment in Maulbronn, and a silk manufactory in Stuttgart. The head of the family, Christoph Adam Schertlin, a strong, successful and clever man, had turned the business, still small and insignificant, into a limited liability company and had given the Countess shares at much less than their value. In this simple manner the powerful favourite's interest in the undertaking had been secured, and she had obtained privileges and commissions for the company. Later, when the Countess fell into disfavour and had to realize her assets in Württemberg, Christoph Adam Schertlin, in negotiation with Isaac Landauer, was able to buy back cheaply all her shares. And then he had retired from business, quitted the Duchy, and bought himself in the free town of Esslingen a patrician house which he redecorated. There he sat now, stately and rich, a Town Councillor, and highly respected.

The factories in Stuttgart, Urach and Maulbronn were now directed by Johann Ulrich Schertlin, a steady, experienced, enterprising man, one of the first captains of industry in Swabia. He had married a Frenchwoman, from the emigrant colony of Pinache in Upper Maulbronn, which had been founded at the end of the previous century by the deported Waldensians, a strange, beautiful woman with a small red mouth in a pale face, and long proud eyes under shining reddish-golden hair. His friends and relations could make nothing of her. She was stylish, that could not be denied, but she was damnably proud, curt and sparing in her answers, and generally silent out of boredom; and although she had been born in Germany she nearly always spoke French, and her German was halting and broken. But she was an indulgence which Johann Ulrich Schertlin could well allow himself; he was rolling in money and dignities, and had a house in Stuttgart and one in Urach beside his factories. Confound it, he could set anyone he liked at the head of his table. And he went proudly about with the wife whom he loved, and his house and his business throve.

Now Süss had a business friend, a certain Daniele Foa in Venice, who was his intermediary for Levantine capital, horses, jewels, stuffs and wine. He it was who had procured the white

134

mare Assjadah. This Daniele Foa had met Süss in the Palatinate, and there his support in the contest with Dom Bartelemi Pancorbo had proved very useful. The Levantine merchant, a daring and cunning man of business, had set going up and down the Rhine a widespread trade in textiles, and now used Süss's influence to get a footing in Swabia. He obtained exemptions and privileges, but came hard up against the competition of the Schertlin factories, which did excellent business everywhere in these regions. Süss, who wanted to oblige his friend, set himself with his usual cold ruthlessness to destroy these rivals. Schertlin's factories were harassed, their privileges qualified until they were worthless, their contracts with the Treasury terminated, their excise and customs duties so increased that they could no longer remain in the running. On the other hand the Finance Director established a factory, ostensibly in his own name but which in reality acted for Daniele Foa, and the excisemen did not dare to apply to the all-powerful man the prescribed high rate of taxation; his bales were only lightly taxed or not at all.

The Schertlins were also harassed in person. One of them was impeached by the Fiscal Bureau on trivial grounds, but in such a way that he could not extricate himself, and two of the younger ones were pressed into the army although they offered large sums to buy themselves off. The old man, Christoph Adam, who sat in the free town of Esslingen, could not be got at certainly, and for the present Johann Ulrich too was left alone. But the Jew's hand was more heavy on this family than on others, and the worry about the degeneration of his business, the humiliation of seeing two young Schertlins pressed into the army, and the pain of not being able to surround his lovely wife with the princely magnificence he had dreamed of for her, all this stuck in Johann Ulrich's throat.

Then at last Süss got hold of a rope with which to catch Johann Ulrich. One of the young Schertlins in the army had obtained leave to go to Esslingen on a visit to his grandfather, and did not return. Negotiations were pending between the Duke and the town about the surrender of deserters, but were not yet concluded. At the behest of the old Councillor the town refused to give up the young man. Then Süss's hussars intercepted a

135

letter from Johann Ulrich supporting the old man in his refusal to hand over the young man to the Duke's commissaries. That was rebellion, high treason.

Süss, with all the trumps in his hands, proceeded slowly and gently. First Johann Ulrich was ordered to attend a Ducal War Inquisition. The proud man stayed at home, gnashing his teeth, and was then arrested and brought to the prison of Hohentwiel. It was whispered that he would be condemned by a court-martial to lifelong captivity.

In the destitute house the Frenchwoman sat with a pale face. She listened in silence, her small red lips firmly compressed, to the inquisitive sympathy of friends and relatives. When they were tired of comforting the arrogant woman, who did not even have the grace to weep, and left her alone, there appeared Councillor Bühler from the Fiscal Bureau, a distant connection of the Schertlins, who had always despised him as a creature of Süss. Now he came very importantly in the role of patronizing benefactor, full of pompous sympathy, to relish his revenge; found the Waldensian isolated in her fixed, proud sorrow, and advised her to go and see Süss. Süss was slandered: in business he was as hard as could be, that was natural, but he was not revengeful.

Nobody knew whether the Waldensian loved her husband or not, and she herself did not know. But when his trial was imminent she went to Süss.

She came of a good family, which preserved traditions of French Court life, of elegance, and of great possessions. She saw the Jew's salons, his wine-red lackeys, his pages; his tapestries, statues, and Chinese pieces. That was something different from the solid comfort of the Schertlins! Here was plenty, superfluity, the superfluity which turned life from a constraint and a burden into something light and lordly, lovely and desirable. Süss was in a good humour, and the lady pleased him. He treated her quite as a great lady, speaking only French since he saw that she preferred it, flattered her with mundane compliments, and said not a word about her difficulties. This was the atmosphere for her; if she had not come as suppliant she might have succumbed to him. But when, suddenly, with cynical gallantry, he suggested the satisfaction at once of her request and of his desire, she stood for a little while motionless and deadly pale. Then she threw his nationality in his face: said that she was ashamed not to have reflected sooner that it was a Jew she had to deal with. Whereupon smoothly and without altering his demeanour he smiled and bowed, saying, "Then the answer is no," and escorted her courteously to the door, kissing her hand as he took his leave.

He released Johann Ulrich from prison, and contented himself with having the affair settled by the Fiscal Bureau. Johann Ulrich got off with a fine, but the fine was so big that his business was crippled by it forever.

Her encounter with Süss inflamed the Waldensian. Up till now she had not known whether she loved her husband or not. Now she knew that she despised him. It was his duty to be successful. He was not worthy of her if he was not successful. She despised him because he could not spread elegance and superfluity and wine-red lackeys and Chinese porcelain before her as the other could, because he had let Süss overcome him, because she had cut such a lamentable figure before Süss on his account. She despised him because for his sake she had rejected Süss's overtures. Süss was of the world, like herself; Johann Ulrich was a petty bourgeois. Of all this she said not one word to Johann Ulrich, not even did she mention her visit to the Jew. He raged against Süss, screamed and swore he would have the bloodthirstiest revenge. But it was empty bluster. She looked at him with her large eyes cold, proudly indifferent, and he knew as well as she that he was broken and powerless and would never do anything.

He sank lower and lower. The factory in Urach was sold by auction, as also the branch establishments in Stuttgart and Maulbronn. The Levantine merchant obtained them. With contemptuous charity Johann Ulrich was offered a managerial post in his former factories. Perhaps he would have accepted had not his wife, guessing the hand of Süss in this offer, sharply and curtly refused to allow it. The other Scherlins too were involved in his downfall. The houses in Urach and Stuttgart were sold, the fields and vineyards were sold. Only old Christoph Adam maintained himself in Esslingen. He carried his large weatherbeaten head higher than ever, and struck his cane more fiercely against

137

the ground, clasping the golden handle firmly in his withered but not trembling hand.

Johann Ulrich, like many others who during Süss's regime had lost both home and money, made preparations for joining a train of emigrants to Pennsylvania. The Waldensian opposed him. There was a sharp, short struggle. He struck her, but he stayed in the country. He opened a store in Urach; degenerated more and more, sat in the public-houses and fuddled himself, venting blashphemous curses on the Duke and the hellish Hebrew government. But although all malcontents were usually severely punished, he was left quietly alone. His store, too, was officially supported in every way. The officials must have had a hint from an influential quarter.

The Waldensian went about in her shabby clothes with as much pride as formerly, casting arrogant glances from her long eyes. When a customer tried to open conversation with her, she was curt and sparing in her answers. Generally she was silent out of boredom. And although she had been born in Germany she nearly always spoke French, and her German was halting and broken.

THROUGH Süss's magnificent rooms Isaac Landauer trailed his caftan, with the Württemberg Jews' badge ostentatiously displayed on his arm, although no one required him to wear it, the 'S' with the horn. The shining mirrors reflected his image among lapis lazuli and gold, his lean shrewd head with the side-curls, the straggling, reddish, faded beard. The Finance Director was showing him his house. The man in the caftan stood before the vases, the Gobelins, the tinkling pagodas, and looked up with an irritatingly mocking smile at the Triumph of Mercury, clapped the white mare Assjadah with his chilly dry hand, and walked between the two pages, the sons of Lamprecht the President of Demesnes, who stood at attention by the door of the private suite. He fingered the expensive upholstery of the furniture, and with stupendous expertness guessed its price. He stood shaking his head before the busts of Moses, Homer, Solomon and Aristotle, with the remark, "Moses our teacher never looked like that in all his life." But

138

from its cage Akiba the parrot screamed, "How did Your Highness condescend to sleep?"

Süss had long been expecting Isaac Landauer. He had prepared his palace for this visit more carefully than for the visit of many a reigning prince. He lay in wait for a moment of surprise or of astonished appreciation; he was stung and tormented by a desire to impress the man in the caftan, him especially. But Isaac Landauer only shook his head, rubbed his chilly hands, smiled and asked: "To what end, Reb Josef Süss?"

Into the small room came inquisitively Sophie Fischer, the daughter of the Attorney to the Treasury, whom the Finance-Director had kept for two weeks as his declared mistress,—a large stately woman, white, wanton, reddish-golden, very lovely and slightly commonplace. When Süss rebuked her for the interruption she excused herself carelessly, looked at Isaac Landauer with compressed lips, and took herself away.

"To what end, Reb Josef Süss?" repeated Isaac Landauer. "Why thirty servants all at once? Can you eat better and sleep better with thirty servants than with three? I understand your keeping the wench, I understand your wanting to eat in a fine room, and to have a broad comfortable bed. But why the parrot? What does a Jew want with a parrot?"

Süss was silent, filled with devouring anger. This was not simplicity, it was a sneer, an open, obvious sneer. What no Minister was bold enough to do, the man in the caftan did, in the most calm and matter-of-fact way, laughed at him to his face. And he was helpless against him, he needed him, he could only hold his tongue. And he would certainly trot out all his old tales again, which had no sense or relevance in the present, the Ravensburg ritual murder and rubbish like that. And he, Süss, would have to listen to them. It was impossible to do business without Isaac Landauer. Oh, if one could only get rid of this compromising fellow! But one had to be thankful to have dealings with him. For the present he could not be circumvented.

They discussed the affairs they had to settle, and bargained sharply and warily. Süss was really the employer throughout; but he had to speak much more than the other, and in spite of his

139

grand gestures felt himself to be on the defensive. No camouflage, however skilful, could deceive Isaac Landauer's eye, he got behind it immediately, and all pretences fell before him; shaking his head in disbelief he cleared away the tempting decorations and laid his chilly hands upon the heart of Süss's affairs, the round figures. The more Süss vaunted himself the more bitterly he was filled with vexation and discomfort. He did not admit it, but the other had him on a string; the man in the caftan made him dance.

When the negotiations were finished and signed, Isaac Landauer did not touch this time upon the Ravensburg ritual murder, but upon another Jewish tale from the past history of Württemberg. That was the affair of the great Jewish artist Abraham Calorno from Italy—a good hundred years ago, under Duke Friedrich I—and of his General Consul Maggino Gabrieli. The Duke had enticed this Italian Jew into the country with grand promises. He was as if bewitched by the amiable nature, the learning, the financial skill of the great Jewish artist, he had boundless confidence in him and rudely and curtly disposed of all the objections raised by the priests, by the Estates, yes, he even banished the chief pontiff Osiander from the country for the Jew's sake, and Abraham Calorno and his people were great and magnificent in Stuttgart. But the story finally ended in terror and cruelty; some of the family were tortured to death and the remainder hunted out of the land in their shirts, and Jews were forbidden to enter the Duchy for years. "They abused us, called us gnawing worms," said Isaac Landauer. "Well, don't they gnaw too? Everything which lives gnaws. One gnaws the other. Now it is your turn, Reb Josef Süss. Gnaw, while you can and while they let you!" And he laughed his small chuckling laugh.

The man in the caftan at last took leave of his unwilling listener and passed through the anteroom amid the mocking and hostile whispering of waiting petitioners. At the door he met fresh visitors, Weissensee, the President of the Ecclesiastical Council and his daughter Magdalen Sibylle who, when she caught sigh of Isaac Landauer, mistook him for Süss. That was how she had imagined the small disgusting emissary of Beelzebub, filthy and in a caftan and with side-curls, like occasional Jewish pictures she had seen.

140

When the Prelate Weissensee paid him a visit of thanks for his appointment as President of the Ecclesiastical Council, Süss had mentioned casually and courteously that he had heard the President had a very amiable daughter. It was not desirable that the flower of the Swabian ladies should bloom afar from the Residence; Ludwigsburg and Stuttgart were not rich enough in beauty to be able to dispense with a lady such as the Demoiselle Weissensee had been described to him as being. Weissensee accepted the compliment graciously, and expressed his pleasure that His Excellence should honour his daughter with his interest. He had then succeeded more easily than he expected in persuading his daughter to go with him to Stuttgart to call upon Süss. She devised in the invitation a call and a mission. Where else could she fulfil her mission, where could she more probably meet with the Devil than at the house of his minion, in the neighbourhood of the Duke and the Jew? So she came with her father to the Residence, alert and in readiness.

When she learned that Isaac Landauer was not the Jew she was slightly disappointed and sat in a tension of expectation. They were admitted before the others. She preceded her father into the cabinet past the lackeys standing at attention, caught sight of Süss, recognized him as the Devil, reeled and swooned away. When she recovered her senses a veiled silken voice was saying in her ear: "I am desolated that mademoiselle your daughter should have an accident just as she was crossing my threshold for the first time." Her father made some reply. A bottle of smelling salts was held under her nose. She must not open her eyes yet, she must not be compelled to speak to him, to look into his eyes. When at last, willy-nilly, she had to come to life again she saw Beelzebub's eyes, his roving, warm, arched eyes, gliding over her breast and her hips, and she was passionately ashamed of herself.

Süss had regarded the girl closely as she lay swooning; he saw that she was beautiful, a virgin, and full of sap. Her swoon, the enormous impression which he had obviously made upon her, was balm and consolation to him after his uneasy interview with Isaac Landauer. How brown in spite of her pallor, and how keen and masculine her face was, how fascinating the sweep of her bold eyebrows! While the lackeys were running for essences and for a doctor he considered whether he dared undo her bodice. There was no need to stand on ceremony with Weissensee, the servile old courtier.

But just then she opened her eyes, deep blue in strange contrast to her dusky hair. He lifted her up, his eyes, his voice, and his tender hands surrounded her with caressing devotion and humble gallantry, he employed all the insinuating arts learned in his long experience. Over the broken stammering words of the girl, whose confused eyes in her pale tawny face were fixed upon him half threateningly and half fascinated, he spread a cloak of adroit conversation. Offered her a litter, a carriage, a doctor. Did not attempt by a single word to detain the President, who was preparing to go. Himself escorted Magdalen Sibylle, supporting her with his arm, through the respectful salutations of the people in his antechamber, to the front door, and into her carriage. While they were passing through the entrance hall Sophie Fischer encountered them. The blonde and wanton creature trailed indolently through the room, casting a glance of curiosity and furtive hatred after Magdalen Sibylle.

In front of the house in the Seegasse there stands a gaping crowd. It is night; a foul mixture of rain and snow, with gusts of wind which whip one's clothes about one's limbs. The people stand squeezed together, waiting to see the carriages, lit up and noisy in the darkness, arriving for Süss's redoute.

Pitch flares are flickering at the entrance. All the windows are illuminated. The door is wide open, a hussar stands towering with his staff, and three footmen to open the carriage doors.

In quick succession come the coaches. This is not one of the public balls where Süss tries to make a profit, and black-lists every one from the Court, the Civil Service, and the populace who is absent. Through these public festivals he has compelled the Capital and Residence of Stuttgart to celebrate a more brilliant Carnival than ever before; he has forced people to spend more money on a seat and to squander more (for his profit) than in weeks of ordinary days; but this select masked ball is to serve exclusively as a private exhibition of his greatness and his pomp. Only the

142

most important gentlemen, only the most beautiful ladies of the Duke's circle, have been invited.

From behind Süss's hussars and the town policemen the people stretch their necks to espy the costumes of the alighting guests beneath their cloaks. The Ministers arrive, the Generals, the courtiers. Very lean, and with his hook-nose looking twice as big above his Spanish ruff, comes Privy Councillor Schütz in a grandee's mantle. And there is Remchingen, solid and red as a lobster, sweating in his carriage under the thick fur coat of his Boyar costume. He is gruffer than ever, because he has knocked up against M. de Riolles in the doorway, one of those wandering cavaliers who are welcome at all the Courts and carry through Europe the gossip of the first circles among the international aristocracy, making and marring all the worldly reputations in high society. Two or three women burst out giggling, and even the policemen cannot help grinning at the sight of the small, meagre, fidgety gentleman, who is got up as a Chinese but has kept his periwig. He looks ridiculous, tripping like a dwarf with his old, vicious, boy's face beside the bulky Remchingen. The General clanks massively and imposingly beside the small foppish Frenchman; but he knows that the Duchess, whether from a desire for change or to make him angry, will prefer the babbling idiot to himself, as she has done for the last few days.

Neuffer, the Estates Advocate, pushes his way on foot through the crowd, in a nondescript costume of some dark colour and scarlet; murmurs of abuse follow him; he and Weissensee are the only Parliamentarians who are invited. He is overtaken by the elegant and studiously inconspicuous carriage of the old Prince Thurn and Taxis. The Prince has come on a visit yesterday from Regensburg; his lean, elegant greyhound head rises from the wine-red suit of a Genoese noble; he is pleased to be the first to introduce this costume, in which he looks particularly slim. But obviously he has abominable luck with this damned Jew! The other time in the Château Monbijou his pale yellow coat was killed by the pale yellow salon, and now the Hebrew brute has stuck his whole domestic staff into wine-red livery, so that the Prince will be taken for a lackey; at least the effect of his wine-red costume will be

143

spoiled. Beside the angry Prince waddles Privy Councillor Fichtel, small, thick-set and insignificant, who has come for two days to Stuttgart with letters from the Bishop of Würzburg; he is like a ball in his baggy breeches and Turkish coat, and his sly face looks pleased under his fez; he waves jovially with his small plump hand to the people, who are whispering about the Catholics.

A dingy ramshackle coach drew up, with a single footman behind, dressed in a very ancient, obsolete style; and a tall gentleman alighted with a remarkably purple, haggard face, and glided through the silent crowd into the doorway: the Palatinate Privy Councillor Dom Bartelemi Pancorbo. The Duke himself had made the reluctant Süss invite the jewel-merchant, who had been living in Stuttgart for some time. Dom Bartelemi Pancorbo appeared in his usual clothes, his compressed death's head stretched out of a shabby, badly-fitting and slovenly Court dress; he had made no other attempt at a costume.

Punctually at the appointed hour the Ducal coach arrived. Karl Alexander descended from it, with only a slight limp on this occasion, enormous and imposing as a hero of antiquity: Marie Auguste, her figure rising like a slender stalk from a sweeping peacock-blue hooped skirt, her lizard-like head lambent as a delicate flame, was the Goddess Minerva. She wore a wig with a magnificent gold helmet on top of it, and round her breast was fitted the merest suggestion of a fine golden corselet; one page carried her shield behind her and another her owl.

The flourish of trumpets was already beginning to greet the Ducal pair, Süss had already appeared at the door of the reception room, in which people were drawn up, but the Duke loitered in the vestibule. Beside the President of his Ecclesiastical Council he had caught sight of a girl of large and beautiful stature, dressed as a Florentine gardener; when for a moment in taking off her cloak she removed her mask to arrange her enormous beribboned straw hat he caught a glimpse of masculine keen brown cheeks, and deep blue eyes in strange contrast to strong dark eyebrows. He felt himself moved as he had not been for years at the sight of a woman, his knees became weak, and he had a sinking feeling in his stomach. With a slight smile the Duchess turned her quick eyes from Karl Alexander to the girl, who had immediately reas-

144

sumed her mask. "I think we ought to go in," she said. Süss was already there to conduct them, slim and elegant in a Saracen costume. "Who is the lady?" asked Karl Alexander. "Mademoiselle the daughter of Weissensee, I imagine," answered the Jew, "Mademoiselle Magdalen Sibylle Weissensee." Then the great personages entered the ball-room, the guests bowed deeply, and the trumpets rang out.

Since the Duchess dearly loved comedy, Süss began the evening with the performance of a small Italian opera, "A Prodigal against his Will." For the occasion the new singer, Graziella Vitali, a Neapolitan, made her first appearance, a small vivacious creature, plump, golden-skinned and pretty, with a somewhat shrewish face and sparkling eyes. Süss had promised himself that she would make a great impression on the Duke, as her type was usually Karl Alexander's fancy. Süss had drawn a glowing picture of her prospects to the singer, and when she was presented to the Duke after the comedy she fluttered assiduously around him, giving him signs and looks of open invitation, only waiting for him to withdraw with her into a private room. But Karl Alexander paid her only a casual and distracted attention; he muttered something like, "Later, later!" It was obvious that for the time he had someone else in his eye.

Magdalen Sibylle had hardly removed her mask during the comedy. She hid her nervous, twitching face behind it under her large straw hat. She had willingly submitted to her father's insistence that she should accompany him, but now she repented it. She did not have the strength to withstand the Devil. It was vanity and presumption to think that she could lead the Devil to God with her own poor hands. Since she had learned that the Jew was the Devil she had had a gnawing pain in her bosom. How she had cried to God! But God was silent. The Books of Humility, of Knowledge, and of Meditation were only so much paper. There were words in Swedenborg, but they had no sound or meaning for her; she ran to Beata Sturmin, the blind holy woman, but she had nothing to give her, the holy saint was a poor sick old-maid, and the atmosphere about her was bleak and soured.

She had not seen the Jew again since that time, and she had hesitated long before coming to the assembly. Now her evening

145

was a disappointment, a vexation. Süss paid no attention to her, he had given her barely a word of cold and courteous greeting. She could not know that this was diplomacy, she only saw that Lucifer had no eyes for her. She removed her mask from her brown, keen, quivering, distorted face; Lucifer had no eyes for her. This prostrated her more than a defeat.

But another was looking for a second time at the quivering brown face, looking at it long, with the relish of a connoisseur, looking it up and down, looking at the deep blue insistent eyes, in strange contrast to the dusky hair. By Jove, that Weissensee girl! So there were people like this! This was a Swabian, his subject! A Swabian of a rare kind. Karl Alexander had never imagined that Weissensee, the fox, had such a lovely flower growing in his house. He had gone to the ball with a vague and aimless longing for something new. He had been working, and was now rested and refreshed. This was something new and different. Now there was some meaning in the Soirée. The Italian actress, whom Süss had praised to him beforehand, only increased his desire for the firm, young Swabian girl.

After the opera they sit down to table. The supper is varied and magnificent. Masks are taken off, the flushed faces look at once strange and familiar above their costumes, and are doubly charming. Highly seasoned foods, strong rare wines, pithy toasts.

Gnomes come dancing in, empty the jewel cabinets, and with comic gestures hand the glittering gifts to the ladies for whom Süss has destined them. Dom Bartelemi watched them keenly as they shared out stone after stone, necklace after necklace, buckle after buckle. The extraordinarily tall man, with his right shoulder curiously raised, his purple fleshless face stretching on the withered neck out of the formal ruff of his old-fashioned Portuguese dress, let his long unblinking narrow eyes rove unceasingly from behind their wrinkled lids. Deepset in their cavities they kept watch in his compressed and death-like head. The Palatinate Privy Councillor—who was also the General Director of Palatinate Commerce and Tobacco Manufacture—examined the ladies' gifts, and appraised them with expert skill. Profound uneasiness seized Süss when he heard the hollow, cold, drawling voice which had so often undercut his prices, hindered so many of his transactions, and for so long reduced him to petty insignificance. With a cold shiver of repulsion he observed the glowing passion with which Dom Bartelemi let the shimmering stones trickle through his long, dry, purple fingers. They looked askance at each other, like two sparring birds of prey, the one old, bleak, and incredibly experienced, the other smaller, younger, rasher and more exuberant.

"Fine stones, good stones," commented Dom Bartelemi. "But rubbish beside the solitaire. Let me look at your solitaire," he said to Süss. And, turning the solitaire tenderly in his spidery fingers, he growled in his pot-house voice across the listening guests, "What's your price for the stone, Finance Director?" "It is not for sale," replied Süss. "I will give you the Palatinate Tobacco Manufactory for it," insisted the Portuguese. "It is not for sale," repeated the Jew emphatically. Reluctantly Dom Bartelemi handed back the diamond, and the Duchess remarked: "Now my Jew is sticking the Palatinate Tobacco Manufactory on his finger!"

After supper, while the ball was beginning, the Duke sat with Magdalen Sibylle apart in the conservatory. Immediately after supper he had given Süss a hint that he would like the use of his bedroom and dressing-room, and that he wanted Magdalen Sibylle to be conveyed there on some pretext or other. Süss felt a sharp stab of pain on hearing this; he remembered how the girl had screamed and run away on first catching sight of him in the wood, and how later in his study she had swooned and lain there, so brown in her pallor, so helpless and so very young; Magdalen Sibylle really belonged to him, it did not need a sharp eye to see that she was drawn irresistibly to him, and when Karl Alexander mentioned her, he felt a wild desire for her. But he was so accustomed to put the Duke and business first, and his own sentiments and lusts for women second, that he was glad to be of service to His Highness. He would only respectfully draw His Highness's attention to the fact that the lady, so far as he knew, was an evangelical enthusiast difficult to handle and easily driven into hysterics; also in his opinion this cask had not yet been broached. "Have you been trying it?" the Duke laughed uproariously, and again, "Have you been trying it?" That was precisely the kind of thing, he added, he was itching for, and the fact that she was a pietest only gave a doubly sharp relish to the dish. And he nodded jovially and graciously to Weissensee, who was not far away, talking to Fichtel and Schütz.

So, sitting with her in the conservatory, he began to chaff her about her pietism. To be sure he was himself a Catholic, and a low renegade; but his Ecclesiastical Council, which should know something about the matter, and her father, too, at the head of it, did not agree with such revivalistic teachings; in fact only the day before he had had to sign an edict prohibiting, under pain of severe punishment, a certain Frau von Molk from holding sectarian conventicles. And when he saw Beata Sturmin, the saint who headed the whole movement, he thought to himself that intercourse with angels did not make a woman exactly charming; but now that he had made the acquaintance of Magdalen Sibylle, he began to think that intercourse with God and the angels had something to say for itself. Magdalen Sibylle listened in torment to his stale witticisms. She was afraid of Karl Alexander, afraid of his heated face, his devouring eyes. She was not amused by his jests; she felt that God had deserted her, else she would have flamed up at such blasphemy and would not have been afraid to throw her contempt and anger in the face even of this raging Nebuchadnezzar. Instead she only felt aversion, she was so sad and weary, and God had hidden Himself in darkness, God did not deign to give her an answer, God had cast her out.

It was terribly hot in the conservatory, the exotic trees and plants stirred like living things in the light of the candles, wild bursts of music floated in, and Magdalen Sibylle had a frightful headache. The eyes and words of the Duke hurt her like something sharp and piercing. She saw the words coming out of his wanton, lecherous and threatening mouth to attack her, piercing her, flaying her soul. She felt tense almost to breaking point, she was on the verge of doing something wild and senseless; then at the very last moment she was delivered by one of the Duchess's pages, who brought her a command to wait upon Her Highness.

Marie Auguste sat in the middle of a fairly large circle. Süss was beside her, M. de Riolles, Privy Councillor Schütz, Götz, the young actuary, in a shepherd costume, yellow-headed, fresh and stupid, belonging to one of the best families, with his mother, wife

148

of a Privy Councillor, and his sister, Elisabeth Salomea. Both the ladies, mother and daughter, were ridiculously like each other; they looked like sisters, both pale, with delicate long limbs, very pretty, with a wealth of bright hair and large, sentimental, foolish eyes. Flaxen and lovely they sat in shepherdess costumes not very original and somewhat out of date, and flattered the Duchess with their naïve clear voices and their amiable unintelligent eyes. Sophie Fischer, stately and indolent, Süss's voluptuous mistress, had just returned to the conservatory, and Marie Auguste could not refrain from teasing her pet Jew about her. He had managed to get her father, Fischer, the Treasury Fiscal, appointed as Transport Director, obviously as a compensation for the use of his daughter. Süss, manly in his slender elegance, stood in his Saracen dress in front of the ladies, and returned jest for jest with unembarrassed readiness; to be sure the Fischer girl had been a delightful and welcome housekeeper for him; but now that Her Highness has deigned to exalt her father to such an honourable position, he could not venture to keep her in his service; the daughter of such a high official—no, that would be quite improper. He smiled, and concluded with impudent indifference, therefore he would send her home next day. The little group was astonished at the open cynicism with which he rewarded and dismissed his mistress. The Duchess was amused, M. de Riolles, too, was clearly delighted at this display of *savoir faire,* but the stupid young actuary Götz was at a loss to know what he ought to do, for he attached great importance to good form, and did not know whether to agree with the Jew or to attack him; he decided finally on saying nothing, and looking fierce.

The sweet and amiable ladies Götz, however, both mother and daughter, were astonished at the elegant superciliousness with which this cavalier ended a love-affair, and looked at him with great admiration and tender interest.

Into this circle came Magdalen Sibylle. The Duchess had noticed the marked attention paid to her by Karl Alexander, she also liked this girl with the brown, keen face and the strange contrast of blue eyes and dark hair. She was curious to find out on a closer inspection what her attractions were. She extended her hand graciously to be kissed, and looked her over indolently and without embarrassment. Magdalen Sibylle had a small, shy, furtive glance for Süss. He had bowed profoundly when she came, and now stood, serious and formal. She was free now that she did not have to listen to the Duke any longer, and felt goodwill radiating towards her from the Duchess, but the indifferent formality in Süss's countenance disturbed her afresh. She sat in silence while the others continued their light and aimless conversation, and suddenly her fear, tension, disappointment, rage and expectation found vent in a fit of wild sobbing at the Duchess's feet. The others were embarrassed, tittered a little, but Marie Auguste stroked with her small delicate hand the great cold hand of the sobbing girl. Süss, however, skilfully made use of the opportunity, and saying that he would look after her until she calmed down, he led her out, shaken and self-conscious. Riolles the Chinaman grinned, Schütz the Spaniard smiled, and Götz the fanciful shepherd again found no reaction but a fierce expression. But the Duchess, calmly going on with the conversation, stole a glance at her husband and noted to her satisfaction that he made a sign to Süss as the girl was taken out past him.

The chamber into which the Jew conducted Magdalen Sibylle was cool after the ball-rooms, which were overheated with candles, wine, and people. It led into his bedroom, and one could see through a portière the state bed with the golden Amoretti. In this place had been collected all the things from the other rooms which had been cleared away for the ball, things which might get broken, porcelain, the Chinese pieces, and the cage with the parrot Akiba. The noise of the festivities was barely audible, and after the crowded salons this little room with its fresher air, its emptiness, quietness and coolness, was comforting and pleasant.

Magdalen Sibylle sat down on a low divan, breathing more quietly relaxed. She looked magnificent sitting there, warm and drooping after the excitement; and Süss, who stood, gentle and kind, beside her, desired her intensely. It was annoying and unfortunate that the other would be coming now; he probably would not be able to appreciate such a rare morsel.

The girl looked up slowly at the man with her large, brimming eyes. Süss felt it incumbent on him to return the look with that air of boundless devotion in which he was so skilled, and to mingle with the devotion a spice of fatherliness suitable to this special occasion. "Poor Lucifer!" thought Magdalen Sibylle. "He is an unhappy and troubled creature. There is no sense in being fanatical and attacking him with wild exorcisms. I will take him quite gently by the hand and persuade him with kind words to turn to God again. How could I doubt that I would have the strength for my mission? He is only waiting for some one to come and reconcile him with God."

"I am inconsolable, Mademoiselle," said the Jew meanwhile with his veiled caressing voice, "that you always meet with an accident in my presence. Is my face really so abominable and repulsive? Or is it perhaps only an unlucky chance?" And he bent towards her as she sat tall and glowing on the divan.

"Please do not pretend any longer," she said suddenly, with a rush of courage, and looking at him gravely and urgently. "I know very well that you are Lucifer, the son of Belial, and you know that I am sent to wrestle with you and bring you back to God."

Süss had much experience of women; he was accustomed to surprises, and never lost his composure, or showed himself at a loss. But this remark was so utterly unexpected that words failed him, and for the first time in his life he had no answer ready. It was lucky for him that Magdalen Sibylle was expecting no answer, but after a short pause went on speaking. She could comprehend very well that he believed that God, his Enemy, would have nothing to do with him, and certainly it needed enormous strength of will to give up the perversity of thousands of years. But when once this perversity and blind frowardness was abandoned, the soul would be freed from its evil accretions and would bathe in God as in pleasant, clear, transparent water. She went on in this fashion with insistence, and in her enthusiasm stretched out her hand to him.

With characteristic adroitness, Süss had adjusted himself to the pietistic vocabulary, and he seized her hand, beginning a quickly composed answer. They were both getting on excellently when the Duke suddenly entered the room. With dilated eyes, terrified and imploring, oppressed and breathing quickly, Magdalen Sibylle stared at Süss. But the Jew observed politely that he must return to his guests, and all at once she was alone with the Duke, and the parrot screamed, *"Ma vie pour mon souverain,"* and in the next room the shameless, magnificent bed leapt more clearly and nakedly into view. Karl Alexander made some aimless and jesting remark in a husky, constrained voice. She saw his red face, slightly bedewed with sweat, she saw his eyes which grew darker and wilder, and she smelt his hot and drunken breath. She forced herself to go to the door, stammering some excuse about following Süss, going back to the others. But the door was locked. Karl Alexander laughed hoarsely, and deliberately undid his priceless antique breastplate, in a silence in which her breathing was audible. He advanced towards her with gruesome affection, and took her hand in his, a curious hand, slim, long, bony and hairy on the back, but fleshy, fat and short on the palm. She summoned her strength and defended herself wildly, but without any prospect of success, against the bulky, powerful, aroused man.

Returning from the little room, Süss flung himself with a kind of grim determination into the whirl of the masked ball. He tried to avoid the Duchess (who with a small, amused and lascivious smile asked after Magdalen Sibylle) and paid court to both the Götz ladies, in whom the Duke was also interested, with such fierce insistence, that the young actuary Götz, seeing that his pugnacious attitude was ignored, fuddled himself in a corner in dumb perplexity, while the two ladies gave themselves up to the cynical gallantries of the Jew and returned them with foolish affection. The little Neapolitan comedienne, golden-skinned, slightly plump and vicious, had made up to the old Prince Thurn and Taxis. She acted as if she did not know who he was, and was only caressing and flattering him because of his elegant and distinguished appearance. The old Prince, seeing that in spite of its similarity to the footmen's liveries his wine-red costume was making an impression after all, recovered his spirits, and visibly threw off his irritation. At the same time Remchingen was trying to attract the lady's attention, but she skilfully gave him the cold shoulder, though he was devouring her with eyes already glassy, and she stuck to the fine, rich, old Prince. But Götz from his corner was gazing at her with transport, his eyes dimmed even more by sentiment than by liquor; and while she kept the General at arm's length and

152

drew on the old Prince, she still found an opportunity of ensnaring the stupid, yellow-headed, young shepherd for ever, with a single but unutterably eloquent look.

Weissensee, Neuffer the advocate, and the Würzburg Privy Councillor Fichtel were sitting at the faro-table with Schütz and M. de Riolles. Weissensee was more distracted than usual. His clever lean head turned restlessly from side to side, and he asked everyone who passed if they had seen Magdalen Sibylle. And his long, fine hands were damp with sweat, and his sceptical eyes had a hunted look as they searched the room right and left.

Suddenly, on catching sight of Süss, he excused himself to the others, and with his silken Venetian mantle fluttering behind him he advanced hastily to the Jew and asked after his daughter. Süss replied carelessly that she had a slight headache, and had withdrawn into a quieter and cooler room. The President of the Ecclesiastical Council, somewhat discomposed, wanted to seek her out. But Süss thought it would be best to leave Mademoiselle alone, especially as His Highness himself was looking after her, so far as he knew. As he said this he regarded Weissensee steadily, with a polite and brazen smile. The latter began to tremble, and had to sit down. After a short silence Süss added of his own accord, with the same smile, that the Duke had spoken with unusual graciousness of the new President of the Ecclesiastical Council, and that promotion and honours would certainly come his way before long. Weissensee nodded once or twice in a strange, preoccupied, senile manner, and stared with a courteous but slightly wry smile at the bustle around him, then, in a wavering voice, without looking at Süss, began quite suddenly to speak of his roomy house in Hirsau. He drew a picture of his comfortable country home among its vineyards, crowned with harvest, well-stocked both in and out and steeped in rustic peace; he told how he had worked there at ease on his New Testament far away from the turmoil of the world, which subsided into stillness and only now and then threw up a touch of spray which he savoured like a connoisseur; and how his daughter had flitted to and fro amid all this in quiet simplicity, preoccupied and matter-of-fact.

In the middle of his reverie, which he unfolded more to himself than to Süss, he stopped as suddenly as he had begun. He looked sunken, his elegant Venetian mantle hung loosely and incongruously upon him like the folded wings of a bat. Standing before him as he sat there sunk in abandonment and helpless, the Jew looked him up and down, and in a light, alert, ruthless tone of voice sent a shaft of mockery into his silence. "I should never have believed that you could be so sentimental." "Not at all, not at all!" returned Weissensee eagerly, pulling himself together. "I do not flee from life, your Excellency. I have never refused any experience in all my time. Curiosity is the principle on which I have regulated my existence." He tried to recover his habitual ready smile. "It must have been a very restless star under which I was born. It has never allowed me to settle, but has hounded me on through many countries and overseas, and has bid me peer into the souls of all the creatures of God and Satan. Ah, my memories!"

But while he was striving to recall his memories, it happened that the pale, smiling face of the Jew before him, with the arched, brown eyes and the voluptuous lips, suddenly lost its outline. Suddenly he knew with certitude that a few paces away, behind a locked door, his daughter was struggling and fighting with failing strength and no hope of success. He saw her, he saw the warmth fading from her keen, brown face, he saw her deep blue eyes becoming fixed and glassy beneath her dusky hair. And in the midst of this vision he heard the sharp and matter-of-fact voice of Süss: "As things stand this evening, I dare promise you quite definitely promotion and honours."

The remarkable thing was that he did not hate this man who bent over him with the polite and brazen smile. He played, but only played, with the desire, the idea, of seeing the other sitting in front of him equally broken and unsteady, while he, Weissensee, stood over him alert and smiling. After that, he behaved quite as usual, only everything he did and said seemed oppressively unreal, vague and puppet-like, as if he were asleep. He kept on bowing, courteously and amiably, he exchanged a jest with the Duchess, he spoke with gentle diplomacy to Privy Councillor Fichtel, and he capped one of M. de Riolles's subtle and indecent stories with one even more subtle and more obscene. But all these voices sounded strangely mechanical and thin, and the people moved like artificial dolls, and everything seemed made of wax. Even the Duke, who was again in the salon, bulky and heavy, limping more than usual with tired, slack, and relaxed limbs, seemed to be only a wax figure behind a veil of smoke and vapour.

But all the same at the sight of the Duke he managed to raise a small new flicker of hope. He dispersed his visions, he suppressed his knowledge and pretended that it was not true. With a quick flutter he gathered his Venetian mantle about him and went to intercept the Duke, his whole being one urgent, imploring entreaty to know whether this had perhaps not happened after all. But the Duke did not see him, he obviously did not want to see him, he had no eyes for him; although Weissensee was quite near him he passed him with a vacant stare and an embarrassed, gruff hiccough.

Weissensee went suddenly old and tired. He sought out a quiet corner for himself, and happened on the table where Götz the actuary was sitting alone and drinking. The young man felt himself very honoured by the President of the Ecclesiastical Council's company, and although he was already half seas over, persisted in standing up ceremoniously and making many formal reverences. And then the two men sat together, the one old, subtle, sad and broken, and the other young, downright, disappointed and stewing himself stupid in helpless sentimentality, and they said nothing, and gazed at the festive and overheated turmoil, and drank.

But Karl Alexander moved through the room, satiated, proud and pleased with himself. True, he often gave a small, embarrassed and defiant laugh, like a boy who has done something wrong and swaggers about it to get over his sense of shame. But precisely for that reason it was clear to everybody that he had just come from an embrace. He waved to his wife, who looked at him as if asking a question, with a lordly gesture which was easily to be interpreted as a proud avowal. He paused at the faro-tables, where the flushed players, secretly outraged at being disturbed, arose respectfully, and assured them that he was extraordinarily, yes, quite extraordinarily delighted with his evening. He thirstily tossed down two glasses of Tokay and became very drunk. He made for his father-in-law, who was now completely absorbed in the Neapolitan, a fact which Karl Alexander recognized with appreciation and benevolence. He fell on the old Prince's neck several times, saying affectionately, "Your Highness! Your Highness! It is glorious that Your Highness should feel so young!" Then he boasted vainly and sentimentally about his young days in Italy, his Lombard companions, and his Venetian adventures. "Your Highness is getting on well," he stuttered, "and so am I. *Suum cuique! Suum cuique!* In this dunghill of a world the Lord has set both of us on a spot which is warm and soft and full of sunlight." And he caressed appreciatively the bare golden ripe arm of the comedienne, and congratulated the old man on the fine chicken he was beginning to pluck.

Süss avoided the Duke. He was soured and jealous; he knew that Karl Alexander would want to describe his affair with Magdalen Sibylle, coarsely and wordily and with all the details, and he was not in the mood to listen to an account of these delights, the first fruits of which should really have been his. To escape from thinking about it he plunged into the flood tide of his festival. It was in his honour, to celebrate his arrival in the world, to celebrate his birthday, that all these lights were kindled, these tables and magnificent salons decorated, these lovely women and grand gentlemen assembled. He had climbed very high, never before in Germany had a Jew risen to such a high and brilliant position. And he would climb higher yet. His application for a patent of nobility was already on the way to the Emperor's court in Vienna; he would be ennobled—Karl Alexander, daily under more obligations to him, would have to put that through. He was no fool like Isaac Landauer, he did not run around in gaberdine and side-curls; but neither did he think of procuring titles and rank for himself by the cheap expedient of changing his religion as his brother had. He would climb to the top by sheer genius, by his luck and his genius alone. He would remain a Jew, and in spite of it—and that would be his triumph—he would become a noble and take his rightful place in the Duchy formally and in face of all the world.

Dancing was going on. His heart and eye and ear were filled with its gay and gratifying noise. His dreams mounted on the runs of the violins, the drums brayed his power into the room, the beauty of the ladies and the silken grandeur of the gentlemen paid homage to him. He looked on at his festivities, dreaming of his court career, his ripe red mouth half open, and a look of rapture on his pale face. But suddenly an invisible something erased the pleased and satisfied enjoyment from his features. The gay rainbow-coloured bubbles were blown away, the radiant hues of the dancers faded; he saw the musicians playing, but he no longer heard the music. He saw himself treading in another shadowy, mocking and terrifying dance. In front of him, holding his hand, moved Rabbi Gabriel, his uncle; behind him, holding his other hand, the Duke haltingly dragged his lame foot. Far ahead of him, linked to him by a chain of many hands—was not that Isaac Landauer, moving his limbs in the dance rhythm and shaking his shrunken head while his absurd caftan fluttered around him?

When he shook himself free of this vision he found Dom Bartelemi Pancorbo standing beside him in his shabby Portuguese dress, fixing upon him his watchful eyes in their deep-set cavities, and slowly into his consciousness wound the strange pot-house voice: "Well, Finance Director, what do you say? I'll add the tax on brandy for a month to the tobacco monopoly; will you give me the solitaire?"

And the dance went on. Nicklas Pfäffle, who in his indifferent, drowsy and precise way was managing the complicated mechanism of the ball, had planned a surprise for the second half of the evening. The ceiling painted with the Triumph of Mercury opened out, and on a flying machine there appeared Dan Cupid, who hovered over the guests strewing roses, and then in elegantly turned Alexandrines greeted the Ducal pair and congratulated Süss on his birthday. He was a very handsome boy and spoke his verses prettily, and even if Cupid had a slight Swabian accent that was at least better, said Remchingen in a loud voice, than if he had a Yiddish one.

When the dance recommenced immediately after, a slight unpleasantness occurred. A suspicious-looking frowsy fellow suddenly appeared in the salon and began shouting. People laughed and gathered round him, thinking that he was disguised in this way for a joke; and he had certainly been admitted on that assumption. But it soon became clear that his wild and abusive onslaughts on Hebrew justice and the whole robbing murdering and filthy Hebrew gang were made in earnest.

This frowsy vituperator was Johann Ulrich Schertlin. He had had some small business to transact in Stuttgart, had been drinking in the Blue Boar, and had fuddled himself among the railing tradesmen, while Benz the confectioner had listened in silence, with venomous satisfaction, saying only once: "Under the last Duke it was a harlot who reigned," whereupon there was a general outburst of growls. So Johann Ulrich had sat there, feeling more at ease than he had done for a long time, for he was no longer under the reproachful and contemptuous eye of the Waldensian; he had drunk a great deal, and had finally come to the Jew's house to give him a piece of his mind. Some of his boon companions had come with him, and now stood outside in the snow in the light of the candles which streamed from the festal rooms into the street; the coachmen of all the carriages which were waiting to take the guests home again had joined them, and there they stood more inquisitive than hostile, expecting to see Johann Ulrich handcuffed and delivered to the police. He meanwhile stood among the silken guests, stinking and filthy, smelling of bad wine, railing endlessly and abusively. People were already calling for the police, but when Süss heard that it was Schertlin he gave instructions to lock him up in the madhouse for the night and to send him home next day to his wife in Urach.

And the dance went on. Karl Alexander was very drunk; he had remarked but little of the affair with Johann Ulrich and had not understood it at all. He had succeeded at last in getting hold of Süss, and now sat apart with him, wishful to retail to such a connoisseur the delights he had enjoyed. He puffed and blew, for he was really very drunk, and had not properly fastened up his antique hero's costume; he was hot and heavy, reeking of wine and red in the face; he laughed and stuttered and clapped the respectfully attentive Jew on the thigh. "A delicate morsel!" and he smacked his lips and clicked his tongue. "You did well, Jew, to invite her to meet me. I will see to it that you are well rewarded. A German Prince doesn't do things shabbily. A delicate morsel!" He described Magdalen Sibylle and sketched with his blunt red hands, which were curious, being slim on the back and fat and short in the palm, the details of her body, her thighs, her breasts. "A wild filly! Hits out and bucks and bites and glows all over. And then so ice-cold when she should be accommodating." He pointed to the small, yellow-skinned, mercurial Neapolitan, who in spite of her preoccupation with the old Prince yet found time to make eyes at him, with her tongue in the corner of her mouth, like a naughty boy. "That one's a humbug, a bit of quicksilver, a whiff of scent. Let His Highness my papa-in-law make himself happy with her." He chuckled a small contemptuous laugh. "But the other, the lady of my heart, she's not an Italian rag. Nothing weak-kneed about her; she doesn't go to pieces in one's arms." He leaned back dreamily and sentimentally. "Mine is like a forest pool," he said with a vague and sweeping gesture. "Like a forest pool," he repeated with a hiccup, sinking his head on his breast, shutting his eyes, and breathing heavily.

Consumed with rage, Süss began cautiously and respectfully to withdraw, but Karl Alexander began again sketching, and brandishing his hands importantly. "What eyes she has, the jade! Eyes! Do you know what I had to think of? You'll never guess, never in all your life." A laugh began to bubble up, quietly at first, then wheezing and chuckling until it overpowered him completely. "I had to think of your Magus, your magic uncle—what eyes she has, the jade! The Magus. 'The first I will not tell you'—" He was suddenly seized with anger. "He wouldn't tell me, the dog of a wizard, the cursed malicious brute! May he swallow it down and choke on it and die of suffocation, the sorcerer, the accursed Jew!"

Terrified and very pale Süss had recoiled a step, breathing quickly, and made an imploring defensive gesture with his hand. But Karl Alexander, drunken and wrathful, rose with difficulty and tried to assume the proud and statuesque military pose attributed to him in the picture of Belgrade and the seven hundred halberdiers, bawled, hiccupped, and screamed: "Any one can prophesy what he likes. I am not afraid. *Attempto!* I'll dare it! I am Karl Alexander, Duke of Württemberg and Teck! By the grace of God! I stand above destiny! The German Achilles! By the grace of God!" And he stood there like his own monument.

But very soon he fell back into his chair, smiled of his own accord. "Like a forest pool," he hiccupped once again, puffed, snored, rattled, wheezed, and fell asleep.

And the dance went on. The sound of it rang out into the street where Johann Ulrich was being led away among his whispering fellows, sobered, weary, and dejected; and rang farther out over the town, over the land, which groaned, writhed and tossed, and then started out of its sleep muttering and growling—and fell asleep again and went on suffering.

Book Three

THE JEWS

THE JEWS

In the cities of the Mediterranean and the Atlantic, the Jews sat in the seats of the mighty. They commanded the trade between the Orient and the Occident. They spread over the seas. They helped to fit out the first ships to the West Indies, organized the trade with South and Middle America, opened up British, established the sugar industry of the West Indies; laid the foundations from which New York developed.

But in Germany they sat in humble and misery seats. In the fourteenth century in nine than three hundred and fifty families they were slain, drowned, burned, broken on the wheel, strangled, buried alive. Most of the survivors had wandered into Poland. Since then their numbers were few in the Holy Roman Empire. To every six hundred Germans there was one Jew. Under the refined extortions of the people and the authorities, they lived anxious, straitened, obscure, at the mercy of every caprice. Hard work and every free vocation was interdicted to them, and the official regulations drove them into the most complicated and difficult forms of chaffering and usury, neglected their purchase of necessaries, and not let them shave their beards, confined them in a ridiculous and shameful garb; pressed them into narrow quarters, barred the gate of their ghettos, locked it up evening after evening, and guarded their going in and coming out. Pressed close together they sat; they multiplied; but they were granted no more space. And because they could not expand their buildings horizontally, they piled them on high, story upon story. Ever narrower, darker, more winding became their streets. Neither free nor grass nor flower had room; they stood in each other's light, without sun, without air, in thick disease-bearing dirt. They were separated

Book Three

THE JEWS

In the cities of the Mediterranean and the Atlantic, the Jews sat in the seats of the mighty. They commanded the trade between the Orient and the Occident. They spread over the seas. They helped to fit out the first ships to the West Indies; organized the trade with South and Middle America, opened up Brazil; established the sugar industry of the Western Hemisphere; laid the foundations from which New York developed.

But in Germany they sat in humble and uneasy seats. In the fourteenth century in more than three hundred and fifty parishes they were slain, drowned, burned, broken on the wheel, strangled, buried alive. Most of the survivors had wandered into Poland. Since then their numbers were few in the Holy Roman Empire. To every six hundred Germans there was one Jew. Under the refined extortions of the people and the authorities, they lived anxious, straitened, obscure, at the mercy of every caprice. Handwork and every free vocation was interdicted to them, and the official regulations drove them into the most complicated and difficult forms of chaffering and usury, restricted their purchase of necessaries, did not let them shave their beards, confined them to a ridiculous and shameful garb, pressed them into narrow quarters, barred the gate of their Ghettos, locked it up, evening after evening, and guarded their going in and coming out. Pressed close together they sat; they multiplied, but they were granted no more space. And because they could not expand their buildings horizontally, they piled them on high, story upon story. Ever narrower, darker, more winding became their streets. Neither tree nor grass nor flower had room; they stood in each other's light, without sun, without air, in thick disease-bearing dirt. They were separated

163

from the fruitful earth, from heaven, from verdure. The wandering wind was trapped in their drab, stinking streets, the high, toppling houses barred their view of the drifting clouds, the blue sky. Their men slunk with bowed heads, their women faded early; of every ten children whom they bore, seven died. They were like dead brackish water, cut off from the freely-flowing life outside, dammed off from the language, the art, the spirit of others. Thick, pressing upon one another, they sat, in wretched intimacy; each knew the other's secrets; slanderous, suspicious, they exacerbated each other, lamed but energetic, chafed each other in pain, each the other's enemy and yet woven into the same net. For a single, trifling error or mischance of one might bring disaster to all.

But with the sure intuition which they had for the new, for the dawn, they surmised the changing aspect of the world outside, the ousting of birth and worth by money. They had experienced it: in insecurity and hazard, outlawry, there was only one shield; among the many tottering and deceptive footholds only one firm ground: money. On the door of the Jew with money no watch was set; the Jew with money stank no more, and no magistracy clapped a ridiculous, pointed cap upon his head. The princes and great lords needed him, they could not make wars and levy regiments without him, they allowed him to spread himself in their sunlight and to grow great and magnificent.

But the dense throng of the oppressed and the proscribed, and the few men of power; the proud Jews of the Levant and the great ocean cities who ruled the trade routes of Europe and the New World and in their counting-houses decided wars and peace, and the filthy, degenerate, downtrodden, ridiculous Jews of the German Ghettos; the Jewish physicians and ministers of the Khalifs and the Persian Shahs and the Sultans of Morocco in all their power and great splendour, and the lousy rabble of the Polish towns in their dirt and misery; the bankers of the Emperor and the princes, courted and hated in their cabinets, and the Jewish peddlers of the countryside hunted by dogs, and by the street boys and police driven into degrading, ludicrous humiliation: all of these had a sure and secret knowledge in common. To many it was not clear; only a very few could have expressed it; some shielded

164

themselves from a definite recognition of it. But it pulsed in their blood, it was in their innermost soul; the deep, mysterious, certain awareness of the senselessness, the inconstancy, the worthlessness of power. They had sat so long, puny and straitened, among the peoples of the earth, like dwarfs, dissipated into absurd atoms. They knew that to exercise power and to endure power is not the real, the important thing. The colossi of force, did they not all go to rack and ruin one after the other? But they, the powerless, had set their seal on the world.

And this lesson of the vanity and triviality of power was known by the great and the small alike among the Jews, the free and the burdened, the distant and the near, not in definite words, not with exact comprehension, but in their blood and their feelings. This mysterious knowledge it was that sometimes brought suddenly upon their lips—that enigmatic, soft, supercilious smile which doubly provoked their enemies, because to them it signified an iconoclastic insolence, and because all their tortures and cruelties were powerless in front of it. This mysterious knowledge it was that united the Jews and smelted them together, nothing else. For this mysterious knowledge was the meaning of the Book.

The Book; yes, their Book. They had no state, holding them together, no country, no soil, no king, no form of life in common. If, in spite of this, they were one, more one than all the other peoples of the world, it was the Book that sweated them into unity. Brown, white, black, yellow Jews, large and small, splendid and in rags, godless and pious, they might crouch and dream all their lives in a quiet room, or fare splendidly in a radiant, golden whirlwind over the earth, but sunk deep in all of them was the lesson of the Book. Manifold is the world, but it is vain and fleeting as wind; but one and only is the God of Israel, the everlasting, the infinite, Jehovah. Sometimes the Book was overgrown by the weeds of life, but it stuck fast in each of them, and in the hours when they were most themselves, at the highest points of their lives, it was there, and when they died it was there, and what flowed out from one to the other was this Word. They bound it with phylacteries round heart and head; they fastened it to their doors; they opened and closed the day with it; as sucklings they learned the Word; and they died with the Word on their

165

lips. From the Word they drew the strength to endure the piled-up afflictions of their way. Pale and secretive they smiled over the might of Edom, over its fury and the madness of its past works and its future plans. All that would pass; what remained was the Word.

They had dragged the Book with them through two thousand years. It was to them race, state, home, inheritance and possessions. They had given it to all peoples, and all peoples had embraced it. But its only legitimate possessors, knowers and judges, were they alone.

Six hundred and forty-seven thousand, three hundred and nineteen written characters had the Book. Each character was counted and weighed, tested and judged. Each character was paid for with blood; thousands had let themselves be tortured and slain for each character. Now the Book was altogether their own. And in their houses of prayer, on their highest holy-day, the proud who walked in power, as well as the humble, bowed and downtrodden, knew it and cried: "We have nothing, except the Book."

KARL ALEXANDER sent Magdalen Sibylle magnificent gifts, Gobelins from Flanders and Venice, golden perfume flasks with Persian attar of roses, an Arabian steed, a necklace of pearls. He was no niggard, he had no intention of being mean, and he regarded Magdalen Sibylle as his declared mistress. Daily came Neuffer, the Groom of the Chambers, and asked formally in the name of the Duke after the demoiselle's health.

Magdalen Sibylle met all this with cold and silent acceptance. She went about as dumb as the dead, her masculine, keen, beautiful face fixed and inflexible, her lips pressed together, her arms strangely rigid. She did not leave the house; she said "Good morning" and "Good evening," but nothing more; she dined alone; she did not trouble herself about household affairs. To no one, not even to her father, had she spoken about her affair with the Duke; and for days on end she did not even see her father.

Weissensee risked no attempt to waken her out of her torpor. He had been promoted to greater rank, he had now the position of a Conference Minister. He was in a vacillating and miserable state; he felt the mistrust of his colleagues on the Sub-Committee;

he would have liked to speak out to Harpprecht, the jurist, and to Bilfinger, who was a just and honourable man, and his friend. He dared not.

Magdalen Sibylle sat for hours benumbed and rigid. She was beyond herself, trampled to pieces, broken up, annihilated. Were these her arms? When she pricked herself was that her blood? The most fearful thing was that she had no hatred towards the Duke. He was like a great animal, a horse or an ox, warm and very big and closed within himself. Sometimes one surmised in the eyes of an animal like this how strange and incomprehensibly alien it was, sometimes one felt akin to it. But one could never hate it. This was the gruesome thing which had destroyed her world and herself, and had reduced them to a senseless and ridiculous rubbish heap: that the other was an animal, whom it was impossible to hate. For she herself must be such an animal, more delicate perhaps, not so red and bellowing and gross-scented, but still an animal. And what she had dreamed, of hovering and soaring to God in bliss, that was all stupid, childish, nonsensical illusion and deception and tomfoolery. One was an animal, not a flower.

She went to Beata Sturmin. She listened to the pious, serene, self-secure words of the holy blind-woman, and it was with difficulty that she refrained from breaking out into pert and ironical laughter. What did *she* know? She was blind. It was meaningless cant and rubbish and nonsense that she preached! You have lived, holy and chaste and in pious diligence, and no filthy thought is in you. And now comes an animal, red, reeking with wine, panting, and tramples upon you, and buries you with filth and dirt: and you cannot hate it. Explain that! Interpret that!

The Duke invited Weissensee and his daughter to the palace. She went to the animal in a kind of deathly curiosity. All was so grotesque and ridiculous. There all the people hurried about and made themselves important and invented the grounds which justified them in rushing and fidgeting about with this importance. And in truth all was without reason, and had no more sense than the sprawling of cockchafers which a boy has imprisoned in a box.

She sat by Karl Alexander. She said, "Good day, Your

167

Highness," and lifted the chocolate to her mouth. He spoke to her graciously, gaily, kindly, as if to a child. She responded trivially, mechanically. What she did and said was as if put on, not belonging to her. He laid himself out still more to please her. She thought, "He is more of a cart-horse than an ox," and waited thereupon in a mute curiosity full of loathing to see whether he would take her. In due course, as he could make nothing of her, he became angry. Certainly a virgin was supposed to be coy, and afterwards had to pretend to be insulted; in all the world it was so. But, after all, it meant something to be the Duke of Württemberg's mistress. No one had ever assumed such high and mighty airs; such a cold, frosty creature he had never encountered before. He became passionate. She looked at him, not with reproach, nor with arrogance, but there was such an abysmal, biting scorn in her glance that he became uncomfortable, and felt like a little ensign who had just had a dressing-down. He became kind and tender again. She remained silent. At last he took her. She endured it coldly, without defending herself, and he remained unsatisfied. As he conducted her down the stairs to the coach, the smirking of the lackeys died upon their faces, so like a corpse or a half-wit did she go.

After that she made no attempt to prevent him from considering her as his declared mistress. She came when he commanded, and showed herself publicly with him. The people were glad that their prince had such a respectable, beautiful and modest mistress, who moreover stood in the odour of sanctity, and was a native of the place. That in addition to his beautiful wife Karl Alexander had such a beautiful and proper and Swabian mistress, did not reconcile the people to his Jew, but it made good again much that was damaging to his popularity. The burghers took off their hats to Magdalen Sibylle, and many shouted: "Hurrah!"

To Weissensee, too, this mood was very auspicious. He rose in consequence, even in Parliament. And though among the Eleven of the Committee of the Estates they still blustered, except for two or three they would all gladly have been in his place, and they envied him heartily for his luck. Even Neuffer regarded him with gloomy deference, as in a sense the vicarious father-in-law of the Duke.

Slowly, after weeks, Magdalen Sibylle found her capacity to feel returning. As one who has been frozen and is brought back to life feels the pain when his blood begins anew to circulate, so she felt painful agitations rise, flow out, ever more wildly through every pore; hate and concupiscence. Karl Alexander remained still the indifferent, strange, astounding, slightly disgusting animal which she must endure, but her thoughts and impulses were all directed to the other, and revolved round him. The Duke, bah! what did he know! what did he understand! He was her misfortune. One hated him as little as the apple rind on the pavement upon which one slipped. But the other was answerable; he knew better than any one else, saw more clearly, judged exactly, was worthy of hate, was in truth the devil and all that was evil. It had been a true intuition, a great, merciful warning, when she had been so fearfully shaken that time in the forest of Hirsau by his appearance. He knew very well, the insolent, smooth, clever, profligate, ice-cold devil that he was, he knew as well as she that for one warm, honourable word she would have gladly slipped away to him, that all her childish, dear, mysterious, vaporous dreams of God and the devil would have been lost in one ardent, human emotion, if he had only had the strength to pursue his feelings, and not abandon them for a smile and a scrap of money or a title from the Duke. For he loved her. No one could look like that, no one could speak and submit himself like that, whose feelings were not true. If driven by one's nature one pressed soldiers, impoverished one's subjects, forced women—that was after the animal kind; one was not answerable. But that other one who bartered his feelings, fie! fie! that was truly devilish and Jewish.

She did not know how mingled, and as it were fused in a thousand others, the sentiment was with which Süss thought of her. Perchance for the fraction of an instant he had truly, honourably and wholly thought only of her; but he was far too divided, parted out into a thousand interests, he was far too much the man of the moment for such a feeling, even if he had wished it, to hold him. And to put to hazard the fundamental theme of his being—his connection with the Duke—for a woman: even the thought of that would have seemed to him absurd.

Once she saw him. Her heart beat high: what would he do?

169

If he would only dare to speak to her! But he did not speak, only saluted her deeply, and with a quiet, serious, deferential glance. And her hate was doubled.

From the first evening the Duchess had interested herself in Magdalen Sibylle. The tall girl with the masculine, keen face pleased her; she sought to become acquainted with her. She remarked that to this woman the Duke was indifferent, and that he did not understand her, and that only with coldness and distaste did she endure him. But this she could not comprehend, and so she pursued with double curiosity the girl with the strange interplay of blue eyes and dark hair. Magdalen Sibylle felt the goodwill which flowed from Marie Auguste, and indifferently accepted it. As if fascinated, the Duchess wheedled and insinuated herself ever closer to her, she behaved like a younger sister, put her arms affectionately round Magdalen's waist, showed quite openly—she who was wont readily to exercise her self-confident, sharp tongue on all women—her friendship for the beautiful mistress of her husband.

She humbled herself, struck pretty attitudes, made mouths. Oh! she was so childish and so simple! Magdalen Sibylle must explain so many things to her! For she was so clever, she had occupied herself with such profound things, like God and the millennium, and the Philadelphian Society. It was lovely to have such an accomplished friend.

She laid her small, rounded hand on the large, warm hand of Magdalen Sibylle, and gave a naughty, amused laugh. "Did you chance to notice, my dear, yesterday, when Lord Suffolk's ruffle was disarranged, that he is all shaggy on the breast? He is as hairy as the Duke."

At this time Marie Auguste was more beautiful than ever. Like black silk gleamed her hair; languidly shone, a superb pastel, her face with the longish eyes under her very clear brows. Her motion was a harmonious, gracious undulation. Her day was full and satisfying, her only wish was ever to live on just like this. Remchingen stood at her door, he so rough and masculine, whom it was so amusing and yet deliciously frightening to anger. Once in real earnest he had aimed a blow at her. And Lord Suffolk stood at her door, who had so little to say, but who, although his duties to his estate clamoured for him, wasted his life in staring at her, moveless and solemn. Perhaps one day she would give him a hearing. Why should one not show grace to a young man who gave such serious proofs of his inclinations? Perhaps, too, she would treat him badly, and he—and that would be perhaps more interesting still—might then shoot himself. And Monsieur de Riolles stood at her door, who was charmingly ugly, and in his soft, high voice made the wickedest jests, above all about fat women. And in the offing stood the Jew, of whom she was very proud, and who knew how, with the greatest deference, to pay her the most insolent compliments.

And she goaded the men on. And she hunted and she held festivals, and she went to see comedies and played them herself, and she travelled to her bathing resort and to Regensburg and to Vienna. And she was very happy.

But to Magdalen Sibylle she was like a tiny, playful kitten. Oh, if only one could skim so lightly over things, nothing would be more than skin-deep, one would be light and without seriousness and one could laugh.

As the crops grew higher, as the fields, meadows and flower-beds took on colour and shape, written characters began to grow out of the soil of the Duchy. It was like a mysterious conspiracy. On the borders of the towns, and everywhere in the country places, the farmers in their fields, meadows and gardens had sown, with cornflower seed, poppy seed, trefoil seed, but also with the seed of nobler flowers, certain written characters. Now they grew high, now they grew out of the black soil into the light with clumsy letters, and with elegantly-turned ones; now they cried it red in poppy blossoms, blue in cornflowers, golden in dandelions, but also in lilies very white and very beautifully disposed: "Süss, Pig-Jew." And also: "Josef Süss, Pig-Jew and Traitor."

Here and there the authorities interfered, but, against their custom, languidly and without severity. People grinned, the Duke laughed, Marie Auguste even drove out of the city to be entertained by the spectacle of one of these curious and artistic arrangements. She gave a detailed description of it to Magdalen Sibylle, who had made a pretext to avoid accompanying her.

171

Even in the forest of Hirsau, in the great clearing near the wooden fence of the house with the flower terraces, a peasant had sown the inscription. He was a young man, and he belonged to the Brotherhood of Master Jaakob Polykarp Schober. In the Bible College everything had seemed stale and unprofitable after the departure of Magdalen Sibylle. True, they were quiet, humble, modest people who dwelt there together. But while the daughter of the prelate was among them they had borne themselves proudly, and now that they had her no longer they felt sad and despondent. There came, too, such extraordinary rumours about Magdalen Sibylle from the Palace, and although it lay far from these pious souls to believe evil of their late sister, yet these rumours had at any rate the effect of nourishing their hatred and loathing against that Herod, the Duke, and his myrmidon the Jew, who, as such, was manifestly Satan in his own person. Inspired by such Christian loathing had the young peasant neatly and conscientiously written in flowers in the forest clearing: "Josef Süss, Pig-Jew and Sathanas."

With the departure of Magdalen Sibylle, a consolation and a great light had been quenched for Master Jaakob Polykarp Schober. He loved his solitude with God, yet he sorely missed Magdalen Sibylle, and it was now that he felt it most acutely, when on account of the demands of the Patronage Bureau his application for the post of librarian had miscarried. And now for the first time there awoke in him, in addition to his general loathing for Süss, an intensely personal, violent hatred—a lack of Christianity with which he often repentantly reproached himself. But he could not rid himself of it, and when he took his pensive walks in the forest, often he stood in the clearing before the floral inscription and followed with satisfaction the lines: "Josef Süss, Pig-Jew and Sathanas."

Once, when it had drawn him back again, his heart quickened to find another spectator before the floral inscription, the girl, the blue-black, languid white Princess of the Heavenly Jerusalem. She lay prostrate and lifeless. A stout person of good-humoured aspect busied herself, perplexed and helpless, over the unconscious, outstretched form.

The bowels of the soft-hearted Master yearned over her for

pity. He strode nearer, stumbling over a root, swept his hat low, and uttered amid manifold reverences: "Demoiselle! Demoiselle!" The stout woman, terrified, flew about, the Princess turned eyes towards him which seemed to be looking at other things and did not see him. He was no great hand at guessing, but he grasped the fact that the agitation of the lady was connected with the floral inscription, and, happy over this knowledge, he said, promptly, gallantly, and with the most tenderly considerate tone in the world: "Has he touched you, too, Demoiselle, the wicked Jew? Yea, that man is indeed a betrayer and a stinking Satan."

But his kindly-intended words had a terrifying effect, for the sweet girl sprang up with cheeks inflamed, and cried with unexpected power: "Slanderer! Miserable slanderer!" When Master Jaakob Polykarp Schober saw the Beloved of the Heavenly Jerusalem weep so forlornly a great uncertainty and distress overcame him. He stammered lamely: "But it was not at all ill-meant, Demoiselle. He is known by his actions, Demoiselle. It is well-known in all the land, Demoiselle." He renewed his reverences, while the sweet, blue-black beauty quietly and helplessly wept on, and the stout person spoke to her and sought to draw her away. Supporting and comforting her, she led her at last away from the accursed flowers.

But the Master could not so easily let himself be saddled with the reproach that he was a poisonous slanderer. He shuffled after her, unhappy, again and again defending himself; it was well-known in all the land, and it had not been ill-meant. But the girl, and her eyes appeared great and wild in her white face, exclaimed passionately: "Satán! He! He Satan! 'He is white and ruddy, the chiefest among ten thousand. His cheeks are as a bed of spices, as sweet flowers; his lips like lilies, dropping sweet-smelling myrrh. His hands are as gold rings set with the beryl. His legs are as pillars of marble, set upon sockets of fine gold.'" And the holiest enthusiasm and conviction shone from her clear brow while she spoke.

When he heard the Scriptural verses, Jaakob Polykarp Schober felt himself at once better and more composed. Now he could piece together the causes of her agitation. Aha! This was one of those whom the Jew had seduced with his magic and witchcraft. Against the mandragora root even the purest heart had no protection; he himself could not hope to prevail against it. The Jew was full of malice towards women. And she, the Princess of the Heavenly Jerusalem, was certainly one of his victims. How pure and frank she was, was manifested by the fact that even now, in her distress and deep misfortune, she cited the Bible. Certainly Beelzebub had appeared to her in a holy, angelical guise when he had enchanted her.

The chubby Master was lifted as on celestial pinions, as he deliberated these thoughts. With the departure of Magdalen Sibylle his life had become stale and arid. Now the grace of God had sent him the congenial task of rescuing this gentle and refined Princess out of the jaws of the libidinous and greedy Satan. Warily and with some prolixity, he began upon the joy that is in Heaven over repentant sinners, proceeded to the contrite Magdalene, and concluded with remarks on the slyness and subtlety of the snares, from which even the purest and gentlest are not secure. For the Enemy, the Satan and seducer—

But then the girl's rage returned a second time and much worse. "My father is no Satan and seducer," she flamed, while the stout person urgently and in despair sought to hold her back.

The kindly, chubby face of the Master became quite yellow and blank. The Jew her father! The mossy turf under his feet rose and sank, the trees fell around him and about him, cut into him, covered him up. The Jew her father! His whole world, God, devil, revelation, was topsy-turvy.

The child noticed quite clearly the Master's confusion. "Ah!" she cried, "now you are horrified because you hear that he is my father. Do not fear! He is too noble even to lift his heel against his wretched calumniators and slanderers."

But that once more Jaakob Polykarp Schober could not let pass. He was humble and unimportant, he said. But fear before men he did not know. And even if the princely Jew, her father, were a raging Nebuchadnezzar and had the power to cast him into a fiery furnace, he would nevertheless always give honour to God.

In such conversation as this they had come to the wooden fence, and the stout person now said he must go. The Master, who usually was very slow in the understanding, and who was

174

confused by the encounter and all its surprises, saw that all his happiness would in a few seconds be gone for ever, and now he made unexpectedly a by no means humble decision. He said it was due to his honour as a Christian to demonstrate to the Demoiselle clearly that he was no rascally slanderer, and on this ground he must absolutely ask to speak with her once more and at length. The stout person suggested irresolutely another day and vanished with the Princess, who cried: "And to defile flowers like that! Poor, innocent flowers!"

From that day, however, a great importance and dignity rested upon Jaakob Polykarp Schober. God had given him a handle to move mighty and grave events. With him it lay now to save the soul of the maiden; yea, in this way perhaps he might attain to the Jew himself, and speak to his conscience; for it was by no means demonstrated *a priori* that a Jew had no conscience. And if the Lord of Sabaoth granted power to his words, then perhaps through him the whole Duchy might find redemption from its disastrous oppression.

In such anticipation the chubby Master went about, and he was full of dignity. His confidence was not shattered even when he heard that the librarian's post had been taken over by an unworthy fellow who, beside his thalers, brought no qualifications with him.

Grace was now visibly upon him; his lectures flowed sweetly from his lips; yea, it happened that the words led him on to rhyme. Thus, immediately after the tidings of the appointment of the librarian, he composed a song which he entitled: "Cares of Life and Faith in God," which began with the verses:

> So long as there's a single crow,
>   So long as one small sparrow sings,
> So long as I see the dumb beasts go,
>   I will not trouble about things.
> If they of food are not beguiled,
> Why should I be, as God's child.

Another was called: "Jesus, the best Reckoner," and was well-known:

My Jesus can add,
And can multiply,
Even where many ciphers are.

In the Bible College both songs were received with humble admiration. The brothers and sisters learned them by heart; they sang them in all circumstances, when they were in great need and when they had good fortune, when they died and when they had children. In all humility Jaakob Polykarp Schober was intensely gratified by this. It consoled him for the loss of Magdalen Sibylle.

It was with a bad conscience that Jantje, the fat waiting-woman, told Rabbi Gabriel of the unfortunate encounter. The Rabbi signed to her to go, and was silent.

The waiting-woman gone, the stony, morose face grew more gloomy than ever, and the three vertical furrows above the nose became more sharply marked. Forbid it, Heaven and all good angels, that the child should enquire further. He did not wish to lie to her. To root out the radiant image of her father, he might have taken upon himself, but with it something final would have slipped from his grasp. Rather than that he would have changed his flower-terraces into a cess-pool.

And the seraphim and cherubim guarded the melancholy, sullen man. Naemi did not ask. Would not a question have implied a doubt? No, her father was magnificent and of great splendour, and the caluminations of the heathen and the Philistine did not defile even the sole of his foot. The heavy characters of the Hebrew Scriptures piled themselves up, the building stones of his fame. He was Samson, who smote the Philistines; he was Solomon, the wisest among all men; he was—and this glided again and again into her dreams—he was Joseph, the mild, the adroit, whom Pharoah set above all people, who imposed tribute on the land for future scarcity. But they were foolish, and did not comprehend his wisdom. Oh! if he would only come, at last! Before his fiery glance the tittle-tattle of this dull young man would burn to ashes.

But Rabbi Gabriel read in the book of Master Isaak Luria Aschkinasi, the Cabbalist: "It may happen that in one human body our earthly destiny may be accomplished by not only one soul,

176

but that at one and the same time two, yea, several souls may associate in one body for a new incarnation. The aim of this federation is mutual assistance in the expiation of guilt, on whose account it has to suffer the new incarnation."

His cheek supported on his hand, he sat and meditated. The room grew dim around him, the book faded before him, so sunk was he in that countenance, testing lineament by lineament. He saw the arched eyes, the small, sensuous mouth, the rich, chestnut-coloured hair. He saw skin and flesh and hair, and nothing more.

Then he shrugged his shoulders, sat limp, weary, dense, breathed heavily, growling, like an animal which is too heavily burdened, and cannot get any further up the hill.

NEAR Heilbronn, among lovely vineyards, lay the castle of Stettenfels. Count Johann Albrecht Fugger sat up there, a product of Jesuit schools, a zealous Catholic, a friend of the Lord Bishop of Würzburg. Already in Eberhard Ludwig's time the enterprising nobleman had several times endeavoured to obtain permission to observe in private the worship of God as it is ordained by the Catholic Church, but always in vain. Now under the Catholic Duke he took without ceremony Capucin priests into his castle, and began to build cloisters and churches far and wide over his mountain.

Open infringement of the laws, storm in Parliament, threatening summons to the Cabinet to put a stop to the glaring scandal. The Duke sat angry and with tied hands. Never, according to the Constitution, could Catholic Churches be set up; Catholic worship was confined to the Duke's own private devotions.

The situation was clear. Harpprecht, the jurist, had jurisdiction over the affair in the Cabinet; his colleague was Bilfinger. Both honourable, plain-dealing men, they were profoundly glad that this affair was out of the competence of the Duke. With deep discomfort they saw the land more and more going to ruin, all officials debauched and corrupt. If they remained in office it was because they did not wish to see Süss's creatures step into their places. Here at last was a situation where no Duke and no Jew dared intervene; here they could show their evangelical brethren that the land, degenerate as it might seem outwardly, bore itself firm and upright and without shadow of turning in

177

matters of conscience and religion. Against the irresolute and doubtful Schütz and Scheffer, Harpprecht and Bilfinger carried a decision that a Commission of Enquiry, a travelling Committee, should be sent to the Count at Gruppenbach, at its head State Councillor Johann Jaakob Moser, the publicist, now for the first time proved by word and deed and writing to be an unyielding Protestant. He was given ample and full powers.

He found the Count scornful, obstinate, not at all inclined to the slightest act of submission. He let the State Commission stand before the Castle in wind and rain, and greeted them ungraciously and arrogantly. When the Commissioners pointed to the newly-built monastery and church, where already men were working at a high tower, and asked how against the expressed legal prohibition and ministerial forewarning he dared erect Catholic edifices on the Ducal soil, the little, energetic, lean nobleman surveyed the Commission grimly, ferociously, arrogantly, and with negligent and deliberate provocation threw them the information that these were his new workshops. Nearer approach he forbade them. Capucins appeared two by two. Ever with the same scorn the little Count explained, this was his new livery, he wished the mode might very soon be in full swing over all the country. With their task unaccomplished the Commission went away to Heilbronn; compelled the Count at last to permit an examination of the buildings; and sent him an official messenger with a plain summons containing a formal command to pull down monastery and church, giving three days of grace for the work to begin. With his own hand the Count hurled the man from the terrace, and hunted him down the mountain with dogs. Then appeared Moser, the stately, important, histrionic man, with a detachment of soldiers, razed church and monastery, and only departed when the Count, hot with cursing, had paid for this work down to the last cent as well as for the calling out of the military. In the foundation stone of the monastery they found a manuscript according to which the monastery of Stettenfels was consecrated to the dissemination of the only true and holy Catholic faith and the conversion of the heretical land of Württemberg.

Jubilation in the country, in Parliament. In the Sub-Committee the rough, massive Burgomaster Johann Friedrich from Brackenheim blustered: "One is still somebody. If one has a mind one can always compel the heretical dogs to eat their own dirt." Among the people loud rejoicing. In the Blue Boar, Benz, the confectioner, allowed himself another glass of wine and exulted: "There are affairs still where no harlot nor no Jew dare interfere." Heartfelt joy of Harpprecht and Bilfinger. Quiet, humble thanksgiving among the inmates of the Bible College of the Pietists. In the Bible College of Hirsau the pious choir sang thrice in succession Master Jaakob Polykarp Schober's song: "Jesus, the best Reckoner."

But far beyond the Swabian frontiers, too, over the whole German Empire, this Stettenfels affair excited the greatest attention. The Lord Bishop of Würzburg laid an official complaint with the Duke through his councillors Fichtel and Raab. The Duke, who thought that with deliberate intention they had tried to make him suspect and contemptible to those of his own faith, was deeply offended. Nevertheless, the very adroit Bishop of Würzburg did not goad him further. He knew that Karl Alexander's attention was claimed by other things, and he reserved energetic action for a later day.

Karl Alexander, indeed, had both hands full with innumerable little exasperating concerns. Süss now thought seriously of having himself ennobled. His position was established sufficiently, he desired in addition to the possession of power its titles and dignities, and he was meditating the taking over in open form of the office of Lord High Steward. Had he consented to be baptized, that might have been done next day. But it was his ambition to occupy the highest position in the Duchy, before Emperor and Empire, in spite of his Jewish status.

After Süss had conducted Magdalen Sibylle to him at his grand reception, the Duke through his Viennese Ambassador, Privy Councillor Keller, had supported the petition of his financial agent, requested a diploma of nobility for him, and offered a thousand ducats for it. But not only the Württemberg Parliament opposed this: Süss's ministerial colleagues, too, intrigued at the Viennese Court, so the matter came to a standstill. To spur the Duke on, and at the same time to show himself indispensable, Süss relaxed his zeal, and under the pretext of urgent personal

179

business asked for leave of absence to go abroad. Immediately the recruiting went to pieces, the revenue for the army came in no more, the women became more difficult, a thousand tiny dissensions, from which the skill of his Finance Minister had protected him, now showed the Duke their unwelcome shapes; there were difficulties in covering his monstrous, personal expenditure, artfully enhanced by Süss, and difficulties over military supplies. Karl Alexander was also exasperated by the unvarying obstinacy of Magdalen Sibylle; and the two ladies Götz, mother and daughter, adroitly and secretly prompted by Süss from a distance, put up an unexpected opposition. Remchingen was wearisome. Bilfinger he did not want to meet, because he was furious over his share in the Stettenfels business; the Frenchman Riolles was too much like a monkey, too clever and sharp. He sighed for his Jew. Had he been there, then certainly the Stettenfels affair would have gone differently; it was a scandal that his ministers could not discharge Christian affairs quietly without the help of the Jew.

The wanderer was received with open arms. He had been in Holland, in England, had holidayed in France; in Darmstadt he had derided his brother, the baron, the baptized; saying that without such contemptible means he would attain the same rank. Moreover in Holland he had become acquainted with a Portuguese lady, a Madame de Castro, an auburn beauty, stately, still young, refined, noble, imperious in aspect and mien, widow of the Portuguese Ambassador to the Netherlands, very well off. He wished to marry her. She did not refuse him; the condition was that he should be ennobled. In any case she would visit him in Stuttgart, and that in a short time. Marie Auguste laughed hysterically when she heard of the project. To the Duke the proposed marriage of his court Jew was not acceptable; he blustered, saying that he would allow him certainly to have mistresses. "You lick out of all my dishes as it is," he growled. But for all his smiling deference Süss would not be moved from his plan, and extorted from the resisting Duke a new letter to Vienna about his ennoblement. Karl Alexander wrote urgently and with his own hand. He emphasized how he could accomplish much more with his court Jew alone than with all his other councillors and servants; how on account

180

of his genius and his marvellous capacity he was equal to every practical contingency; and how he, the Duke, absolutely owed him the diploma of nobility as a proof of his own princely power. After this letter Süss believed that everything would go well.

He rode through the streets on his white mare, Assjadah. He looked ten years younger than he was, he was easily the first cavalier in Swabia. Supple and slender and easy he sat on his horse, his very red lips slightly parted in his pale face, his chestnut-coloured hair falling gracefully under his wide hat, his whip glittering with precious stones, his fawnlike eyes arched under his serene brows; the heads of the women were turned; he was here again! The Götz ladies reclined on their balcony, gazing with delight, while full of respect he sent a greeting up to them: he was here again! He is here again! snarled the people; but he pleased them. And Dom Bartelemi Pancorbo saw on the hand which answered his greeting the gigantic, glittering solitaire. He is here again! he smiled with his fleshless lips, and over the ceremonial ruff at the throat of his antique Portuguese court dress, his small, expressionless, shifty eyes followed enviously and watchfully the disappearing rider.

But the mare Assjadah tossed her head high, and neighed clear and triumphantly to the watching citizens, the scornful, envious cavaliers, and the infatuated women: He is here again!

In the Schertlin factory in Urach there was employed a certain Kaspar Dieterle, a forty-year-old man, with a bloated face, watery blue eyes, reddish walrus moustache, and no back to his head. When the factory passed into the hands of the Foa-Oppenheimer Corporation, this man was retained as master weaver. He carried himself submissively and with humility, but in private only abused the more obscenely the pigs of Jews, his employers, engineered occasionally petty mutinies, and, himself extremely servile, made the others refractory; was at the same time rough and shabby to his underlings; and was finally, when his double-dealing came out, dismissed.

He could not bring himself to seek work elsewhere, deteriorated more and more, brought himself to dire poverty with a miserable

181

house-to-house hawking trade diversified with the occasional smuggling of prohibited, unauthorized wares, was several times imprisoned, and once even flogged.

He had taken to himself a distant cousin, a tiny little orphan girl, who together with his aged dog, pulled his hawking cart, and was otherwise useful; fifteen years old, a dirty child, small, sturdy, shy, impudent, sullen, depraved, thievish, and in addition to all this, in her primitive way a coquette. He treated the child badly, and thrashed her with fiendish cruelty, so that sometimes she fell, lamed and covered with blood. But when the authorities intervened, and sought to take the child from him, she stuck to him, denied all mistreatment, and would not let herself be parted from him. The fact was that this man kept the defenceless, scrubby little creature in plain terms as his mistress. She was attached to him, she loved him in a certain sense; his brutality and his fringed walrus moustache were to her signs of his great masculinity; she loved him when he was gentle to her and when he struck her. Gradually she became ever more indispensable to him; he enjoyed himself, brawling at markets and fairs, bargaining and drinking with niggardly customers and those who never bought; till at last the maintenance of them both lay entirely upon her shoulders.

When she saw how necessary she was to him, and guessed her power over him, she began to be intractable, she mocked him, but what fascinated her most was to play dangerous tricks upon him when he was drunk. Ever oftener it happened now that he would thrash her until she lay unconscious. Once or twice she ran away, but always she returned to him again; in the end he was the only man over whom she had unquestionable power and who depended on her.

In this manner the strange pair slouched about the roads, stole, hawked, in more than deplorable straits. Kaspar Dieterle could curse frightfully, and with more obscenity than anybody else in the whole country. This impressed the girl prodigiously, and seemed to her especially virile and manly. But he was best when he cursed the Jews. Cascades of venom and filth spouted then from under the red moustache, the blank face swelled round the watery blue eyes, and the girl listened in rapture. Sometimes, too, in a good mood, and as a reward for the little one, he would mimic

182

a Jew, walk bent, and amid the child's shrieks of enjoyment, attempt to hang his moustaches over his ears as ritual curls. But it was a red-letter day when at markets and fairs he ran up against Jews. True, within the Ducal jurisdiction the police, under the influence of Süss, usually, if reluctantly, took the Jews under their protection. But in the free cities he could torment in peace these helpless people, and play all sorts of ill-natured jests on them which his weak brain was in a state to invent.

Now he had set great hopes on the Easter Fair at Esslingen. There, however, a Jew, Jecheskel Seligmann, had appeared, a Jew formerly protected by the Countess, now tolerated in silence in Freudenthal, one of her former possessions. He dealt in products of the Süss-Foa factory, and as he had a far greater selection, put up a competition which the primitive trumpery of Kaspar Dieterle could not stand against. Jecheskel Seligmann Freudenthal was an elderly, meagre, bent, ugly man. Kaspar Dieterle found a thousand grounds for mocking him; he smeared the bench of his stall with swine-fat, which afterwards stuck to the old man's caftan; he set the children on him, he made him hop and cry "Down with the Jews," and he had the laugh on his side. The Jew put up with it all, he looked ugly, meagre and weary, and, when finally, among his wares, he got back his breath, he had a painful, exhausted smile on his face. The crowd had certainly had pleasure in Kaspar Dieterle's jests, and had laughed heartily at the Jew along with him; all the same they bought from the Jew, for in spite of the special tax his wares were cheaper and more various than the poor trumpery of the other. Kaspar Dieterle was filled with a gloomy, senseless fury against Jecheskel Seligmann; he decided that night to maul and trample him until he was half-dead, but he had not enough money to pay for his night's lodgings at the inn where the Jews and pedlars stayed, and he had to leave the town before the gates closed.

The pair passed the night in a sparse wood. They were, the girl as well as the man, embittered and in the worst mood. Moreover, rain set in; they were frozen and hungry. He had promised to buy a coral bracelet for her at the Esslingen Fair, she had even reserved the small takings which she had for this purpose, but he had snatched the money from her and bought schnapps with it.

Now she asked that at least he should let her drink some of it. He jeered at her, swore that, lousy, whorish brat that she was, she was to blame that he had not earned more. She swore back, she would report him; he had raped her, robbed and stolen as well; he was certain of the gallows. He struck her, she screamed and cursed on; he struck her harder, she bit him. And because she would not let go, but in spite of all his blows only bit more wildly, he hit her a heavy blow on the brow with the schnapps bottle. She fell down, stretched her limbs out, and remained lying. That had happened often enough already, so he let her lie, took a deep breath, licked the splintered bottle out, wrapped himself in a few rags, and slept like a log, snoring blatantly. But the rain beat through and soon woke him again. He hiccupped that she must wriggle close to him, give him another coverlet, warm him. When she did not reply, he kicked her and swore. As even now she did not stir, he stood up stiff and cold, touched her with his foot; at last, sighing, hiccupping, he lighted fussily and after many vain attempts the blind, battered lantern, ran its light over the motionless form, saw it, the jaw fallen, the eyes wide open, wet, and stiff.

He stood for a long time in the sparse wood, frozen, stupid, without intelligence, alone with the dead girl and the softly whining dog. The wind had blown out the light almost at once; it was dark and freezing. From the tree against which he leaned the rain dropped down on him, it ran over his poor, straight skull and down his neck; his ruddy blond walrus moustache dripped steadily. Thus he stood for a long time, and could not grasp how or why Babette, the one creature dear to his heart, was dead now. At last he set up an inhuman, fearful howling, the dog joined in; he lifted his foot to kick him, desisted.

After a while he knelt beside the corpse; undressed, not without care, the stiff, ugly, unwashed body, made incisions here and there in the flesh, with clumsy, but not unskilful method. He employed for this purpose splinters of the bottle, although he might have done it more easily with a knife. He then—the rain coming down still—bundled the naked, mutilated body on to the cart, piled rags and rubbish over it, and with his dog hauled it back again to the town, arriving there in the early morning, as the gate was being

184

opened. To the guard he said that he had still some business with the Jew Seligmann. They let him pass.

As if impelled from within, with a strange, indifferent certainty of his goal, he hauled his cart to the inn where the Jew Jecheskel Seligmann Freudenthal stayed. He stood his cart in the yard of the inn, sold for a little cash his last necessaries, drank, jumped up meanwhile ever and again to look to his cart, until at last, with only the pigs to see him, he managed hastily to bury the corpse in the dung-hill. It still rained. Then he went back again to the tap-room, drank, drew out the garments of his little companion, and told a story, slowly, inarticulately, bit by bit. Yes, it was known what trouble he and his Babette had had the day before with the Jew Jecheskel Seligmann Freudenthal. But the Jew had afterwards promised the child a string of coral beads. She had wanted to return for them. He, Kaspar, had prevented her, beaten her. During the night the Jew had presumably given her something, at any rate she had been away. Sometimes a man must sleep; then he cannot look after other people, can he? And now among the wares of the Jew out there he had found a bundle of clothes; they were Babette's. Now the child must be running about naked apparently, except for her string of coral. Aye, and this was the Passover Festival of the Jews.

All this Kaspar Dieterle related, while he drank away his last possessions. He related it several times, and always more people listened. And ever they grew more insatiable as they listened, and ever they stared more fascinated and horrified at the mouth of this man, where under the tangled, reddish moustache, stinking with schnapps, from between the foul, black teeth, the gruesome story was insidiously whined out.

And then they found the mutilated corpse on the dung-heap; the swine already were eating it. On bats' wings, embellished with fantastic horrors, the news flew through the town. The people gathered; in the houses, in the streets, all work ceased; the gates were closed; the Councillors were called to assembly. Horror upon horror! An innocent Christian child murdered by the Jews, her blood drained for the Passover feast, her mangled corpse cast to the swine. So far had things gone through the Jewish dealings of the Württemberg Duke, that such a black murder could happen

185

in the free, imperial city of Esslingen, to the disgrace and shame of the whole Swabian province.

A storm of excitement throughout the whole city. For forty, nay, for three hundred and forty years, such a gruesome crime had not been known in the Holy Roman Empire. One had come to believe that such stories were only to be found in books. In their vicinity nothing of the kind had happened since the Ravensburg child-murder. Oh, how wise their fathers had been in hunting the Jews beyond the Esslingen pale! Since Salomo von Hechingen, the physician, they had not allowed one of them to pollute the pure air of their good city with his villainous breath. Proud and confident they could reply, when the Emperor demanded the tax on Jews, that for two centuries none had dwelt within these walls. Now the Duke, the heretic, the Herod, had brought into the country these knaves, these murdering villains, that lie in wait for innocent Christian children and drain their blood. The mothers, anguished, warned their children. Ever more horrifying details went round. What happened to-day to a strange child, might happen to-morrow to one's own. For a long time the poor, little terrified mites would fly from every stranger, and have horrible dreams of blood and knives and rough beards.

Meanwhile the Jew Jecheskel Seligmann Freudenthal went about the suburbs on his business. He was arrested just when, humbly but perseveringly, he was trying to extract money from an unwilling debtor. He had absolutely no notion what it was for, and protested without ceasing; he had spoken back yesterday neither to Kaspar Dieterle nor to anybody else, he had not even opened his mouth. For this was one of the favourite devices against Jewish competitors; by word and deed one provoked them to a retort, and then had them locked up on the charge that by insolent abuse of their faith they had sought to bring discredit on Christians. But the beadle struck him over the mouth, seized him fast, manacled him. Outside, the wizened, trembling, terrified man was received by a multitude; he saw a hundred arms lifted, howling throats; mud and stones flew against him; he was torn to the ground, trampled upon, spat upon; his hair and his beard were plucked out. He sought continuously to expostulate with the people who pressed around him; panting still under his mistreat-

186

ment, while blood and spittle ran from his mouth, he protested he had uttered no abuse, no, not even one word. It was only from the screams of a woman who continually jabbed him in the groin with a distaff, that at last he suddenly became aware of the accusation, and lost his senses. Unconscious he was taken to the tower.

But among the Town Councillors there was great, fierce, derisive joy. The Duke's friends, the Jew's friends, were guilty of this abominable deed. How they would rub it into them, how they would make them swallow it! Now at last they could give the Duke and his Jew tit for tat. Were they not continually plagued and harassed by them? While the Duke's wild boars and deer and all the beasts of his forests destroyed their fields, the insolent heretic complained that the Esslingen citizens were poaching—yes, and how could they help themselves else?—and he was high and mighty about it. And did he not groan continually that the Esslingen streets were bad, and not up to regulation. Ha! you high and mighty lords! what is a hole in the street against such a gruesome murder? Over the Neckar regulations, too, it was impossible to please him. Had he not even mortgaged the revenues of Esslingen Hospital clean outside the Württemberg border? And first and foremost, his Jew, the insolent knave, the malefactor! Of course the city had revoked its covering agreement with the Duke, but only *pro forma*, and in order to secure easier terms. Yet the lousy pig of a Jew behaved as if he took it in earnest. Simply treated the Esslingers like any other foreigners, as if there were in truth no covering agreement! He was always harassing them, always putting his finger into their industries and their traffic. Every one of the councillors had been done by him out of several thousand thalers. But only wait, my lord Jew! Now we will pay you back! We will pay it back upon your black and accursed brother in the faith. We will lace him up in Spanish boots, make the blood spurt out from under his nails, tear him with red-hot pincers. Already those among the Councillors who dwelt in the market-place were congratulating themselves—for he would be burned there solemnly—and were promising window seats to their friends and relatives. The only pity was that he could only be executed once. They would have liked at the same time to hang him, break him on the wheel, quarter him, and burn him.

187

The oldest among the Councillors was Christoph Adam Schertlin, who in his time had founded the Urach workshops, and who,
in his patrician's house in Esslingen, had for a long time seen his
works slowly and irrecoverably sinking, and slipping into the hands
of the Jews, and his sons degenerating and going to the dogs. He
was well on in the seventies. This was a savage and unexpected
pleasure for him before the coming of death. From the hollow
cavity of his breast he drew thunderous words against the Jewish
abominations, spat them before the judge into the face of one who
was, alas, absent. He carried high his great weatherbeaten head;
with a sturdy step he went through the streets; violently, as if the
fiend coursed in his body, he struck his bamboo cane against the
ground, grasping the golden knob with his withered but not shaking hand.

In the tap-room, however, sat Kaspar Dieterle. He had no
need more to sell anything to obtain schnapps. Continually a
packed crowd sat round him, horrified and fascinated. He who
had earlier been hunted from every threshold as a vagabond and
ne'er-do-well, was valued now as an important man and treated
with great respect. He related details which ever became more
highly coloured, and at last he came to believe himself that the
wicked Jew had maliciously killed his sole prop and stay. As the
strongest proof, he adduced the fact that the child had been born
on Christmas Eve, and all hung fascinated and charmed on his lips,
when, his watery blue eyes wide open with wonder, he brought
this out. For it was a demonstrable fact, and to be seen in
many books for the reading, that whoever was born on Christmas
Eve stood in especial danger of being murdered by the Jews.

The women, particularly, had great pity for the man. Had
he not given them warning, given them cause to protect their children all the more anxiously? They pressed baked and roasted
foods upon him, bacon and lard-cake. His bloated cheeks took on
colour, his walrus moustache was combed out and not so bushy;
only his teeth remained blackened and foul. And a baker's widow
occupied herself seriously with the thought of marrying the poor,
forsaken man, with whom the Jews had played so cruelly.

DOCTOR WENDELIN BREYER, the Court Physician, examined the

Duke. A tall, withered man, immensely diligent, anxious and meritorious, with clumsy, apologetic movements, whose strained, sepulchral voice resounded hollowly in his chest. He smiled much and deferentially, begged pardon countless times, and tried to lighten his communications with tiny, bashful, ineffectual jests. The Duke was a difficult patient; he had beaten Doctor Breyer's colleague, Georg Burkhard Seeger, half-dead with the flat of his sword; also he was not averse to the smashing of medicine bottles on the heads of his doctors.

"Well then?" hectored the Duke. With a few fluttering movements the doctor sought to bring himself beyond Karl Alexander's range. "A touch of *goutte militaire!*" he mumbled in his smothered voice, and bleated on; "a very tiny, insignificant touch of *goutte militaire.*" As the Duke remained darkly silent, he added quickly: "Your Excellency need not be depressed or have black thoughts over it. Your Excellency's indisposition is only to be regarded as temporary, as in a certain sense a slight catarrh of your royal bladder. With God's help your Excellency will be rid of it in some three months. With the greatest submission may I say now that the said little indisposition has been in the fashion with all the great military leaders of Christendom? According to the chronicles, the great antique generals, too, Alexander and Julius Cæsar, laboured under it."

The Duke waved a gloomy dismissal, and, with many clumsy and apologetic gestures, the doctor took himself off.

The doctor gone, Karl Alexander snorted, and with his marshal's staff angrily smashed a small porcelain figure in two. In earlier days he had twice had this filthy disease, and at that time he had not known from whom. This time he knew. The sow, the filthy sow! How dainty and exquisite she had appeared on the stage, how brightly her eyes had sparkled, how experienced and cozening she had been with her tongue, how appetizing was she, all of her, the trollop! A humbug, a bit of quicksilver, a whiff of scent. And she had filth and poison and the devil in her flesh. The damned, dirty whore! But he would have her flogged, have her whipped with rods out of the country.

He contented himself later with making her cart a load of dung through the city as was customary with baggages who were caught in unchastity. In a rough smock the tiny, plump, yellow-haired Neapolitan was conveyed through the streets; slowly she dragged her cart-load of filth, her vivacious eyes helpless and wild, a huge board with the inscription "Whore" hung round her neck. The burghers smacked their lips regretfully: one should have known this before. Ere it went sour the juice must have tasted very sweet; then one would gladly have run off one's little glass. But the woman spat on her and pelted her with offal. So, ill and penniless, she was hunted out of the city.

From the same malady as the Duke, however, General Remchingen and the Duke's brown slave were suffering too.

Remchingen and Karl Alexander sat together and abused women. The Duke pursued Süss with grim pleasantries. He, too, had had her, but first of all, perhaps, and he had come clean away, the devil knew through what black Jewish art.

But flaxen-haired and in deep perplexity sat Transport Officer Götz. He was the only one who was able to survey all the ramifications of this affair. He had contracted the malady from the waitress in the Blue Boar. He had bequeathed it in turn to the Italian, whom with great simplicity he regarded as his beloved princess and sweetheart. In other circumstances he would have held it to be his absolute duty to make everything good, yes, even perhaps to marry the Italian. But now, when at the court they were whispering with discreet amusement about the Duke's little gallant indisposition, when he slowly grasped, when he recognized that he, the humblest and most reverential of subjects, had brought this heavy and abominable affliction upon his sovereign; his world was shattered about his ears. That in his loyalty he could be guilty of such a foul wrong to his prince, that it was possible innocently to be entangled in such guilt—this confounded him. He decided to shoot himself. But later he said to himself that certainly the Neapolitan was to blame for everything; she had brought him into this entanglement with his divinely-ordained prince; he washed his hands of all guilt and threw it upon the singer; and as she drew along her cart of offal, he looked on with grim satisfaction.

Now the Neapolitan really loved the helpless, flaxen-haired man. She had not betrayed him, in spite of the fact that by doing so she might probably have saved herself. While she was being conveyed through the streets in dire need and amid curses, she only thought of him. Her lips moved; the people thought she prayed; but she only murmured, tonelessly and disjointedly, his name and a host of endearments. Old fairy tales haunted her of the prince who raised the beggar girl, and made her his princess. Now, just now, he would come forward, and all this horror would pass like a nightmare, an evil dream. Only when she was driven over the frontier, without the slightest sign from him, did she break down.

The news of the Duke's sickness trickled through. In the Bible College it was whispered that this was punishment from God, and Nebuchadnezzar was recalled, who near his evil end was made to eat grass like the oxen. But among the courtiers the gallant malady only brought the Duke great respect. The Tübingen court poet presented him with a poem in which he said that sometimes one must pay for one's victories in the realm of Amor with tiny wounds, which, however, were no less honourable than those of the battle-field. Amor shoots sometimes with poisoned arrows. In conclusion he proclaimed that he who had overcome the Turks and the French would also overcome the smaller enemy; and soon Swabia's Alexander would be Swabia's Paris again.

The Duchess saw pretext and opportunity in the indisposition of her spouse. The young Lord Suffolk still stood continually at her doors with his red, inglorious, boundlessly infatuated face. At his own court and on his own estates he had made his position impossible by his absence; obstinate, dumb and shy, he continued to worship her; it was only a matter of days before he made an end of himself. Now that her husband could not come to her, was it not an excuse? And, amused, smiling, she took pity on the poor, faithful, obstinate man.

But the young Englishman was manifestly destined for mischance. Usually Karl Alexander was not at all prone to jealousy; it never came into his thoughts that one could go behind him, him! But whether it was that his sickness has made him mistrustful, or that others had instigated him, he burst unexpectedly into the Duchess's room just before the young lord, half-clothed and ridiculous, had managed to escape. The Duke made a terrible scene, smashed mirrors and perfume flasks, hacked at the costly

191

sheets with his sword, called Marie Auguste street-names, even struck her on the elegant little lizard-like face, which was of the colour of ancient, noble marble. The Duchess related it, weeping and indignant, to Magdalen Sibylle; theatrically she protested her innocence, but soon a light, smiling amusement stole into her indignation; she mimicked maliciously the stormy wrath of the Duke, diverted herself with the remarkable, rough-sounding oaths, and sought to find their equivalents in French and Italian. At last she smilingly opined it was strange: now if Riolles or Remchingen had come to her she was sure they would never have been caught, no not on the four-and-twentieth time, but the poor, awkward youth naturally the very first time, before he was finished and hardly knowing how to set about it.

As it was not expedient that the sovereign should embroil himself with the nobleman, Remchingen must challenge him to a duel, whether he were guilty or not. Remchingen growled to himself that in truth he had abundant grounds for offence. Nevertheless, as the affair became more serious, he showed no particular haste. Suddenly the Englishman departed, without any attempt at secrecy, ceremoniously and in state, but his faith in God wavering, his simple, untroubled image of the world in pieces, his belief in himself and in men shattered. His brief enjoyment had profoundly shaken him, his memory of everything was indistinct; the only token of remembrance left him was a somewhat damaged garter of the Duchess, for which truly it would not have been worth while to imperil life, fame, and his position at home.

Karl Alexander had a mass of circumstantial evidence, but no absolute concrete proof of Marie Auguste's infidelity. In other circumstances he would soon have been placated; now his exasperation over the inaction forced upon him by his illness made him quarrelsome and sulky. Marie Auguste, soon weary of the continual suspicion and espionage, played at first the rôle of a Geneviève, quickly changed her tune, however, and confronted the harshness of her husband with a biting, exasperating, ironical calm, threatening at last that she would return to her father. Whereupon Karl Alexander retorted bluntly: on that day he would have all the bells rung, fire the cannons, and feast all his subjects with wine and good cheer.

To the aristocratic old Prince of Thurn and Taxis the quarrel seemed highly inopportune. Certainly, his daughter had amused herself a little with an Englishman. Why should one not amuse oneself with an Englishman? They talked badly and their appearance was wooden, but in freshness, health, and above all in discretion, they were superior to the Latins. If he were a wife, he too would seek out an Englishman. There was no need to make such a noise, such a song about it. But indeed, his princely son-in-law was a general and as such accustomed to arrive on the scene with great éclat. And then one expected victories from a strategist, not milk-and-water manners. Sighing he wrote thus to his friend, the Lord Bishop of Würzburg, with a request to put the childish affair right as quickly as possible.

To the adroit, sly, stout nobleman this invitation came very opportunely. He had not forgotten the Stettenfels affair; the defeat of the Church was a thorn in his flesh; he retained Count Fugger at his court; he awaited only the opportunity for an innocent visit to Stuttgart, and there personally he would find smoother and speedier means for the winning of the country for Rome. So his Eminence allowed himself to be persuaded without much difficulty, and soon with his Privy Councillors Fichtel and Raab, and with an ostentatious train of coaches, made a comfortable and merry entrance into Stuttgart.

With a slight smirk he enquired after the Duke's affliction, heard with pleasure that he was as good as recovered, advised him for the present at least to stick to the coffee beverage of his councillor, Fichtel, rather than to his Tokay, stroked paternally the tiny, white, plump hand of the doll-like, pouting Duchess. Soon he had Duke and Duchess in such a good mood that they honourably resolved, as soon as the Duke was recovered, to present themselves and the Church with an heir.

The Lord Bishop insisted that they should let him see at closer hand the famous Privy Councillor and Court Jew. Karl Alexander did this unwillingly. He was very afraid lest he should be deprived of his indispensable Jew. But in the long run he could not refuse this harmless request to his friend. Süss appeared before the Lord Bishop; with practiced, immeasurably humble devotion, he kissed the princely ring, and strewed adroit compliments before the great worldly oracle, the secret Emperor, the inspirer and prime mover of all politics. But his Würzburg Eminence was not so easy to catch. The two foxes scented each other knowingly, and neither trusted the other. Smoothly, cheerfully, but undeceived, the sly, fat man chatted with the sly, slender one, and neither came nearer the other.

With indefatigable labour the Lord Bishop and his two Councillors advanced their projects. Incessantly they goaded on the Duke and Remchingen. Open and secret conferences with Weissensee, with the various ecclesiastics who in defiance of the constitution and arousing secret resentment had established religious orders in Weil the Stadt, and over all the Duchy. When, satisfied, the Lord Bishop left the Duchy, he had paid back Stettenfels, with something to spare, secured great things, and laid the foundations of greater. The chapel of the castle in Ludwigsdorf was now prepared for Catholic worship, and priests officially brought into the country. The Catholic army chaplains openly held mass, baptized children. Further, a Catholic military scheme had been worked out to the last detail, and an extraordinarily subtle and intricate interpretation prepared of certain constitutional guarantees, which rendered the Parliamentary liberties illusory. Finally they had ready a formal recognition of the equality of the Catholic worship with the Lutheran. Thirty years before this religious equality had led in the Kurpfalz to the suppression of Protestantism.

In flowing, elegant Latin, and with pious joy, Privy Councillor Fichtel sent word to Remchingen's brother, chamberlain in the Papal court at Rome, of all that the Lord Bishop had achieved through his visit to Stuttgart. He spoke then of the pretext for the journey, the sickness of the Duke, and concluded: "So you see, esteemed lord and brother, that the heavenly Providence often uses strange means to strengthen the only true Church and to disseminate the right faith."

Süss was worried and tormented. The process of his ennoblement proved to be more difficult and tedious than he had expected. Madame de Castro remained cold, and he could not bring the adroit, calculating woman to a decision.

The projects, too, of the Würzburg Bishop spoiled his temper.

194

He had known quite well that he had not succeeded in winning the confidence of his Eminence, and that he was not wanted in the grandiose plan which was now regarded as the cornerstone of Swabian politics for the next decade. In this province, moreover, Süss did not feel himself so competent, so firm in the saddle, as elsewhere. He did not like to mix with ecclesiastical affairs; these questions which made others so bitter appeared to him discreditable and unworthy of, a grown man. His clear, keen, incisive mind recognized that behind them lay very real things, the putting aside of the constitution and the parliament, the military autocracy of the Duke; but he did not comprehend why even expert politicians should so painfully confine themselves to such prolix, scurrilous, roundabout ways of speech. His means and his ways were far more direct, swift and immediate; he could not abide the soft, gradual, soporific methods of the Jesuits. He saw with astonishment that even in the most intimate circles these people scrupulously avoided calling things by their names; that, even if here were but two of them, they employed, with pious prudence, every conceivable moral and disarming circumlocution, and when he or Remchingen gave, sharp and incisive, a thing its right name, they cast round mild, disapproving glances.

So the Jew felt at a loss, and needed corroboration and support.

He managed to get Karl Alexander to commission him to convey personally in his name an unusually splendid present to Magdalen Sibylle. He gave the Demoiselle a day's notice of his arrival, and appeared in great pomp, with pages and servants. It would have been an insult to the Duke had Magdalen Sibylle snubbed an embassy so announced. She received it.

Magdalen Sibylle dwelt now in a little castle outside the town. Golden cupids on the ceiling upheld fluttering festoons, on priceless Gobelins rode elegant hunting-parties, superb mirrors lengthened the magnificent rooms which were filled with the knick-knacks of a great lady. Two coaches, a sledge, sedan-chairs, riding horses were at her disposal. Superfluous lackeys yawned, elegant and idle, about the corridors. Karl Alexander had an open hand for his mistress; even the King of Poland could not surround his mistresses with more pomp and splendour.

In the midst of all this magnificence Magdalen Sibylle maintained a frozen calm. Splendour hung and stood, as it were, lifeless around her; the little castle was like the tomb of a dead woman laid upon her pompous bier.

With frigid courtesy she received Süss in an ample maroon dress of brocade, with long, close-fitting sleeves, high at the neck. The brown cheeks, the blue eyes, were set in formal politeness as if to receive the Baden-Durlach business agent, with whose court one was on strained terms; the black hair was ceremoniously concealed under the peruke. Süss sought at first to make an impression on her coldness by extravagant, merry persiflage and boundless gallantry. She gave him only disdainful and curt answers. Then he tried other ways, provoked her to retaliate, thanked her with ironical rapture for having resolved to receive him. She retorted that she had done so on the order of his Excellency, and was silent for a little; but she could not keep herself from adding that she had borne so much already, and she could endure this, too, with patience.

Now Süss was in his element. Borne so much! Endure with patience! To be the mistress of the Duke of Württemberg, what a misfortune! The daughters of the whole Swabian nobility longed for that fate. A splendid castle, hundreds of lackeys, to call hunting-parties and assemblies when she liked, poor Demoiselle, ah, how ill it went with her!

Magdalen Sibylle took off the mask. So he would have war; he believed apparently that she had forgotten already, and that he could begin where he had left off before; chaffering, devilish Jew that he was, he had sold her to the Duke. She stood up abruptly, let the tiny, modish, Asiatic dog, a present from Karl Alexander, slide ungently to the floor, so that it yelped, and flashed at him: he should not simulate. He knew well enough how things were, and what he had done to her. "Yes, you are to blame for everything!" she cried, and the blood rushed into her brown, keen, masculine cheeks, giving them a bloom of animation.

Süss saw the firm smooth neck rising and falling. He had her now where he wanted. She should not under-value herself, he urged with his soft, caressing, persuasive voice. She had fired the Duke's blood of herself, and his help had not really been needed. But even supposing that he was really the cause (and smiling dryly he looked her up and down), what harm had he done her then? Here it was no use uttering the copy-book maxims of bourgeois morality; they should speak sensibly and as people of the world.

She breathed stormily, made more energetic gestures than the stately, stiff dress really allowed, so that her inborn vigour burst through. What he had done to her? Hypocrite and wicked Jew! He had turned into falsehod and theatricality all she said, all she did! Stifled the living breath of God in her!

But this was still not what she wished to say. Why, why did she lie, why did she not throw full and clean in his face his betrayal, his love for gold, and all his ignominy? Why, in God's name, did she lie?

But he had already perceived what her words did not say. He told her they were only subterfuge and self-delusions. The Bible College of Hirsau, and the breath of God, and apparitions and dreams; that was only mummery and play-acting; all very well for weaklings and men without spirit or guts, and infirm and ugly virgins. He looked her up and down with his impudent, insistent, appraising eyes. "Anyone with your form, Demoiselle," he cried, "anyone with your eyes, and your hair, even if you do hide it, has no need of God. Only be honest! Do not lie to yourself! Your holiness was only a pretext, while you waited."

She defended herself, she struck back. "You have been able to steal from me what I had," she said, "but your devilish art will not have the satisfaction of soiling it as well. Talk away! Declare all your frivolities and profligacies! You will not be able to talk down my God as the dream of a love-mad fool." She called back the rich full hours when she read Swedenborg, the simple, pious faith of the Brotherhood; she forced herself back to the credulous inspirations of the holy blind-woman, and for an instant she was sure and without doubt, and God lived. "Even if He despises me," she cried, and the other was astounded at the pious ardour of her voice, "God lives!" and once more she cried, "God lives!" and truly He appeared and was risen in her.

But, ah! for a moment only. The Jew held his peace, enjoying her zeal, the glow of her ardour. Then with his smooth hand he wiped it away. "If that is so," he said, easily, "why did you

197

flee from me once in the forest of Hirsau? Why then did your God not help you against the Duke? I believe in very little; but I believe this, that no one can have power over a woman who is filled with God." And while the light went out of her face, and while she stared after her vanishing God, he stepped nearer to her and said to her now what she had feared he would say. He spoke good-humouredly, in his most caressing voice: "I will tell you why that time in the forest you fled from me. Because you loved me. And all that you have done and felt since, hate and doubt, and revenge and numbness and wrong; all that you have done and felt for that reason. And I will say further: I, too, have not had a day since in which I have not seen and thought of your face."

Magdalen Sibylle had thought that she would die if ever he spoke these words. And now he stripped her naked, now he called her holy zeal to lead the devil upward to God, by its downright, small and ridiculous name. It was of course quite easy to bring everything within his simple and idiotic formula. She was only a stupid Swabian country girl who had been smitten with the first cavalier that crossed her road, and her awakening, her ardour towards God, were nothing but quite ordinary, common lewdness. But for some extraordinary reason she did not die at all when he said this to her face. Instead she held herself more proudly, she stood over against him, and all at once she found her voice, and in unvarnished, scornful words she upbraided him; yes, she had perhaps masked her feelings, but he had done the most despicable, shabby, disgusting, Jewish thing that any man could do; he had chaffered away his emotions.

From her words he licked only the honey for which his vanity was greedy, observed only with satiated pride how completely he filled her. And he would have liked to have her a credulous girl again, so that he might parade still more splendidly before her. With practised sophistry—it had been prepared, indeed, long before—he unfolded at once the argument that was bound to bring her to him. Expertly and with many flatteries he laid it before her. Yes, he knew that then he could easily have had her heart at his disposal, and that she would willingly have given herself to him. But he was no lover of easy shifts. With his power and his consequence to make an impression on a Swabian country girl—this would have seeemed too cheap to him. Thus it had been like a sudden opportunity for him when the Duke had asked for her. Now she had tasted what power was, now they stood equal to equal, and he battled with honourable weapons. And he congratulated himself on the subtlety, the brilliance, with which he had turned the business to his advantage.

In her heart Magdalen Sibylle knew that these were phrases, gallant excuses. Yet his words were sweet to her, she had fought long, she was glad to let herself be deceived so pleasantly. Meanwhile he became drunk with his own eloquence, soared still higher. He did not see, or he refused to see, the incongruity between the straightforward, naturally-bred country girl, beautiful through her simplicity, and the courtly, ceremonious, over-rich grandeur of her clothes. No longer did he see that in concealing her dark hair under the peruke she had taken away an essential part of herself; that the maroon brocade puffed out and laced the living, breathing girl until she appeared a doll; that the easy movement of her limbs, the innocent, untamed fire of her eyes, now artificially curbed and arranged, reduced her to one among the many. He wanted to see her as he wanted her to be, so that he could plume himself before her, could plant his statue on her pedestal. He stood behind her chair, his elbow supported on the back, leaned over her, spoke to her, not loud, but with his urgent, penetrating voice, the arched eyes ardently fixed on her: "Have you not realized now what it means to have power? Only try it! Go back again to your Bible College! Garner pears in your free time; knit stockings! Only try it! You can never do it again!" he ended triumphantly. "You have tasted your destiny now, and know what it is."

She had sprung up, panting, her hands raised in half repulsion. The little dog had crept fearfully into a corner. Hostile, incredulous, yet, now that he ceased, eager for more, she confronted him, agitated and tense, from the opposite corner of the tiny room crammed with knick-knacks, of whose restricted space in her ample court dress she took up a large portion. Slender, insinuating, his feet noiseless on the rich carpet, he came nearer and nearer. "Leave your naïve dreams behind you, Magdalen Sibylle! They were all right for the forest of Hirsau. Now the castle of Lud-

199

wigsdorf is your reality. Regard it well! Take a firm grip of it! It is a good and a beautiful reality. I am proud that I directed you to it. We have both the same destiny, Magdalen Sibylle, you and I, and it is power."

And while, with her last mistrust of him scared into a remote corner of her being, she looked at him with amazement and apprehension, he began to show off like a rope dancer. To impress his mother, who from the beginning had believed in him, oh, that was easy, that was no task. But to wheedle over this mistrustful, hostile girl here, that would be fascinating; if it succeeded that would be a triumph, his longed-for, his needed confirmation to himself. Even as on the lighted stage a great comedian, piqued by a frigid, unresponsive audience, gives ever more and more of himself, just to carry away that obstinate mass, so Süss rose higher and higher, expanding beyond his own being, recklessly unfolding his most secret desires.

Mute, bewildered, she listened as he said: "Thus finally, we stand equal to equal, Magdalen Sibylle. You and I, each with a hand on the lever of power. It is not the Duke who has a claim on you. Who is he then, this Duke?"

The excited man then began to miscall the Duke in terms which before he had never permitted himself, and which made him pale when he returned to his senses, lest they should be divulged.

"This Duke believes one can rule a country with army regulations! He has no notion of the interdependence of things: no eyes of his own, no brain of his own, hardly a heart of his own; measures his enjoyment by the number of his women and his bottles; mistakes the barbarous brawling of his Remchingen for Dionysian joy. It is a pure chance that you please him. He sees absolutely nothing, and understands as little of your charm. I have the claim on you, I! I have admired you from the first, I know what you are. I have clambered up by my own help, I, a Jew, despised and poor, rung by rung, step by step, so that now I stand above these Swabian louts as my mare Assjadah stands above their lumbering plough-horses. And therefore I have set you higher than the other worthy, honest, home-bred Swabian misses. Thus I stand before you, equal before equal. Thus I state my claim, and ask your assent. Had you glided into my bed, unawakened, unaware, as you were when you came from the forest of Hirsau, the triumph would have seemed too easy to me, and like a betrayal. Now, experienced, knowing who I am and who you are, you shall decide. Now you shall say to me: I belong to you, I come."

She stood in deep bewilderment and was silent. But he, to avoid weakening the impression, turned adroitly and without warning from his ardour back to a cold conversational tone. And ere she had well come back to herself, he had bowed, ceremoniously, kissed her hand, and left the distracted, bewildered woman alone.

Relieved and cheerful he returned with his retinue to the city. He had the confirmation of his power that he needed. He felt himself high and secure above those who imperilled his career. Ho, let one of them try to emulate him, the raw Remchingen, or the fat Lord Bishop! The others had birth, but he had got the lady before them. Birth was easier to acquire. He was the stronger.

And the mare Assjadah felt him lighter, more victorious, now that he returned than he had been as he went. It was a joy to carry him, and she neighed clear his renown to the city.

THE Esslingen child murder excited a great sensation and stir all through the Empire. Ever more thrilling details were related, how the Jew had cruelly drained the girl's blood and baked it in his Passover cakes so that he might attain power over all Christians with whom he might have dealings. All the old stories came to life again; the legend of the holy Simon Martyr of Trier, the child who was slain by the Jews in the same way; and of the boy, Ludwig Etterlein of Ravensburg. Even more radiant mounted the image of the dead girl; what a sweet, angelic little virgin she had been! In the public-houses strolling musicians celebrated the deed in song; newspapers and occasional sheets told of it in rough verses and bloodthirsty woodcuts.

Already there was a movement among the people to revenge themselves upon the Jews. A mob collected at the gates of the Ghetto, and whoever dared to show himself was received with stones, mud and curses. Trade stood still, the Christian debtor poured contempt on the Jewish creditor, plucked his beard, spat on him. The justices lingered out the ensuing law-suit, until it petered out. In Bavaria, in the neighbourhood of Rosenheim, on the great trade route from Vienna to the West, a corn dealer whose business had been injured by the Jews, together with an absconding clerk, had organized a band which lay in wait for Jewish merchants and plundered their transports. The Electoral Prince's administration looked on idly, not displeased. At last the sharp protests of Swabia and energetic representations from the Vienna Chancellory put an end to the mischief.

Even in courts and cabinets the Esslingen affair was followed with the greatest interest. It was seen how weak and full of lacunæ the circumstantial evidence was, and people chuckled to see in what a primitive manner the Imperial Town was trying to reach the Duke of Württemberg and his Finance Councillor through the dead child; but, with malicious satisfaction, found this naïveté very effective. The strongest piece of evidence was still merely the exploitation of the belief that whoever was born on Christmas Eve stood in special danger of the Jews, since the murdered child had indeed been born on that sacred night.

Against the Jews rose now heavy, oppressive, leaden clouds. The anxious, cowed people crept into their corners and gazed on the formless and approaching calamity. Ai! Ai! whenever one of them was seized on some stupid, malicious charge, thousands were butchered, thousands were burned and hanged, tens of thousands were hunted hither and thither over the earth. Terrified they crouched in their holes and corners; around them lay a stillness, fearful, pregnant with murder, inexorable, to be named with no name, not to be touched, as if the air fainted out of their streets, and they gasped in vain to draw breath. The fearfullest of all was the first week: that waiting, that awful, helpless crouching, and not knowing what, where or how. Those of most consequence rushed to the authorities. Usually, when they were in request they were flattered there; but now they were not admitted. This shoulder-shrugging in the ante-chambers, this delight in their agony, this lowering contempt, this desertion, this refusal to extend a hand to them, defenceless people that they were! Ai! these authorities who made them pay dearly for their safe-conducts, and yet had no time to spare for the peril and dire need of their Jews! Ai, these two cool and languid city guards at the gate of the Ghetto, what protection would they be against a horde of a thousand robbers and murderers? Ai! they saw clearly now how the officials and councillors closed their eyes and put their hánds behind their backs, that unhindered the rabble might fall upon the defenceless Jews! Ai, the dire need! Almighty God would keep them, praised be His name! Ai, thou poor Israel! Ai, the defenceless and riven tents of Jacob!

Black-pinioned, vulture-beaked, paralysing, the news flew through all the Jewish communities, from Poland to Alsace, from Mantua to Amsterdam. A prisoner lies in Swabia, in Esslingen, the evil city, parent-city of evil and vileness. The Goim say that he has slaughtered one of their children. Edom is making ready, and will fall on us to-day, to-morrow, who knows? Hear, Israel!

The men went about pallid and grey, their business forgotten; dressed in their finery, terrified, with foolish, bewildered eyes, their beautiful wives fluttered in corners, and gazed at their husbands full of trust, ready to do blindly whatever they counselled. All Jewry, in the Roman Empire and far beyond its frontiers, held its breath. They gathered in their synagogues, beat their breasts, acknowledged their sins, fasted on Monday, on Thursday and again on Monday, from sunset to sunset; ate nothing, drank nothing, did not touch their wives. They stood crammed tight, in their evil-smelling synagogues, wrapped in their prayer mantles, or in their grave clothes, frantically rocking or grovelling. They cried to God, they cried to Adonai Elohim with shrill, despairing voices which reminded one of the shrill, discordant sound of the ram's horn which they blew at the festival of the New Year. They reckoned up their sins, they cried; "Not for our sake, Oh Lord, be gracious to us, not for our sake! But for our forefathers' sake." They reckoned up the endless lists of their predecessors who had sealed their faith in the divine name with death, those who had been tortured by the Syrians, stretched on the rack by the Romans, slaughtered, strangled, exiled by the Christians, the martyrs from the Polish communities to those of Trier, Speyer, Worms. They stood veiled in their white grave-shrouds, their heads strewn with ashes, all their limbs jerking ecstatically until they were exhausted; they bargained with God, importuned him with loud outcries, when the day dawned greyly; and when in the melancholy dusk it faded

203

away, they still stood and cried with their discordant, shrieking voices: "Remember the covenant with Abraham and the offering of Isaac." But by a hundred ways all their prayers returned always to the wild, shrill chorus of avowal: "One and eternal is Adonai Elohim, one and eternal is the God of Israel, the everlasting, the infinite, Jehovah."

But the women were invisible, sitting behind lattices, separated. Scared, with great eyes, they sat like birds ranged on the transverse bar of a cage, and babbled softly and piously and foolishly out of their prayer books which, in Rabbinical letters and in a hotch-potch of German and Hebrew, related the Biblical stories and other pious legends.

In every temple and synagogue from Mantua to Amsterdam, from Poland to Alsace, the men stood thus, fasted and prayed. At the same hour, when the day dawned and when it departed, all Jewry stood, turned towards the east, towards Zion, phylactery on heart and brow, clothed in their grave-shrouds; they stood and acknowledged: "Naught is left us but the Book"; they stood and cried: "One and eternal is the God of Israel, the everlasting, the infinite, Jehovah."

But as the first days of horror went by, it was seen that the Free City of Esslingen intended to prolong the process against the Jew Jecheskel Seligmann Freudenthal. Was it on political grounds—perhaps they wished to keep it up their sleeves as a card to play against the ducal cabinet?—was it out of simple pleasure in the long, lingering torment, was it that they hoped still to obtain some stronger evidence; months passed and the Jew lay still in his prison, and his case had not advanced beyond the preliminary stages and the first degree of torture.

But accustomed to every description of persecution for two thousand years, the Jews, gathering themselves together out of their first paralysing anguish, rushed, flew, bored holes in every nook to creep into when the terror should break out. They had their letters of protection ratified, engaged armed men and townspeople to take their part; their couriers flew through all the streets, organizing a general campaign of defence; in every court, in every council-chamber their agents laboured to persuade the well-disposed to take steps; a great part of their capital went abroad securely in letters of credit and bills.

But over all that they thought and did lay the leaden cloud. The approaching terror disturbed their sleep, turned their food into insipid, tasteless scraps, soured their wine, took the flavour from their spices, crippled their assiduous, hearty, zealous, well-beloved disputes over the Talmud, so that in the middle of a sentence they would fall silent and stare blankly before them. Yes, even within them hung the leaden cloud, in their proud Sabbaths, which once, dreaming of the glory of their fallen kingdom and their future Messiah, even their poorest beggars celebrated royally. They had taken all possible measures to secure themselves, but these were as straw, or as the fir lintels and palm-leaf roofs of their tabernacles. The cloud was there, and all this was of no avail against the cloud. And when they followed their daily worship, when they celebrated their feasts, from every corner the strangling apprehension sprang out on them.

The Rabbi of Frankfurt, Rabbi Jaakob Joshua Falk, sat over the Scriptures. And involuntarily his frail, wrinkled hand unrolled that chapter in the fifth book of Moses which contains the most terrible curse that ever the brain of man conceived. That curse the Jew is accustomed to pass over apprehensively, and the reader in the yearly reading of the Scriptures glides over it with a shy, startled, hasty voice, so as not to bring ill-luck with it. But the eyes of the aged Rabbi remained glued to the threatening, blockish characters, and he read:

"The Lord shall send upon thee cursing, vexation, and rebuke, in all that thou settest thine hand unto for to do.

"Thou shalt betroth a wife, and another man shall lie with her: thou shalt build a house, and thou shalt not dwell therein.

"The Lord shall cause thee to be smitten before thine enemies: thou shalt go out one way against them, and flee seven ways before them.

"And thou shalt eat the fruit of thine own body, the flesh of thy sons and of thy daughters, which the Lord

205

thy God hath given thee, in the siege, and in the straitness, wherewith thine enemies shall distress thee.

"The tender and delicate woman among you, which would not adventure to set the sole of her foot upon the ground for delicateness and tenderness, her eye shall be evil toward the husband of her bosom, and toward her son and toward her daughter,

"And toward her young one that cometh out from between her feet, and toward her children which she shall bear: for she shall eat them for want of all things secretly in the siege and straitness, wherewith thine enemy shall distress thee in the gates.

"And the Lord shall scatter thee among all people, and among those nations shalt thou find no ease, neither shall the sole of thy foot have rest: but the Lord shall give thee there a trembling heart, and failing of eyes, and sorrow of mind.

"And thy life shall hang in doubt before thee; and thou shalt fear day and night, and shalt have none assurance of thy life:

"In the morning thou shalt say, Would God it were even! And at even thou shalt say, Would God it were morning! for the fear of thine heart wherewith thou shalt fear, and for the sight of thine eyes which thou shalt see!"

Thus read the old man, and he threw his prayer mantle over his head, so that he might see no more the great threatening letters, and he wept and groaned. His wife, who never dared to disturb him at his studies, stood terrified in the doorway, and her aged heart beat with apprehension until it almost stifled her. But she did not dare to disturb him.

But Rabbi Jaakob Joshua Falk wept out of his sunken, aged eyes, and his prayer mantle was wet with tears.

THE High Church Councillor Philip Heinrich Weissensee, von Weissensee now, had changed sadly since the night when Magdalen Sibylle had fallen to the lot of the Duke. True, there was no political affair in the Empire and in the Swabian province in particular, into which he had not stuck his covetously sniffing nose and his fine, intriguing finger. But his diligence had now something careless, strangely lifeless and mechanical. It happened sometimes that this accomplished man, well-versed in all social arts, would divagate in the middle of a conversation, and begin to talk about irrelevant things. Again, dressed scrupulously in the latest mode, he would appear without his garters or make some other incomprehensible blunder. His behaviour towards women was very noteworthy. He spoke and demeaned himself to them with the greatest courtesy, but it sometimes happened that with the greatest apparent deference he would say something so lewd that even General Remchingen was taken aback. People would have it, too, that he, of whom there had never been a whisper before, now had gallant liaisons. Strangely enough he favoured specially such ladies as by common knowledge had passed already through the hands of Süss.

He attached himself to Süss more than ever. This astonished people. For in the immediate entourage of the Duke it was known that the Jew did not sit so immediately at the hub of power now as he had months before. Nor in the position of trust which he enjoyed as head of the Catholic project had Weissensee any need of all this fawning and toadying towards the Finance Director. Yet he let no opportunity escape of speaking to Süss, of touching him; he was so familiar that the suspicious Jew began to believe that he wanted to wheedle information out of him and ruin him, and he behaved with scrupulous care.

One evening the Church Councillor suddenly and with urgency begged Bilfinger and Harpprecht, his old friends, to come to him. The gentlemen went at once, asked solicitously and sympathetically what was wrong. But there was nothing: Weissensee made use of subterfuges transparent to anyone. The gentlemen, puzzled, gazed at him, gazed at him again, recognized the sad state he was in, and remained. There they sat now, school-fellows, very busy men all three of them, gifted by nature all three and enriched with all the culture of their age, respected names, and in positions of power. There they sat and drank, and the two stout and comfortable men spoke in monosyllables, while the slender, elegant Weissensee poured out indifferent witticisms, and set himself anxiously to prevent any moment of silence intervening. Bilfinger asked him direct how far his Bible commentary had advanced. The books of Andreas Adam Hochstetter, Christian Eberhard Weissmann, Johann Reinhard Hedinger on this subject were really only mediocre at the best, and his friend's projected work was urgently needed. With a faint, uneasy smile and a blind movement of his hand, Weissensee replied that it might perhaps have been better if he had never left Hirsau and had sat all his life over his commentary. "Aye," said Harpprecht, and truly it was no rejoinder, "it is a filthy age, all the ways are filthy, and it is cursed hard to keep oneself clean."

Weissensee's political position became ever more ambiguous. He combined irreconcilables. He sat in the Sub-Committee of Parliament; he formulated and drew up the grievances of the democracy against the despotic rule of the Duke; and he was the Duke's illegitimate father-in-law and trusted friend. He conferred with Süss, with the Jesuits, with generals, and composed spirited defences of the constitution and evangelical liberties. He had his finger in every pie, his snares in every thicket. The earlier Weissensee would have been happy to be the lever, the moving force, in so many plots, intrigues, conventicles, complicated machinations. The President of the Church Council had even now his eye and hand on every act; but to the astonishment of all, in the very middle of his multifarious and important activities, he suddenly withdrew, declared he must rest, and sat himself down over his Bible commentary in his desolate house at Hirsau.

He did not advance with it. Peevishly he gazed at the tomes of Weissmann, Hedinger and Hochstetter, who valiantly and ceremoniously had ploughed the same field. Ah, for a long time still students would have to practise their teeth on those tough chunks of wisdom. Oh, it would take a good while yet before he could fill that giant body with life and give it a heart.

So, the work did not advance. The lamp burned amid his books deep into the night; but his eyes did not see the letters, neither the crisp Greek, nor the firm German, nor the stocky Hebrew. They saw one who was not there; duskily glowing, masculinely keen cheeks, unflinching blue eyes in strange contrast with the dark

208

hair. He saw her in the still circle of lamp-light, rapt, with her childishly-important expression. During the day he shambled through the rooms—how big and empty they were!—in his slippers, without his peruke, shiftless; prowled into the corners, stroked gently with his fine withered hand a table-cover, or the back of a sofa, absent, with a wry smile.

Then he commanded Jaakob Polykarp Schober to visit him. The master was mightily afraid. Certainly the President of the Church Council was going to give him a talking to about his beliefs, accuse him of sectarianism, drag him before the tribunal, incarcerate him, hunt him, a restless fugitive, over the earth. Now that his daughter was no longer in the Bible College, he could let prudence go. The sweat broke out on the chubby-cheeked man, his childish, pious eyes became very round and anxious, he trotted to and fro with short steps, his breathing was oppressed. But very soon he mastered his fear. If God had destined him for a martyr, then he would take this election thankfully upon himself. So he went before the prelate, perspiring but upright, with manly courage, and began straightway to talk in a warlike strain about the three men in the fiery furnace. But Weissensee, at first astonished, soon interrupted him, explained courteously that he had not invited him to come in his official capacity, he had only wished once more to see and speak with his daughter's old friend. Much relieved, the Master spoke simply, warmly and respectfully of Magdalen Sibylle, and how the whole circle missed that pious, noble and learned sister. Weissensee listened greedily. He was visibly pleased with the Master's simple and amiable chatter; he met him often, the two men even went walks together in the forest. At last Schober began timidly to speak of his verses; he recited his poem "The Cares of Life and Trust in God," and that other one about Jesus the Best Reckoner. Weissensee listened graciously, he even let something be hinted about publication, and the affability of the great and learned man won over the young Master completely, so much so that he whose heart had for long been overflowing entrusted to him his secret of the Princess of the Heavenly Jerusalem and the wicked Jew, her father.

Then Weissensee pricked up his ears; his weariness, his indifference fell from him. Day-long he ranged through the forest with the Master, who was radiant with such signs of honour. He stood by the wooden fence, and had every detail related and related again. He enquired after the old man, the Hollander, Mynheer Gabriel Oppenheimer van Straaten. He pieced things together. True, he did not manage to get a glimpse of Naemi, but out of the mosaic he assembled a fairly true notion of things.

Now, too, his lamp burned long into the night. But the prelate shambled no longer with uncertain, erratic steps. Elastic and young he went through his large, white rooms, his busy dreams filled with human figures and future events. His fine, very mobile lips smiled deeply, amusedly, and sometimes he even spoke aloud, actor of his dream: *"Voyons donc,* my Lord, Privy Financial Councillor!" or "Eh, eh, who would have suspected that, your Excellence?"

Yes, who would have suspected that! Here he was, an old fox; he had scented and smelt life and humanity from all sides, and flattered himself he could read the faces of men. And now he had to recognize again that on this great world-theatre there are always more disguises and masks than ever the most hard-baked sceptic supposes. Who would have guessed that? He called up the Jew's face before him in the stillness of the night in his lonely room. He closed his eyes and searched it, feature by feature; the voluptuous, very red mouth, the pale, cold, elegant cheeks, the pitiless, inexorable chin, the watchful, quick, mobile eyes, the smooth, dreamless brow with the bumps of calculation above the eyebrows. Behind this icy-cold, icy-clear business man and man of action, who would have looked for the sentimental idyll in the forest of Hirsau? Ho, ho, my Lord Finance Director! How you stood before me on that horrible evening in your palace! What a vigilant, immaculate, malicious bearing you had! Ho, ho, my lord Hebrew, I should have gathered myself together a little better. I babbled a little foolishly, it is true, and did not carry myself quite *à la mode* that evening. I sat very wretched and scattered on my chair while you stood before me, slim and slender and cutting, and the marrow crumbled away in the most singular manner within my bones. Now I would like very much to know how your Excellency would carry yourself in a similar situation. The President of the Church Council Philip Heinrich von Weissensee halted in his march through the room. The lamp shone serenely in the large room, a night moth buzzed, the rows of books around gazed out mutely and calmly; through the open window streamed in the night scents of the woods. Was it revenge that he gave himself up to, then? Was it plans of revenge? *Fi donc,* he did not befoul himself with such common, bourgeois feelings. He was only—yes, what was he?—he was curious to know how the Jew would conduct himself. Whether he too would suddenly become so defeated and old, and what, in short, he would do. Ho! yes, that would be very much worth seeing, that would be full of edification, much more interesting than what one usually read in novels or saw on the stage.

"*Voyons donc,* your Excellency! Eh, *voilà,* my Lord Privy Councillor!" said the fine, elegant prelate to himself, deeply amusd and smiling. Then he sat down to his Bible Commentary with great animation; his depreciatory, mocking eyes glided over the valiant labours of Hochstetter, Weissmann, Hedinger, the admirable, prolix, learned men, and diligently and merrily the work proceeded now.

MEANWHILE the emissaries of the Würzburg Bishop in Stuttgart laboured on silently but stubbornly. Clear in the public eye now stood new men, military chiefly, who took no pains to be deferential to Süss, and though outwardly courteous did not hide their contempt for the Jews. There was General Margrave von Röder, a boor; then there was the Commandant of Asperg, Lieutenant Colonel von Bouwighausen; further, a mob of noisy and brilliantly-uniformed officers, who now were like a perpetual hedge round the Duke, the Colonels Tornacka and Laubsky, Cavalry Captain Buckow. There was still another officer who was particularly hostile to Süss, Major von Röder, a cousin of the Margrave, Commander of the Stuttgart Mounted Militia, the city cavalry, a surly man with a low brow, a hard mouth, and coarse hands, doubly uncouth in their gloves. But the one who hated and loathed the Jew most was still that Dom Bartelemi Pancorbo, the Palatinate Privy Councillor, General Director of the Tobacco Manufactory, and jewel dealer, who now again stepped into the light, the right shoulder as ever curiously drawn up, clothed always in the strictly ceremonious, obsolete Portuguese court dress, showing over the gigantic ruff at his throat the purple, distorted, fleshless face with the vulture beak, and the dyed and curled moustache, and eyeing Süss behind his heavy eyelids with lingering, expressionless, small eyes.

All these, and in addition his other ancient enemy, Remchingen, threw themselves now into the Catholic Plot. With his thorough grasp of the whole affair, which he saw much more clearly than the stupid and arrogant officers, Süss saw that he was left outside these plans. Matters of importance were divulged to him only casually or not at all. Only when his technical knowledge of finance was absolutely needed, did they impart to him drily and condescendingly this or that detail. And once, when he had quietly tried to probe something further, the Duke bellowed at him, saying that he should cease this espionage once and for all. When it was time to let the cat out of the bag, then, perhaps, they might tell him!

Karl Alexander, fully restored to health, and more quickly than he had hoped, laboured mightily and was in a good mood. The result was that the reconciliation with Marie Auguste effected by the Würzburg Bishop had the wished effect: the Duchess was pregnant. The country heard this news with dissatisfaction. Had the Duke died childless, then the Protestant line would have come again into power; but now the people saw themselves delivered up interminably to Rome and the Jesuits. The officially-decreed services of intercession for the Duchess were badly patronized; those only went who had to go.

But the Duke was awkwardly glad. He spoke to every one of the awaited heir, broad pleasure on his fleshly, sanguine face; he made uncouth witticisms and encumbered Marie Auguste with clumsy attentions. To her the pregnancy came most inopportunely. She feared the disfigurement, she feared also that the child would be a hindrance to her, she had apprehension and loathing for her confinement; moreover motherhood in itself appeared to her to be something vulgar, plebeian, not fit for an aristocrat. She even thought of taking steps to avoid the consequences of her pregnancy, and she made representations to Dr. Wendelin Breyer to that effect. But the physician did not or

212

would not understand. With clumsy, apologetic gestures he spoke in his hollow, muffled voice of the joy of motherhood, referred to the ancients, cited the mother of the Gracchi, and that other heroic matron who would rather see her son return borne on his shield than return without it. With a sigh, thinking too that now the Duke's attentions must cease, Marie Auguste gave it up.

On the contrary she listened greedily and pleasantly scandalized when Süss on one occasion told her the story of the demon queen, Lilith. She, the long-haired, the winged, Adam's first wife, had a quarrel with her spouse, for in carnal intercourse he was not so much to her liking as she would have desired. Then, practising black arts, she called on God by His forbidden name and fled to Egypt, the land of all evil magic. Since then, hating Eve and every proper marriage, she threatens the woman on child-bed and the suckling with curses and dire injury. But she was overtaken in Egypt by the three angels whom God had sent after her, Senoi, Sansenoi, and Semangelof. First, they thought of drowning her, but then they let her free after she had been made to swear with the oath of the demons that she would injure no woman on child-bed and no suckling who was guarded by the names of the three angels. For this reason the Jewish wives guard themselves when they are confined by an amulet inscribed with the names of the three angels.

Tickled, deliciously afraid, the Duchess asked the Jew confidentially whether he could not procure such an amulet. Certainly he could do that, he assured her with zealous devotion. Afterwards she chanced to relate this to her confessor, Father Florian. He warned her violently and urgently against it. But she resolved, all the same, to allow herself the amulet. It might do good, and if she used it she could always confess afterwards.

For the most part she took her pregnancy, according to her usual custom, with light mockery. She behaved like someone who, caught in a shower in her light summer attire, exchanges her wet clothes for a peasant costume, and amuses herself magnanimously over the piece of mummery.

So she sat on Christmas Eve, frail and delicate, all in white foamy lace, out of which, of the hue of an old and noble marble, the lizard-like face flickered maliciously under the gleaming black

213

hair. Around her was the small band of friends who had been invited for Christmas Eve. The Duke had wished to exclude Süss. But since the night he had told her the story of the amulet to be used against Lilith, Marie Auguste had had with her amusing and gallant Court Jew a strange, secret and unspoken understanding, and she did not wish to be without him on this evening. In his isolation of this time he accepted the invitation as a sort of amends. In respectful gratitude he proffered the Duchess as a present a very pretty cameo on which a new-born child was carved, and an exquisite Chinese child's rattle of porcelain and ivory; pigtailed men, carved with marvellous delicacy, clambered up the handle with nodding heads, and tiny pagodas trilled and rang. But as third present he handed her, with a smile full of secrecy and respect, a little golden box; she knew that the amulet was inside.

But the others, displeased because Süss was still so firmly in favour, received him precisely on this evening as an intruder, and fell on him with coarse, ill-natured jests. The Duke, taking up a sentence of Remchingen, warned Marie Auguste that she should not look at the Jew, lest Württemberg should be presented with a hook-nosed duke: Marie Auguste only smiled. Secretly she fondled the tiny box; secretly, unseen by the others, she took out the amulet and regarded it—a strip of parchment, inscribed with red, blocky Hebrew characters, amid which wound and writhed disturbing, intricate figures, while absurd, threatening, primitive-looking birds crouched among them.

Meanwhile Süss listened with the same observant and careless politeness to jeer and blunt attack. Later he turned to the Duke and Weissensee. He had heard, he said, that the Duke and the President of the Church Council had occasionally debated over the Catholic and the Evangelical meanings given to the text about Christmas Eve, whether the Evangelical version "and goodwill to men," or the Catholic "to men of goodwill," be the correct one. He was glad to be able to bring, as a trifling Christmas present, a contribution to the solution of this question. Somewhat taken aback the gentlemen gazed at him, the others, too, ceased talking and listened, sceptically and mocking, while Süss courteously and imperturbably continued. Since the time of Professor Baruch

214

Spinoza, whom his Excellency the Elector Palatine had desired to call to his university at Heidelberg, the partakers in his faith had also turned their attention to the scientific study of the New. Testament. So he had written to a business friend in Amsterdam regarding the text mentioned, and had received the following information. In the Greek text it is written "eudokias" which the Vulgate and the Catholics rightly translate with "bonæ Voluntatis, of good will." But Erasmus had his Bible printed from a manuscript in which "eudokia," without the s, was wrongly set down, and using that, Luther translated it as "an act of good will." Erasmus would certainly have come upon this error if he had not been in such haste. But, out of vanity, he wished his Bible to appear before that of Cardinal Ximenes. From this it followed, with all respect to the erudition of the President of the Church Council, that the Lutheran text on Christmas Eve was not right in this respect, and that his Excellency held the correct text.

Süss expounded his explanation modestly, courteously and incisively. What he said was so obvious that even among the officers there were one or two who understood it, and Marie Auguste congratulated herself on the cleverness of her Court Jew. But all the others were exasperated that on Christmas Eve the Jew should pick the gospel to pieces, and Remchingen growled; now, it seemed, the Jews haggled not only over money and jewels, but also over the Word of God.

Weissensee enlarged upon the position of woman in the Old and in the New Testament. This was a theme with which, under the influence of the painful knowledge and experience of the last few months, he had been savagely obsessed, too, in writing his Bible Commentary. In the New Testament, the Madonna: in the Old, the thousand wives of Solomon. He spoke smoothly, elegantly, deftly, agreeably, as his habit was. But there was something hidden, which made his words sound so malignant that Magdalen Sibylle became very pale, and her hands felt quite cold.

Beautiful and stately, she sat beside the lovely and wayward Marie Auguste. The Duchess held her hand and stroked it; it did her good to stroke with her small, manicured, plump hand the strong hand of the other. Magdalen Sibylle wrestled anew and more passionately for Süss. She did not clearly apprehend the political constellation, but she saw that he stood alone; she saw a host of enemies around him; she thought of him as a slender, sinuous panther among clumsy, shaggy bears. And she surmised, too, the strange entanglement between him and the Duke, and between him and her father.

Süss remarked lightly that neither the ladies of the Old nor of the New Testament were after his taste. The one type was too heroic, the other, too sentimental. And his eyes glided with eloquent flattery from the Duchess, whose inquisitive, lascivious goodwill agreeably flattered him, to Magdalen Sibylle, who had been his longed-for rehabilitation and firm prop; from the auburn, magnificent Madame de Castro, the clever, calculating woman who, although visibly cooler, had never quite given up the idea of marrying him, to the sweet Götz ladies, the daughter the very image of the mother, who still refused themselves to the Duke.

Remchingen remained constant to the theme of the Old Testament. In the singing Viennese to which he, a born Augsburger, had used himself, because he considered it aristocratic, he held that judging from the Yiddish one heard from time to time, the Holy Scriptures in the original must have sounded like an evil and odious kind of quacking and gibbering. "Do you think, your Excellency," asked Süss—very politely in reply, "that our Lord spoke Viennese with Adam in Paradise, or did he speak Hebrew?" The Duchess laughed; proud of her Jew's readiness with his tongue, and glad at Remchingen's discomfiture, she surreptitiously fondled the box with the amulet; and in a temporary lull in the talk made the child's rattle sound out, gently and delicately. But the Margrave Röder thought it necessary to second Remchingen. He turned to the Duchess and remarked that it was a good thing her Excellency was not yet far advanced in her pregnancy. The children who were born to-night would find it no laughing matter. And now they were all at the point where they had wished to be, and they spoke exhaustively, circumstantially and weightily of the Esslingen child-murder, while Süss remained tenaciously silent. The officers above all had been quite convinced by the argument that the girl had been born on Christmas Eve. But now Monsieur de Riolles, who was a free-thinker, interpolated that if truly those who were born on Christmas Eve stood in danger of the Jews,

216

then obviously Jesus of Nazareth should have chosen another night for his birth; then the cross had been spared him, and they had been spared the whole of Christendom.

Meanwhile the Privy Councillor Pancorbo had begged the Duchess to allow him to inspect Süss's gifts more closely. With his withered, purple, gouty hands he fingered them, held them up before his lifeless, oval, deeply-sunken eyes, until they almost touched his vulturine nose; then he said incisively and exhaustively that the material of the cameo and of the child's rattle was worthless, adding that in the jewel trade it was usual to throw in such toys gratuitously. Spitefully he pointed out what a monstrous sum, on the contrary, the solitaire was worth which Süss himself wore on his finger, and out of their deep cavities his tiny eyes glittered behind their hooded lids with lust for the ring. But Marie Auguste defended her Jew. These were not all the presents he had given her, she said in her smooth, careless, lightly mocking tone, and she produced the amulet and related the story of Lilith, the queen of demons. They listened, embarrassed but tickled, and contemplated the primitive-looking, threatening birds, and the blocky, uncanny characters on the parchment. Until Karl Alexander with a loud, somewhat forced laugh, good-humoured and noisily bantering, broke the silence by swearing that she would become a Jewess yet.

But after supper he drew Süss aside, clapped him on the shoulder, and was very gracious. That about the Catholic and the Evangelical versions, that had been a round and lucid explanation, that had been very amusing, and he was indeed one in a thousand. Of his own accord then he asked the flattered Süss about the Magus, whether one might not manage to see him once more. He knew quite well why; it was about the matter the old man had not wished to reveal. Süss was uncomfortable and tried to evade the demand. Karl Alexander did not persist; he said it was indeed true, the Magus was difficult to approach, he was a hard uncle. But one thing Süss must procure for him: a horoscope from the Magus telling what evil or good he might expect in the future from women. After the affair with the Neapolitan, after the shilly-shallying of the Duchess, and the present imbecile, affected hesitations of the Götz ladies, he wanted some explanation.

217

It was only right and fair that Süss should get the Cabbalist to draw his horoscope and find this out. After obtaining the amulet for the Duchess, he could very well do him also a good turn; and after performing such difficult work as Scriptural interpretation, this must be easy for him. Süss could not well refuse; he hesitated, and assented.

They parted soon. The Catholic gentlemen wished to proceed to the castle chapel for mass. Weissensee asked Süss to give him his company.

The gentlemen sent the carriages in front and went on foot. The night was sultry, there was a strong, gusty wind. Weissensee came back to his theme—how strange it was that the eastern legends should have established themselves so firmly over the whole world. He spoke of the German woods, how curious it would seem if one were suddenly to find an oriental building set among them. In his neighborhood, in the forest of Hirsau, a Dutchman had had that strange intention. Amid such talk they reached the Jew's house in the Seegasse, and the Church Councillor departed with unusual ceremoniousness and courtesy. As soon as his Bible Commentary, in which Süss's kindly proffered information would find an honoured place, was ready, he would accord himself the honour of presenting the first copy to the Finance Director.

Süss strode through the dimly-lit hall. In his ears rang: 'Oh thou happy, oh thou blessed peace-bringing Christmastide.' Soft-footed, the valet appeared, and enquired whether his Excellency would undress. Süss dismissed him. He could not sleep. Had the south wind got into his blood? And what that old fox had said about Hirsau, it sounded harmless enough, and his uncle's house, moreover, was not really oriental; but was there not some catch in Weissensee's words?

He sat down to his papers. But the figures did not seem to have the cold incisiveness which they had had. The white house with the flowers seemed to muffle them in sinuous tendrils. He threw down his pen and walked up and down in restless, anxious thought, while the bells sounded, calling the people to mass.

Uncomfortable and awkward, Isaac Landauer sat on one of Süss's magnificent chairs. They had talked out their business concerns, and Süss, exasperated by the dingy presence of the other, waited nervously for his departure. But Isaac Landauer did not make a move; instead he combed his reddish, faded beard and said: "Ay, the process against Reb Jecheskel Seligmann Freudenthal is in four weeks now. Uncomfortable, Reb Josef Süss. It must be peculiarly uncomfortable for you. Here you have your lackeys, your Chinese, your golden robes, your parrot. But the Esslingers spit on them and you, and will murder Reb Jecheskel Seligmann Freudenthal."

Seeing the other silent, he continued: "When I spoke to you of the Ravensburg child-murder you made a wry face, arrogant like a Goi, and said: 'Old fables.' Now you see what the old fables are; now you can feel their truth yourself."

But Josef Süss remained obstinately silent. When the first news came of the measures taken by the Esslingers, he recognized at once, naturally, that they were directed against him, and against him alone. He wanted to fly at them, but compelled himself to sleep upon his indignation, so as to consider in complete calm the pros and cons for an intervention. If he took the part of Jecheskel Seligmann, he would imperil his ennoblement and the marriage with the Portuguese lady, would cumber himself with a thousand galling disputes with Parliament, and would have to renounce as compensation the manifold advantages he held against the Esslingers. So far his policy was clear. He did not know the Jew Jecheskel Seligmann. If the Esslingers, simply to spite him, chose to compromise their reputation for justice by a manifestly wrong verdict, they could. Their affair. He would not meddle. He would remain strictly neutral; be as silent as a log.

He behaved accordingly. He confined himself to actual measures for the protection of the Jews under his jurisdiction in the Duchy, and of their questionable rights. Above all, he did not allow himself to be drawn out of his passivity by jeers or abuse.

And so, though it incensed him greatly, he had no reply for Isaac Landauer's speech. But the other persisted obstinately: "I have bought up with one or two others all the claims on the city of Esslingen. If they stand by the process, then eight days in advance I put in my claims. If they let be, I let be. If they put on the screw, then I put on the screw. But one can never know," he concluded anxiously, rubbing his chilly hands. "These Goim are smitten with all evil and stupidity. When they are after a Jew they would rather have blood than money. And you, Reb Josef Süss?" he asked bluntly, seeing that no word could be wrung from him.

Long forearmed, Süss responded evasively: "I do not know the Jew Seligmann. In my own province I will know how to protect myself."

But Isaac Landauer became excited: "Do not know! Will be able to protect yourself! What does that mean? He sits there with his lackeys, his Chinese, his golden clothes, and knows nothing! Will know how to protect himself! Allow an old business man to say to you: Of what good is all this rubbish, who will be impressed by all this rubbish, who will allow himself to be blinded by it, if you are unable to protect Reb Jecheskel Seligmann Freudenthal?" And enraged he flourished his hands before the other's face, his caftan fluttering angrily: "Parrots, Gobelins, busts! Of what use are busts?" he jeered bitingly. "Moses the prophet and Solomon the king never looked like your white busts in all their lives! And their eyes were not always closed, either. Otherwise they would never have got so far." And, exasperated by the heedless silence of the other, he stared with choleric eyes in front of him.

"A good Jew will think twice before he has dealings with you in future"; suddenly icy, lowering, malignant, he played his last trump. But Süss only shrugged his shoulders: "I allow nothing to force me," and offended and hostile, turned away. There remained nothing for Isaac Landauer except to depart muttering angrily and tugging his beard.

Some weeks later, on the eve of the Esslingen process, ten Jewish men stood in Süss's ante-chamber, at their head Jaakob Joshua Falk, the little shrivelled Rabbi of Frankfurt with the sunken eyes, and with him the patron and the three most prominent members of his community, and a deputation of Jews from Fürth, similarly constituted. They had met together in Freudenthal, where since the time of the Countess there had been a tiny Jewish community; they had sought out the wife of Jecheskel Seligmann, but she was dazed, and no words of comfort could reach her. They had then journeyed to Stuttgart amid the angry growls of the people, and had alighted at the Jewish inn, where the innkeeper was reluctant to receive them. They had prayed, morning, afternoon and evening, in grand and ceremonious order, for ten constituted a congregation in which all the refinements and windings of the prayer ritual could be gone through. They had stood solemnly before the scroll of the Holy Scriptures—which they had borne with them; they had kissed it, exalted and united, shrouded in their prayer mantles, the phylactery on heart and brow, their faces directed towards the east, towards Zion. Thus, in great and dubious need and perplexity, they had prayed with hands and lips and all their limbs. And now they stood, faint and exalted in their ritual curls and heavy caftans, the pointed Jewish caps on their heads, their badges on their sleeves, in Süss's ante-chamber, amid busts, knick-knacks, Gobelins, gold and lapis lazuli. They sweated, and spoke now and then a whispered, passionately murmured word. A clock struck the full hour, and played a thin, silvery, trickling melody, and they waited until the Privy Financial Councillor would receive them.

On this day, however, all the Jews in Germany who were over thirteen years fasted, eighty thousand in number.

Süss would gladly not have received the deputation. These people were foolish. They must know quite well that if he had wished to intervene he would have done it of his own accord. As it was, they could only compromise him. The Parliament was referring more energetically than ever to laws not observed for a long time, but formally still valid, which permitted the presence of Jews in the Duchy only on special grounds and with many qualifications. From the Duke he had obtained nothing more than a declaration that with reference to his Finance Director and the Jews under his control, he would not let his hands be bound; as for the others, they must remain by the old regulations. Utilizing the Esslingen incident, the estates had thereupon promulgated anew and with vigour these ancient and strict laws. It was remarkable that at the head of this agitation in Parliament stood

221

Weissensee. Did he wish to hide his Catholic intrigues under a war on the Jews?

In such circumstances, at any rate, the Jewish deputation was superfluous if not scandalous. On the other hand, it was the most prominent men in German Jewry who wished to speak with him; he must certainly receive them. Had he been able to grant their prayers, then it would have flattered him to listen to them in the rôle of their noble protector. Thus he received them unwillingly, firmly resolved to dismiss them with an evasive answer.

The ten Jews entered, awkward, scraping, coughing, ceremonious, filling the tiny cabinet. Slender, elegant, formal, Süss confronted the clumsy, heavily-breathing, inarticulately-moved men.

Jaakob Joshua Falk spoke, the Rabbi from Frankfurt: "We have worked together, all Jewry, and have laboured with money and with presents. But it has been fruitless. For the people are very furious, and the Councillors of Esslingen are resolved to torture their Jews; and this is also to spite you, because you are so powerful with your Duke. The iniquity of the blasphemer is great, the malice of Edom is mightily lifted up against Israel. They devour money, but they are not softened."

Seeing that Süss did not answer, but waited in silence, the Rabbi of Fürth, a corpulent, fretful, persistent man, began: "There is no help more, Reb Josef Süss, except in you. Reb Jecheskel Seligmann Freudenthal belongs to Württemberg. We beg you to request his discharge to the Duke, so that his case may be tried according to Württemberg law. There is no other hope," he concluded, urgently, pleading, stuttering, almost touching Süss.

But Süss leaned against his writing table, courteous, elegant, unmoved. "The Jew Jecheskel Seligmann," he replied positively, "has no regularized papers from me; his name is not on my lists; it is doubtful whether he belongs to the Duchy. The City of Esslingen will oppose me at the Imperial Court in Vienna, the Estates will mingle in the dispute. It is not opportune for me to request his discharge."

"Not opportune!" exclaimed the zealous Rabbi of Fürth. But the tiny, mild, shrivelled Rabbi of Frankfurt interposed; "You have done much for us. So we had hoped that you would help

222

us this time also, that the blood of the innocent might not be shed."
But the stout, fiery Rabbi of Fürth would not be silenced. "Not
opportune!" he cried excitedly. "To save a human life, to save a
Jew, who has been guilty of nothing but being a Jew! Not opportune!"

"You see only one thing always, Rabbi our teacher," replied
Süss, and he remained courteous and quiet, and gave the other
his title, "I must see more largely, see the implications. Assuming
that I could save Reb Jecheskel Seligmann, then for it I should
have to pay with concessions to the city of Esslingen and to the
Emperor. I cannot permit myself this softness of heart. You
have your simple, clear principle; here is a Jew, who should not
die. I dare not deal so simply; I must reckon, count, weigh. You
have only your Jewish anxieties, I have a thousand others."

In his mild quavering voice responded Jaakob Joshua Falk,
Rabbi of Frankfurt: "How many in Israel would give all their
possessions, all their property, and more than these, that this innocent blood might not be shed! You could prevent it with one
single stroke of your pen. Do not close your heart, Reb Josef
Süss!" And the fat Rabbi of Fürth added: "Would you leave
the whole of Jewry in the lurch because you are apprehensive about
one or two insipid speeches which they may make in Parliament?"

Süss leant still against his writing table, slender, elegant,
courteous, and his calm was a dam against the agitation of the
others, breathing heavily and deeply moved, who filled the small
cabinet. He flashed a quick, haughty glance from his brown, oval
eyes at the fat, zealous rabbi; but he had the rein upon himself
again and replied calmly: "I have done enough for the Jews in
Germany for anyone to see that I do not fail in goodwill. Had
I become a Christian, had I turned away from Jewry, after the
Emperor I would have been the first man in the Empire. But I
was not a coward; I have set myself as a representative of Jewry:
I have not bawled it out, but I have never denied that I am a Jew."

"Then show yourself to be one now! Now! Now!" stuttered
the Rabbi of Fürth impetuously, urgently, sticking forward his
massive, obstinate head.

But Süss replied with greater coldness: "Usually you can
measure and weigh well enough. Just measure now! Just weigh

now! Look further than the instant! Demand the release of Reb Jecheskel Seligmann Freudenthal? I weigh in my right hand his death, and in my left the trouble, abuse, danger, complications I will have to encounter if I save him." He paused, looked quietly in the ten faces which—attentive, agitated, tense—stared into his. He concluded lightly: "I will not make a decision to-day. But it is possible, at least, that on reflection I will not risk a storm on account of a bagatelle."

This roused them. Indignant hands gesticulated in the air, their mouths were opened. Little cries, Ai! Ai! broke out, tumbling over themselves, half-sentences. Above them, spluttering, threatening, the unruly, obstinate prophet-voice of the Rabbi of Fürth: "Bagatelle! A man like you, a Jew, your brother, will be tortured, will be executed in misery and shame, all for nothing and again nothing. My heart stands still when I think that I must look on idly. And you shrug your shoulders: Bagatelle!" And panting, obese and angry he pressed towards him.

But the little Rabbi of Frankfurt pushed him back. In his very old, soft voice he said: "We do not wish to press you, Reb Josef Süss; we only wish to ask you. God has visibly exalted you as never yet a Jew has been exalted in Germany. He has made the heart of your prince as wax in your hand: may yours not be hardened against the need of your brother!"

The others had become quite still, while the old man said this in his not very loud voice. Even the Rabbi of Fürth was silent. After a pause Süss replied, and his voice sounded less assured than at first: he had not by any means declined to intervene. Only if after ripe consideration he found he could not interfere, they should not impute it to ill-will, but would understand his grounds.

Thereupon they went, and he conducted them courteously through the ante-chamber.

Alone, he was vexed at himself. He had been more cordial than he intended. He had shown them some of his real grounds. Why, truly, and to what end? He should have remained cool and polite; he should have promised more and with less amiability. They were not in the least accessible to the finer points. They kept their eyes obstinately fixed and as if bewitched on the one

224

thing: they must have their rascally Jecheskel Seligmann released.

He went to and fro in ever deeper vexation in his cabinet. That they should grasp nothing of it at all! Had he not granted them colossal bounties in Frankfurt? Did he not advance their trade wherever he could? Procure facilities for them, here, there, everywhere? If in spite of the laws of the country several hundreds of Jews dwelt in the Duchy to-day, he alone was responsible. How they had acclaimed him that time in Frankfurt and clapped their hands! And now all that went for nothing, and they took no account of his services simply because in this one case he was not of their mind.

All the same it would have given him a very pleasant feeling to have been able to show them, this time, too, his omnipotence. It struck him as stupid that he could not, without all this bother, take the Jew out of the hands of the Esslingers. In future, certainly, his prestige in the whole of Jewry would be far less. This fretted him.

He decided energetically not to think more about it, and flung himself into his work. He unchained a new whirl of women round him. But his nights passed badly. He dreamed that before him passed slowly and solemnly the executioner's procession with the Jew Jecheskel Seligmann Freudenthal. He, Süss, burst in on his mare, Assjadah, and tried to bring the procession to a stand-still. But slowly as the procession crept immediately in front of him, and hard as he spurred hs swift steed, he could never overtake it. He shouted, and flourished energetically a document prohibiting the ceremony. But there was a great wind, and the thing before him went on and on. Suddenly Dom Bartelemi Pancorbo was there. With his cadaverous face, the one shoulder high, in his great obsolete ruff, he stood in front of him and said that if he would give the solitaire on his finger, he, Pancorbo, would bring the procession to a halt. Perspiring and apprehensive, Süss consented. But when he tried to draw the ring from off his finger, it sat there as if it had grown into his flesh, and Dom Bartelemi said, Yes, then he must even hack off his hand.

At that Süss awoke, unrefreshed, and with a headache. But though he was always tired, now he was afraid of going to sleep. For Red Jecheskel Seligmann Freudenthal, who did not trouble his days, filled with work and women, insinuated himself into his short and wretched nights.

BEFORE the scared and terrified Süss sat, crouched together and morose, the Rabbi Gabriel. He sat there, burly, troubled, the three sharp vertical clefts in his brow. He told his story in laconic, old Frankish, expressive, menacing words.

Rumours, it seemed, had reached the child, evil, corroding rumours about Süss. The child had said nothing, but she had lost her peace, was troubled. Anxious and terrified, Süss asked: What could he do, then? And Rabbi Gabriel retorted, morose and grim: Here words were useless, evasions useless. He must present himself before the child. He must let her read what was in his face. Perhaps, he added, scornfully, the child would discover more than he had, the Rabbi. Perhaps she would find more in Süss's face than flesh and skin and bone.

When he was alone Süss passed from exaltation to despair. Torn from his foundations he was flung hither and thither. But still, fundamentally, his mind had been made up from the beginning. For that reason, this menacing and scornful demand of the Rabbi's came to him fundamentally as a sign and a great light and something intensely desired.

He would present himself to the child, and show her a face clear and shining through and through. That he was constrained to do so just at this moment was an indication and a sign even for the most sceptical. He was no cowardly hypocrite, that was certain; he could let himself be seen, at any time and by anybody; and even if there should be a God who judged and kept an account and held the balance, he could be assured and need have no anxiety in front of the final balance sheet. All the same, if he had to go to the child now—a child like that has strange eyes; she has only seen flowers and the lighted heavens, she has no notion of human complications, and she may see offence and uncleanness where our hearts and hands appear tolerably clean. And if rumours had flown to her already, if she was full of anxiety and doubt as it was, then it would certainly be for the best to examine oneself fundamentally once more, before one appeared before her.

He went up and down, his head sunk, his full lips compressed, his arms tense. He was, devil take it! not the man to make sacrifices. He gave far and wide, he scattered gifts around him, because he was generous and a great lord and cavalier. But sacrifices? No one had ever made sacrifices to him; in human life steel met steel, hammer struck on anvil, and whoever was afraid or soft-hearted had to remain below and let the others spit on his head. He had no fear, either before the surly populace, or insolent great lords, or an eventual Lord God. Nevertheless, to make a sacrifice in this one case would be like a titillating voluptuous smart; then one could appear before the child resplendent, and even an eye which had only been accustomed to flowers and the clear heavens would be able to find not the tinest fleck in one.

But how much would be lost for ever if he made the sacrifice! It was senseless, it was, politically speaking, sheer idiocy, to save Jecheskel Seligmann, simply to drive away a few perplexing thoughts from the child's mind. His marriage with the Portuguese lady would go under, his ennoblement would go under, a good piece of the solid ground on which he stood, would go under. No, no! And even supposing it were an indication and a sign, he would not yield so far, he would not fling away for the mood of a child so much that had been won in blood.

In his heart he knew he would do it. In his heart he knew it from the first moment he saw Rabbi Gabriel. And he had great difficulty in preventing certain inchoate fancies, which ever again thronged up in his mind, from becoming pictures only too comprehensible; how from now on he would impress the whole of Jewry, how over all Europe he would be exalted and lauded as the first Jew in the Roman Empire, how he would bring to pass a deed unique and inconceivable, to snatch away from a whole city of Christians, he, a single Jew, an unfortunate man.

And while these vain and swelling pictures thronged up in his mind, he found it difficult to play before himself the grave drama of his sacrificial resolve.

Next day he went to the Duke. He was less ceremonious than usual, less deferential, and made his demands more urgently. He maintained that it did not accord with the duke's dignity to leave one of his Jews without further protest to the mercies of the Esslingers; Süss's authority, too, suffered under the continual scorns and jeers of that insolent people. Karl Alexander burst out rudely, he should leave him in peace with his idiotic Jewish tales, he had had sufficient annoyance over them with his Parliament, he was called down through the whole Empire as a pro-Semite, and now Süss should hold his impudent tongue. But against his custom Süss stuck to his theme; he did not weaken, but, in spite of the Duke's renewed outcries, went on piling up his arguments. He requested that at least the judgment of Johann Daniel Harpprecht, the first jurist in the country, should be heard on the competence of the Esslinger trial, if he, Süss, was to continue his arduous and dangerous labours for the Duke. For if his authority were to be weakened further as it had been by the Esslingers, he would humbly have to beg to be released from his functions. Scarlet and breathing heavily, Karl Alexander growled out that he could go to the devil.

Süss went away pleased and smiling. He knew that these were phrases; to-morrow the Duke would behave as if nothing had happened. Karl Alexander could not dispense with him, he would have to consent, would have to grant him the favour. So he divulged the same day to Rabbi Gabriel that he had as good as secured the release of Jecheskel Seligmann, swaggered and boasted, saying what a great burden this had cast on him. While, garru-lous and magnificent, he set this forth to the stonily silent cabbalist, the Duke, coming from parade in full uniform with cross and band burst suddenly into the cabinet. Was it chance that he encountered the Magus now? Had he heard of his presence, and did he want to have things as once before in Wildbad? At any rate, he was there now, filling the cabinet with noise and glitter and din. Eh, how he valued himself, he cried with assumed affability to the Magus. Or perhaps he absolutely refused to take the horoscope of the uncircumcised? Süss interposed, poured oil on the waters. The Duke was referring to the horoscope, showing his fortune with women; he, Süss, had written several times and pressingly to his uncle about it. He had in fact written once only, and then but tentatively, lightly touching it; but Rabbi Gabriel grasped how things stood. He remained silent, however, looked in the urgent, slowly-darkening face of the Duke, and was silent.

228

At last the Duke pulled himself together again, and asked, always with an assumed, supercilious jocularity, whether perhaps his destiny with women might have some connection with the fatal denouement which the Magus on their first encounter foretold, or more correctly, did not foretell? The Duke expected no answer to this question; even Süss expected that his uncle would give none. But Rabbi Gabriel, his stony eyes ever on the Duke, responded with a surly, grumbling, emphatic "Yes." Karl Alexander, not prepared for such a round answer, felt his heart thump, breathed heavily: silence lay thick and oppressive in the room. At last, still with faint mockery, Karl Alexander exclaimed: See there, now he had his answer; broke off and spoke of other things. He threw at Süss: Yes, the reason he had come; he had charged Harpprecht to prepare a judgment on his rascally Esslinger Jew. What an affliction and a nuisance the fellow was! He called for his coach and departed in an ill mood, after a bad and scandalous witticism about the bust of Moses.

The Duke gone, Süss preened himself magnificently. Now he had the Jew, Jecheskel Seligmann Freudenthal, happily out of the hands of Edom. What till now had never been accomplished in the Holy Roman Empire, Süss had achieved. Did his uncle regard his life and great labours now as vanity and catching at straws? Was not the act which he had done now in itself a sufficient justification for one's life? And what if this deed, this achievement were only one pearl in a chain of pearls? If his whole life, interpreted in this light, were nothing but renunciation, the working out of a pious, ultimate idea?

He paused in his walk through the room, clamped himself faster to this thought. It pleased him, the man of the moment, the grand comedian of his own personality, to contemplate his life sentimentally from this standpoint. He forced himself to believe in a deep, fateful, pious meaning for his life, to find in his rise to power a lesson and a symbol. Full of ardour he strode to and fro, with the low and mysterious tones of his practised voice striving to convince the silent listener. With persuasive eloquence, with the diligence with which he might plead a State's plea, he fired off before the Rabbi a brilliant display of pious vanity.

If he had only thought of making a career for himself, why,

tell him, should he have remained a Jew? Why, then, had he not let himself be baptized like his brother? No, his uncle did him great injustice, if he regarded his life so pettily and contemptuously. Certainly not through mere lust for gold or power did he stand there, on such a lofty, envied and perilous station.

He clasped the idea to him, for it flattered him; he had suggested it to himself so as to be able to suggest it to the other. He played before himself almost more than before the other, destiny, conviction, a mission. How? What if he had been chosen out to avenge Israel on Edom? It could not be blind chance that he stood there like Joseph, whom Pharaoh had exalted. If he was so high now, and in great splendour, so that those who were used to spit on Israel and tread it beneath their feet, and draw their robes aside when they met a Jew, had to bend their backs before him and lick the dust—was not that revenge? To-day he hung over the country, the Jew, and sucked of its blood and grew fat on its marrow. And if one of his people were oppressed, his hand was over him to shield him, and Edom slunk away, his tail between his legs like a beaten hound. Was that not sufficient core and meaning and justification for a life?

But Rabbi Gabriel was silent, and when he regarded the silent man, Süss's flowing periods became ever more halting, and at last they fell into blank silence. He stood there as tongue-tied as a school boy who has learned his lesson badly and cannot repeat it to the end, and his words were like a poor, ill-smelling cosmetic, quickly drying up and falling off in scales.

The cabbalist did not reply to Süss's long, fiery and high-flown speech. He stood up and said: "Before you show yourself to the child, go to your mother in Frankfurt."

With that he went. Süss remained in dull rage. Now he had made his sacrifice, now he had accomplished the deed. What did the old man want of him still? What more could he do? Why was he silent over his achievement, with his arrogant, belittling silence? And what was this about Frankfurt? Oh, certainly he would go to Frankfurt, to his mother. The Frankfurters would have more appreciation of what he had done. His mother would hang on his words admiringly. And the Frankfurt Jews, the wise little Rabbi Jaakob Joshua Falk, and the other prominent

230

men and all, how he would sun himself in their whispered praises, their blessings and wonderment! Let Rabbi Gabriel keep silence—ten thousand other mouths would only speak the louder and bear witness for him and his deed.

In his library, sitting over deeds and documents, Professor Johann Daniel Harpprecht smiled amiably and knowingly at his friend, the Privy Councillor Bilfinger. In the spacious solidly-furnished room the sun slanted a shaft of light in which danced a myriad of motes.

Both these influential men had discussed seriously and exhaustively the affairs of Württemberg, in particular the desire of the Estates Committee, advocated with great prolixity and zeal, and brought forward by Weissensee, in no circumstances to mix themselves in the Esslingen affair. "Look you, brother," said Harpprecht, and laid his hand on his friend's massive shoulder; "it would warm my heart more, too, if I could let the Jew Jecheskel remain sitting in the mud and wipe out part of our account with Süss; and I would not grudge Weissensee his triumph. And when I reflect what we will have to pay in compensation for the release of this stinking Jew, and what in emoluments and well-earned claims we will have to fling into the greedy maws of the Esslingen shopkeepers, while we will have no return for it except the pleasure of being slandered and jeered at over the whole Empire as pro-Semites, brother, I need not say to you that the gall rises in me to think of it. But the Duke has asked me for a juristic verdict, not a political one. And if I were twice as vexed over it, if I were doubly willing to fling all the compendiums and commentaries in the Jew's insolent, filthy face, Jecheskel belongs to us; and if right and justice are to prevail, then all the small points that could be casuistically interpreted *in contrarium* count for nothing. As jurist I must adjudge; Jecheskel must be handed over to the Ducal authority."

Bilfinger bowed his massive head. He had known it, all had known it; the Duke, too, had certainly known it, and when he had commanded Harpprecht to give his judgment the matter was already settled. But it would have been fine if Harpprecht had decided differently. The Duke would probably still have demanded

231

the release, but the Jew would have received a shrewd knock. "He stands secure up there," he groaned, "and laughs to see how we must constrain ourselves to do him a favour."

But he made no further appeal, he knew that the jurist would hack off his fingers before he would insert one word in a judgment that would deviate one hair's-breadth from justice. He parted from his friend, saddened and without hope, but with a warm and friendly hand-grasp.

Alone, Harpprecht was not disposed to sit down again to his labour. He filled his glass anew, gazed at the slanting pillar of light and the dancing motes, and thought. He was accustomed to survey things from a height. He set the case in perspective. He saw beyond the frontiers of the Duchy. He saw the affair of the petty Jewish trader as a wave in the ocean of European events and forces.

For the petty Jewish pedlar, tortured, lying under an arbitrary accusation of murder, and Süss, the omnipotent, universally-envied Finance Minister, an important factor in the calculations of the Courts of Europe, rocked on the same wave. How strangely the lot of these two was bound together! Had Süss not been pre-eminent and in favour the Esslingers would certainly have let the poor devil go. Had Süss not been pre-eminent and in favour he could not have secured the poor devil's release. What bound the Finance Minister to the Jewish pedlar? The same blood? Stuff and nonsense! A common faith? Pooh! Nothing was in common between the two, except one thing: the hatred that raged against the great Jews as against the small.

Reflectively Harpprecht dipped into the chronicles and historical documents of Gabelkhover, Magnus Hessenthaler, Johann Ulrich Pregizer, and into the ordinances, rescripts and governmental resolutions which lay piled before him. Therein was shown how hitherto the Jews had been dealt with in the country; there were the legislative measures of the Swabian Dukes and Estates concerning the Jews; there were the history and the rights of the Swabian Jews.

From ancient times they had been there. Ever again they had been accused of murder, poisoning wells, blaspheming the Host, and above all of their intolerable usury, corrupting the people.

232

Ever again they had been butchered and their claims declared null and void, in Calw, in Weil the Stadt, in Bulach, Tübingen, Kirchheim, Horb, Nagold, Oehringen, Cannstadt, Stuttgart. But ever again·they had been recalled. Throughout the whole Empire their goods should be seized, so it stood in an imperial decree, and their lives in addition, and they should be slain except for a small number who should remain immune, so that their memory might survive. Another time, in a decree of the Consistorial Court, it was declared that next to the devil Christians had no greater enemies than the Jews. In a treaty between the German Emperor and Count Ulrich the Much-Beloved, measures were promulgated on account of the manifold complaints against the Jews, who in accordance with their usual recalcitrancy did excessively and intolerably oppress through their usury the spiritual and temporal subjects of the Empire, and did also conduct themselves in such a disorderly and stubborn manner that thereby disunion, war and confusion did arise. And in the last testament of Count Eberhard the Bearded, the Jews were declared to be hateful to God the Almighty, Nature and the Christian dispensation, despicable and offensive, as gnawing worms, to the poor man destructive and intolerable, and for the honour of God the Almighty and the common good they were sent with sharp rebuke out of the country.

But why, after all these judgments, were they ever allowed back into the Duchy, or called back into it? Why did Eberhard the Quarrelsome protect them and Count Ulrich? Why, when Eberhard the Bearded, and the dukes, Ulrich, Christoph, Ludwig, drove them out, did Friedrich the First and Eberhard Ludwig call them back again into the country? It was too easy to call them an accursed people, spurned by God. Why could one not be indifferent to them as to other foreigners, the French immigrants, for instance, who had come in? Why did they always repel or attract, or even were loathsome and charming at once?

Johann Daniel Harpprecht raised his head from his papers. In the dancing dust of the slanting shaft of sunlight the image of the Duke and that of the Jew formed before his eyes, the one mysteriously melting into the other. Both of them of ill-omen. Against the Duke there was a bulwark, the Constitution; but it was full of holes and profited nobody. Against the Jew there were

233

laws, rescripts; but they were of no use. The gnawing worms, so it stood in the decrees, the prohibitions. The land decayed; poverty, misery, hatred, corruption, despair broke in. The gnawing worms crawled over the land, fed on its marrow, gnawed and waxed fat. Up above, melting into each other, the Duke and the Jew, strutting in arrogant, stall-fed nakedness, iridescent, voluptuous.

The simple, direct, matter-of-fact man sat in great confusion of thought. Here it was so difficult to find firm ground; these Jews and all they implied were disturbing and enigmatic. To drive them out availed nothing, for they would always be called back again; no, not even the primitive measure of exterminating them brought any solution. The enigma continued to torture one even after that, and then, suddenly, one could not tell from where, it would emerge again.

You see a Jewish pedlar; he goes about, waddling, hideous, filthy, bent, secretive, crooked in body and soul; you have a feeling of loathing for him, and take care not to brush against his unclean caftan; but sometimes in his countenance an immemorial, wide world opens its eyes and gazes at you mildly and in perplexity, and the lousy pig of a Jew, even now so wretched that you might have trampled him in the mud with your stout boots, lifts himself like a cloud, and hovers over you, lofty, smiling, unattainably distant.

It was discomforting, disgusting, to think that such a dirty rag-and-bones Jew should be of the seed of Abraham. It was disturbing, a vexation, that a world-renowned philosopher like Benedict Spinoza should belong to the accursed race. It was as if this race had resolved to demonstrate by way of example how high a man might raise himself, even to the stars, and how deep he might sink in the slime.

Gnawing worms. Gnawing, noxious worms. Professor Johann Daniel Harpprecht forced himself back to his papers, but behold, the good, reasonable man had the face of a dreamer. The letters themselves turned into worms, crawling, loathsome, elongating, moist, clammy, with the heads of the Duke and Süss. Gnawing worms, gnawing worms. He made a wry mouth and spat.

234

He steered his thoughts into the sphere in which apparitions and hallucinations can most easily be brought to book, into his particular sphere, that of political economy. What kept the Jews alive was economic necessity. The world was changing. Once a man's worth was determined by rank and birth, now it was determined by money. When they had made the despised and hated race the monopolists and controllers of money, they had flung them the line by means of which they were to climb so high. Now the money machine had become the living blood of the State and of Society, and the Jews were the most important wheel in this machine, were the starting and decisive point in all the complicated machinery. Take this wheel away, Society and State would go to pieces. The Duke, badge and symbol of the old order, of rank and of birth, and the Jew, badge and symbol of the new order of money, reached their hands to each other, were linked together, fell upon the people in concert, and sucked their marrow, the one for the other.

Gnawing worms, gnawing worms. Sighing deeply, Harpprecht turned again to his work. Before the onset of his firm will the loathsome brood changed again into clear, dry letters, and incisively, carefully, deliberately, formally, he wrote down his judgment.

AFTER stiff bargaining and against fat compensations, the Esslingers handed over the Jew Jecheskel Seligmann to the Ducal Court, outwardly with deep curses, but inwardly very pleased. The Württemberg justices, after a few days, set him free. Broken, tottering, deranged by the horror of awaited death and of the rack, Jecheskel returned to Freudenthal, for the rest of his life a wreck, struck to the marrow by his experience. Frequently he was subject to a nervous twitching which shook him, made his shoulders work and his arms flap absurdly to and fro, and distorted his face; often too, he suddenly whimpered, or howled softly, like an animal. Other Jews took care of him, and sent him out of the country to Amsterdam.

Before he left Germany he wrote the Finance Minister to ask if he might speak to him, to thank him. Süss considered, hesitated. It would have been a triumph to parade before the Stuttgarters the booty which he had torn from the Esslingers. But, on the other hand, that booty looked so shabby and decayed, the Stuttgarters, if they did not curse openly, would at least make coarse witticisms, and then he did not dare aggravate the Duke further, who was angry and vexed over the whole business, by a public display of Jecheskel. With a grand gesture therefore he renounced the pleasure of receiving the thanks of the released prisoner in person. But, as had been his custom latterly, he did not let the real grounds for this decision appear, but strutted in front of himself; it was proved now that he had done the deed not for the sake of thanks, but out of the purest and noblest motives!

All the more richly he fattened his vanity in Frankfurt. Eh, how the Jews thronged the narrow streets of the Ghetto to see him, how they muttered their admiration, called all the blessings of God down upon him, lifted up their children, that with their exotic, beautiful, oval eyes they might drink in his holy and gladdening image. As over a carpet he walked amid their boundless admiration and good wishes. Eh, what a redeemer and great sage had the Lord, praised be His name, sent Israel now in its dire need. And he stood in the synagogue, and they called upon him to read the Scriptures, and while the hum which usually filled the crowded hall was so still that the tense silence of those newly delivered from terror almost burst asunder the walls, the withered Rabbi in his quavering voice let the beautiful, tender, old blessings fall over him as from a noble urn of warm and goodly-smelling water.

There was only one who did not surround him with her admiration so softly and eagerly as he had expected; his mother. She, usually his humblest, most devoted supporter, appeared on this occasion curt, anxious, constrained; certainly she found ever new praises for him, how great and lordly and slender and rich and high-spirited and elegant and clever and profound and powerful he was, how rich he was in all the gifts of the world, in money and courage and beauty of form and nobility and the admiration of women. But she was not so absorbed in him as usual. The great, foolish eyes in the beautiful, pale face would suddenly be averted from him as if in deep fear; her hands, which had loved to fondle her clever, elegant, very powerful son, were without explanation withheld. The beautiful, cheerful, light-hearted old lady, who loved to chatter, was, against her nature, disturbed, nervously afraid, repressed.

While they sat together, constrained, the air heavy about them, Rabbi Gabriel appeared. Michaele sprang to her feet with a little cry, and lifted her hands as if in supplication and wavering defence.

"Have you given it to him?" asked the Cabbalist. Michaele, white, her eyes wide open, retreated a step.

"Give it to him now!" said the Rabbi, without raising his voice, but in such a way that opposition died. Michaele went, with tottering limbs, stifling her sobs.

"What is this?" asked Süss, taken aback, annoyed. "Why do you torment her, what do you want of her?"

"You have told me," replied the Rabbi, "what you intend to present before the child as your meaning and justification. I take your justification in my hand and show it to you as it really is."

Dragging, as if drawn unwillingly, Michaele returned. She brought a packet of papers—letters, as it appeared.

"Must I remain?" she asked painfully, in a small voice which seemed full of fear.

"No, go!" said the Rabbi, almost kindly.

As soon as she had hurriedly disappeared Süss hesitatingly lifted the papers, held them in his hand, undecided, at last began to read. Gallant letters, slightly old-fashioned, indifferent stuff. He wondered, he did not understand. What was it about? At last he saw light, put two and two together, gazed up from the papers as if struck by a sudden, startling illumination, and glanced towards the Rabbi. He was not here; Süss was alone in the room.

He sprang up, and walked up and down; his eyes clear, again darkened, again clear; flying clouds, then sun, then night over his face. Rambling, absurd movements with his arms, his feet reeling as if drunken. Senseless, disconnected words; then, while his whole body stiffened, a clear phrase. And again he had fallen back, slack, tottering, all his limbs helpless. Overmastered, he was like a comedian learning a rôle which lifted him to all the stars and dashed him down into the deepest abysses—till he collapsed like a sack, seated, his mind working feverishly, his face and limbs motionless. A long, eternal space, as if dead.

Thus, then, everything fitted in. Thus, in one flash, all these shadowy, dark corners had become clear. They, the accursed, magic-practising Rabbi and his mother, had betrayed him, scurvily, contemptibly, infamously, in having hidden this and wrapped it in mystery for so long. It was an evil jest, a truly Jewish, malicious, rascally trick to bind him so long to this shabby, miserable, common, ridiculous and despised community. It was true that, God be thanked, by means of his genius and his inborn noble blood, he had not allowed himself to be kept under. His genius had flowered magnificently in spite of every wretched repression and prohibition. But how many maddening, self-poisoning humiliations, how many degrading, tortuous paths he might have been spared, how many bizarre, idiotic edges and corners might have become smooth and straight, if they had not criminally left him in this false and vulgar rank and faith.

But how? Steady now! No agitation! Weigh everything quietly and consider it. Did his way really lie so smooth and obvious before him now?

So the petty musician and comedian, Issachar Süss, had not been his father. It was clearly and irrefragably proved that his father was Georg Eberhard von Heydersdorff, baron and Field Marshal. He was not of poor blood, his *allure,* his *tenue,* his temperament, had not been adopted arbitrarily, were not conned and artificial. His chivalrous instincts, his rise, his aristocratic, noble view of life, were self-evident and broke inevitably through all trammels, for they came from his blood and his innermost nature. He was a Christian and an aristocrat by birth.

Bastard? Well, they were the most capable and the best who were conceived in those wild beds of unbridled desire, where no cold and prudent consideration was interposed between flower and fruit. If not on the throne itself, then on the highest places round it, there sat, everywhere in Europe, bastards. It was to the honour of his father that he had chosen as the mother of his son no sour aristocrat, but the beautiful Jewess.

Heydersdorff, his father; Georg Eberhard von Heydersdorff. A beautiful name. A wild name. A bloody, calamitous, fatal name. He knew portraits of this man. In fine shamelessness his

238

mother had hung his picture in her room, even when the man was slandered and hunted from pillar to post. How often as a boy he had stood before the picture of the grand general! With that name his mother had taught him to speak first; the sonorous name of Georg Eberhard von Heydersdorff was among the first which the precocious child could utter without making a mistake; his mother had put a sugar lump into his mouth when he succeeded for the first time. Ah, so it was from him that he had his chestnut-brown hair, from him that he had the aristocratic, slender figure; and it had been that red fine uniform that had dazzled him, had ever drawn him on towards the height which so fabulously he nad scaled.

Georg Eberhard Heydersdorff; a fate which ascending abruptly in triumph had plunged precipitately down again. Field Marshal, distinguishing himself in the Turkish Wars, leader of the Order of German Knights at Heilbronn, commander at Heidelberg in the French War. After the fall of the fortress, envy and jealousy dragged him before the court martial. He had surrendered it hastily, had shown cowardice; he should have held it until the arrival of Ludwig from Baden. Death sentence. The Emperor pardoned him. But how? The boy had seen pictures showing how the pardon was consummated. Even now he could still see every detail of the picture. Along the right bank of the Neckar the jealous Margrave had stationed troops. How rigidly he held himself on his lean horse! That was his father who was paraded there in front of the whole Imperial Army. An endless line; the soldiers went through the unending list of their evolutions. And his father crouched in the hangman's cart, driven out with curses from the Order of German Knights, all his honours taken from him, and conducted by the Heilbronn executioner and his menials.

He had seen still other prints and wood-cuts which had been hawked around. But they were not so clear in his memory. In one he could see quite distinctly still a sword being broken. That was evidently when, before the regiment which carried his name, the Field Marshal had his death sentence read, and its commutation to banishment. As a traitorous knave he was banished from Austria and Swabia. The executioner tore the sword from his side, struck the delinquent three times over the face with it, and broke it. Loudly lamenting the exile was conveyed over the Neckar in a skiff.

For the rest there remained rumours. He had fled to the Capucins in Neckarsulm, had died as a Capucin in Hildesheim. His mother certainly knew more. In any case his name was no longer in bad odour. The sentence had been the result of jealousy and injustice. To the people, Heydersdorff the soldier was a hero, Heydersdorff the monk, a martyr.

Such was the man, then, who was his father. A wild name, a wild destiny. The Cabbalist might divine all his fate from the excessive and restless star of his father.

Away with those dreams! Send them packing! What now? What would happen now? What would he do now?

He would go to the Duke with these papers, request legal recognition, acknowledgment of his Christian birth. Perhaps he would go himself to Vienna. He would press through now without difficulty his ennoblement; he would then be High Steward in all the forms, even President of the Council. This he would be. Yes, but then?

Would he be other then, than he was now? It would be easier for him to get his hand into the Catholic project. The Lord Bishop of Würzburg would no longer remain taciturn before him, the impudent mouths of the officers would be closed. To the actual possession of power he would have added its name and its appearance. Yes, and then?

Would he be more then than he was now? He would be less. There were scores of diplomatists in the Empire such as he would be then. The singular thing, the unique, the unexampled, which was his now, would not be there. Now he was the Jewish Minister. That was something. People laughed, people jeered; but under their laughter they disguised their appreciation, their admiration. That an aristocrat should be minister, was that much? But a Jew, who climbs so high and alone; that is more than a score of aristocrats. Should he throw this away? What for? To what end? Yes, he should have consented long before this to be baptized. Then perhaps he might have achieved more than if now he declared himself as a Christian by birth. To be a Christian, that was to be one among many. But there was only one Jew for every six hundred Christians. To be a Jew, that meant to be despised, persecuted, humiliated, but also to be unique, always knowing that all eyes were upon one, always to be on the strain, tense, gathered up, every sense alive and on the alert.

Why did the Rabbi show him these papers now, without warning, when he was well on into the second half of his life? Did he not want to accord him the triumph which he had won over the affair of Jecheskel Seligmann? Did they seek with their cunning to trick him of his most precious heritage? Slyly and despitefully to lie in wait for his worthiest possession?

The great magnate saw himself involved in an affair where he could not get any further with mere figures and calculations, where even his adroit art of reading men was defeated. What the devil did this Rabbi want in laying the papers before him now? What was his intention? If Süss appeared now as a Christian, what would Rabbi Gabriel gain by it? He could not detach himself from his business principles according to which in every transaction the man tries to win something for himself, and to cheat his opponent.

The Polish Jews, even the lousiest of them, if they would be baptized, would be held in honour. Why did they not do so? Why did they disdain, these cunning chafferers, such an easy advantage, letting themselves be butchered rather than take it? Piety? Faith? Conviction? Could there be anything, then, in these words? And was it conceivable that one of these filthy Polish Jews possessed the things which were hidden behind these profound and sonorous words? Was it conceivable that one of these wretches was wiser in his primitive feeling, better prepared for a shadowy beyond, than he in his intricate adroitness? He felt himself as unsure as a child, and without counsel or help.

To-day he was the first among the German Jews. They lifted up their children when he passed in the street, and moved deeply and with urgent voices called down upon him all the blessings of Heaven. He thought of when he had stood in the synagogue, amid the intense silence of a crowd usually talking and vivacious, the gentle, quavering blessings of the Rabbi falling round him; and a warm, sweet, languid feeling overcame him. It needed decision, he had to set his teeth, to renounce all that. Whenever he had won a triumph then, truly, it had been fine to parade it before his jeering enemies, to fling it in their wry faces; it had been good to shine with this triumph before the women, before Magdalen Sibylle; but the fullest triumph of all had been to display it before Isaac Landauer in the Judengasse and before his mother. There without fear of spiteful words and looks, one could savour one's success in comfort, drink it to the drains, and know that in their hearts the others rejoiced with him. There one was at home, there one could expand and blossom in deportment, gestures, words. There one was at rest and softly-bedded.

His mother. She had then—how did they put it?—gone astray. Strange that through this she had not changed for him even by a hair. Him whom he had held to be his father, the gentle-hearted, courteous, quick, worthy, engaging singer and comedian, him he ought certainly to despise. Extraordinary; he could evoke no feeling for him but tenderness. How that man must have loved his mother, when he never made her suffer for the bastard! He had never heard one evil word from him to her. And how gentle and sympathetic and fatherly had that man been all his life to Süss himself. To think of him except as his father was impossible.

And his noble impulse in the affair of Jecheskel Seligmann, his sacrifice, that was all self-deception, then, hypocrisy? He had acted it all before himself? He shied at the thought. The exultation which he felt then, when he had achieved the deed, that ineffable floating on air and deliverance from himself and soaring and flowing away; that must all have been deceit and vanity? And that about Edom, the revenge on Edom, that was only wind, pretty speeches, to get the ear of the Rabbi? But all the same it had lifted him beyond his limitations, out of himself! Yes, he had believed in it, he had known, in spite of all, that it was true! And the child? If he had not been shown these papers, then he would have gone to the child with this lie, would have believed himself in the lie, and through that would have seduced the child, too, into believing in the lie. No, no, that was not possible. What he felt then, himself as the champion of Judah against Edom, its guardian and avenger, that must have been an honourable and unsullied feeling. That was already his life's meaning and motive principle. Yes, he was his mother's son, not his father's.

But that he only felt himself at home amid magnificence and power? It was by right, it was on account of his ancestry and his blood, that things bent themselves to his will! That gold, splendour, power, came to him of themselves, fitted him like a robe carefully prepared for him, was his rightful inheritance from his father. It was this that drew the Duke to him, so that without fear he laid his heart in Süss's hand. He was his father's son. It was his right and his duty to emerge from the ranks of the needy and the despised, to stand acknowledged in the light, to lay his hand upon his name, inheritance and position.

His thoughts perplexed him. What was he to do? Where recognize himself? Power drew him with golden cords, but the temptation to remain among the despised was as obstinate as it was soft and gentle.

He saw himself in a dream which he sometimes had. He saw himself treading a spectral dance; the Rabbi held one of his hands, the Duke the other. Was that not his father, the Field Marshal, who stalked before him, his epaulettes torn off, clattering along in time with his broken sword, waving towards Süss the deeds of his inheritance? But the monk behind there, the Capucin, that was also his father! Strange, that one could not tell whether it was a broken sword or a rosary which hung by his side. But the form that hopped along ridiculously in front in a caftan, with the towzled beard, that was Isaac Landauer. No, it was not Isaac Landauer, but Jecheskel Seligmann. He came to give his thanks, and he bowed himself grotesquely, and he curtsied deeply and kissed the hem of Süss's coat, and he was altogether comical and abased, as continuously he smiled out of his face distorted by the rack, and then, curtsying again, swept the ground with his caftan.

Süss tore himself violently out of his waking trance. He must see his mother now. He would not decide yet: one could get no further here with figures and calculations. And he had had enough of these thoughts, and he would have rest from these idiotic dreams; and he must see the face of his mother.

But when he went Rabbi Gabriel stopped him on the threshold

of her room. His massive face seemed less stony than usual; the furrows over his flat nose were less sharp, even his ill-humour seemed more frank, forthright, human.

"Will you arrest me?" he asked mockingly. "It will only help on your career if you hand me over to a Church Court for keeping a born Christian so long in the false faith."

And as Süss made an impetuous step forward: "Or will you accuse your mother? Give her a scolding because she has been silent so long? Or thank her because she gave you such a knightly father?"

A wild, senseless fit of rage rose in Süss. How came this man to assume without further thought that now he would slip cannily into the comfort of Christendom? How jeeringly he stood there with his melancholy grey eyes which looked down upon one as from a summit, as if he were a tutor detecting a dense pupil in some wretched, stupid evasion. Did he want now to gainsay his Jewish birth, annul his sacrifice, his great intuitions, as rhetoric and lies, and cheat him out of his best possession?

His indignation against the Rabbi, stupid as it was, was honourable. For the first time, he divined, he was, without casuistry, in the right; for the first time the other scorned him without reason. The disabling constriction which the Rabbi always imposed upon him had disappeared, and suddenly his decision was there, which for so long had concealed itself formless in the darkness; it sprang clear and certain into the light, was there, self-evident, impregnable.

His voice frank and emphatic, he said: "I am going to Hirsau. To Naemi."

Taken unawares the Rabbi advanced towards Süss. His face clearer, half incredulous, he asked almost good-humouredly: "As avenger on Edom?"

But Süss remained calm. Without irritation, steadily and firmly, he said: "She wants to see me; I will go to her."

Rabbi Gabriel took his hand, looked into his face, and saw impurity, untruth, corruption, but under these something else, under skin, flesh and bone something else, for the first time something clear and bright.

"So be it!" he said, and again his voice rang as ill-tempered as ever. "Come with me to the child!"

244

Book Four

THE DUKE

Book Four

THE DUKE

By the Lake of Tiberias the Master of the Cabbala, Rabbi Isaak
Luria, walked with his favourite pupil, Chajjim Vital Calabrese.
The men drank out of the Fountain of Miriam, fared out on the
Lake. The Master spoke of his wisdom. The Spirit brooded over
the waters, the skiff stood still. It was a marvel that it did not sink,
for heavy with the lives of millions was the Rabbi and his word.

Back to the Fountain of Miriam the men returned again. And
again they drank. Then suddenly the fountain changed its course.
It formed a bow in the air, with two vertical rays, a cross ray
above them. Into the bow strode the Rabbi to be a third vertical
ray. So out of him and the Fountain came the character Shin,
the beginning of the most exalted of the names of God, Shaddai.
And the character waxed, and spanned itself over the lake, and
spanned itself over the world. When the pupil Chajjim Vital returned out of his trance, the fountain flowed as before, but the
Rabbi Isaak Luria was no longer there.

But this middle column in the sacred character was the only
thing he had written down of his learning. For the words of his
wisdom fell from his lips and were like snow. They were there,
they were white and glittered and were cooling; but no one could
catch hold of them. So his wisdom fell from his mouth and no one
could lay hold upon it. The Rabbi did not write it down and did
not even suffer that others should write it. Because what is written
is changed, and becomes the death of the spoken word. Therefore,
even the Scriptures are not the word of God, but a mask and a
distortion, what wood is to the living tree. Only in the mouth of
the wise does it rise up and live.

Yet after the Rabbi had gone, his pupil could not refrain from

247

setting down his wisdom on paper in the vain and lying symbols of the written word. And he wrote the Book of the Tree of Life, and he wrote the Book of the Metamorphoses of the Soul.

Oh, how wise had been the Master in that he had not soiled his knowledge with the written word, in that he had not twisted his wisdom by means of the evil magic of letters! Elias, the prophet, had appeared to him by day, Simon ben Jochai by night. The language of birds had been revealed to him, of trees, of fire, of stone. The souls of the buried he could see and the souls of the living when on Sabbath Eve they soared to Paradise; also he could decipher the souls of men on their brows, draw them to him, speak with them, and then release them again to return to their places. The Cabbala had opened itself widely before him, so that the bodies of things were like glass to him; he saw in One, body, spirit and soul; air, water and earth were full of voices and shapes, he saw God's shuttle weaving the world, the angels came and held discourse with him. He knew that over all there was mystery, but for him mystery opened its eyes, fawned on him like an obedient dog. Marvels bloomed on his way. The Tree of the Cabbala entered into him and broke through him, its roots were deep in the bowels of the earth, its crest in Heaven fanned the countenance of God.

But oh, how this wisdom was changed in the books of his pupil! In wild confusion foolishness and wisdom sprouted from them. False prophets and Messiahs grew out of the characters; magic and thaumaturgy, wonders and miracles and harlotry and ostentation and falseness flowed from them into the world. The pallid countenance of Simon ben Jochai looked out of these characters, and in the thicket of his silvery beard lay snared and destroyed myriads of saints and holy men; and out of the symbols of these books gleamed naked and impudent the breasts of Lilith, and at her nipples hung lisping and babbling and with drunken senses the children of lust and of power.

And this is one passage from the secret wisdom of Rabbi Isaak Luria Aschkinasi:

"It may happen that in one human body more than one soul may suffer a new incarnation, and that at one time two, yea several souls, may unite themselves by means of this body in a new earthly fate. It may be that the one is balsam, the other poison; it may be that the one is an animal's, the other a priest's or devoted anchorite's. Now they are confined in one place, belonging to one body as the right and the left hand. They interpenetrate, they bite into each other, they impregnate each other, they flow into each other like water. But though ever bruising each other, recreating each other, always this union is the means by which one soul aids another, that the guilt might be expiated on whose account they suffer the new incarnation."

These are a few sentences from the secret wisdom of the Rabbi Isaak Luria, the eagle of Cabbalists, who was born in Jerusalem, for seven years mortified himself, alone, on the banks of the Nile, brought back his wisdom to Galilee and performed miracles among the people, never defiled his wisdom with writing and paper, and mysteriously vanished on the Lake of Tiberias in the thirty-eighth year of his life.

THE Lord Bishop of Würzburg travelled in comfort through the rich land. Leaning back luxuriously amid the soft cushions of the well-sprung carriage, the stout gentleman breathed in contentedly the mild scenes of the first fruit blossoms; everything swam in the young sunshine; tender and fresh the new green lay on field, tree and branch. The Bishop was travelling to Stuttgart for the baptism of the Crown Prince. He was in a jovial mood. What a splendid land! What a richly blessed land! It was made safe now for Rome and the Church.

Friedrich Karl von Schönborn, Lord Bishop of Würzburg and Bamberg, the first diplomatist of the Church, celebrated by the Catholics as the World Oracle, the German Ulysses, aspersed and slandered by the Evangelicals as a malignant serpent, a Haman and Herod, was a jovial, portly man. Very much a man of the world, at home equally at the Viennese and the Papal court, widely travelled and versatile, he had a comprehensive and kindly contempt for mankind, and he saw in a benevolent absolutism and a cheerful Catholicism the salvation of the world. The masses were dull, stupid, without intelligence; that was the will of heaven; God had so decreed it, and worldly wisdom demanded that one should take it into account. It was sad that there was so much misery in the world; yes, that was indeed to be deplored. But it sufficed if one occasionally gave it a sigh; forever to be lamenting over trouble or, blindly mistaken, to think of altering a law of nature such as this—that was a matter for fools and gloomy visionaries. He, Schönborn, had spent his best years in Italy, had learnt the arts of diplomacy in Venice; he loved the clear southern air, he found it again in his Würzburg. His Catholicism had its origin deep in his blood; his eating and drinking, the way he stood and walked, were Catholic. He saw the Church as he had seen it in Italy, when with all his senses he had drunk it in. The assemblies at the Vatican were a part of it, the diplomacy of Venice was a part of it, the Alban hills themselves were a part of it. All that was beautiful in the world, and that, thank God, was a great deal; masses and churches and wine and works of art and *coups d'état* and a beautiful sermon and a well-developed woman; all that was clear and cheerful in the world, was Roman and Catholic. But whatever was dull and warped and misty and cob-webby, was Evangelical, Saxon, Brandenburg. He did not hate Protestantism, for he hated nothing in the world. But he was deeply hostile to it. Its grey, utilitarian liturgy, its pale, pinched misty theology; these were like bad air, the rabble's wisdom, sterile growths. The Apostles themselves, if they returned, would understand nothing of the things about which these so-called theologians disputed. One could not breathe in that dull, grey world. But, *gloria in excelsis,* the mist was rising now from these cheerful Swabian fields; he, Friedrich Karl, had taken a good part in bringing into the land the clear Catholic air which was so much better for it. Now he was hastening to baptize a new Duke in the true faith. Oh, it was a well-ordered world! Oh, it was a pleasure to be alive! And joyously he breathed in the mild air and jested with his adroit councillors and flung coins to the children by the wayside and gazed benevolently on the pretty chambermaid at the inn. And his heavy body lolled comfortably, and his fat, clever face beamed cheerfulness on everybody around him.

But to the country his coming was like the rising of a blood-red full moon, presaging misfortune. Alas, the triumph they had won in the Stettenfels affair had only been a false dawn. Now it became clear that the country was encompassed, that the meshes

250

of the net had been drawn tight all round it. Of what avail were all these clauses and reciprocal rights against the hellishly sly arts of interpretation of the Würzburg councillors? And even if one opposed them, if one refuted them soberly point by point, it would not be of any use; for behind the Würzburgers stood the military, the bayonets of the Ducal army. If the Jew had seized their bodies and possessions, now came the Catholics and devoured their souls. Catholicism, that meant renunciation of everything, renunciation of every human and political liberty. That meant military absolutism, meant the destruction of all civic duty and capacity, meant a vast, stupefied mass of slaves and a tiny little excrescence of licentious and unbridled courtiers on top of it. Like a blind creature the country struck out around it on all sides. But it was a hopeless convulsion. The Jew had prepared the way well, and the Catholics found their path easy. Resigned and apathetic, overawed by the imperious bearing of the officials and the clattering of Catholic officers, the burghers slunk in the tap-rooms, and for the fresh arrival of the Würzburger had only impotent, jeering, apathetic laughter. Yes, there it was! Yes, they could see it! But their rage could find no further expression, and they all sat now like the pig-eyed pastry-cook Benz, venomous and helpless.

The Catholics suffered only one serious rebuff. The Sub-Committee of Eleven utilized a slight indisposition of Weissensee to elect in place of that equivocal man a trustworthy Evangelical and democrat, the State Councillor Moser, the publicist, who had distinguished himself so prominently in the Stettenfels affair. He was the youngest member of the Sub-Committee, but though just in the beginning of his thirties, was a busy man; ardent, consequential, with an adventurous desire for change, a lover of impetuous, great words and pathetic gestures, very accomplished with his pen, a passionate publicist. He wrote continuously and voluminously; there was no concern of the day or of eternity, on which he had not employed his tongue and his pen. At first sceptic, then Deist, he found amidst all this leisure to become an initiate and to range himself in the army of Luther, Arndt, Spener, Francke.

He had excited great attention by his swift and daring termination of the Stettenfels affair, and felt himself now to be the divinely-called redeemer of Württemberg. Trusting in his rhetoric, he resolved to go simply and without ceremony to the Duke, like Nathan the prophet to David, as man to man, and speak strongly and urgently to the conscience of his Prince. Convinced of the power and impressiveness of his personality, he begged for an audience and went full of hope, as publicist, advocate, prophet, in his best form, confident, keyed up to the occasion, like an actor congratulating himself on a well-practised part which he likes. But the audience was not up to his expectations. Karl Alexander received him in the presence of Süss. Moser did not allow this to divert him from his purpose. He spoke learnedly, earnestly, with conviction, brought forward moral theological arguments, examples out of sacred, ancient and modern history, tempered the theoretical with the practical, borrowed illustrations from nature; in short, he found himself irresistible. The Duke and the Jew listened attentively; when the orator, striding up and down in his ardour, found a chair in his way, the Duke removed it with his own hand, so that he might not be stopped in his flow. But when after twenty minutes the publicist took a breath, one arm curved and lifted in a fine gesture, the Duke clapped him on the shoulder and said appreciatively: "If the child that the Duchess is expecting is a boy you must ground him in rhetoric." Süss put in a few observations on the difference between German and Latin eloquence. And when, dumbfounded and sweating, the publicist was dismissed by the grinning Karl Alexander, he had to own: "Poor land! Poor Fatherland! No, not even I can help you!"

Thus the Bishop had reason to be in the best of moods as he drew near to Stuttgart. The baptism under such favourable auspices of the heir to the Swabian throne was a triumph for Catholic policy which would have reverberations far beyond the Württemberg frontiers. It was therefore celebrated with the greatest solemnity and amid an impressive assemblage of Catholic princes and nobles. The Pope recognized the occasion by decorating the Duchess, by the hand of a special ambassador, with the Cross of the Order of Malta. Besides her only two ladies possessed this decoration; the Queen of Spain, and the Princess Ucella in Rome.

Elegant and pale, her face like a pastel, now quite transparent, Marie Auguste lay on her colossal bed. In spite of the refusal of her confessor, Süss's amulet with the primitive, menacing birds and the rough-hewn uncanny letters, lay under her pillow; she laughed maliciously when she thought how that would enrage the priest if he but knew. She was firmly convinced that only the amulet had saved her, for the delivery had been long drawn out and agonizing. Now that it was over she was terrified lest she might be permanently disfigured, and the physicians, Doctor Wendelin Breyer and Doctor Georg Burkhart Seeger, had always to be assuring her that not one scar, not one silvery wrinkle would be left on the body of Her Excellency. But more than to the consolations of the doctors she listened to those of old Barbara Holzin, who, tremendously knowing and authoritative, confirmed them. For the rest Marie Auguste found the situation in the highest degree comic. Curious and amused, she regarded this little human being whom she had brought into the world. So she had presented the country with an heir! She contemplated herself curiously in the mirror with the great frame of beaten gold; now she was to all intents and in the truest sense the mother of her people. It was curious, curious.

So the Lord Bishop of Würzburg baptized the heir-apparent, Crown Prince of Württenburg and Teck, Count of Mömpelgard, Count of Urach, Earl of Heidenheim and Forbach, etc., etc., by the name of Karl Eugene.

And the cannons roared, the bells chimed. Gala, fireworks. Free meats, free wine, to be eaten and drunk to the good fortune of the heir. And deeply as the people cursed over the Catholic heir-apparent, early in the afternoon there was no shred of meat left, and in the monstrous, numberless ranks of barrels not a drop of wine.

During these solemnities Süss remained severely in the shadow. Before, he had made up in every way he could think of to the Bishop and the Würzburg dignitaries; now it looked as if he intentionally avoided them. The Catholic plot, now the decisive centre of Swabian policy, lay wholly in the hands of the Würzburg diplomatists and the military. As these gentlemen had been prepared to find it difficult, and a business involving all sorts of quibbles and pretexts, to keep the Finance Minister out of it, they now saw with astonishment that he shunned everything connected

253

with the question. Earlier, recognizing that everything finally was related in some way to money, he had controlled, as Finance Minister, every tiniest wheel in the administrative machine; now he referred back almost everything that was laid before him, as not belonging to his province. The heads of the administration regarded him with suspicion, scented mysterious and dangerous motives in his policy, felt uncomfortable and apprehensive, thought that this apparent passivity masked the preparation for a great *coup*.

If, as once before, the indifference of the Jew was not brought home acutely to the Duke in a stoppage of his revenues, he had to thank for this the Palatinate Councillor who was now permanently about him, Dom Bartelemi Pancorbo. With frantic eagerness the haggard man with the purple, fleshless face flung himself on everything that Süss let out of his hands; dug himself firmly, menacingly, as if for eternity, into every post which the other resigned, threw himself greedily upon everything on which the other relaxed his hold. He managed, almost by himself, the difficult, complicated and confused finances of the Catholic Plot; in this way the chief control of affairs of state glided into his hands.

Süss withdrew, too, from the whirl of social life of which earlier he had been the vortex. Sometimes it would happen that after beginning an affair, he would break it off, weary and bored, before it came to a point. Among the countless women whom he had possessed, forsaken, and in part forgotten, were some who joined in the jeers which blackened him; there were some who preserved the memory as something titillating, forbidden but precious, like a jewel which, ah! only in a closed room before the mirror, one would dare to put on, and they were silent when he was mentioned; there were some who put themselves in his way when he rode by, smiled with wide eyes, remained standing until he was out of sight, and they did not set it against him that he had cast them off so soon, they thanked him daily for their brief hour, they cherished as their most precious possession the words which, who knew to how many, he had said and long since forgotten.

About this time Josef Süss began to take note of his secretary, Nicklas Pfäffle. He had always treated well the fat, even-tempered, slow and indefatigable lad, as one had, indeed, to treat such an unusually capable and dependable person. But that his man had, besides his capacity and reliability, other faculties, that he had impulses and experiences which had nothing to do with his master, Süss now for the first time had leisure to recognize. Nevertheless, he spoke to Nicklas Pfäffle much the same as before. It would have been impracticable, yes, quite impossible, to utter a word to the pale, stout youth which went beyond the matter of fact indispensable. But his tone was different, his glance different; he spoke as man to man.

Even the mare Assjadah felt that a changed master bestrode her. Perhaps he did not ride now in such great magnificence as before; perhaps the people round about him divined that his hand was no longer the only one on the lever of power; but the mare Assjadah felt that she was something different to him now from his clothes and his jewels and his furniture, that now he saw her eyes, and saw that one life flowed through him and her.

While in Stuttgart and Ludwigsburg they worked feverishly on the execution of the Catholic Plot, intrigued with the other Catholic courts and noblemen; concluded military treaties which should put the Estates in the wrong with Emperor and empire; strove to appease the Evangelical courts; while Pancorbo, seeking out new sources of revenue, ever pressed closer upon the province of the Jew, the enigmatical man retired completely from affairs, took a holiday, entrusted Nicklas Pfäffle with the management of the most important things, and left the capital unattended and for an unknown destination.

He went to Hirsau. During this unusual and solitary journey he saw himself as tremendously noble and exalted. To think that with one single word, with one single revelation, he could win the Duke over completely to him, plant himself in the centre of the Catholic Plot, and fling his malicious, triumphant, jeering rivals back to the periphery! To think that he had simply opened his hand and dropped as if it were worthless the painfully achieved, the unique, the final, most longed for goal in all the world. How noble he was, how unworldly, how proud in sacrifice!

Usually he chose times for his visits when he believed the Rabbi to be away, but now he sought his company. The unconditional devotion of the child seemed to him perfectly comprehensible, almost the due recompense of fate. Naemi, though the face, voice, bearing of her father on his first appearance had made the Master's slanders seem doubly empty and foundationless, was slightly confused by his new mask. She saw her father as Samson who had smitten the Philistines, as David who had slain Goliath. His new expression did not chime harmoniously with this, and, if but fleetingly, yet again and ever again, there broke into her vision that face which hung from the rich hair of Absalom entangled among the branches, and its features were those of her father.

In the silence of the white house with the flowery terraces Süss took his father's destiny in his hand, regarded it, turned it this way and that. In this long pause in his life the restless man was overcome by the old temptation. If now he acknowledged his paternity who would dare to blame him? He had shown sufficiently that he could be submissive; after such a trial had he not the right to emerge out of his submissiveness into the magnificence which rightly belonged to him? If he were to take his beautiful daughter by the hand, slip out of his mummery like an Arabian Khalif, and glittering, so that their jeers died, step out among his insolent opponents, not only the first of them in genius, no, a Christian as well, and a nobleman by birth?

Full and proud rose the tulips amid his dreams; a white, blinding square lay the house. Fleetingly appeared in his deliberations the strange, magical figures, the blocky Hebraic characters; the Divine Man stood abstract and motionless, the Cabbalistic Tree bloomed.

His father. In tumult he lived, in shame he fell, in the cloister he died. Verily, luck had forsaken him, life had driven him out; he had had no success. What remained for him but to search for his soul? Those who have no success must creep within themselves, turn their gaze inward. With him, Süss, things were otherwise. He had success. Life fawned on him, bowed to him, submissive.

He looked up. His uncle stood before him. Ho, had he been trying to surprise him? The slinker, the spy, hunting out every thought that he could use against one. Ah, he would never be able to live so free and unburdened again as he had done before. If he

256

did what was his natural good right to do, if he acknowledged himself as a Christian, forever he would feel, like an icy wind on the back of his neck, the disdain of this ridiculous, ill-clothed man. If he could only drive it out of his blood, the poisonously sweet, sickly allurement which this house sent out of other-worldliness and humility and renunciation!

Naemi came. And quickly he fled behind his mask of serenity and calm.

While he was torn hither and thither between this ostentatious humility which cramped him and this exacerbated thirst for action and glory, Nicklas Pfäffle unexpectedly arrived. He declared that a Ducal commission had confiscated Süss's books and moneys for the purpose of inspecting them. The Finance Director was suspected of a formidable series of frauds in his state and private affairs, and a strict examination had been ordered.

The enemies of Süss had utilized his absence as an opportunity for making a general advance. Of friends on whom he could depend he had hardly any left. The Court Chancellor Scheffer, the Privy Councillor Pfau, had gone over openly to the Catholic military party, and attacked him now in public. The Steward of Demesnes, Lamprechts, removed his boys from their service as pages in Süss's house, on the count that they were too old now. Remchingen, the two Röders, the general and the major, captains Laubsky and Tornacka, the chamberlain Neuffer, filled the Duke's ears perpetually with suspicions about the Jew. In Karl Alexander's entourage only Bilfinger and Harpprecht took no part in the persecution. To them these emissaries of the Jesuits were still more obnoxious than the Jew.

Now Dom Bartelemi Pancorbo had for a long time watched vigilantly Süss's trade in jewels. He represented to the Duke that the Jew made all his purchases in the jewel market in the Duke's name. The prices, however, were very variable; if they fell, then, often almost a year later, Süss declared them to be the property of the Duke; if they rose, then he kept them himself. So that the Jew threw all the risk upon the Duke, let his prince bear the loss, and put the profit in his own pocket. But to the great vexation of the Portuguese, these allegations made no impression on

257

Karl Alexander; he remarked equably that this only showed Süss was a Jew; for the rest he would be more on his guard in future. He was not in the least inclined to draw further inferences.

Extraordinarily enough it was quite an unimportant action of Süss that enabled his enemies to bring him down. The Finance Director had made the sweeping of chimneys a state service, arranging that in return for the payment of a general tax the authorities should undertake this function. This order had excited derision and discontent, and the chamberlain waved a lampoon about it before Karl Alexander, a crudely-illustrated broadside with the title: "Humble and grateful thanksgiving of the assembled witches and wizards to his Jewish Witchellence, Jew Josef Süss Oppenheimer, in the name of the universally respected and acknowledged great-grandmother of the United Night-Loving Society, the Witch of Endor."

While the Duke read this sheet he was overcome by the old memory. He saw himself treading that enigmatical, rhythmical dance, he heard the surly, ill-tempered voice of the Magus, he heard, heard physically, his silence, saw the silent man creep towards him, many-armed, formless. He wanted to be rid of this cursed sorcery. Why, then, did he keep the Jew? He had nothing but mockery and evasions from him. Purple in the face, fuming, one of his feet lame, he stamped up and down. He would show him, the scoundrel, the swindler, with his impostures and black art! Still hot and furious, he dictated the order which commanded the examination and strict scrutiny of the Finance Director's accounts and books.

And the Court Chancellor ran, the generals ran, the Portuguese ran, stretched his withered neck over the gigantic ruff, set to work with his purple, fleshless poll. The examiners crouched full of zeal, sweating, lost to everything else, goggling through their glasses, their pens rustling over sheets of paper. They calculated, pried, smelt about, built columns of figures, forests of figures. They shook them out, collected them together again. They spied, sniffed, sweated.

Meantime the Finance Director was driving post haste to Stuttgart, changing horses at every station. This inquisition, this blow, this fall, he saw as an opportunity. Luck, fate, had to be seized upon, compelled. If one did not embrace it with all one's faculties, if one did not direct intrepidly one's courage and will upon it, it broke down, it was lost. If the rabble in Stuttgart had not divined his lassitude, they would never have dared such an insolent attack.

Thus he had broken out stormily in his first excitement when he heard the news from Nicklas Pfäffle. He saw no more the stony massive face of his uncle, had no thought more whether out of the troubled grey eyes mockery or sorrow looked at him, wiped hastily from his mind his child's sorrow. One thing only he thought of; on horse-back, in his carriage, he considered it from all sides: what was to be done?

By the time his horse brought him in sight of the capital his decision was already clearly formed. Every step of his way, every word he would speak, was distinct in his mind. He would not be clever, or expedient, or politic. He would dare to challenge fate: go to the Duke, demand his demission. If the Prince granted it, good; fate had spoken. Then he would resign himself to live somewhere in retirement, bury himself as his father had done. If the Duke stuck to him, then, yes then—he would live as enemy, as avenger. Then he would pay back all his humiliations. His hands on the throats of his enemies! Throttle them! Strangle them!

At the court they had expected that Süss would defend himself, fawn with many words, turn advocate; or refer to his virtues, or pathetically maintain his innocence; or strike about him, enraged. Nothing of the kind. Cool and collected he went to the Duke; returned to his spluttering, raging insults not a syllable; and when, snorting with fury, the Duke at last was silent, asked calmly and formally for his demission. For any conceivable financial errors he might have made there remained his gross property, fixed and floating. Courteously and with deadly calm he repeated his request to the Duke, who, at first speechless, broke at last into senseless cursing and raging. When on his limping foot Karl Alexander rushed at him with arm upraised, he continued to press in set terms for a quick decision on his well-considered and submissive desire.

Karl Alexander had the accusers called before him; asked, his voice inarticulate with rage, if they have found proofs; overwhelmed the stammering, evasive, trembling witness with coarse, popular, obscene oaths, until his voice cracked. The Jew had more brains in his arse than they in their muddy skulls. He could not conceive why he had allowed himself to be drawn into their impotent, envious, idiotic, venomous wranglings. He would rather have the Jew than these stupid pigs of Christian scoundrels.

Sullenly he sent the books back to Süss with a huge *douceur* and papers granting him rich estates. Pale with fright his enemies crept back into their holes. Almost without a stroke Süss won back his lost positions. He still remained aloof from the Catholic Plot; but in every other department he let his hand be heavily felt whenever his interests were threatened.

There he sat now in all his old power, kept the bridle tight, and every one in the Duchy felt his hand. Whatever had been done in the interregnum was qualified, corrected. The chimney-cleaning regulation, which had been repealed, was now law; the broadsides vanished, and only in secret, in the closet of the Blue Boar, could the pastry-cook Benz show his intimates the testimonial of the Society of Night Lovers to his Jewish Witchellence. The Steward of Demesnes, too, sent his sons back to the service of the Jew; he had thought over it twice; they were not too old, after all.

Outwardly, then, Süss's position in Stuttgart seemed the same as before. He went into the whirl of Society, too, as he had once done. But he was more imperious, less amiable. He permitted himself biting, injurious witticisms, and did not remain silent when any one made merry at his expense. Once when General Remchingen uttered one of his accustomed coarse jests about the Jews, he looked him up and down, up and down again, and as under his strangely compelling, menacing look the grins of the General disappeared, the Jew in his turn laughed suddenly in his face, a dreadful and disturbing laugh.

Marie Auguste admitted with regret that her court Jew was not nearly so nice and amusing as before. Ah, so many things had become less amusing!

The relations between the Duke and Süss, too, had changed. Karl Alexander was very communicative when they were together, and showed him clumsy graces and favours to make up for his previous mistrust. But often he said to himself that it would really be better to be rid of the Jew. If, nevertheless, he did nothing, it was because he feared that Süss knew too much, and could compromise him too easily; and it would be foolish, too, to allow him to decamp over the frontier with all the wealth he had grown fat upon in the country. He would not admit that what bound him to the Jew as what made him hostile to him, was more mysterious and lay deeper in his blood.

Now, too, it would sometimes happen that Süss would suddenly let his arms fall, would sink within himself, would have fits of strange absentness and incapacity. Then Dom Bartelemi Pancorbo would stretch out of the hole into which he had been scared his fleshless, purple face, and under his heavy lids cast his eyes after the solitaire on the Jew's hand. He would blink, his fingers would twitch. But he had become very prudent, and contented himself with eyeing and gloating.

MARIE AUGUSTE stood before the mirror, naked, stretching and regarding herself, anxiously, exhaustively, feature by feature, limb by limb. She drew a breath of relief and smiled. No, no, she had remained unmarred, she was not disfigured. She was smooth and slender as ever. With her tiny, plump hands she felt herself, massaged her body. It was soft as before and yet firm. With her long, oval eyes she scrutinized in the mirror, serious and without pity, the small, lizard-like head. The inconveniences of her long pregnancy, the wild agonies of her delivery, had left behind not a mark, not a flaw. Clear and light and without a furrow, the rounded brow appeared beneath her gleaming, black hair; there was no wrinkle cut in her cheeks above her very red lips. Naked, she lifted with half-hieratic, half-obscene bearing both arms stiffly to her head, so that the black tufts under her armpits were visible, and softly breathing, smiling, she went with lithe steps, dancing almost, through the room. Oh, still she could glide like flowing water over the ground, still all her limbs could play harmoniously and supply, obedient to her! And she stretched voluptuously and she smiled more deeply and the day lay blue and untroubled before her.

But that night the same anxiety slipped again upon her, crept in, laid hold on her ever more closely, oppressed her breathing. And the next day she stood still longer before the mirror, scrutinized still longer every curve of her body, flesh and skin. She suffered from a sick, terrifying horror of age. It was not conceivable that her hair should lose its colour, the skin should wrinkle up, the flesh decay. She would hobble about painfully, cough, spit, and the men would be glad when they got over the ceremonious greeting and the few words of conversation; the women would not envy her. Her eyes became veiled while she thought of this; she was defiled by such imaginations.

When she reflected that the birth of the child would hasten her decay, she felt hostile to it. It was alien to her, it was no part of her; it was incomprehensible that it should have grown within her body. He was a big, healthy child; from his father he had the strong nose, the swelling underlip; all the same he looked pretty and lively. People assured Marie Auguste that the child became her very well, as mother she made a tender and charming picture; but she could feel nothing deeper for her baby than she could for her tiny fox terrier, now the fashion, of which she knew that it looked pretty, crouching under the border of her white dress.

As before, her days were filled to the brim with bright, noisy gaiety. But now she was more restless, more nervous. Riolles began to weary her, she was not always equal to his sharp witticisms; the Jew was less amusing and did not enter so willingly into every jest; Remchingen with his crude obscenities she had an actual aversion for. So now she drew Deputy Johann Jaakob Moser into her circle, thinking to become the Omphale of that dignified, pathetic publicist.

For the Councillor this was a great stroke of luck. Even if, magnanimous in their way, the Duke and Süss had enjoyed his downfall in silence and had not babbled about it, yet his self-consequence was deeply wounded. Now under the favours and gracious attentions of the Duchess, it sprang up again like bedded corn in good weather. Damn it all! he really must be something of a gallant when someone like Marie Auguste, renowned through all Europe for her beauty, the first lady in Germany, showed—to him, her opponent—her grace, and so openly! The members of Parliament, with their shopkeepers' souls, might not quite like it that he, the democrat, the mighty hater of tyrants, should go so much to the court. But let the poor fools think what they list; he felt himself Ulysses enough to withstand the Swabian Circe.

So the consequential, pompous man spent every hour that he could with the Duchess. He was at her levées; when she was in her bath he sat on the wooden board which covered it, only leaving a space for the bather's head to emerge. He declaimed indefatigably and ardently, his great eyes flashed in his massive Cæsarian head, his sword swung rhythmically to and fro; rolling and sonorous the words flowed from his mouth. There he sat, Swabia's Demosthenes, and his mighty head wagged until the powder rained from his peruke. He perorated to the Duchess on everything possible; he read her manuscripts intended for journals, and great works and brochures, theological, juridical, political, economical, and essays on questions of the day, but also on things æsthetic, botanical, mineralogical—for Johann Jaakob Moser was very learned. He recited everything with the same fire and with much expression. Usually Marie Auguste did not make much show of listening; she had her hair done while he spoke, or her fingers manicured, or read the *Mercure galant;* often she could not have said whether he read German to her, or Latin. But the uniform volume of sound which this Cicero provided so assiduously was pleasant to the ear; it was amusing, too, to have before one's eyes the important, bustling form of the excitable, histrionic man; and it tickled her that this democrat and enemy of princes should have such a puerile and self-lacerating infatuation for her. Sometimes when he turned his great, rather vacant eyes upon her, calf-like and ardent, she would let a slow, lingering glance slide into them, and would laugh when, reddening, he breathed more heavily. But in the bosom of his home he would describe to his wife, circumstantially and in a sweeping torrent of words, the beauty of the Duchess, and how openly she found pleasure in him, but how his heart was armoured in triple iron. And he would throw himself on his knees and together with his wife would pray ardently and in excellently-chosen words that God might in future, too, grant him strength, if the occasion should arise, to leave his mantle behind in the house of the Duchess.

As before, Marie Auguste made one particular intimate

among the Court ladies, Magdalen Sibylle. She fawned on her, spoke to her as a silly little sister to her omniscient elder. Ah, Magdalen Sibylle, how serious she was, and accomplished, and full of experience and knowledge. In the Duchess's little head everything flitted about gay and entangled and confused together like coloured moths, and everything slid off her like water and nothing stuck. But Magdalen Sibylle considered everything that was said or that happened, scrupulously studied it and gave herself to it and made it her property. It was this that made her so rich in experience and knowledge of life, and she, the Duchess, was so silly and stupid beside her, even though she wore a crown and in a certain sense was the mother of her people and even the possessor of the Cross of Malta.

Magdalen Sibylle was friendly but reserved, and sought as well as she could to enter into the mind of this inconsistent and changeable creature. Sometimes, indeed, a sort of horror overcame her at such boundless triviality. Was this woman, off whom everything glided, whom neither husband, nor country, nor child could move, and who only existed as a corporeal appearance; was she real, then, was she not a form of air, a phantom, something discarnate, a coloured shadow?

The tall girl with the brown, masculinely keen face was weary. The deep gleam of her blue eyes, so unearthly and strange beneath her dark hair, had become feebler, the movements of her tense limbs more languid, more feminine. She had fought and lost, she was finished; now she was calm, and no longer disposed to flame out wildly and indignantly.

In rapture and humility she had gone into the Brotherhood, the Scriptures had had meaning for her, had spoken to her, she had seen God, the Apostles had sat by her bed and held speech with her. Then in the forest she had beheld the Devil; she, holy brand and torch, had advanced to combat him. And then the Duke and the Jew had come, and like a great deluge of mud had overflowed her garden and wasted it. Blossom and fruit and tree and green were dead and defiled, and when the flood had disappeared nothing remained but wet, sterile mud.

And then had happened the courtship of Süss. In spite of her first disappointment she had looked upon him as upon a great, life-giving sun, and would have thrown open to him all the secrets of her body and her soul, freely and deliberately, in a boundless abnegation. But he had become a sun which did not warm, which impassive and pitiless and unattainable went on its way. She had tried with all her will to understand him, she had tried to identify herself with him; she had divined, too, better than any one else, something of the change in him, had understood better than any one else his isolation, his struggles, his humiliations, his paralysing weakness, his new rise to power. But her courtship of him, direct and indirect, remained without reward; to her he showed the most courteous, intimate friendliness, but all masculine ardour had been burned out of it.

She did not hesitate a second time; she came to a decision. Clear, firm, matter-of-fact, she deliberated; she would have been a good wife for a land-owner; a large landed proprietor, or something like that, who did not close himself away from the world, but was most at home and secure on his own lands and among his peasants, would have been the right man for her. But an evil star had sent her into the false world. She herself was not guiltless; Beelzebub did not appear if he was not called, and whoever saw him, as she had that time in the forest, must have longed for him in the deepest, most hidden centre of his being. But however it was, it was foolish to brood over it further. Now at any rate she was imprisoned in this court, which to her seemed a senseless whirl and confusion of gaudy animals, and the only human being among them to whom she was bound by a thousand ties had through his courteous, unfailing friendliness become, oh, a thousand times more remote than the devil in the forest of Hirsau.

Often she went to Beata Sturmin. The blind seer was no longer a foolish old woman to her; the silence in which she lived herself became less chilly and blank in the presence of the contented, pious, blessed woman; yes, sometimes she could almost feel her silence corporeally, like a good, warm cloak.

At Beata Sturmin's she often met the city deacon, Johann Konrad Rieger, Stuttgart's best preacher, and his younger brother, Immanuel Rieger, Transport Officer. Even in the quiet cabinet of the seer, Johann Konrad, the preacher, could not bridle his flowing eloquence. He was a good-natured, upright man, but why should

he not exploit the talent which the grace of God had granted him?
And he spread his beautiful, deep-resounding periods before his
hearers like costly samite, to regale them with it. The orator reminded Magdalen Sibylle of Johann Jaakob Moser, whom she
sometimes met when she visited Marie Auguste, and once she
mentioned the publicist, and said harmlessly what an accomplished
rhetorician he was, without really being interested much. But then
the amiable preacher actually swelled with venom, declaimed against
the Satanic conceit of that orator, saying how such profane rhetoric
was a deception and an invention of the devil; and it was with
difficulty that the blind woman could restrain the man's rage against
his secular rival, until finally, still growling, he went.

Immanuel Rieger, the Transport Officer, listened reverentially
and devoutly when his celebrated brother was speaking. He was a
little, meagre, insignificant man; to give his diffident, boyish face a
touch of virility, he wore, against the fashion, a tiny moustache.
Very much inclined to see only the good in every man, he was
deeply troubled that his brother should express disapproval of one
so generally held in honour as the publicist; but his diffidence was
such that he did not dare show his dissent except by slight, protesting motions of his hands. To the diligent and conscientious
official it was a deep, inner need, it was his refreshment, his one
pleasure, to be allowed to honour great men, and it was not difficult to rise to his conception of a great man. There were so many
people whom God had richly endowed with high gifts; he looked
up to them eagerly, full of submission and genuine admiration;
he was happy to be able to meet so many truly important men and
women in the circle of the blind prophetess.

To Magdalen Sibylle he looked up with boundless veneration,
adored her in his heart. What a woman! What a martyr! This
woman, the purest and most virtuous in the whole Swabian realm,
—what must she have suffered, how many thousand deaths she
must have died, when the heretic of a Duke cast his eyes upon her!
Cast his eyes upon her; any more daring phraseology he would
not have ventured upon in his boldest dreams. And with what
dignity she bore her crown of thorns, this saint endowed with every
gift in body and in soul!

Shyly the little, insignificant man would sometimes dare to

address a word to her. He did not speak of his immense admiration—that he would never have risked; he spoke of a mutual acquaintance, Master Jaakob Polykarp Schober, of Hirsau. Magdalen Sibylle smiled a tiny, melancholy smile. Ah, Hirsau! The stout, good-humoured, chubby master! The smell of baked apples and the devoutly droned song of the Heavenly Jerusalem came back into her mind together. Meanwhile, Transport Officer Rieger spoke further of the Master; he told modestly, circumstantially and with great respect, of his poems, of the song "Cares of Life and Faith in God" and also of that other one, "Jesus, the Best Reckoner," and Magdalen Sibylle listened to the respectful words of the Transport Officer, silent and peaceful.

The boundless, devout veneration which his whole being radiated so naïvely, did her good. Her life at the court, though it was confined to the receiving and returning only of visits she could not avoid, had thrown countless types in her way, who in her eyes seemed artificial and cramped, masqueraders and mummers, who did not know how to approach her in her very peculiar position. She was the Duke's mistress, and a Pietist, and the friend of the Catholic Duchess; that did not make sense; no one could ever make it out. And so from the people she encountered there arose to her a confused babble of mockery and embarrassment and sardonic curiosity and servility, with the result that she rarely heard a straightforward, simple human word. So the naïve, unconcealed admiration of this man was welcome to her.

She longed more and more for peace and an unobtrusive life. To her distaste for the empty gaieties of the court and all the irritating paraphernalia of power, she had to add now that Süss had no real interest in her; the whole business became more and more unbearable. Something woke in her of the dull hatred for the great and the lordly which she had inherited from her forebears; a relative of her mother had been a leader in the rebellion of the unfortunate Konrad and had been shamefully executed. She conducted her household ever more simply, became in her appearance ever more matronly and bourgeois, disdained the peruke even on the occasions when it was customary. Karl Alexander, who hardly knew what to say to her, and kept her still only because he believed the liaison stood him in good stead and was popular, was astounded, but contented himself, on seeing that the Duchess seemed more pleased than shocked, with a shrug of incomprehension.

But one person observed with deep, helpless and embittered disappointment the change in Magdalen Sibylle: Weissensee. He had never been intimate with his daughter; indeed during the years at Hirsau he had felt uncomfortable with the serious, melancholy girl. Yet she had meant fulfilment for him; he had a secret pride in her. She was of finer clay than the others. She had her own atmosphere around her, and even if he smiled sceptically, he spoke gently to her and involuntarily with more respect than was his wont. The clever and discerning man knew well enough that he lacked the final gift of seriousness, that he had no core; and Magdalen Sibylle had this core to her life; her walk, her voice, her very breathing, had a natural inner force; he saw in her his complement: that she was the child of his loins seemed to him his justification to himself. Even in his secret heart he did not venture to criticize her. Whatever she was, woman or saint, she was something remote and unattainable to ordinary people; she was different, the manifestation and goal of a higher, inviolate world. When the Duke came and trampled her into the mire, this, though it broke him down and undermined him, could not alter his inward image of her. She was Athene in the form of a Swabian maiden, mingling with mortals; or a demi-goddess at least.

But as she became more bourgeois in dress, conduct and speech, this his most treasured thought, stoutest support and argument against self-reproach and comfortlessness, broke to pieces. She did not merely seem to be in bourgeois; she was one. The enthusiast for the Philadelphian Society, the marble-cold mistress of the Duke, ignoring power and glory, her soul at home in another star —these had been chrysalis stages. The prudent burgher dame, busying herself complacently with everyday affairs and perfectly content, was the ridiculous, banal, definitive, final development. Had she become an actress, a vagabond, Duchess, whore, saint, it would not have destroyed his faith in her. Only this one thing could not be; she could not dwindle into the ranks of the ordinary, cheerful, common souls; these narrow ways, this bad, stifling air, could not be hers. Intuitively he divined that for this final change to prudence in Magdalen Sibylle, too, the Jew was responsible. But even now he was not overcome by a cheap lust for revenge. Only his curiosity became stronger, his fine, enigmatical, tickling, tunnelling curiosity: What would the other do in the same contingency? What change would be visible in his expression, his gestures, his hands? His curiosity goaded him keenly, swelled up in him when he slept, drove him itching and scratching from pillar to post, filled him completely.

With his faith in his daughter his last restraints broke down. He had to reckon now with the fact that his position at court, his participation in the Catholic plot could not be permanently reconciled with his membership of the Committee of Eleven. But when, taking advantage of his indisposition, they had excluded him in the mildest way from the Committee, he had been deeply and painfully wounded. Now without further regard for the consequences he ranged himself more and more openly on the side of the Duke's Government. Clever, with a finer power of intuition than the dense Remchingen or the greedy Pancorbo, he had not taken part in the persecution of Süss, not trusting the Jew's apparent impotence. So that he could the more easily act as mediator between the heads of the Catholic project and the Finance Minister, without whom it was clear now that it could not go on. He became more and more estranged from his old friends, Bilfinger and Harpprecht; serious, saddened and without hate, they saw him sinking into unholy and infamous toils.

Day by day he insinuated himself closer into the Duke's confidence, and used now without scruple his strange position as illegitimate father-in-law. He called up all his knowledge of men to please the moods of Karl Alexander, and the Duke, still growling against his intimate counsellors for their intrigues against Süss, and uncomfortable and without his old trust in the latter, allowed himself to be easily pleased with Weissensee's flattery and willingness. Many of the little services which the Jew had rendered formerly, the evasion of personal obligations, procuration and dismissal of women, and more of the same kind, the President of the Church Council unobtrusively and adroitly took upon himself. To fetter Karl Alexander more closely, he seduced him into byways of refined, artificially stimulated profligacy, and the poor man, healthy enough in his tastes, who really found little savour in such banquets and preferred plainer fare, thought it due to his reputation as a prince and a man of the world to eat, too, from those tables. The prelate sent him women in whom he had in reality no pleasure, but who were become a fashion among the *blasé* Parisians; he sent him, too, Italian secret recipes and aphrodisiacs; he conducted his victim ever deeper into the poisonous garden and as mentor made himself indispensable. Strangely enough the Duchess was uneasy about this collaboration. She was no prude, she loved to be told about forbidden things, and would take on a strained, thoughtful, dreamy expression while she listened; she loved, too, in her way, to observe her father's face, which was lined with corrupt knowledge. But the face of Weissensee, perhaps because corruption in him was not natural, but put on, was among the few which she could not endure.

Karl Alexander was in the habit of giving great and splendid hunting-parties, and spent gigantic sums on them. In one of his forests he had constructed an artificial lake, to attract the game. Weissensee used this pretext to suggest that for once the Duke should go hunting with quite a small party. Hunting-parties such as he had been giving were demonstrations, not diversions. The Duke agreed. Later the President of the Church Council would occasionally speak of the lovely forest of Hirsau, so rich in game; it would probably be a welcome change to go there sometime for a couple of days without the paraphernalia of the hunt, without attendants, incognito, only accompanied by two or three gentlemen; have a complete rest, forget his crown, give himself like a country gentleman to the pleasures of the chase. What an honour it would be for him to welcome his excellency as guest in his poor house, he need not say. Karl Alexander accepted gladly and without hesitation. Weissensee had chosen day and hour with great skill; it turned out, too, to his joy, that the Duke had only been twice in the famous monastery. So in great secrecy, that the incognito should be observed, the excursion was arranged for the immediate future.

From then on Weissensee showed remarkable industry and cheerfulness. He became more youthful, his walk grew more buoyant and nimble, his keen eyes had a more comprehensive glance for men and things. He sought persistently the company of Süss; whenever he could be, he was with him. A tiny, voluptuous smile on his fine, fastidious mouth, he listened when Süss spoke, his small, well-shaped head diligently inclined as if to let nothing escape. When Süss was unaware, he would look him up and down, greedily devour him with his gaze, and the Jew, chilled without knowing why, would at last come to a complete pause, uncomfortable and awkward.

RABBI GABRIEL left the house with the flower terraces, and went on one of his usual lonely journeys.

He traversed Swabia from West to East, wandered through Augsburg's stately old streets, gazed at by everybody. Followed by stupid and suspicious stares, he visited the residential city of the reigning prince of Bavaria. He bent his way then to the South, to the mountains. By the river a market was spread out, noisy and gay. From there on the valley became narrower, more winding, and the road followed in endless curves the rapid, whitish-green stream. High aloft, on a level space between great, pale brown, gigantically towering walls, lay a hunting-seat of the reigning prince.

The road forked. Rabbi Gabriel plunged into a dense, endless forest. He kept by the diminishing, clattering stream, which clear and cheerful tore on its way through the gloomy wood. The Cabbalist crossed the frontier, stood on the Imperial soil. Still and very lonely the landscape lay; where the river valley widened, and after he had walked for almost two days, he came upon a few miserable houses huddled round a tiny church. Here he passed the night.

A few miles further on, a high wall of rock closed the river valley which he had followed till now. From here three smaller valleys branched off, carrying torrents which issued in the main stream. He followed the first. It did not ascend very rapidly, and had a homely look; the mountain walls high aloft were wooded. He took the second. It was very short, rose rugged and steep and ended soon in a circus-like amphitheatre of gigantic, dreadfully bare, pale brown, rocky walls. He took the third. This was longer and wider than the others. The brook which flowed through it was not so rapid; often it lost itself altogether, flowed underground. Rabbi Gabriel came upon willow plantations and marshy bogs. Further up stood a forsaken, very tiny hut, obviously the last one in this neighbourhood.

The day was cloudy, not warm, but sultry. The stout man breathed heavily, walked with difficulty up the pathless valley.

Behind the hut, unexpectedly the valley widened. Suddenly he came upon a maple tree up there, then several, a whole grove. The ancient trees stood very still and tall; there was not a breath of wind, not a leaf moved. One could only see indistinctly through the branches the gigantic, white mountain walls which, vast and inexorable, closed the valley on every side; and they were so high that through the branches their summits could not be seen. The air lay oppressively upon the place; the grove of ancient, solemn, pale-coloured trees stood among these peaks like a part of a southern landscape transplanted by magic; the deep, crushing stillness lay almost like a corporeal weight; the motionless valley was enchanted; one was imprisoned in it as if in the uttermost end of the world.

The Rabbi crouched under a tree, weary, exhausted, groaning slightly. He took out a letter of Süss's in Hebraic characters, a serious letter, tinged with an almost morbid piety. He buried himself in the hand-writing, absorbed, his head on his knees, and called the man's face before him whose soul went with his, the man to whom he was fettered. To help him! To help the imprisoned soul into the light, that his own, chained to it, might also be able to breathe.

But this valley was not the right place for meditation. Oh, this weight of motionless air! Had Samael, the Ill-omened, sent his mighty spirits hither, to crib and confine him and seduce him from his task? Rescue my soul from the sword and my life out of the power of the dog!

Uncannily motionless, corpse-like, stood the strange, unexpected trees. Ei! demons everywhere, formless and in myriad forms, were around men and led astray him who sought the higher world. Imprisoned in a thousand things the souls of the dead expiated their sins; imprisoned in animal and plant and stone. In

272

the soul of the humming bee is incarnated the soul of the babbler who misuses the Word; in the quivering flame that of the unchaste, in the dumb stone that of the slanderer and liar. Rabbi Isaak Luria, who was wiser than other men, saw the souls as they left the body, also those of the living when on Sabbath Eve they soared aloft to Paradise.

Oh, could he but see this man's soul! Speak to it, speak with it, help it! The soul of the man who quests over the earth only for the goods of the earth, is consigned after death to the waters. On the waters it is restlessly driven hither and thither, whirled, ground, crushed to a hundred pieces every moment. If men but knew this agony, they would never cease weeping.

But the feeling of oppression weighed upon him, more suffocatingly; he breathed in gasps. He was compelled to look up. From among the foliage a thousand eyes were upon him, the eyes of a child, golden-brown, filled with tears; yes—his heart stopped beating—Naemi's eyes. And they cried, prayed with urgent, anguished instancy: "Help!"

"Help!" they cried ever more urgent and imploring, and would not let him be. He lifted his hand to his brow and tried to wipe the dream away, leant his head back and gazed up at the sky. There he saw ragged clouds, strangely shaped; they stood still and did not move. Suddenly he recognized that they formed Hebrew letters which read: "Help!" He tore his eyes away; then he saw that the branches of the tree under which he sat formed the same letters: "Help!" The roots said: "Help!" Up he sprang, breathing heavily, sweating, his tongue dry, his skin prickling, his heart in his mouth. He started to go back. The water courses on the rocks, the leap of the brooks, all formed again and again the same letters; the whole, silent valley was a mouth; its walls, rocks, streams implored him, cried in need and terror: "Help!"

Then in his heavy clothes the stout man hastened down the valley, panted, stumbled, fell, hastened on again. He came among men, flew on his road, on mules, horses, in coaches. He felt on him the golden-brown, agonized eyes of the child, felt in his brain the urgent, imploring, shouting letters: "Help!"

At Hirsau, in the still, spacious chamber in Weissensee's house, the chamber with the great curtains, sat the Duke with his host, the insinuating Privy Councillor Schütz with the hare-lip, and the surly Major von Röder with the clumsy paws, almost always gloved. The image of Magdalen Sibylle with her childishly ardent face still hung about the room, and the father could see the girl sitting over her book, in the still circle cast by the lamp, childlike importance on her face, absorbed. He saw her as she had been earlier: the brown, glowing, masculinely keen cheeks, the blue, unwavering eyes in their strange contrast to the dark hair. How much light, how much hope, he had drunk from that face! How sad, how cold, now that it was extinguished!

In the room which had once been filled with his expectations, with his work on the Bible Commentary and the dreams of the girl, the Duke tippled and swore, pleased with his company. Karl Alexander felt young, fresh, in gross health. His green coat was wide open, his doublet unbuttoned, his fair, greying hair untied. It had been a rare thought, to come and hunt here. In Stuttgart and Ludwigsburg things were going excellently, the Catholic plot was in good train. Then the new singer in the opera, Ilonka, pleased him marvellously; really he might have taken her with him. But no, it was better as it was. By day only the wind in your face, in the evening wine and good, strong masculine talk. No women! No politics! No Parliamentary rabble! How young he was! *Mille tonnerre!* he did not feel his fifty years at all! He could still laugh and find pleasure in nothing but a bit of forest and a good shooting.

Neuffer went to and fro and poured out wine. In the shadow, beyond the circle of light cast by the lamp, crouched the Turkish servant. Karl Alexander drank deeply, stretched his limbs, laughed hoarsely over the course obscenities of Röder and the subtle ones of Weissensee, and the very filthy anecdotes which Herr von Schütz snuffled with great aplomb and a copious intermixture of French. He related, then, stories out of the camp, adventures out of his Venetian period.

Weissensee listened with fierce pleasure. When one thought of it, the Jew was responsible that his quiet chamber was being defiled with this vulgar and disgusting talk. Well, when one

274

desired to know something, when one was inquisitive, then one must pay for one's curiosity. But it would repay him, it would repay him!

As the gentlemen, heavy with wine, were going to bed, Weissensee remarked to the Duke that he had prepared a surprise for the next afternoon. He advised with submission that to-morrow they should sleep all the morning, then dine well, and then he would conduct His Excellence to the forest and show him his grand surprise.

"Weissensee!" laughed the Duke. "Old fox! Excellence! President! I am pleased with you. You know something new for every day. You are a very useful prelate." And he clapped him on the shoulder and staggered into his bed-room.

Next day, replete with food and the old wine which Weissensee had cunningly provided, they set out. First they took the main road, then turned into a cart track. There they left the carriage, followed a foot-path, and stood at last before a lofty and strong wooden fence. Trees barred their further view.

There they stood before the fence. The south wind was blowing. The wine had not yet evaporated from their brains. They puffed and sweated and joked. The surprise was hidden behind there, then; would it be worth while? would not Weissensee give them a hint? He begged them not to shy at the trouble, and clambered over the fence. They followed with difficulty, chuckling, pressed on farther, curious, intrigued, amused.

They reached the flower terraces and the white square house, and were astonished. Confused pictures rose before Karl Alexander; of Venice and Belgrade. But none of them knew what to make of this white, strange house in the middle of the Swabian forest.

"The house belongs to the Magus," said Weissensee, "the uncle of the Finance Director."

They gaped dumbfounded. A nasty aftertaste of the wine arose in Karl Alexander, he felt suddenly heavier in spirit, was conscious of his lame foot, of the wretched, rough path he had come. In an inexplicable embarrassment he gazed at the house, with a vague feeling that stony, troubled grey eyes looked at him

275

out of it. "The Magus! Well! Well!" he said in a hoarse muffled voice. "This is truly a surprise."

"That is not all," Weissensee smiled, his fine, fastidious mouth a little wry. "Does your Excellency permit us to go on?"

Karl Alexander pulled himself together, cleared his throat. "The old sorcerer is due me a talk anyway," he shouted. "Let us give the owl a fright in his own nest."

The gentlemen went nearer, knocked, and nobody stirred, went into the house. The aged, broken-down serving-man intercepted them: What did they want? His master. He was not there. Moreover he received nobody, he added with irritation. Then they would like to look round the house for a little, said Weissensee. What an idea, growled the servant surlily. They should clear out. Nobody had any business there.

"Hold your jaw!" shouted Major Röder angrily.

But the old man repeated with a growl: "Nobody has any business here. Nobody commands here, but my master."

"And the Duke of Württemberg," said Karl Alexander. And the gentlemen passed the gaping servant and entered the Rabbi's chambers. They regarded timidly and jeeringly the folios, the symbols of the Cabbalistic Tree, the Divine Man, the strange inscriptions, and exchanged ironical comments. But the uncanny room subdued their customary exuberance, and made them abashed and quiet.

"Damn it all!" cried Karl Alexander suddenly, "it is as if we were in a church. Wine, Neuffer! Seeing the old sorcerer is not at home, we will find out if his spirits will perform magic at our table for a good glass of wine."

"Should we not have a look at the other rooms first?" suggested Weissensee. "Perhaps we will be able to smell something more out still!" And his fine, long nose seemed to sniff, and his keen restless eyes to search every nook.

While Neuffer set out the wine they looked through the few remaining rooms of the little house. Before a door stood Jantje, the stout, garrulous maid; she sought to keep the gentlemen back. But they thrust her aside and pressed into the room. There in the farthest corner sat the girl, anxious, large-eyed, at bay, dressed in her Eastern costume. Before the loveliness of her clear, pale face and black hair, her eloquent, brimming eyes, they recoiled. "What the devil!" the Duke swore half aloud to himself. "So my Jew has kept this to himself! He has concealed all this from me, the scoundrel! He wanted to keep this peach for his private delectation."

There was still a little space between the girl and the Duke's party. A silence fell. Naemi had sprung up, stood behind the chair, crouching into the corner of the room. The men, struck mute by the strangeness of the apparition, remained near the door and stared.

Into the silence the insinuating voice of the Consistorial President broke smoothly: "The demoiselle is the daughter of the Finance Director." And smiling amiably upon the dumbfounded gentlemen; "Yes, that was my surprise."

"Well, I'm damned! Well, I'm damned!" muttered Major Röder over and over; but nothing else escaped him. But the Duke, recovered from his surprise, became enthusiastic, and devouring the girl with his large blue eyes, grew voluble in extravagantly conventional comparisons. "A masterpiece of a girl! A head as if made of ebony and ivory! Like a fable of the orient!" Privy Councillor Schütz chimed in adroitly: the Finance Director was a genius, but the productions of his loins were still better than those of his brain.

Weissensee was silent. To please the Duke he could have praised the girl better even than he, or than the dry Schütz or the coarse Röder, who could find no better compliment than his raucous: "Well, I'm damned! Well, I'm damned!" But Weissensee was mute. He only gazed at the girl, looked her up and down, a deep smile round his fastidious mouth. Eh, my lord Privy Finance Director, certainly this is a jewel and well worth to be preserved inviolate. The eighth wonder of the world. A Hebrew Venus! She had eyes that came out of the Old Testament, and she did not look as if she were only lovely to behold. The Apostles came to Magdalen Sibylle and spoke to her. To this girl the prophets might well come. You were slyer than I, my Lord Finance Director, but not sly enough. You should have hidden her farther away and in greater secrecy. *Voila!* Now we will see what curious faces you will make.

Meanwhile the others had been exclaiming over the great beauty of the girl. Even Herr von Röder found something to say, and growled: "Who would have credited the old fox with such a cub?" But Naemi stood in the corner, her whole body tense with fear and repugnance, and looked at them. "What do they call you, then, Demoiselle?" the Duke asked at last. And, as she did not reply: "Shulamite? Salome? Shall we lay someone's head at your feet?"

But Naemi remained silent, her repulsion and fear wringing her with almost physical pain. "It is not from her father that she has this shyness," opined Herr von Schütz. But Major von Röder, rough and impatient, broke out: "Answer, Jewish brat, when your prince asks a question!"

"Hold your tongue, Röder!" said Karl Alexander. And to the terrified girl, pressing into the corner, he said kindly, as to a child: "I won't harm you; I won't eat you. Shy little dear! Mimosa! Do not be so coy!"

Meantime Jantje, the maid, had pushed her away to the girl, and stout and courageous remained near her, but in obvious anxiety and perplexity. "I am really your sovereign," continued Karl Alexander a little impatiently, "your and your father's well-affected Duke and lord. And now tell me what your name is."

"The demoiselle is called Naemi," replied the maid.

"Now we know it!" grunted Röder, relieved. "Naemi, a comical name!" and spluttered with laughter.

But the Duke commanded: "Come here, Naemi! Kiss the hand of your Sovereign!"

The maid whispered to the child and pushed her gently forward. Slowly, as if drawn against her will, her eyes on the ground, she advanced, and with greedy eyes, pleasantly excited, Weissensee looked.

They went into the study and drank; compelled the child to pledge them. On the walls the Cabbalistic Tree bloomed, blocky characters and confused symbols interwoven; the Divine Man gazed immovable. The child took a sip, but further she would not go. She fled and locked herself in her room, terrified, trembling in every limb, and icy cold.

But in the study, among the drinkers, Herr von Schütz re-

278

marked, apropos the magical symbols: "First this place savoured of the Jewish College and the churchyard. Now it is redolent of Paris and perfume and the *Mercure galant,* and the whole ghostly atmosphere has fled. It is extraordinary how a little piece of fresh femininity can destroy the prestige of the most learned Magus."

The party broke up. Röder and Schütz went first, then the Duke with Weissensee, last of all Neuffer. The massive Duke supported himself graciously on the arm of the frail and slender Weissensee. "You arranged that cunningly," he congratulated him. "We will have some fun out of that for a long time. Such a secretive sly-boots, my Jew. We will baste him, until he turns all colours." But that was not Weissensee's intention, to go away now and have a little fun in future at the expense of the Jew, that was not enough for him. He had not taken all his trouble for that. The Jew was sly, the Jew knew what he possessed in his child. He would send her out of the country, far away; in any case he would not bring his daughter to court, as Weissensee had done. The Jew had his wits about him; and even when they were flattered, there was always the Magus to restrain him. And if the Duke went now, he would not be brought a second time to Hirsau. Then Weissensee's great, consuming curiosity would have to remain forever unsatisfied.

The President of the Church Council saw the child before him, crouching into the corner, her great eyes in her pale face with a horrified disgust in them, and a soft, gentle feeling overcame him. But this feeling perished in the wild, tormenting curiosity which filled him completely, which lay like a sickly oppression on his heart and caught his breath.

He walked more slowly, begged the Duke not to over-exert himself, advised him to rest for a little. Neuffer had wine still; Weissensee attended upon the Duke. Karl Alexander drank. Weissensee turned the conversation perpetually on the girl; in his courteous, insinuating voice, in half hints, the complete connoisseur, he praised her charm, how young and yet how ripe she was. In their bloom these Jewesses were beautiful, were unique, the best of all, with a cool fire like the wines of the South. But their bloom was very brief, afterwards they withered and were loathsome.

They must be taken when they were as shy and ardent as this one; whoever drank the cream of this had tasted a unique joy which would remain with him all his days.

So he dropped his poison into the Duke's ears. Karl Alexander drank and felt his blood careering through his veins, mounting, falling. Evening came, the wind blew in warm gusts, among the trees the image of the girl floated before him, her shy, tender form; he sighed softly. "So might the women have looked," Weissensee spoke his thoughts aloud and they were the Duke's as well, "the women whom King Solomon took to himself. He had a thousand wives. Thus lived the Kings in the Old Testament. The Testament of the Finance Director." And he laughed his tiny, quiet laugh.

Suddenly Karl Alexander stood up, brushed from his coat a few dried leaves and twigs, and said to Weissensee in a smothered voice that he wished to walk for a little in the forest alone. Weissensee would make his excuses to the other gentlemen; they should not wait for him; they were to go home and send the carriage back; Neuffer he kept with him. The Consistorial President bowed and went. As soon as he was alone he breathed freely, lifted his arms in triumph, his mobile face contorted, strange, smothered, babbling sounds coming from his lips.

Meanwhile Karl Alexander, followed by his Chamberlain, went, as fast as his lame foot allowed him, back through the forest; night was falling. When he came to the house with the terraces it was already dusk; dark, ragged clouds hurried across the sky; there was no moon; he struggled for breath against the strong, warm gusts of wind. A great adventure! He was young, young! He clambered over the fence, and stole like a thief through the trees. Oh, this was good, better than wrangling over clauses with the lousy rabble in Parliament. If one had only a mask on, one might feel as young as in Venice.

Was there a dog about the house? Perhaps the Magus had drawn a magic circle, closed the threshold with sorcery, so that whoever crossed it would not be able to stir.

He told Neuffer to remain behind, and surreptitiously surveyed the house. He had noted the simple ground plan of the building. There lay the girl's room; it was dark. Where the light burned,

280

that was the room with the magical drawings. Would she be there? It would be easy to climb the espalier. He would look.

Softly groaning he climbed up to the window. "Yes, there she sat, her arms rigid, quite still, with her great, anxious, helpless eyes. "Hst!" he whispered to her, smirking, blinking, sly.

She leapt up in terror, saw the red massive face, the blue, greedy, insistent eyes, and recoiled, her body convulsed, her eyes fixed on the panting Duke. He laughed. "Have I scared you? Stupid child! Have no fear!" He swung himself completely into the room and came towards her, panting and sweating: "Look, that shows you how good your sovereign is at climbing." She, feeling her last moment had arrived, fluttered in to the farthest corner of the room, babbling senseless, inaudible prayers, cowering into herself. Coming nearer he spoke with pacifying words as to a child, but his horrible kindness only added to her terror. Her eyes like frozen pools, her lips white, she stared at him, until at last, impatient, brutal, he wrested her to him, showered kisses upon her, fumbled for her breasts. Then she slipped from between his hands, cried with little, toneless, childish cries for her uncle, tore herself free, reached the door, fluttered up a ladder. The ladder led to the roof.

Once up there, she inhaled deep, quick breaths of the warm night wind. The moist, sultry wind took her in its arms, carried her forward. She listened for a sound behind her; all was still. She extended her arms, she felt free; her uncle had helped; now the good, moist wind carried the fumes and exhalations of that beast away. She walked forward, almost dancing, to the edge of the flat roof. Were not those voices coming out of the forest? The deep, silkily caressing voice of her father, and the surly, ill-tempered, but oh! so comforting voice of her uncle. And she smiled into the night.

Then up the ladder stumbled the beast, panting, softly cursing. But now she had no fear. Hither it floated from the forest, a coach drawn by aerial horses, and stopped at the roof. Smiling, with a noiseless movement, she stepped in.

When he reached the top Karl Alexander saw nothing. She had gone up the ladder, and there was no other exit. Hell and damnation! had she, practised in the magical arts of the old man, changed herself into a night bird? Was she floating up there like the black ragged clouds and laughing at him? Cursed little creature! He stood grim and disabused; a strong wind blew, and tore at his coat and his hair, matted with sweat. Old ass that he was! If he had only taken the Jewish brat below there, the little prude, and thrown her over the table, not heeding her pretences and affectations! Of what use, devil take it, was his sovereignty? Now he had been done out of his night, and the people at Hirsau would be justified if they laughed at him.

In deep vexation he groped his way down the ladder again. His foot pained him and he was dog-tired. Painfully and with difficulty he got through the window and out of the house. Then he heard the Chamberlain's voice sunk to a hoarse whisper, frightened and agitated: "She is lying among the flowers!" He thought she had hidden herself there, laughed: "The rogue," and stumbled hastily through the uncertain darkness in the direction which Neuffer indicated.

Yes, there she lay among the flowers. The flowers were tossed wildly to and fro by the wind; they shook a thousand arms; but she lay quite motionless. He cried playfully to her: "You rogue! How did you manage to get here?" As she did not reply he gripped her cautiously by the arm, bent her head back, felt it hastily, recoiled in horror; recognized that she was dead, but did not understand.

Rags of clouds flew above. Hard coloured, the curve of the new moon appeared, giving a little light. The Chamberlain stood apart timidly. But the Duke of Württemberg knelt by the corpse of the young Jewess, in the wind, among the flowers, in stupid, perplexed discomfort, a poor insignificant human being amid the wind and the night.

Had this really happened? Had she stepped into space? Had it been intentional? In some way he was connected with this dead girl, was the cause of her death.

Bah! He had jested a little. Who could have guessed that the girl was so prudish? With others of the same age he had had very different luck, and what had they been? Daughters of the highest Swabian blood! So the Jewess had no need to treasure herself so highly. It often happened that children, only if one

282

gave them a bad word, would throw themselves into a pool, or do something to themselves. That often happened. They were insane, they did not know what life was. And those who were, perhaps, the cause of such things could surely not be blamed for them.

Nevertheless he could not rid himself of his oppressive, over-powering discomfort. The Jew had hidden her, hidden her so deep and so securely, and yet there she lay now, rigid and stiff, and all his cunning had not been able to keep her safe. A gust came from somewhere, who knew whence? and the light was quenched. Singular, that, and very perplexing. There she had sat in the light a little while ago, her eyes glowing with life, and now she lay in the night and no warm wind could keep her from growing cold.

The forest lay dark, hostile and full of mystery. Voices came out of it, confused, mocking. The man kneeling in the wind was afraid. The fairy-tales of his childhood wavered before him, thronged round him—figures in a magical forest, filled with the spirits of the damned; they tore him by the neck, by the hair; long, ghostly arms stretched towards him. And suddenly he entered again into that dumb, shadowy dance; before him the Magus held his right hand, behind, Süss held his left. And there, curtsying, almost bowing to the ground, was that not the girl too, in the ring? And he heard the surly, ill-tempered voice of the Magus. He heard every sound distinctly, and strained his mind to understand; but he could not. And all was so melancholy, mist-like, colourless!

With a snarling curse he tore himself out of his trance. He was dog-tired, now he would sleep. There lay a corpse in the wind. Well, he had seen many a corpse. When he ordered an attack, and the dead fell around him, he was ultimately responsible there too. It was madness, it was over-fastidious, to think so long about it. Why should he think so much more of the dead Jewess than of thousands of gallant Christian officers and soldiers who had died beside him and through his agency? For this he was Duke. God had so disposed it that where he went life bloomed or death fell.

He would go now and sleep. And the girl? Should he let

her lie like that? Truly wind or rain could not hurt her any more. If he went now, the affair would be done with, concluded, *finito*. To-morrow the domestics would discover the girl, send word to Süss. Süss would rack his brains to discover how and by what agency she had died. But probably he would not go any further. He would hold his tongue. He would bury his girl in all secrecy and hold his tongue. And those who were with him, the Duke, Weissensee and the others, would do the same. The affair would be done with, dead and dumb and buried; an end of it.

So he would—no, he would not! Should he turn tail? Hoho! that might look as if he feared the Jew. He would awaken the domestics, send a messenger on horseback to Süss, await him here, and say to him: "Fine tales you tell, you rascal! Your daughter has been found here, dead, in the wind. If you had not concealed her, you Jew, you secretive, crafty fellow, if you had brought her safe to Stuttgart, this would never have happened."

Yes, this must be a great blow, a deep affliction, for the Jew. The cursed, uncanny, incomprehensible pack! First he brings one into ridicule and contempt with the Esslinger affair. And then he has this strange child, and before one can touch her, she is dead. There would never be an end to the story even if he were simply to go away now and return to Stuttgart and never speak a word of it to anyone. This child's face was harder to forget than the faces of a thousand dead, distorted, disfigured soldiers. He recalled the Jew's face, very pale, with the red, small, voluptuous mouth, the quick, arched eyebrows. It was smooth and white like the face of the child. Even from the first the fellow had made up to him, insinuated himself into his confidence, with his cursed, slavish, oriental dog's eyes. Truly, when one thought of it, there was nothing much to be got out of him at that time. A petty prince whom the Parliament would not even grant a trifling advance; no great capital or profit was to be wrung out of him. And if eventually things turned out differently and Süss's trust had been paid back with usury, the business had not turned out well for him in the end. If he was so concerned for the Jew Jecheskel, he must be far more concerned for his child, so tenderly cherished. And there she lay now on the ground, a little morsel for the worms, lay in the wind and was dead.

To be rid of him! To be rid of the Jew! He would dismiss him. He might keep his savings and gold and precious stones and bonds and what he had embezzled at the expense of the country, might take them with him, unhindered. He, the Duke, would add a monster *douceur* to it. But he must go! He must go!

But no, he should not go. That would seem as if he, the Duke, had a guilty, oppressive feeling in his presence. No, he would not dismiss him.

But an end now! He would think it over later! Meanwhile, devil take it, he would sleep. He went to the door, knocked loudly, brutally pointed out the corpse to the old, sleepy, surly servant who opened; without further explanation went past the mute, staring man. The old servant broke out in animal howls, the maid babbled and moaned and whined her grief. Karl Alexander paid no attention to their cries, went into the house, and had only a scornful grimace for the fearful imaginations of Neuffer, who was terrified of the bewitched house with the corpse. The Duke threw himself on an ottoman in his clothes, and slept, snoring, rattling in his throat, in deathly profound slumber.

When he awoke, sunshine was streaming into the room. He felt stiff and dirty. In a corner, asleep, cowered Neuffer. Karl Alexander stretched his limbs. Ah, now he would leave the cursed house, return to Hirsau, have a bath in Weissensee's comfortable rooms, eat a good breakfast. But he would await the Jew first, clap him on the shoulder, say a few princely and gracious words of comfort. And with that this hunting party would be over, and it was only a pity that it had not ended as pleasantly as it had begun. He stood up heavily, and Neuffer started out of his sleep and saluted. He went then into the study, until the other should be ready. There lay the dead girl; the windows were curtained; large candles burned; the magical drawing of the Divine Man was curtained too. At the girl's head stood Rabbi Gabriel. The melancholy, grey eyes above the flat nose were not raised when the Duke entered. The Rabbi asked no question, made no enquiry. In his surly, ill-tempered voice, he said: "Go, my lord Duke!" And, taken by surprise, the Duke went. He did not rage even; there was a great stupor and numbness upon him; he left the house and did not see how cheerful and festive the flowers stood

285

in the bright sunshine; he did not speak to Neuffer, who, in anguish, and greedy for a human word, followed him; he went hurriedly through the forest and until he came to the cart track where the carriage waited, he did not speak a word.

During the night, without warning, Rabbi Gabriel had arrived. He did not seem greatly surprised; his very thick eye-brows became more forbidding, the three vertical clefts in his not very lofty forehead were more marked. He said the blessing which should be uttered on seeing the dead: "Praised be thou, Jehovah, God, righteous Judge." He laid the dead girl on her bed, folded her stiff arms over her breast, arranged the index, middle and third finger so that they represented the letter Shin, the first in the holiest of names: Shaddai. He darkened the window with hangings, lit candles, curtained off the picture of the Divine Man. He sprinkled water behind him when he entered the death-chamber, water, too, at the head and the feet of the girl. For water scares away the demons whom death attracts. Only Samael, the Ill-omened, the angel of death, cannot be driven away. So the Rabbi remained alone with the dead girl and with Samael, the Ill-omened.

He sunk his head between his knees; spoke, bent towards the ground, the three hymns—of the great sanctification, of the raptures of the third Heaven, of the multitudes of the dead. Then was the soul of the girl there with him, and Samael could not hide it. Ah, Rabbi Gabriel had known she was still there, that she had not straightway, in direct flight, entered in to the upper world; a task still awaited her spirit in this world, and for that reason she had cried to him. But he could not reach her, and so she had perished before he had come.

A small, forlorn heap, the thick-set man crouched in the room, which was filled by Samael, the Ill-omened, and the shy, fluttering soul of the child. And he spoke to her with his surly, ill-tempered voice; but he could not say anything to her, she was already over the threshold of the third world, and though she desired it, he could not keep her.

And when he divined how she was being carried away and how Samael had her in his shadow, then he cried after her in those words of the Scriptures which she loved: "How dear wert

286

thou to me, Naemi, my daughter! Love! Beloved! Lily of the valley! Rose of Sharon!"

Then he felt a last, fluttering greeting coming to him. But Samael was stronger than he, and carried her farther off. Then he fell on his face; never had he been so heavy in spirit and so earthy as now; and he lay for hours in dire weakness. And the candles burned, and the dead girl's fingers were arranged to form the symbol Shin; but no symbol availed, no one was in the room, and he remained alone and helpless, in heart-oppressing need, with Samael, the Ill-omened.

In half hints the Duke let Weissensee know what had happened. The messenger to Süss was long on his way. While he awaited the Jew, Karl Alexander seemed noisily cheerful, ate mightily, drank, made obscene jests, hunted.

Weissensee had only heard that the child was dead. Before the Duke, he succeeded in being courteous and self-possessed. Alone, he splintered to pieces like glass. The Jew was too much for him. Again the Jew had won. The child was dead. She was not smirched, defiled, crushed, she was simply dead; she had escaped unsullied and from the height smiled, a lovely apparition. The Jew was no ridiculous, crumpled, beaten pander like him; the Jew was tragic almost, and a martyr; his jewel was not tarnished and beslimed. When another had reached after her with filthy hands, she had freed herself in the pure ether of God. Now there was no sense in being curious, now he was pricked no more with the desire to see the Jew's face. He sat limp, annulled, crouched on his chair, and babbled stupidly and without ceasing: "Thou hast conquered, oh Judean! Thou has conquered, oh Judean!"

Meanwhile, Süss was driving frantically to Hirsau. When he received the news that the Duke was at Hirsau, and that he should go there at once and without an instant's delay, he became cold to the marrow with fear. It was clear to him that something threatened the child, perhaps had already happened to her. But, arrived at Weissensee's house in Hirsau, they told him the Duke had gone out, was in the forest: would he speak with the Consistorial President? But Süss did not wait for the hesitating, helplessly confused man, he hurried at once into the forest again. The cart-track. The wooden fence. The tall trees. The flower terraces. The white house. No servant. No Duke. No Rabbi. As if drawn forward, without considering what he was doing, without hesitation, without faltering, he went at once to the study. Curtained windows. Great candles. The dead child, her arms over her breast, index, middle, and third finger making the symbol of Shin. Süss fell to the ground, and lay for many hours unconscious.

When he opened his eyes the Rabbi stood before him. The Rabbi saw a ruined, grey-haired man. The slim, elastic back was limp and bent, the smooth, pale cheeks hollowed and dingy, colourless and vile the brown hair. The Rabbi had anointed the dead girl with balsam; now he went to and fro, relit the candles, sprinkled water to scare away the demons.

After an interminable silence Süss asked: "Is the Duke guilty of her death?"

"You are guilty of her death," said Rabbi Gabriel.

"If I had gone away with her," asked Süss, "far away, very far, in solitude, would she not have died then?"

"You are guilty of her death," said Rabbi Gabriel.

"Can one speak with the dead?" asked Süss.

Rabbi Gabriel trembled. Then he said: "It says in the Book of the multitudes of the dead: Think but rightly of one who has died, and he is there. You may summon him inwardly, and he must come; hold him, and he must remain. Think of him in love or in hate, he feels it. Think of him in stronger love or in stronger hate, he feels it more strongly. In every festival that you dedicate to the dead, they arise; they flutter round every image you consecrate to them, listen to every word that tells of them."

"Can I speak with her?" asked Süss.

Rabbi Gabriel trembled more violently. Then he said: "Be pure, and she will have peace. When you soar to the Third World, with you she will bathe in the sea of the Third World."

Then Süss was silent. He ate nothing, drank nothing. Night fell, day dawned, he did not stir.

The Rabbi said: "The Duke wishes to speak to you." Süss

did not reply. Karl Alexander entered, then started back; he had hardly recognized this man. This man with the dirty, dark stubble round his mouth and over his cheeks, with the dirty colourless hair, the sunken, red, fixed, bleared eyes; was this Süss, his Jew, his Finance Director, the great cavalier, the man longed for in women's dreams?

In his rough, hoarse voice, having cleared his throat, and after several false starts, Karl Alexander began: "Be a man, Süss! Do not bury yourself in your grief. I have seen the girl, I know what she was. I understand very well what you have lost in her. But consider, you have still many other things in your life. You have the favour, you have the love, of your Duke. Let this be a comfort to you."

With a sort of quiet, monotonous, frozen humility, the ugly, untidy man responded: "Yes, my Lord Duke."

At this quiet "yes" Karl Alexander became uncomfortable. He would have liked it better if Süss had shown his bitterness and he, the Duke, had been able to shout a little and then relent. This monklike behaviour did not suit him at all. What had Schütz said: it reeked of the Jewish Seminary and the churchyard. A vague remembrance arose in him of the Magus's surly voice, of what he had been silent about. He must have a clear field before him; he would take the bull by the horns. With a certain good-humoured, rough nobility, he said: "It was stupid that it should have happened just when I was there. What kind of accident it was no man and no Jew and no Christian and no Magus can ferret out. I found her; there she lay dead among the flowers. You will naturally suppose that I was responsible for it. But I assure you you are on the wrong track."

As Süss was silent, he added: "Sincerely and truly, Jew, I am sorry for you in my very soul. You cannot take me for a debauchee, who, *coûte que coûte,* must have his will. Naturally I paid her a little attention. But if I had foreseen this, I would have marched off. I would not even have asked one kiss of her hand. *Parole d'honneur!* Who would have thought that the girl would misunderstand a little joke!"

With the same quiet, frozen humility, Süss said: "Yes, your Excellence, who could have thought it?"

Embarrassed, Karl Alexander was silent. Then, making a new start, he said, "I do not think that I am guilty towards you. But if I am I beg your pardon freely. I do not want anything to come between us. Do not bear me a grudge. Give me true service as hitherto. Give me your hand!"

Then Süss laid his hand, which was very cold, in the great hand of the Duke. A little while the two men stood thus, their hands slack, without pressure, and an oppressive, painful impotence went from the one to the other. The windows were curtained, in the flickering light of the candles the magical figures danced and changed their shapes; Samael, the Ill-omened, was in the room. So they stood, in reality now figures in that pale dance which in dream and fantasy they had danced.

The Duke tore himself out of his constraint: *"Bien!"* said he. "Now bury your dead. Go then to Ludwigsburg! There are things to be done."

With that he went. The painful business behind him, he drank in with pleasure the sunny air. God knew, he had carried himself like a prince by nature and by birth. Gratified, very pleased with himself, he broke off one of the festive, cheerful flowers from the terrace. The white house behind him, he tramped whistling through the forest, pleased with the dancing light, and travelled back in the best of tempers to his capital.

Beside the dead girl crouched Süss. His white lips surrounded by the unsightly stubble smiled a deep and crafty smile. Without words he called the child, and the child heard. He told the dead girl how sly he had become, and he told her of his purposed revenge. Was he not a man? Had he not curbed himself and remained cold? Not only had he not sprung at the throat of that man; he had said friendly words to him, and his tongue had not been struck dumb. He had reached him his hand and had not strangled him; he had breathed his atmosphere and had not been suffocated. How confused he had been, the other! So he really could not comprehend that the child had fled, had quite simply gone away, ere he could slake his noble lust.

What had he said at the finish? There were things to be done at Ludwigsburg? Did he want to buy him off, through commissions; with affairs to repay him for the death of his child! The fool, the sevenfold blinded fool! But he had remained quiet; had answered amiably and humbly, and had remained quiet. He congratulated himself, the other, that he had come off so cheaply. There lay the child, a bundle of dead flesh, a poor little heap of accusation and putrefaction. Oh, yes, the other thought perhaps; if in the presence of this dead child he does not spring at my throat, then it is because he is too wretched. Wrong, my lord Duke! Wrong, my most exalted lord murderer! Süss is not so simple and dense; he is no serf or peasant or yokel, that an ordinary obvious revenge should content him. He plans his vengeance more subtly. He seethes and stews and cooks it with great care.

He smiled more deeply, he grinned with his pale lips, and his teeth, once snowy white, appeared dry and yellow bone.

Rabbi Gabriel went through the room, thick-set, with lagging steps. "That is not the way, Josef," he said suddenly in his surly, grating voice.

Süss looked up, gazed at him with hostility. Ho! Was he there again? Was he going to lecture him again? What else remained to him, then, but revenge? Would he stand between him and it with his noble speeches? Throw someone over a precipice and tell him: Do not fall! And he looked at the Rabbi with his hateful, tired, quenched eyes. But he said nothing.

Rabbi Gabriel, too, was silent. Both of them sat mute beside the corpse. Their thoughts were very different. But Samael, the Ill-omened, was in the room, and by diverse ways their thoughts always returned to Samael, the Ill-omened.

THROUGH the Jewish communities of the Holy Roman Empire the news flew; Reb Josef Süss Oppenheimer, a great man, high in favour with the Duke of Württemberg, Israel's saviour in dire and terrible need, has lost a child. He had one daughter, an only child. The child is dead. He will go and bury her in Frankfurt. Praised be thou, Jehovah, God, righteous Judge!

Then from all the Jewish communities, from east and west and north and south, men set out to attend the burial of the child of Reb Josef Süss Oppenheimer, saviour of Israel out of great need. The rabbis of Fürth and Prague and Worms came; and from Hamburg came Our Teacher Rabbi Jonathan Eybeschütz himself, the hated and feared, the secret disciple and follower of the Cabbalistic Messiah, Sabbatai Zewi.

To Hirsau, to the white house with the flower terraces, came the Rabbi of Frankfurt and with him Isaac Landauer, the great financier. He gripped Süss's hand warmly and in silence. In reality he was somewhat pleased that the Finance Director of Württemberg had now completely lost his foppish look, and no longer seemed like a Goi and a cavalier; no, with his unsightly, neglected beard and his dirty creased clothes he looked very Jewish and reeked of the Ghetto. But, much as this pleased him, Isaac Landauer refrained from remark: he rubbed his chilly hands, nodded his head, fingered his reddish-blond, greying beard, gulped and remained dumb.

Then they coffined the dead child. Rabbi Gabriel fastened a tiny, golden amulet round her neck, the shield of David inscribed with the word Shaddai. He nodded to Süss; with yellow, bloodless hand the father lifted the dead girl's head, and under the gleaming black hair, which was not yet dulled and lifeless, he strewed a little heap of earth, fat, black, crumbling earth, earth from Palestine, earth of Zion. Then the coffin was nailed up; on their shoulders they bore it, the four men, the thick-set Rabbi Gabriel, the broken, filthy-bearded Süss, the mild, withered Jaakob Joshua Falk, Rabbi of Frankfurt, and Isaac Landauer, shambling in his caftan. On their shoulders they bore the dead girl out of the white house, through the festive and cheerful flowers, through the trees to the wooden fence. There waited other men; they took up the light burden, bore it on their shoulders farther, and after a half-mile others awaited them, and after another half-mile still others. So they bore the child of Josef Süss Oppenheimer through the land and over the frontier and as far as the city of Frankfurt. And the tiny coffin did not touch the ground, was not borne on any car, but was shifted from one living shoulder to another living shoulder, until it reached the city of Frankfurt. Behind the coffin went a large carriage. And as the coffin went by, and as the silent procession passed, many Jews stood in the streets and cried: "Praised be thou, Jehovah, God, righteous Judge!" And each of them strewed a handful of earth on the carriage, fat, black, crumbling earth, earth from Palestine, earth of Zion. It was intended for their own heads in their own coffins; but they strewed it on the carriage and gave it gladly. By this means the child of their teacher and lord, Reb Josef Süss Oppenheimer, who had saved Israel out of dire and terrible need, could be buried wholly in the sacred earth of her land.

But in the city of Frankfurt the cemetery of the Jews was black with people. They stood silent, these vivacious, shouting people, when Josef Süss standing by the coffin declared: "Praised be thou, Jehovah, God, righteous Judge!" And they answered in chorus: "Vain and diverse and fleeting as wind is the world; but one and eternal is the God of Israel, the everlasting, the transcendent, Jehovah." And then sank the tiny coffin in earth of Zion, and earth of Zion covered it. And amid the silence of thousands Süss spoke in a dry and toneless voice the prayer hallowing the divine name. And they plucked grass and threw it behind them. And they said: "We are like the grass that withers." And they said: "We remember that we are dust." And then they washed their hands in flowing, demon-scaring water, and left the graveyard.

And for thirty days there was said in all the Jewish Communities in the Holy Roman Empire the prayer in sanctification of the divine name, for the sake of the virgin Naemi, daughter of Josef Süss Oppenheimer, their teacher and lord.

BACK in Stuttgart, Süss flung himself with wild fury into his work. He burst recklessly now into the Catholic plot, seized upon everything that happened to fall within the utmost reach of his competence. He cast away his crutches of servility and amiability. With immeasurable, mocking arrogance he ruled his whole entourage, made ministers skip like lackeys. There flared out of him a gloomy, sardonic contempt for all that is usually called human worth, freedom and responsibility. In a kind of dreadful play he imposed upon his subordinates ever new, superfluous humiliations, and when they stood exposed, their little scrap of manhood ruined and in tatters, he sneered at them with his quiet, open scorn, and feasted his abysmal contempt for mankind on their ignoble patience.

Quite openly, now, and with both hands, he plundered the Ducal money-chest. He abstracted monstrous percentages for himself, sold the Duke worthless baubles at colossal prices. He laid new burdens on the groaning, fainting land, and what he extorted in this way he put openly into his own revenues, not Karl Alexander's. If hitherto he had oppressed the Duchy with business-like efficiency to extort money, now he throttled and strangled it out of a perverse joy in extortion. He did all this with the most audacious effrontery, did it so openly that Karl Alexander must notice it, and sought in every way to exasperate the Duke by his conduct of affairs. But the Duke was silent.

The Jew's appearance was altered. His graceful, elastic step was harder, with an officer-like brutality. Harder, more decisive, too, his jaw; and the rich, chestnut-brown hair, which earlier he had worn free wherever he went, he concealed now always under a severe peruke. The whole man was older, more hard. His gloomy voice had lost all its insinuating sweetness; often now it barked imperiously, roughly—with a Jewish intonation, said his enemies. His eyes remained keen and attentive, even full of untiring devotion usually; but when he was off his guard, they had something biting and venomous, and subdued only with pains their hostile, yellow, gloomy fire.

More heavily stepped under her rider the mare Assjadah. No more did she carry her radiant, hated and yet admired, nobly free lord; she carried a load, a sullen task-master, sunk into himself, the enemy of all and hated by all.

He gave splendid parties as before. But their atmosphere was poisoned, and brought no enjoyment to the guests. On such occasions he loved to pursue this one or that with well-aimed, humiliating jests, either in fun or otherwise, and expose their domestic or political misery; and he knew very well how to hit the place that hurt most.

To women he gave a mocking, supercilious gallantry. One there had been; her skin was white, in her eyes were the dreams of thousands of years; if she spoke the song of the nightingale was like a croaking compared to her tiny voice. Now she lay in Frankfurt, earth over her, earth beneath her. What did the others want here? They existed, tattled, laughed and gave themselves in return for a little flattery. That was their existence, but the other one had lived.

Weissensee had emerged out of his profound confusion and perplexity of mind, and now always hung about Süss. Something fermented and worked in that monstrous, exorbitant man, who was unlike everybody else; something was growing in him, a grandiose, thousand-hued catastrophe. He was not like him; he was not the man to cringe and submit. In voluptuous expectation the Consistorial President smelt already the sulphurous fumes of the approaching eruption, and only the lust to see it, to be in it, kept the broken man going.

And Süss's challenging arrogance grew. He behaved openly as if he were lord of the country, and recognized no limitations.

At this time happened the affair of young Michael Koppenhöfer. It was like this:

After two years' travel for the purpose of study through Flanders, France and England, the young man, nephew of Professor Johann Daniel Harpprecht, related, too, to Philip Heinrich von Weissensee, returned to his native Swabia, to enter as actuary into the service of the Ducal authority. With a strong, brown, keen face, clear blue eyes under dark hair, the young man—he was twenty-three—looked like a brother of Magdalen Sibylle. From his travels he had brought back mad ideas about human freedom and human responsibility, with an intense hatred of all despotism; all the young, spring-like, pure thoughts of a new and better state, a more just and humane order, filled him with exuberant ardour, almost burst the bosom of the young, enthusiastic man.

He stayed with Harpprecht. The aging man, whose wife had died very young after a few months of marriage, had brought up the nephew; he had missed him bitterly during his two years abroad; he showered now all his inarticulate love upon the youth.

During his tour Michael Koppenhöfer had become doubly proud of the constitution of his native land, freer than that of any other German state. True, he had always known of the military autocracy of the Duke, the Jesuitical autocracy of the Würzburgers, the economical of the Jew. But it was one thing to read of it in letters and brochures, and another to be in the midst of it, to see with one's eyes, to feel with one's mind the insolent oppression, the naked, derisive presence of tyranny. The young man saw the trade in official posts, the sale of justice, the oppression of the people. The rich, lovely, fertile land, bled white and eaten up; thousands pressed to the colours; tens of thousands in hunger and misery; hundreds of thousands corrupted in body and mind. An unbridled court vaunting itself in intemperance and lust; power swaggering in gay uniforms, with mocking casuistries maliciously setting aside the clear and noble provisions of the constitution. The administration corrupt, justice a harlot, freedom, his dear, much-prized freedom, a mockery, a rag with which the Duke, the Jesuit and the Jew wiped themselves.

A holy consuming indignation filled the youth, gave his brown, keen face the look of manhood, burned more urgently in his keen, blue eyes. Oh, his slender young eloquence! Oh, his noble rage and exaltation! Consuming grief over the foulness of his native land had shaken badly and crippled old Johann Daniel Harpprecht. Now the simple, straight-forward man put all his hopes in the youth, and his sterile, lonely evenings bloomed and became young in that fresh young presence.

Süss felt unsympathetic to the actuary from the first. The tall stature of the young man, his stiff, angular dignity, in which nevertheless there was nothing of the lout or the yokel; all this exasperated him. Even the transparent honesty of the young man's political convictions put him into a temper. But before the catastrophe at Hirsau he would have feared the youthful impetuosity of the actuary, Michael Koppenhöfer, as little as he had feared the hackneyed pathos of the publicist Moser; would have let the one as he had let the other go free without question: officials of the most revolutionary temper had not been visited with the slightest reprimand.

But now, after the happening at Hirsau, Süss's poisoned nature burned with a more gloomy fire against the unbroken freedom of spirit and generous daring of the youth. He fixed his gloomy gaze upon him, and maliciously, playfully, crouched for a spring. The young man's imprudence provided him very soon with grounds for a sharp and severe warning.

For a long time old Johann Daniel Harpprecht had foreseen a conflict of this kind; but he could not bring himself to throw water on Michael's fine ardours. It was the right of youth to be imprudent, to straighten out what was crooked, even if it should

296

break its arm in the attempt. But he felt a load on his breast, a bitter taste in his mouth, when he thought that his weary evenings would again be solitary, without the warming glow of the youth's presence. Always he hoped that his own great prestige would prevent Süss from proceeding more strongly against Michael.

Amid the misery of his fatherland, the waste of corruption around him, the actuary Michael Koppenhöfer saw a great and gentle light. This was Demoiselle Elisabeth Salomea Götz, the daughter. Her blond, pastel-like loveliness impressed deeply the enthusiastic, easily-fired young man. As soon as he heard that she gently but persistently rejected Karl Alexander's advances, she became to him the symbol of human freedom. Their images swam into each other, and he spoke of his beloved freedom and the dear Demoiselle Elisabeth Salomea Götz in the same breath.

By this time Süss thought he need pay no more attention even to Harpprecht. On the grounds that in spite of being warned he had not kept in mind his due respect for the Duke, and had delivered unseemly, godless and blasphemous speeches against him, young Michael Koppenhöfer was deprived of his post. By an act of special clemency and grace, he was not proceeded against as a criminal. But he had to leave the country within fourteen days, and his banishment was to last all his life-time.

This had always been on the horizon. But now that it had come it was unexpected and broke old Harpprecht to pieces. Oh, to sit alone and dull in the great, empty room, only with books and parchments, his company only the shadows beyond the lamplight! They formed themselves into images of haggard, bent exiles, hungered and ragged; or they stretched thin, covetous Jewish fingers towards him. Whatever they were they oppressed and stifled him. And if the youth were to be there, obstinate and living, and were to lift his thick dark eyebrows, the shadows would fly away; his piercing blue eyes would drive out of every corner the menacing, chilly twilight. But he is not here; the Jew has banished him out of the country; the Jew will not let him come back.

In heaviness of spirit the old man wrestled with himself, came to a decision, stood before the Duke. He had never begged for anything, he had never asked for more than his just due, he was accustomed to have others come to him and beg. It was an acute trial for the upright man to stand there as a suppliant, and his words came awkwardly and with difficulty. The judgment was right, and not at all too severe. Yet the Duke should reflect that many things in the land were not in a good way, and if the young man spoke out his disaffection openly, that was better perhaps than if he had dealt, like others, in hidden poison. Karl Alexander listened gloomily, pressed Harpprecht's hand warmly, promised hesitatingly that he would think it over.

Brusquely he demanded a report of the case. Süss himself came. Yes, it was exactly as the professor had related. Only Süss and the professor had different opinions about what was needed for the protection of a prince's dignity. The Duke was vexed, cast upon Süss the blame for getting him into such a distressing position, from which he must either retreat now or else refuse a faithful and highly-esteemed man his first and only request. Impudent and venomous, Süss retorted that he knew it would vex His Excellency more to have to refuse a request by the German professor than one by his Jewish Finance Director. He had had other and very good grounds, however, for putting the actuary out of the way. If, to come to the point, he added, pert and confidential, the Duke did not advance much with the Götz ladies, the young man was the chief cause that His Excellency, at least with Demoiselle Elisabeth Salomea, was so much at sea. Growling darkly, the Duke relapsed into silence.

Alone, he decided in spite of all to let the actuary remain in the country. The Jew was off his head as well as insolent. Ho! would he, then, Karl Alexander, have any fear that a rascally democrat and rebel should put his nose out of joint with the lady? Or did the Jew imply that now, after Hirsau, the Duke was scared before every little virgin, and trusted no more in his manhood? A ferocious lust came over him. *Mille tonnerre!* He was Karl Alexander, Duke of Württemberg and Teck, and, in spite of every rebellious scoundrel, he would make this virgin small and humble. In any case the rivalry did not scare him, and he would annul the sentence now.

But when he was about to dictate the order, it occurred to him to think it over one more time, and leave the decision to the next day. Next day he went to Ludwigsburg. Amusements, presentations, other political activities thronged upon him. The day arrived when the sentence came into force, and no counter order had appeared. Young Michael Koppenhöfer must go out of the country, and the evening of Professor Johann Daniel Harpprecht's life was left barren and lightless.

Now Karl Alexander could take no retrospective measures that would help. When he thought of the Götz ladies he was very relieved on the whole. But this he would not admit. He was seized, rather, with a sullen rage against the Jew. He was responsible for everything; he had set the choice before him; Harpprecht or him, the Jew.

Süss knew that Karl Alexander had never committed a deliberate piece of trickery, and that he would not admit his real motives for this banishment. This made him itch to pester the Duke continually, so that this verdict might become a thorn in his flesh. He would drop casually: "Now your affair with the Götz ladies will go better, seeing we have got rid of young Koppenhöfer." The Duke would be on the point of breaking out, but he would content himself with a growl, and respond without much vigour: "We? We?" But Süss would only smile, and remain silent.

It came to the ears of Süss's enemies that his proceedings against young Koppenhöfer had been too hasty for the Duke's taste, and not desired by him. They could not understand the long-suffering of the Duke, and utilized the opportunity to raise a protest against his incomprehensible patience. They brought up the fact, and garnished it with statistics, that Süss oppressed the land and sucked it dry only for his own purse, without anything accruing to the Duke; that over every transaction the Duke was cheated and plundered. They spoke for almost two hours, and Karl Alexander did not repulse them; he heard them to the end, he even listened while they explained details which he did not quite understand; he listened most attentively of all to Dom Bartelemi Pancorbo, who showed at great length how shamelessly Süss humbugged and swindled him over inferior precious stones. When the gentlemen were finished he courteously dismissed them without expressing any opinion.

Next day, without being summoned, Süss appeared at the

palace. He heard, he said, they were intriguing anew against him. He wished to be spared the shame of having his papers shuffled through a second time. He reiterated his request therefore, most submissively but resolutely, to be given his demission.

"Listen, Jew," said Karl Alexander. "You bought a stone for me in October for more than five thousand ducats. What is the stone worth?"

"To-day hardly five hundred," said the Jew. And his eye meeting the Duke's, he added with an impudent, provocative smile: "Yes, such stones as these have collectors' prices, and their value changes."

"Very well," said Karl Alexander. Then both were silent. The Duke rang, and commanded Court Chancellor Scheffer to come, at once. Twenty minutes passed, however, before the Chancellor came, and during these twenty minutes neither of the two men spoke a word. They did not even think of one another. There was a deep, wonderful, complete silence in the spacious and glittering room. Pictures and dreams came and went between the Duke and Süss, Süss and the Duke. The surly voice of the Magus was in these dreams, and the dead child was in them, her fingers arranged to make the symbol of Shin.

At last Herr von Scheffer came. He was counted now among the enemies of Süss; he sweated when he saw the Jew, imagining that the Duke wished to confront him with the Jew, and conjecturing that he would have a hard task against that diabolical man.

But it happened differently. Hardly had the Chancellor entered before the Duke took up a position, and severe, military, cold and imperious, addressed the confused Minister: "The Finance Director, present now, complains of slanders touching his conduct of affairs, and demands his resignation. In recognition of his services, performed to our full and gracious satisfaction, we wish that everything should be done to retain him. Will you, then, Your Excellence, prepare immediately a deed, a deed of legitimation or absolution or whatever you like to call it, a Ducal order, that the Finance Director in all his transactions, past and future, is answerable to nobody. By no one, whoever it may be, can he be brought to book for any of his actions. Will you prepare this document immediately and in proper form, and give to us for

300

signature, so that next week it may be published in the official gazette. We are waiting."

Karl Alexander's voice while he said this was so icily precise, that the terrified Chancellor did not venture upon any remonstrance. Neither the Duke nor the Jew spoke a single word while Scheffer drew up the document. Without speaking, too, Karl Alexander signed his name. Then, scarcely able to constrain himself any longer, he ordered the Chancellor: "To the official gazette with the rubbish!" The Minister retired trembling.

Süss gave thanks with the most servile, devout protestations for this enormous, unearned favour, this extraordinary proof of trust. But his eyes were not grateful, they were bold and challenging and sardonic. Dumb and hostile the two men surveyed each other, and Karl Alexander recognized that he had not bought himself off.

"Go, Jew!" he cried at last, raging. And Süss went, but not like the Chancellor. He went slowly with his head lifted high, consciousness of his power in his deep, malignant smile.

But the Duke, alone, foamed and raged; tore, tugged, chafed himself sore against the invisible, inextricable, horrible thing which bound him to that man.

THE flaxened-haired Transport Officer Götz, who now, very young for the post, had been advanced to be Chamber Procurator in the Privy Council, saw with discomfort the Duke's gallant attentions to his mother, Johanna Ulrike Götz, and his sister, Demoiselle Elisabeth Salomea. He did not quite know how he should demean himself. On the one hand it was a mark of honour when the sovereign paid his court to a lady, and it was the duty of the subject to be at the disposal of her divinely chosen ruler with body and soul; for his career too, this inclination of his sovereign could only be advantageous. On the other hand the road to and from the Duke took one always past the horrible Jew; yes, he had the impression that Elisabeth Salomea had eyes for the Jew even more than for the Duke. And even if, through his position at court, Süss was to a certain extent purified of the bad odour in which Jews were held, yet it remained painful to his imagination to think of his sister and mother in closer relationship with a declared Jew. The Transport Officer would probably have made a quick end of his inner conflict, said good-bye to Stuttgart, and withdrawn with his mother and sister to his property near Heilbronn; but the affair with the Neapolitan and the illness of Karl Alexander had cast him into a profound confusion, he saw himself under a heavy load of guilt towards his prince, and his conscience did not allow him to take this way out. Dumb, not knowing what to do, he let things go.

But they went at first heavily and clumsily enough. Süss was always putting on the brake and preventing the Duke from making progress. The latter sometimes played with the idea of plucking the fruit with force this time, too, as he had often done before; but he wanted to show the Jew that with only the weapons of gallantry he could win an entry into the fortified castle. So he waited; but the long wait fanned his ardour ever higher.

He sent beautiful gifts to the mother and daughter alternately. His dusky servant brought them, the mameluke, who was so silent that people took him for a mute. This sinuous, dusky, gleaming figure was pleasing to women; he looked so remote and melancholy and like an animal; with the maids in the castle, and with others in much higher positions, he had had great success. The sweet, blond, tender Götz ladies fascinated him; when he brought the gifts he would feast his deep, savagely sad eyes in silence upon their pastel-like loveliness. But when Demoiselle Elisabeth Salomea was aware of his urgent, lascivious gaze, she would laugh with the callousness of a school-girl straight in his face.

Süss kept both women well under his thumb. They both loved him measurelessly, to distraction, and without being jealous of each other. Rather they emulated each other in rhapsodies on his manifold virtues. While the mother praised his genius, saying that she had long recognized that he and not Karl Alexander ruled in the Duchy, and while she lauded him, finding him so powerful, fearsome and feared, and yet so amiable; the daughter found him manly, strong, and at the same time not rough and rude-tongued. How different he was from the turbulent Michael Koppenhöfer; but how different too, from the vulgar, brutal officers! And leaning against each other, like sisters, they rhapsodized over him, they enjoyed together the knowledge that the first two men in the country, the Duke and the Jew, courted them; while the Transport Officer maintained an uncomfortable silence.

Süss could have enjoyed both ladies before the Duke got the chance. But he smiled darkly, when he thought of this; he behaved as if they were too high to be touched by him, pretended not to see their advances, and contented himself with so leading them on that they would not yield to the Duke.

It happened about this time that a Dutch jewel merchant offered for sale an unusually costly stone, called the Eye of Paradise. It came from India; an English adventurer had brought it with him from there; it had been procured by somewhat questionable means. However that might be, the Eye of Paradise was the most beautiful and pure stone of its kind in Europe. The Grand Vizier was willing to pay a gigantic price for it; but before this treasure vanished once more into the Orient, the Amsterdam merchant enquired of all the great princes of Christendom if none would bid higher than the heathen.

Once when the Götz ladies were lauding Karl Alexander's presents, Süss mentioned the Eye of Paradise, which was now for sale. The man who should present his lady with such a gift would prove that he truly loved her; whoever bid such a price, on him no lady's favour would be squandered.

It happened as Süss had wished. Demoiselle Elisabeth Salomea spoke lightly but appreciatively to the Duke about the Eye of Paradise. Karl Alexander asked Dom Bartelemi Pancorbo about the stone and how much it cost. Eh, that would certainly be a diamond of great price! exclaimed the Portuguese in his husky voice, and stretched his neck yearningly out of his gigantic ruff. But what it cost! And he named the price which the Grand Vizier had offered. One could have bought five castles and the accompanying villages with it. Karl Alexander drew back when he heard the monstrous figure, and did not give the commission.

He guessed, he knew quite well, who had inflamed this covetous mood in her silly, blond head. But he was no fool to throw away good money—how much land, how many soldiers one might purchase with it!—on a woman, whom at any rate he could if he liked fling on a bed; and no one dared blame him for it, after

303

spending so much in time, gallantry and presents upon her. The only thing was that now the Jew would take him for a niggard and miser. He would, in his impenetrable, smooth, scoundrelly way, put such freaks in women's heads, so that he, the Duke, should stand before them, a miser and a Harpagon. His lust, too, was rising high. Death and damnation! Could a woman do with pleasure the will of any one who stood before her like a filthy miser? He summoned Dom Bartelemi, and gave the exultant man the order to obtain the stone.

But alas, when, hurried and desirous, Pancorbo reached the merchant, the stone was sold. To whom? The merchant did not know. Without troubling to bargain, a middle-man had excessively over-bid the offer of the Grand Vizier.

"All the better," grinned the Duke, related the affair to the Götz ladies, and regretted that he had not been able to give them the pleasure.

Two days later Süss presented the Eye of Paradise to Demoiselle Elisabeth Salomea. It was a present costly out of all measure; in the whole of Western Germany it was spoken about; young Transport Officer Götz was in greater perplexity than ever.

Süss appeared without being summoned before the dark-browed Duke. In the style which Karl Alexander was accustomed to practise, he lauded impudently, unctuously, garrulously and in great detail the prepossessing charms of the Demoiselle.

His clenched fist upraised, raging, Karl Alexander stamped, massive and threatening, against the Jew. The latter stood and did not stir, but gazed at him.

But Karl Alexander restrained himself, panting hard. "We are quit, Jew!" he said at last, hoarsely.

But the Jew was silent. And the Duke knew that he was not ransomed.

MEANWHILE at the headquarters of the Lord Bishop of Würzburg they had engineered a remarkably fine, intricate plan. After the model of the administration obtaining in the Austrian Netherlands, Württemberg was to be divided into twelve military constituencies. The commander of each should be given a regiment of soldiers, the officials should be immediately under his control.

That meant the complete military control of the country, the legalization of a military autocracy.

Karl Alexander worked ceaselessly, feverishly; held conferences, wrote countless letters himself, visited the troops. He flung himself into the Catholic plot as into a healing bath. The bleeding and cupping prescribed by the doctors, Breyer and Seeger, had not helped him when his dull rage at the Jew had sent his blood, thick and heavy, to his head. Now he had a vague feeling that in the Catholic plot he might find freedom, deliverance.

The Duke was not in the least pious. God knew it was not the Divine Mary on whose account he had gone over to the Roman Church, but Marie Auguste of Thurn and Taxis, and a sackful of ducats. But in spite of his occasional jests in the free-thinking vein, he was not inclined to a convinced and thorough-going atheism *à la mode.*

Now his languid faith became earnest, grew a core. Before, his religious protestations had been nothing more than political means, the practical preliminary conditions of a military autocracy supported by Vienna and Rome, at the best a decoration; but now the laboured-for absolutism began to take on mystic hues. He saw himself in the service of a great, divine idea; the power for which he strove was something holy, the struggle for it the service of God. To the joy of his confessor, Father Kaspar, and his friend the spiritual prince, he became visibly more pious and strict in his observances.

The cause for this, which he would not admit to himself, was that in such service of God he saw the expiation for his strange, hateful, undeviating inclination towards the Jew. With sly casuistry, learned from the Jesuits, he persuaded himself that the Jew was necessary to him on political grounds, and that only for that reason did he tolerate his exasperating presence. But as soon as he attained his goal, he would knock the rascal on the head and lodge him in the tower. Sometimes he would say to himself that if he achieved a triumph for the Church in Swabia, God would certainly reward him and free him from his painful bond to the Jew.

ALTHOUGH Süss had been there before him, Karl Alexander was

not able to withstand the temptation on his part, too, to try the Götz ladies, whom the Jew handed over to him with easy contempt. But, even in memory, he had not the expected pleasure. Ever more furiously attaching himself to the Catholic plot, soon he was totally neglecting the ladies. There they sat in humiliation; they could not conceal the cares which sat on their tender, pastel-like faces: the mother, in particular, aged visibly. The Transport Officer gnashed his teeth and could hardly contain himself. He thought seriously now of retiring to his estate near Heilbronn, and as he rose in the Duke's service his rage went with him.

But the sufferings of the lovely, blond ladies grieved most of all the dusky Otman, the mameluke. As usual he had lain before the door on the night when Johann Ulrike had come to the Duke, and on the worse one when had come Elisabeth Salomea. On that second night he had not slept; cowering by the door he had listened keenly for the faintest sound, and when Elisabeth Salomea left the castle, his impassive face was transfigured suddenly behind the back of the Duke, who was noisily conducting her; and he glared at Karl Alexander with such savage, animal-like hatred, that in involuntary fear the Duke humped his back.

The Duke's dusky servant knew very well how things were. He knew from whom Elisabeth Salomea had had the Eye of Paradise, and he knew what her possession of it signified. Strangely enough he did not hate the Jew for this; he even felt a curious satisfaction that this man, and not a Christian, had had her first. And all the deeper was his consuming hatred of Karl Alexander.

The Duke treated his mameluke like a good dog. He believed, too, that his servant understood his affairs no better than an animal, and he had no secrets from him. Wherever Karl Alexander was, Otman always stood, sat, leant, crouched, cowered, or lay in a corner; even at night he lay in the corner of the bedroom, or before the door. But he could piece things together better than the Duke guessed, he kept his eyes and ears open, and even quite subtle things he could understand. In his impassive, noiseless way he appeared at times now in Süss's room; in his impassive, quiet way, lazily, he revealed this or that secret of the Prince to the Jew, which the latter could not and should not know. And then the two men

306

would look at each other; the quick eyes of the one, now less arched than before, would sink into the still, beastlike eyes of the other, and in both would be the same savage, stubborn hatred.

Süss took advantage of a few quiet days to go to Hirsau. The white house now lay perfectly silent. Rabbi Gabriel spoke no word; the men greeted each other, but for the rest they never met. At last, after days, the Rabbi was compelled to speak: "I see your face, Josef, under flesh and bones."

"Have I become different?" asked Süss. And he added grimly: "Now in truth I look like a real Jew. Or am I still my father's son?"

"Suffering scratches the varnish off the face," said Rabbi Gabriel. "You have a look of suffering, you have a Jewish look. Your way is false, Josef," he said again after a while; "you must turn back over it." But Süss was silent; his face was impassive, and one could not have known whether he listened or not. Of the child they did not speak.

Süss went among the festively gay flowers which the child had loved; he stared at the pictures of the Cabbalistic Tree and the Divine Man, on which she had feasted her eyes; he stared at the pages containing the great, blocky characters of the Song of Songs, which she had loved more than the other books of the Bible.

Unexpectedly, in the forest, he encountered the President of the Church Council. Weissensee had applied himself again to his Bible Commentary, slouched about in his spacious room with the white curtains, had reflective conversations with Master Schober. Now he begged Süss to let him accompany him. When the Jew did not reply he took this for consent, and joined him. Slowly, on his guard, saying little, he went with him through the sun-flecked forest, and followed him, seeing he made no objection, through the flower terraces into the white house. They sat, mute, in a strange embarrassment, in the room with the magic figures. Presently Rabbi Gabriel added himself to the company. There the three men crouched, round-backed, sad, weary. They recognized that they were old, they felt that life was leaving their bodies, flowing from them into the past, minute by minute; they felt it

307

distinctly, physically, with a painful voluptuousness, like one who sick with fatigue stretches his limbs; they felt each other's pain, and did not seek to hide their grievous lassitude.

Next day Rabbi Gabriel said good-bye to Süss. He was resolved not to return to Württemberg again. Süss was gentler, more ductile than usual. Much as he exclaimed against the Rabbi, scornfully as he rejected as weak spiritual nonsense his exhortation to retrace his course, he was always glad to know he was near. On the face of the thick-set, ugly man there was an afterglow from the child; Naemi's dreams were behind his broad, not lofty, beetling forehead with the cloven lines of the letter Shin.

He stood with a divided mind beside the Cabbalist, and very willing to give and receive a softer word. But the Rabbi was morose and ill-tempered as ever. His books and Cabbalistic paraphernalia were almost all gone already. In his grumbling voice he gave the old servant this or that final direction. Then, his face towards the East, towards Zion, he spoke the prayer for the beginning of a long journey, reiterating three times the declaration of trust in the help of Jehovah. Once more he turned his troubled, grey, stony eyes upon Süss, growled, sharp and discordant, his last greeting: "Peace be with thee!" Then he went, followed by Jantje, the stout, waddling maid-servant, whom he purposed to take back with him. Süss saw his broad, solid, rounded back in the old Frankish costume pass down the flower terraces, then vanish into the forest. Very faintly he had hoped that the Rabbi would turn round once. But with his clumsy but steady, unerring step he tramped straight in front of him and away.

A few days later Süss and the old man-servant, too, left the white house. Now the tiny, foreign-looking building lay quite silent in sunny solitude. The rooms stood sad and forlorn; the white windows, nailed up, looked forbidding and spectral; the festively gay flowers rotted and no one tended them. The forsaken, strange, arrogant house gave rise to whisperings; childish, blood-curdling legends were woven round it, and circulated as far as the capital. In the Blue Boar, the pastry cook Benz, his pig-eyes wide open, full of importance, whispered to the customers the latest mystery: in a wood his Hebraic Excellence had a hidden workshop where he worked magic. Out of the blood of Christian

308

virgins, whom he cast after torture from the roof, so that they spitted themselves on iron flowers beneath, he brewed a devil's broth, by which he sought ever to retain the favour of the Duke.

The maid Jantje had had a cat, an old, dark grey, plebeian beast. Rabbi Gabriel could not abide this cat, and Jantje did not dare to take it with her on such a long journey. Considering who would look after it best, she hit upon Master Jaakob Polykarp Schober. The Master had often met Naemi when she was out walking, had spoken pious, respectful words to her, had also made a few, tentative attempts to convert her to his sober, earnest faith; above all he had employed for this end certain fervent recitations of his verses. But when she rejected his advances with burning indignation, he had refrained and was content to refresh himself in a chastened spirit in her angelical beauty. When she at length was so sudddenly torn from his sight the chubby man went about for days in the deepest, most painful depression, pale, his childish eyes troubled, filled with self-reproach that he had not striven with greater zeal to steer her out of the false, poisoned dream of her life into the goodly ocean of God. He had been standing by the roadside with a wreathe of simple flowers when the tiny coffin was carried out of the white house, and he was troubled to the very soul that the four gloomy men who bore it and who looked like dark and false prophets, would not accept his friendly offering. Cast down he returned to his house, took pen and paper and wrote a rhymed "Death lament, entitled Naemi, for the late Demoiselle Naemi Süss, Jewess, but virtuous," a poem which began with the verses,

"Now has unpitying death, The source of so much ill,
Ta'en tribute, too, of thee, Hebraic Demoiselle."

This poem he recited later to the maid Jantje, at which both shed heavy and bitter tears.

So the maid entrusted her dark grey cat to the good-humoured, honest man, and he accepted it willingly and with kind intentions. By this chance Süss encountered the Master. For a few days the Jew went about in intense restlessness and activity, before the house with the flower terraces should be forsaken and sink forever into white silence and oblivion. He stood among the tulips, before the wall on which the Divine Man and the Cabbalistic Tree were depicted. When he saw the Master he made him an imperious sign to approach, threw a few rude and arrogant questions at him. Jaakob Polykarp Schober, whom kindness could make shy and mild, saw in the violent and gloomy demeanour of the Jew a test and a temptation, before which he strove to banish to the remotest nook of his being his native cowardice. With pounding heart, panting but valiant, the chubby man turned and prepared, the cat in his arms, to withstand the Sathanas, the Finance Director, with the good, sharp weapon of faith, and bring him to the right way. Süss, who knew of the Master through Magdalen Sibylle and had also been told of his encounter with Naemi, listened to him for a while in silence, not ironically as was his custom, but rather pensively, so that the Master began to have hopes and his zeal strengthened, with the result that his gestures becoming more violent, the cat escaped. While, without interrupting his fervent homily, he sought to regain possession of the cat, the Finance Minister seemed to come to a decision; he suddenly cut short the Master, but mildly, and spoke of other things. He strove warmly to gain the young man's confidence, led him on. Thus very soon he came to know something of the Master's private circumstances and wishes, also of the iniquitous way in which he had been refused the post in the library.

To Schober's wonderment he did not show himself as the furious Holofernes that he was universally called. Patiently he let the garrulous young man come to his conclusion, showed interest in his verses, assured the gratified bard, after hearing that Weissensee approved of them, that the *poemata* would be guaranteed publication. The library post, he ended by saying, was definitely disposed of, but perhaps there was a way out, something else might be substituted for it. The very next day he asked Schober to call again and laid before him the proposition that he should enter his service as secretary; for this, honesty and eloquence were necessary, and both the Master possessed in an illustrious degree. Jaakob Polykarp Schober saw himself thus entering, in splendour, by a way opened by God, into the capital and the gracious circle of Sister Magdalen Sibylle; saw himself in the Stuttgart Brotherhood, with the Holy Beata Sturmin and the good, kindly Immanuel Rieger. He saw the possibility of speaking with pious urgency to the Jew, yes, even perhaps to the misled Duke; he heard all the angels in Heaven singing; and, radiant, he said yes. Then he searched for the cat which yesterday he had forgotten in his happy bewilderment, and carried heedfully the dark unlovely beast home in his arms.

But in Stuttgart, in the splendid house in the Seegasse, there was nothing of his hoped-for bliss; on the contrary his diligence in Süss's service brought him only distress and confusion of mind, for Süss dictated to him documents of the most dangerous nature, which even to the most guileless must plainly reveal the whole black plot for the destruction of Evangelical and Parliamentary liberty, papers in which every line heavily compromised the Duke and the Finance Director, documents which put into the Master's hands the most secret, important, crucial details of the Catholic plot.

Within the unhappy Jaakob Polykarp Schober everything turned and whirled in confusion. Süss dictated his black, infamous plots with a smooth, impassive brow and voice; surely he must put boundless confidence in his secretary! Schober was bound to him by his office and by duty. Should he now go and break his word, betray his knowledge, coldly prove false to the Jew's trust in him? He was only a Jew, certainly; but then would not every knave and villain have a right to call him, Schober, a scoundrel and a double-tongued rascal? But if on the other hand he looked on in silence while the faith and liberty of his country were being craftily and shamefully strangled to death and hundreds of thousands of Evangelical souls were being cast into the abyss, the last gulf of hell, would he not then be still more a villain, one of the damned?

The Master was rent and torn by all the hounds of doubt. He had thought of himself at Hirsau as one chosen, when he had felt the faint hope that God had put his hand to the lever of great destinies and of redemption. And now his audacious, presumptuous wish went in such a gruesome, dubious way towards its accomplishment, that he could save the hundreds of thousands of Evangelical souls in Swabia only by a renunciation of his own.

He went about in misery and shivered like a shorn dog. His fat fell from him; a sudden flush of heat would run over him during the day, followed by cold sweat; at night his misery kept sleep away; he would start up, stumbling over the old, unsightly cat, and run to and fro groaning.

BRUSQUELY, hardly concealing his displeasure, Karl Alexander dismissed from the private sitting the gentlemen to whom he had entrusted the conduct of the Catholic plot. With an impatient sign he told the Jew to remain. "You have said nothing at all, Jew," he said accusingly to Süss, who waited courteously.

"It was not worth while to reply," retorted Süss, and with a slight shrug wiped away what had been spoken at the conference.

Karl Alexander groaned softly, lifted with his clenched fingers the table at which he sat. Hell and fury! It was damnable, but the Jew was right.

Once more the latter took up his secret thoughts for him and formulated them. "The gentlemen dance about," he said in his insinuating, jeering voice. "They manage details, spin threads, but they have no eye for the whole. What do *they* know?" And his tones consigned them to the nethermost regions of incapacity and stupidity. "As if it all could be done by threadbare lawyers' tricks, stealing a comma here and a full stop there from the Constitution. What miserable shabby shopkeepers' dodges! A rescript, only one, would be enough. 'We, Karl Alexander, Duke of Württemberg and Teck, take the right which God gave us and which cunningly, maliciously, and seditiously has been stolen from us, back to ourselves again. From this day we are in reality ruler of the country. We are Württemberg!' But before that these poltroons draw back with their tails between their legs. They cannot understand this, they shake their heads and become thoughtful and tongue-tied, and can only say 'Oh!' and 'Ah!' and 'But!' The thought is too simple for them, too great, too princely, too royal."

In spite of the dull anger which Karl Alexander nourished against the Jew, he felt again that only he understood him, that only he knew what was what. In reluctant, sullen wonderment he said to himself that only through him and with him could the

312

Catholic plot be carried to a finish. Whatever Süss took into his strong, uncannily capable hands, he kneaded as if by magic till it was round and adaptable. Before his fanatical, smouldering fire, the valiant and scrupulous labours, the fidgetting and plotting of the others and their half-successes, seemed ridiculous. But after all, what did these others know? For them the Catholic plot was a business, a task, perhaps a praiseworthy task. But that in truth it was much more, that this *coup d'etat* was his, Karl Alexander's, life and meaning—that only he and the Jew knew and felt.

For this the project had gradually become transformed in his mind; thus under Süss's urgent and pressing incitements it had burned itself into his blood. First it had been for him merely a political matter, sinews of power, a decoration, nothing more; then it became a mystical thing, a longed-for deliverance out of bondage, a religion. Now it had been transmuted into his very life, his blood. He would now—that was the meaning, the crown of his plan—he would now become the country itself. Not a servant or a prince of the country, not a law-giver or military leader: all that was wretched illusion and nonsense. He would subsume in himself the whole country, would so interpenetrate it that he would be the country itself. The country could only breathe when he breathed, move when he moved, be still when he was still. This fancy became to him almost physical, corporeal. Stuttgart was his heart, the Neckar his great artery; the Swabian mountains were his breast, the Swabian forests his hair. He was Württemberg, corporeally: Württemberg nothing but him.

Such a great, such a sweet, burgeoning, living change could not be engineered by petty lawyers' tricks. Was that his own thought? Or had the Jew uttered it? In any case now Süss went on: "It must be done in one blow, in one inspiration. It must happen in such a way that one morning the country will awaken and quite simply be planted and grounded in its Duke, in its prince by divine right; nothing but its prince's skin and flesh and blood. No petty bickerings and skirmishes, no stupid, pitiable hesitation and dubiety before it happens. No, it must come obviously and naturally, as a bud springs open when it is ready."

Yes, yes, yes! The Jew was right. It was impossible, un-

313

imaginable, that there should be disputes and discussions about it. For then he would be a Merry Andrew, a clown and coxcomb, and his whole life an empty, inflated bladder. But they did not grasp this, Remchingen and Fichtel and Pancorbo. They were faithful servants, good officers, and adroit diplomats; but they had not the genius, the something living, to grasp a thing so wonderful in its complete, sacred inevitability. That—it was the very devil, it made one's brain boil, but it was simply true—that only the Jew had.

All this was not said in so many words by the Duke to the Jew. But it flowed in waves from the one to the other, it pulsed, unuttered, between them. So it had always been during these last weeks. There was one life in them; in silence the Jew answered with deeds the unspoken questions and demands of Karl Alexander; it was as if one breathed out the air which the other drank in; they were parts of one body, inextricably bound.

Always more madly the Jew had goaded the Duke on in his illusion of godlike power, in his measureless Cæsarian dream; had burned all his smouldering, fanatical fire into his blood. The corrupted prince sought greedily for corroboration, for fresh, wilder instigation, in the Jew's uncannily comprehending gaze. Sometimes, it is true, he emerged for a moment out of his fever, reconsidered whither this strange, bewitching companionship would lead him. It was unimaginably terrible to have beside him all his life such an uncanny reader of his blood and most secret thoughts. One hardly knew oneself how much muddy and poisonous stuff was buried deep down in one's heart; one struck it down when sometimes it thronged up, and did not acknowledge it even to oneself. Another man in whom so many of his own dark thoughts were transfused; no, it was not to be thought of that such a one walked in the common day, in the light, lived. Now he needed him, the plot could not be carried through without him: the conference to-day had only proved it again. But once it was accomplished, he would silence him; he would entomb him in one of the deepest dungeons of some fortress, as one buries from the light the wild, destructive, arch-evil notions of one's own heart.

He looked across to the Jew, mistrustful, full of hatred. Did this man know already of these thoughts of his? "Set out the rescript, then, as seems good to you," he commanded. Süss bowed

314

courteously, full of diligence, while the distraught prince breathed heavily. But his eyes were veiled in scornfully, insatiable anticipation, sure of its triumph.

THE country groaned in a state of suspense and anxiety which could hardly be longer endured. It was clear that the Catholics were almost ready with their preparations and that any day the blow would fall. On every side the people were menaced; this left no ground more for mere conjecture; even the most careless had it forced upon them. Near the frontier soldiers from various foreign states were assembled, Bavarian soldiers, Würzburg soldiers. The Committee of Eleven had definite information that nineteen thousand auxiliaries from Würzburg alone had been assigned to the Duke; their advance guard lay ready at Mergentheim, the seat of the Teutonic Order of Knights, waited there for the order to advance. In the country itself, too, the number of soldiers increased who spoke foreign dialects, Bavarian, Frankish. They marched at night in small divisions. The Ducal castles and forts were bursting with troops. All the fortresses, Asperg, Neuffer, Urach, Hohentwiel, the strongly fortified castle of Tübingen, were being put in order with all the arts of modern strategy: the bad road on the Asperg had had to be improved by the forced labour of men who worked day and night. A beautifully-organized news-service which employed certain couriers, maintained the communications between the various fortresses. The powder mills of the country, chief among them the enlarged factory of Hans Semminger, worked day and night, preparing shot and powder. In endless transports cannons and munitions went past; when they saw the mysterious trucks, the people supposed that they contained rosaries for the approaching conversion of the land; but it was beads of another kind that they held!

This open menace to their faith goaded even the most peaceable out of their submission. Everywhere arose conventicles and secret societies for the maintenance of Protestantism; citizen and peasant provided themselves in secret with weapons; the considerable corporation of shoemakers and coopers in the capital borrowed rifles and muskets from their guild-fellows in the free city of Esslingen; from Stuttgart arsenal itself weapons vanished several times in great number and by mysterious ways; the most peaceable petty burghers, however, would show their friends hidden weapons, smirking, and with anxious pride.

On his side the Duke imposed a severe course of drill on the Stuttgart militia, a body of cavalry. The commander of this, the strongest regiment of militia in the Duchy, was Major von Röder, an officer belonging to Karl Alexander's most intimate circle. He was a good Protestant, and at the same time Remchingen's best adjutant in the military organization of the Catholic plot. This dense, one-idea'd man found the planned *coup d'ètat* quite in order, did not understand the fuss people made about it; could only see in their discontent sedition and bad-will. If the Duke wanted to give the Catholics more liberty, well, why not? The country was large, there was space enough for churches. Constitution? Parliament? Freedom? Nonsense. Conceit and discontent of those who wanted to eat more and work less. What were they crying out for? He was himself, by God! a good Protestant, and yet nobody had ever troubled him. Everyone could go to church, when and how he pleased, and the black-frocked gentlemen—so he called the prelates and preachers—made a big enough song, without bothering the Duke and his Cabinet with their intrigues. The world was very simple. One only needed to have a little good-will, be faithful, be brave, and above all be obedient to one's divinely-appointed prince. It was remarkable that in spite of such opinions, his intimate friendship with the Duke, and his prominent part in the Catholic plot, Herr von Röder was loved by the people. His rough, banal jokes were repeated, anecdotes of him which showed a certain boorish joviality became popular and elicited approving laughter. At any rate, as appeared from time to time, the entire sympathy of the people was given without obvious reason to this massive man with the low brow, the hard mouth, the formless hands forever gloved, the brutal, cutting voice; he was beyond question the most popular officer in Stuttgart. It was only thanks to his popularity that the institution of intensive drill for the city cavalry did not lead to riots.

Meanwhile the whole city lay in suspense. The higher authorities of the Church ordained a week of humiliation and prayer. Many made their last testament. On Sunday such a multitude

316

thronged to partake of the sacrament that the churches remained lighted far into the night.

In their distress and need the burghers decided to send one more deputation to the Duke, to make representations to him earnestly, but with the due humility of subjects. So as not to exasperate him, they chose no member of the Committee of Eleven (whose very appearance sent him into a fury), but three quiet worthy citizens, of established name and good parts. They journeyed to Ludwigsburg, where the Duke was pressing forward his preparations. Before they ventured to approach the castle, they took a bite of food and a glass of wine at the inn. One said: "This is poor preparation for such a hard job." "If the Duke's temper is as gloomy as the sky to-day," said the second, "then there will be no sun for us." "God's will be done!" said the third.

Before the door of the chamber in which Karl Alexander received them crouched Otman, the dusky servant. He heard within the Prince's voice, thick with rage, hoarse: "Heretics! Murderers! Traitors!" Then feet stamping, gradually ceasing. In a few minutes he saw the men coming out again, first two of them, very soon the third also. He saw how horrified and disordered they were, and he gazed after them with his great, brown, animal's eyes, and smiled deeply and softly. Hastily the men stumbled down the stairs, and sprang into the waiting coach, not giving themselves time to rescue a cap which had fallen off the head of one of them. They sat taciturn during the journey; only the oldest prayed once aloud and in great distress. "Lord God of Sabaoth, out of the depths we cry to thee. Send us help from thy mountain!" In Stuttgart many awaited the return of the deputation. When the crowd saw the men's faces they dispersed with hanging heads and heavy hearts.

Very different from that of the Ducal towns was the protest of the free cities against the plots of the Catholics. In Esslingen especially, Karl Alexander was now cursed and execrated openly and every day. Here was a great colony of emigrants from the Duchy: of the oppressed, the unjustly pillaged, the banished. Johannes Kraus had fled here, young Michael Koppenhöfer was here, and old Christoph Adam Schertlin, whom hate held more upright than ever. Here was gathered the consuming, heart-burning contempt of them all, shown in their glowing, smouldering speeches, full of hatred. The few supporters of the Duke shut themselves apprehensively within their houses; an occasional Catholic travelling through was cudgelled. Transport Officer Fischer, earlier Treasury Fiscal, father of Sophie Fischer, a discarded mistress of Süss—Transport Officer Fischer, who was in the town on business, was almost lynched by Esslingen's burgher sons, after they had howled for a while round his hostel; it was with great difficulty that the city guard managed to save the terrified, half-clad man, and to conduct him with all haste, stumbling on his fat legs, to the city boundary.

It came to open scandal and open conflict with the Duke on the Sunday of the week of prayer. In the night before, several youths, unmolested by the police, who turned a blind eye on their doings, had bound on the pillory two straw effigies, representing the Duke and the Jew, and written on them certain disrespectful and lewd comments. All Sunday the whole city, from the grey-haired elders to the school-boys, regarded the scarecrows, laughing, groaning, booing, shouting, whistling, slapping their thighs. Towards evening a bonfire was prepared, the effigies were fastened to a stake, smeared with mud; a few copies of the picture in which the Duke stormed Belgrade with his seven hundred halberdiers, were disposed in a row, and the whole was finally ignited with mock ceremonial. The effigies blazed up, and the delighted people shrieked and yelled, and danced to and fro in panting, howling enjoyment.

Among the crowd stood young Michael Koppenhöfer; his keen blue eyes in his brown face burned with enthusiasm; he breathed deeply: Oh, that all tyrants might end thus! In the crowd also stood old Christoph Adam Schertlin, his voice rattling deep in his throat, his cane beating against the ground, rhythmically as if in a dance, his mummy-like, brown, wasted face lighted up with wild hate. And in the crowd, finally, stood, beautiful and alien, the wife of Johann Ulrich Schertlin, the Frenchwoman, the Waldensian. She was poorly clad; her husband was now quite demoralized, a homeless drunkard; but she carried her face with the little, red mouth as high as ever. From her oval eyes she cast contemptuous glances on this wildly shrieking crowd who burned the effigies and bowed their backs in front of the originals. The woman next to her said a few words; she looked down at her, distant, contemptuous, said not a word, and slowly left the square with superb and arrogant steps.

In the large, sober, bare chamber of Beata Sturmin there sat, grouped round the blind seer, Magdalen Sibylle, Johann Konrad Rieger, the preacher, his brother Immanuel, the Transport Officer, and Master Schober. Magdalen Sibylle wore a light grey dress, the stuff very expensive, the cut and style very plain. She had become more comfortable, the keen blue eyes were duller, the brown cheeks slacker, all her limbs more languid. Slightly fat, complacent almost, she sat now, a bourgeoise, and listened attentively to the preacher who told of his yesterday's sermon, of its mighty effect, pleasing to God, and who repeated passages from it, in a sonorous and practised voice.

Jaakob Polykarp Schober sat timidly in a corner. The poor, hunted man, suffering on account of his ambiguous position with Süss, sought here a little peace from his unrest. From his corner he gazed at the preacher, who strode up and down declaiming, satisfied; he looked from him to the blind seer, who—mild, grey, colourless—crouched and listened; he looked from her to Transport Officer Immanuel, who hung full of reverence on the words of his great and important brother. But he saw, too, from his corner, how with all reverence the eyes of the meagre, timid man, whose moustache could not hide his insignificance, gradually left his brother, glided over to Magdalen Sibylle, and paused with dog-like humility on her as she sat there, comfortable, almost matronly, her big, rather plump and yet childlike hands resting in her mighty lap over the ample, silver-grey dress. He saw that humbly yearning look, he read that look, and gradually he saw a way to mollify a little his pangs of conscience through a difficult action, but one pleasing to God. Had he not on account of his honourable and submissive deference to the demoiselle during the long Hirsau years a certain claim on her? But he would submit his will, he would, hard as it was, give no more rein to his wishes; he would resign his claims, and leave the way open and free for his brother Immanuel Rieger.

319

Meanwhile the clergyman had finished his narrative with excerpts, and then happened a curious thing. Magdalen Sibylle said, and this simply as if it were a matter of course, without affectation or shyness, that, spurred by the example of their dear brother Jaakob Polykarp Schober, she, too, for her part, had written verses. And now she would read her *Carmina* to the pious brothers and sisters. What she read was lame, melancholy, banal, empty, shallow, moralizing doggerel. But the hearers did not remark anything of the tediousness of the verses; their homely natures were genuinely moved; and tears of sensibility and admiration fell from the eyes of Transport Officer Immanuel Rieger and wetted his moustache.

When they left, the Master attached himself to Immanuel Rieger. The latter rhapsodized in his timid, helpless way over Magdalen Sibylle. Then Schober pulled himself together, swallowed hastily, and, deeply moved, revealed to the other his resolve, his renunciation. The watery eyes of the Transport Officer grew wet; in his thin voice, almost inarticulate with emotion, he asked his friend if he thought, then, that there was any possibility: if he lifted his eyes to her would not that great, sublime, illustrious woman look at him in astonishment, and turn away with disapproval from such presumption? But Schober thought he might comfort himself, and this made the poor man happy.

Magdalen Sibylle listened to his stuttered proposal gravely, but not unwillingly. She asked for time to consider, then set herself to reply in verse. Sitting at a writing table, waiting on rhyme and metre—thus now her happiest hours were passed. This carried her away, lifted her up, led her on. Vaguely somewhere in her mind she thought: In the beginning was the Word, and the Word was God. How sweet to let oneself be carried on the flood of words, to swim on rhyme and metre in an endless dream, to sink in the Godhead! The world was without order, without authority or reason; it was savage, stupid, senseless, filthy. Here were meaning and reason and purity, here one glided gently over all this disintegration, over slime and menacing abysses, rippling, softly dreaming. The heat which once had poisoned one's blood evaporated, harmless, lukewarm, comfortable, in the smooth alternation of lines. The peaks and the abysses of the world became a uniform plain, dwindled into flat, very. correct Alexandrines.

So she sat to-day replying to Immanuel Rieger. Her thoughts and languid inspirations swayed softly up and down, shaped themselves at last, in a wordy, prolix, serious, very bad poem, to an affirmative at first hesitating but ever growing more assured. The rhymes set forth at length and circumstantially all the arguments for and against, passed on to the questions of freedom and responsibility, and lauded order, law, peace, the need for strict limitation.

There came, in fact, while she set down those adroit, collected and ingenuous observations, a moment when suddenly rhyme and metre deserted her. Her limbs relaxed in an unending, melancholy weariness; she saw full, quick eyes fixed hotly upon her; felt herself deliciously bathed in the tones of an urgent, intimate voice which went over her like good warm water; and for a second she knew what a poor, empty sham her silly poetizing was. But quickly she put this thought aside as an evil temptation, and with gloomy resolution, with an almost fanatical passion of sobriety, she wrote the poem to the end.

Such a marriage for Demoiselle Weissensee, even though, naturally enough, her dwindling into a bourgeoise had shocked people, was everywhere greeted with amazement. The Duke was furious that now for all time he would have a stupid, insignificant pedant and subaltern officially sitting at his table. Nevertheless, it did not make him miserly, and he presented them on their betrothal with the castle of Würtigheim, renowned for its fruit culture. Even Süss was startled out of his obsession, which brooded always on the same thing. This was the world then; stupid, small, empty, sour, pitiable everything showed itself at heart which at first had glittered and seemed so strong and so sweet. Had not this woman too, moreover, been trampled by Karl Alexander into the slime, into wretchedness? Well! it had not been his intention, but in the end he would certainly rid the world of an evil and dangerous animal, if he only followed his private impulse. Not the slightest idea that he had any share in the demoralization of Magdalen Sibylle occurred to him. He ordered the mare Assjadah to be saddled; arrogant and in great splendour he rode to Magdalen

Sibylle's tiny castle; a gloomy, savage greatness went out from this man who, embittered and worn with passion, displayed his gallantry for a last time before the lady. Magdalen Sibylle emerged with difficulty, and only after days had passed, from the deep agitation caused by this visit of congratulation.

The Duchess said to Weissensee—the words came nimbly, lightly mocking out of her tiny, red, pouting mouth—"You do not seem pleased, your excellence, with Magdalen Sibylle's choice!" And suddenly turning upon him her elegant, lizard-like face which shone palely like an old and fine marble under her gleaming black hair, she smiled maliciously: "Should she have married the Court Jew, perhaps?"

"Yes, your Grace," said Weissensee. "A hundred times rather." And it sounded so bitter and frantic and so like a cry in the mouth of that fine, amiable man, that the Duchess looked up inquiringly and a little embarrassed. And after a short pause she began to speak of other things.

In the ante-room Chamberlain Neuffer closed the door behind Süss as the latter entered the Duke's cabinet. Behind the Finance Director's back the Chamberlain became in a moment hideous, almost unrecognizable; the formal, lackey-like gravity of his face changed into brutal, crude, impotent rage. The Jew! Always the Jew! Certainly once, as Neuffer undressed him, the Duke had broken out into a fit of senseless, foaming rage; he would cast the Jew in prison, put him in chains for three years, and then hang him. But that had not changed anything. The Jew was and remained regent of the country. The Duke swore at his counsel, praised that of the others; but when it came to a point he only did what the Jew suggested.

In the other corner of the ante-chamber, on a rug, crouched the Turkish servant. He had seen quite well how the Chamberlain's face had for a moment lost its mask, and inwardly he was amused by the downright exposure of his Christian colleague. But he remained silent, crouching like an indolent animal, his face impassive.

Meanwhile Süss took counsel with the Duke. In two days the conspiracy would be sprung; all the preparations were finished.

Officially the Duke would be on tour; in his capacity as Field Marshal of the Empire he would go at first to inspect the fortresses of Kehl and Philipsburg, then on account of his bad foot to Dantzig, to consult the physician Hulderop, the greatest orthopedist of his time. For the period of his absence Karl Alexander had appointed a regency; among the chief in it were the Duchess —who played her rôle with great gravity—the ministers Scheffer and Pfau, the State Councillor Lanz, the generals Remchingen and Röder. This regime should carry through the *coup d' état* in Karl Alexander's absence; after seizing all the strategic positions in the country they should proclaim by law the equality of the Catholic religion with the Protestant, disarming of the burghers, the deletion of certain clauses in the Constitution, imposition of church fees, compulsory handing over of all silver to the Ducal mint, and more measures of the same kind.

Süss once more summarized the issue; the accomplishment of the project in a single night without friction or conflict. Karl Alexander would leave the country as constitutional prince; he would be called back in a few hours as absolute sovereign. If the accomplishment of the plan were drawn out, protracted, if friction, opposition, bloodshed intervened, then all was lost, and the doubters and croakers would have been justified. For they had strained the Constitution so far, that it could bear nothing more; all the arts of Jesuitry could extract nothing more from it. There only remained one thing, to break it, and that could not be done gradually; only by one stroke could it be accomplished. If that miscarried in the very least, then the very fact of their employment of force demonstrated how much they felt themselves in the wrong; the *corpus evangelicorum* would fall upon them, the restrictions of the constitution would then become still more unyielding and severe. If conflict once set in, then the constitutional party had too many and too powerful supporters in the Empire. The country would only acknowledge a successful surprisal; the one party grinning, the other gnashing their teeth. Hitherto he had always been for gentle, gradual measures, when the others' were for brutal directness; in this case there was only one choice, open, impetuous, decisive action, which might spell either success or disaster.

With inexorable logic, objectivity, clarity, Süss elucidated all this once more for the Duke. More fiery and eloquent then, he went on to say how impossibly circumscribed the idea became, the great idea of the godlikeness of princely power, when once it was plotted and nibbled away by disputes and legal tricks and petty skirmishes with the citizen guards, and ridiculous, miserable wrangling. Here in truth, it was a question of all or nothing. Either the Duchy returned back naturally into the person of its prince, or this stuff was too poor for the great idea to work itself out in.

Karl Alexander was filled with dull anger. The Jew was right, as always, and he had spoken well. But how abysmally he could see into one! Yes, he must go, he must be cast for ever into darkness! And what had he said just now: this stuff was too poor for the great idea? What stuff? It was of course impossible that the project should miscarry: but all the same—what stuff was too poor? The country? Or did he dare, did the Jew dare, even to hint it?—or he, the prince? Of course he dared! Behind his courteous, deferential mask there was concealed, scornful and peering, this impudent, supercilious, exasperating doubt. The shameless, pert rebel! He was a hundred times worse than the stiff-necked, intractable imbeciles in Parliament. They were confirmed asses. But this smiling, courteous Jew knew, and his grinning, unashamed doubt went like poison into one. He must go! Into darkness with him! Forever into the darkness!

"Has your Highness decided the password yet?" asked the Jew in unmoved, objective tones.

"Yes," replied Karl Alexander, terse, brusque, military. "It is: *Attempto!*"

Pleased and surprised Süss looked up with a faint, appreciative smile. *"Attempto! I dare!"* that was an insolent, a daring witticism: it was almost genius. *"Attempto! I dare!"*—Eberhard the Bearded had said, and first among German princes had given his land a constitution. *"Attempto! I dare!"* was the sublime inscription on the arms of this prince, the trunk of a cedar, which he had brought home with him from the crusades. So his picture hung in almost every house in the Duchy. With this gallant motto he had given away the greater part of his power and reinstated it in the people. Those in the country who knew no other word

324

in Latin understood this word *Attempto;* for it was the cornerstone of the constitution and of all civil freedom. And this same *"Attempto!* I dare!" Karl Alexander chose now as watch-word, to destroy this very Constitution founded by his ancestor, to seize again the ancient power, to set in place of the most finished democracy a naked absolutism! That showed as much spirit as wit. This Karl Alexander had something in him, after all!

Elated, his breast swelling with keen pleasure, Süss went home. He had made this man, lighted the flame in him, kneaded out of a hot, sensual, brutal piece of flesh—a prince. Oh, his way had been the right one. How crude and simple it would have been to have sprung at his throat that time! Now he had fattened his victim, had raised it up, made it conspicuous and worthy. A famished animal is displeasing to priests as to God. The victim whose blood he proffered now could stand the test.

He walked up and down in his study, excited, elated; all the candles blazed, in the adjoining rooms as well. What had Rabbi Gabriel said? At every feast you give for the dead, they arise; they hover round every image you dedicate to them, listen to every word that tells of them. With all his thoughts, with his blood and his nerves, he had called upon the dead; but she had not come, and only in twilight and dusk could he divine her presence. Now he was preparing a sacrificial feast for her, which would compel her to arise. He would not only offer her the Duke's body; his soul, too, he had so prepared, that it should separate itself from the flesh just at the moment when it exulted in the flower of its arrogance. And the soul of the haughty was incorporated in fire; in fire it palpitated, torn into a thousand pieces every second, through a new eternity. Rise up, Naemi! Arise, child, my dearest, my purest, lily of the valley, arise! The monument of a shattered kingdom I set up for thee, a prince I offer thee; a soul I incorporate in everlastingly palpitating fire! Thus I call thee Naemi, my child! Arise! Thou dove among the secret places of the rocks! Let me see thy face, let me hear thy voice! For thy voice is sweet, and lovely thy presence.

He paused, collected himself. All that had still to happen. He did not desire, in no circumstances did he desire, that it should seem that in his affair against Karl Alexander he was actuated by any wish for personal security, or even that he derived any advantage from it. In his own mind and in that of others, he could not suffer the least suspicion of this nature to arise. If any profit accrued from it, that was secondary importance, neither to be sought nor avoided; any gain for himself he would in any case discount in advance. He was there to feed the heart of this prince, Karl Alexander of Württemberg, until it was fat and haughty, and, when it swelled and strutted in its fatness, to crush it. For this sacrifice, this act of expiation, he was there. What came afterwards, oh, how far away that was, and how unimportant!

He commanded Master Schober to come. The latter appeared, terrified, disturbed out of his sleep, apprehensive lest the Finance Director should goad his conscience still further with new commissions. Unhappy, clad in a trailing dressing-gown, for Süss's command had given him little time—he stood before his master with round, frightened, childish eyes. Süss was merry, complacent, amiable as he had not been for long. He asked after the Master's poems, and how it was the edition was so long in coming out: the money had been sent to the printers weeks before. "Has your Excellency condescended to sleep well?" asked the parrot Akiba. The Master stuttered something: he was at present making corrections, and in two or three weeks the poems would be printed and ready. Suddenly changing the subject, Süss laid his hand on the Master's shoulder, his lips pursed in a sly, pleased smile, and he said confidentially, jovially: "Devil take it, you are a bad Protestant, Master!" And as the trembling man only stammered inarticulate words, he went on: "With my Jewish calculating morality, I would have said in your position: If I betray the Jew, then I betray only one man and only a Jew at that; but if I do not betray the Jew, then I betray a million evangelical Christians. And then I would have gone and told the story from beginning to end to Sturm or Jäger, or at least to somebody in the Committee of Eleven. I must say, Master, that you are of a fidelity and and discretion that stink to the heavens."

Jaakob Polykarp Schober stood shaking amid the bright candles, hardly daring to wipe away the deadly sweat which broke out on his white, fat, childish face, and stared with round, shocked, child-like eyes at the Jew. "Now you fancy I am crazy?" the latter asked after a while, good-humouredly. "No, Master, I am not in the least crazy," he said, drily; and again, after a pause, "or at least no more than everybody else."

It was as still as death in the bright room. Outside they heard the beat of the night-watch's footsteps. Süss had seated himself, and though the room was overheated, crouched as if almost freezing; he seemed to have forgotten Schober, who stood motionless, in a strangely crumpled-up, uncomfortable attitude. Unexpectedly he began again: "I will help you out of your dilemma. Go to the gentlemen in Parliament and say to them: the time is the night of Tuesday, the password '*Attempto!*' and if the gentlemen wish to avoid bloodshed, and to disable the whole project like a marionette when the wires have been cut, then they should send a deputation on Monday evening to Ludwigsburg. The mame-luke will await them at the side entry of the left wing, and will take them to the Duke."

While Süss in a calm and business-like tone spoke thus, Schober's eyes were almost starting out of his head with strained attention, excitement, and lack of understanding. "There is one condition," Süss went on, with the same business-like coolness, "and this condition you must swear on your oath to observe; that no human soul will ever come to know that I have said this to you or that I sent you."

"Your Excellency," stammered Schober at last, "I do not understand this; I do not understand this at all. I am very glad that the Lord has spoken to you, and that you wish to save the Evangelical faith. But if the heretical project comes to grief and no one knows that you have thwarted it, then, with your grace's permission, the Estates will take criminal action against you first of all. I am not strong *in politics,* but *then* the Duke will not be able to protect you."

"No, the Duke will not protect me," said Süss drily. "Let it well alone, Master," he proceeded, gentle, mild, almost paternal. "The affair is too curious. A Catholic Duke wants to turn a Protestant country Catholic, and a Jew would rather go to a criminal's death on the gallows than permit it. You could not make rhyme and reason out of that, even if you were twice as much a poet and magician."

Reeling and giddy, his knees trembling, Jaakob Polykarp Schober slunk, his dressing-gown trailing after him, through the dim corridors of the house. His excitement kept him pacing his room until morning. He could not see his way clearly; everything was indecisive, unreal. But one thing was certain: God had distinguished him, after all, had chosen him out. He trailed through the room, restless; the hem and the tassels of his dressing-gown swept the floor. The old grey cat awoke and accompanied him. It was a spoiled old cat, and wanted to be taken into his arms or laid on the bed, as often before, and it mewed. But he went backwards and forwards and did not hear it.

As soon as the Master had left, the Jew stretched himself and yawned, showing his strong teeth. Over his desk hung a portrait of the Duke under which with his own hand Karl Alexander had set his crude signature along with a few very gracious words. Süss paused before this, and said softly: "Adieu, Louis Quatorze! Farewell, German Achilles!" And again, more fervidly: "Farewell, German Achilles, Adieu, Louis Quatorze!"

He thought no longer of the child. It was a matter only between him and Karl Alexander; the child was not in it. He swam on a dark, violet-red sea of hatred, filling his heart, all his senses. How it roared! How it penetrated his ears, his inmost, inmost heart! What a wild, what a maddening and soothing perfume arose from it! He heard the cry of rage of the prince betrayed to his death, saw the bloody spectacle of the man out of whose hand he struck the supreme triumph of his violent, impetuous life, just as, with a sigh of relief, he was about to close his fingers on it. It was glorious to set one's knee on the breast of the enemy, glorious and sweet to press one's thumb on his throat, and when the mouth snapped for the good air, to press more firmly, gradually, one's eyes jeeringly triumphant on the beaten eyes of the other. That was life! That made life worth while!

Into his wild fantasy glided suddenly, corporeal, noiseless and terrifying, a human being. Otman, the Turkish servant. He bowed, imparting the news that the Duke had given General Remchingen the order.—What order?—The list.—It was the list of those who were to be arrested, which Süss had compiled for the Duke. But would Karl Alexander send word of such a trifle in the middle of the night? Improbable. Certainly the dusky fellow had something more essential, more mysterious to communicate. Süss looked attentively into his impassive face. Then the man began immediately to recite names. Johann Georg Andrea, Johann Friedrich Bellon. Oh yes, the list of arrests, beautifully, neatly, alphabetically arranged. But what about it? He knew it, he had compiled it himself. The Turk went on further: Friedrich Ludwig Stöfflen, Johann Heinrich Sturm, Josef Süss Oppenheimer. Süss made no movement, nor did the Turk. The list ended, he said no word further, bowed and went.

Alone, Süss whistled through his teeth and smiled, almost pleased. It was splendid to have this further corroboration. He was deeply amused. By God, this Karl Alexander was something of a wit. If at least he had given Remchingen a special order to apprehend him! But simply to include him *generally* in the list, in the self-same list which he had compiled, that was—that was supremely witty. He saw the two of them, the Duke and Remchingen, as they sat bowed over the list, saw how the Duke scribbled between the lines in his clumsy, crude hand: Josef Süss Oppenheimer, Finance Director. He saw then how they gazed, the prince and his general, into each other's eyes, silent, the Duke smiling grimly, Remchingen widely grinning. Good Karl Alexander! Well-affected, great-hearted prince! There you sit now and amuse yourself over your stupid Jew, who once he has neatly pulled the crown down out of the sky for you—you will put in the tower for his reward. Hoho! Too late thought of, Your Highness! Your Jew sits still a circle higher up, has thrown his cord round your neck already, and amuses himself with your unsuspecting amusement. You prince! You great potentate and hero! You lewd, stupid fool! you raper and butcher and scoundrel!

He walked about restlessly, in fevered thought. He remembered one time playing with a dog, and snatching away a piece of meat from the hungry beast just when he was going to swallow

329

it—until the cur bit him sharply in the hand. He saw still the blind hatred, the red, bloody rage in the eyes of the exasperated and repeatedly betrayed animal. With you I play a keener game, Karl Alexander. I snatch a more precious morsel away from you. Crouch, stretch your sinews in your lust for your prey, like a beast that is about to spring. Gaze till your dog's eyes are like saucers! Catch, Prince! Snap, my lord Duke!

Two days still, not even two days: only forty-five hours. He smiled more deeply, walked lonely and solitary through his rooms bright with candles. Motionless and white stood the busts of Solon, Homer, Aristotle, of Moses and Solomon; under the tiny pagodas walked the pigtailed Chinese figures; on the ceiling in intricate patterns proceeded the triumph of Mercury; from the glass cabinet glittered costly ornaments; and in his golden cage the parrot Akiba croaked: *"Bon jour, madame!"* and *"Ma vie pour mon souverain!"* But the lonely man wandering restless through his bright rooms heard nothing, saw nothing, was filled completely with his thoughts, images, visions.

When about the same time the mameluke arrived at the castle and stretched himself on his mat in a corner of the Duke's bedroom, he heard Karl Alexander groaning, striking round him, and making strange noises in his sleep.

It was already late in the evening when Our Teacher Rabbi Gabriel Oppenheimer van Straaten arrived at the house of his friend, Our Teacher Rabbi Jonathan Eybeschütz in Hamburg. The house was full of people who had come to see the Rabbi, to pay him honour, to seek his advice, and although his pupils perpetually explained that the Rabbi was among his books, in meditation, that there was no prospect he would receive them, they would not give in, and always hoped at least to have a glimpse of him. Many had come from a distance to see him, from communities where he had been before, Cracow, Metz, Prague; but many, too, had come from still farther, from Provence, yes, from the Black Sea. For the name of Rabbi Jonathan Eybeschütz, Rabbi of Hamburg, was held in humble reverence in many lands.

But he was also hated and combatted with the sharpest weapons in many lands. Ah, how Our Teacher Rabbi Jaakob Hirschel

330

Emden, Rabbi of Amsterdam, had jeered at him, had torn him to pieces in icy scorn, branded him, held him up to ridicule, as the enemy of Israel, of the Talmud, of the Rabbis, and of the true Word! Rabbi Jonathan Eybeschütz: the name split the whole of Jewry asunder; in every school and synagogue, at every synod, there was strife over this name; it was greeted with blessings and pæans, with jeers and maledictions.

Who was this man? Was he a learned Talmudist, zealous, quarrelsome, furious at any neglect of the rites, venomously angry over an iota, defending word by word the lofty table of the law with jealous and wild vituperation? Or had his philosophical, historical, mathematical, astronomical erudition gnawed away his belief in the true faith, proved by the Word and by works, and turned him into a mocker and contemner of Rabbinical ritual? Did he really believe in the teaching of the Cabbala and practise it, he the secret pupil and disciple of the Messiah Sabbatai Zewi, blessing, cursing, working miracles in the name of that redeemer? But why then did he publicly curse the followers of Sabbatai, and solemnly put them in ban? And why again did he send his sons to the Frankists in Poland, to the fanatical disciples of that enigmatical Messiah? Did this zealous, orthodox Talmudist really write letters to the French cardinals, to the Jesuit fathers in Rome, begging them to make him censor for Hebrew books? Was it arrogance, or what did it mean, that he suffered his strict, rabbinical orthodoxy to be defended against all suspicions of this kind by the Helmstatt Professor, Karl Anton, his former pupil, but now become a Christian and an apologist of the Christian evangel?

Rabbi Jonathan's scholars bowed deeply to Rabbi Gabriel when he entered. "Peace be with thee!" they said, and the closed door of the Master's room sprang open before him. In his study, in the circle of lamp-light, sat Rabbi Jonathan Eybeschütz, a mild figure, the wisest and craftiest of men. Cordially, whimsically, in soft, self-mockery, very pleased, he smiled out of his mighty, milky-white beard, more broad than long, and only slightly forked in the Cabbalistic fashion, to the beardless, morose, stony newcomer. All about him was round and comfortable, and accentuated his dignity. His long elegant caftan was of a heavy silk of incalculable value; his very small hand, white and manicured, was lifted out of the wide sleeve in greeting. From out the mighty, flowing, white beard smiled hospitably a countenance almost rosy, and hardly at all troubled by age. Only over the small, elegant nose, and the mild, sagacious, sly and yet deep eyebrows, there were cloven vertically in the white, fleshy, full brow, three furrows, representing Shin, the first letter in the holiest of names, Shaddai.

"My brother and Master will not be reproachful or angry?" he greeted his guest in Hebrew. He smiled, and there was in his smile knowledge and frailty, and coquetry, and consciousness of guilt, and even a little roguery. But above all a magical, lulling charm.

But on Rabbi Gabriel this magic missed fire. Over his tiny, flattened nose the far too large, troubled, grey eyes smouldered with sadness, and from his heavy, broad, not very high brow, went out an oppressive melancholy. But Rabbi Jonathan Eybeschütz was not willing that this melancholy should touch him. "Have you," he asked lightly, almost merrily, "have you read, Gabriel, the new polemic of the Krethi and Plethi man?" This was the most important work of that same Jaakob Hirschel Emden, Rabbi of Amsterdam, his fiercest antagonist. "Now the good man has happily let fly twelve lampoons against me, one for each tribe of Israel," he went on, and his brown, wise, crafty eyes laughed in mocking enjoyment. "Jaakob Hirschel has twelve tines on his antlers now." With his small manicured hand he turned the great pages of the polemic. "The poor, dull man," he said, pitying and amused, "all must be clear, all must be bright, all must be daylight! He does not suspect, the threadbare, arid mocker, he does not comprehend that a withered flower is only hay and good only for an ox." And, scornful and amused, he wagged his mild head with the prodigious, flowing white beard.

But Rabbi Gabriel did not enter into the other's mood. "Why have you excommunicated Sabbatai's disciples?" he asked in his surly voice. "Why do you turn and twist and shuffle and disclaim? Why do you let yourself be defended by a Goi with stupid and idiotic sophistries? Why do you not resign? Is it so important that you should be Rabbi of Hamburg, and have your rooms full of

332

people? Why have you— " and there was accusation and menace in his voice—"why have you excommunicated yourself?"

Jonathan Eybeschütz let a little, pleasant, comfortable burst of laughter out of his beard.

"Let well alone, Gabriel," he said. "You have not become milder in these two years, nor I stricter. I might say: is it not immaterial whether one is Jew or Goi or Moslem, if one but knows of the Upper World? I might say: Certainly Karl Anton, my scholar, has been baptized; but is there not more fellowship and intimacy between him and me than there is between me and Reb Jaakob Hirschel Emden, who is a good Jew with a sharp, gifted head, but unfortunately a narrow-minded worldling, stone-blind to the Upper World, and stone-deaf to its voices? I might say: The Messiah Sabbatai Zewi himself became a Moslem, to save the principle, the idea, and his disciple Frank has been baptized: shall it not be permitted to me, then, to assume the mummery of a snuffling rabbi, and pronounce with angry lips, but laughing in my heart, empty excommunications which recoil upon myself? I might say: it is easy to be a martyr; it is far harder to endure misunderstanding for the sake of the idea.

"All this I might say; but I will not say it to you, Gabriel." He stood up and came forward, splendid and hospitable in his silken caftan, to the thick-set gloomy man in his old Frankish clothes, which might have belonged to any humble official. With great charm, with almost boyish warmth, he said: "I admit I am weak and foolish and vain. The stars meant well by me, they shaped me to be the vessel for a great wisdom; I might have been a channel through which in mighty streams the breath of God might have flowed from the Upper to the Nether World. But I am an imperfect vessel. I know, and nobody can feel it more intensely in his deepest spirit, what blessed peace it is to rest in God, and that the Nether World is vanity and coloured foam and fleeting as wind. But I must plunge into it, always again. Action is foolish, action is stupid and filthy and bestial, and its aftertaste is stale and leaves a very evil flavour. But I must always plunge again into action and vanity and commotion! Let me be stupid, dear friend! Let me be filthy and bestial! Let me care

333

more for my beard than for my soul!" And with a blasphemous jest he concluded: "My soul I will find, and wash it clean in myriads of years; but who will guarantee that I will find such a lovely beard a second time?"

These blasphemies rippled softly from the sweet, persuasive, eloquent lips of the wise, frivolous, lost Rabbi. The other heard them, melancholy, stony, unmoved. Suddenly he saw a landscape. Stone, waste, broken ice; a tender, mocking light over it, overshadowing clouds, vulture flocks, dark madness and violence, gigantic blocks cast up by the ice. Almost unmanned by the picture, he recognized the same correspondence here as there. This presentiment had driven him from the man to whom he was most bound, to this other. One lay on the insolent, naked bosom of Lilith, but he yearned and longed for the Upper World. Among the saints and prophets this other reclined, the silvery beard of Simon ben Jochai on his chin, but he thirsted after the nipples of Lilith. The same picture, uttering the same thing. But that man was nearer his fulfillment than this.

He did not reply when Jonathan Eybeschütz paused at last. He only said: "Peace be with thee, my brother and master!" and went into the bedroom which had been prepared for him. Jonathan Eybeschütz watched the round, solid, slightly bowed back recede, and his mild, frivolous smile slowly disappeared, and in spite of his milky white beard, he looked less dignified and supercilious when he turned again to his books and parchments.

TIRED and nervous, Karl Alexander sat in his carriage. He was driving to Ludwigsburg, from there to go abroad and return only after the *coup* was accomplished. In the early morning he had taken leave of the Duchess. He had spent the night with her, had raved with boundless enthusiasm over his great project. This was the last night that she would dream as a petty German princess; henceforward she would be reckoned among the sovereigns of Europe, and soon, too, people would greet her with other titles than a shabby "Your Grace." Hot and excited he had whispered his fantasies to the beautiful tender Duchess; and she had listened, half-mocking, half-carried away by his ardour, responding to his embraces more passionately than she had for a long time. Now wearied out by his exhausting and definitive leave-taking, feeling stale, nervous and feverish, he leaned back in his carriage. Yet he had faced many an enterprise before in icy cold blood, had not been nervous in the battle-field, even when his horse was shot dead under him. But to-day, hell and fury! all his limbs were prickly, and it was as if he had ants in his veins. His cursed foot, too, throbbed and beat, and would not be still. No wonder, the weather was atrocious. Now sun, now hailstones; the elements were at war. A strong moist wind blew, ragged clouds raced madly across the sky. Moreover, a fire had broken out in Eglosheim, and its glow irritated the horses. A vague memory returned to Karl Alexander. In such a gusty wind he had stood, not so long ago; like the red light there a hard moon had curved down in the sky—it had come spectral, disquieting, out of a black, hostile forest; a pale dead girl lay on the ground, among flowers, in the strong wind. Senseless memories. What use were they now? He had, God knew, better things to think of.

In Ludwigsburg at last. Even there no peace. Couriers, despatches from the more distant garrisons. Vexation, worry. He suddenly discovered he was hungry, asked for soup, greedily began to swallow it down, found it was too hot, flung the dish against the wall. On top of this, the melancholy bell ringing for the fire at Eglosheim. The wind coming in gusts, the chimney smoking. Everywhere in the castle windows rattling, doors banging. The Duke could find peace nowhere. In this way evening came at last.

In Stuttgart it was very quiet that evening. Nowhere a light was to be seen. But in the darkness there was the tramp of many feet, subdued rattling of iron and wood, bustle and commotion. All the citizenry knew that this hour must decide the issue. Schober's tidings had had their effect. All were prepared, armed, full of gloomy, subdued tension, not without dubiety, but willing to fight. No one slept in Stuttgart that night, except tiny children. Meanwhile in the castle at Ludwigsburg all the candles were blazing. Before his going abroad, the Duke was giving a court ball for the special ambassador of the Emperor, Count Palffy, and the Würzburg party. The company was not numerous; it was restricted to those who were implicated in the *coup d'état*. A good many officers were there; the two Röders, the general and the major. With a grin, Karl Alexander had invited the surly, low-browed man to Ludwigsburg; the Stuttgart Citizen Cavalry, of which he was commander, would hardly need him on this night. Without entering into the joke—for he took his position in the City Cavalry very seriously—the major, dumb and staring, his formless, gloved paw at a military salute, had accepted the gracious invitation. In the reception room the purple vulture-beaked, flesh-less countenance of Dom Bartelemi Pancorbo looked over the colossal, antique ruff; Weissensee, a ruined man now, kept near to Süss; he snuffled, his clever eyes blinked, he foresaw fire, fury, ruin, devastation. Süss himself had a radiant evening recalling his best times; his full, quick eyes were everywhere; he was gallant, witty, irresistible; his assured, festive mood was in striking con-trast to the flickering restlessness of Karl Alexander. Sometimes the brown, animal-like eyes of the mameluke sought his; he had given the mute and bowing Turk a few brief, quiet instructions, and after that it went in a triumphant question and answer between the two pairs of eyes.

In the dead of night the leaders of the constitutional party in Stuttgart would be arrested, and the Würzburg and Bavarian troops would break into the Duchy. Until the courier came with the news that the *coup* had been successful so far according to plan, Karl Alexander would remain among his guests, and go to bed with the certain tidings in his mind. He had installed the new prima donna in his bedroom suite, the Demoiselle Teresa, a lively, hot-eyed, fiery-blooded person. For the last two years, from considerations of vanity, he had been accustomed to make use of an aphrodisiac. To-night, after his parting with Marie Auguste, he ordered the Turkish servant to strengthen the dose.

The courier with the happy news did not come, and did not come. The restlessness of the Duke infected all his guests, made them uncomfortable, was felt through the whole room. Outside the tempest remained as violent as ever; rain beat against the window panes, once, too, there was a rattle of hail; the smoke from the badly-drawing chimney could not be quite banished from the rooms. True, myriads of candles blazed; music rang, ever

336

more voluptuously; the rarest wines were decanted out of the oldest casks; they had donned their most magnificent dresses, their most festive moods; but they could not get beyond a feverish, forced gaiety.

Karl Alexander held audiences, put noisy, gracious questions to his guests, suddenly to sink in himself, ignore their responses, abruptly break off. The mameluke glided in softly, with the information that Demoiselle Teresa was in the private cabinet. The Duke replied unceremoniously: "The woman must wait!" and sat down with Süss to play. The mameluke brought him the aphrodisiac in a silver vessel and stood still, submissive. "Have you made it strong enough?" asked Karl Alexander. "Yes, Your Highness," replied the mameluke in his rough, indifferent voice.

Karl Alexander gulped the potion down. Played. Won fast. Remained uninterested, absent. His green gala coat thrown back, a hand resting now on his yellow-breeched knee, now playing nervously with his golden chain, he made long pauses between stroke and stroke.

"Why does the courier not come?" he asked feverishly. "The storm," Süss reassured him, "the bad roads." The Turkish servant was there again, with his quick, gliding step. He said that the Demoiselle was still waiting. "She shall undress meanwhile," cried the Duke. "I cannot bring my despatches here by magic."

A circle of deferential spectators stood round the players and accompanied the play with artificial and forced witticisms. The Duke turned up a winning card, hauled in again a pile of ducats. "To-night you must give me a part, Jew," he laughed, "of what you have done me out of." "To-night I do it gladly," said Süss. The hostile voice of Major Röder growled: "When he is face to face, like this, the Jew does not bleed one so easily. When one works from a distance with papers and dodges, and without having to look the other in the eye—that is easier." Süss lost the next trick, too. The Duke noticed the architect Retti among the spectators, and threw at him: "If my luck lasts like this, we will build the extension to the gallery you talked of." The architect laughed loudly, appreciatively. Dom Bartelemi Pancorbo said unexpectedly in his rough, husky voice: "He will not lose the stone, the Jew." And they all stared greedily, lost in reverie, at the solitaire on the Finance Director's hand, and saw how in alternation, in perpetual change, the rays shot from it.

The mameluke was once more behind the Duke and announced: "They are here." With simulated carelessness Karl Alexander flung the cards on the table, and shoved his considerable heap of winnings across to Süss: "There, Jew! The gallery I will build later. I make a present of this to you." Almost grateful, amused, Süss thought: "Look at that! He is not giving anything away. He pays me, when he thinks I have helped him to his goal, and he adds a tip too. Then he flings me in a dungeon, and sticks both payment and tip in his pocket again." Attentively, urgently, he gazed at the Duke, and the latter, as if compelled by his look, said cursorily: "You may come with me." The dark servant in advance, then Karl Alexander, red, limping, panting; last of all the Jew, elated, pale, youthful: so they went.

Through the bowing lackeys in the antechamber first, then through silent coridors in which there only sounded the fitful gusts of the storm, so towards the other wing of the castle, where was the Duke's private suite: a study, a small dressing-room, and the bed-room with the waiting lady. The mameluke flung open the door of the study. The courier whom Karl Alexander expected was not there, but four men whom he did not know. Two of them were old, with silver grey hair, thin as rakes; the others, thick-set, loutish, of proletarian bearing. All four were silent; they bowed, the younger men awkwardly and bluntly, the older hastily and several times; the draught from the open door made the candles flicker wildly, casting an uncertain light.

The Duke, foaming, his expectations disappointed, his voice almost inarticulate with rage, cried to the mameluke: "Are you crazy? To let the rabble in on me in the night, and this night?" With one kick he sent him sprawling into the corner. "The courier," he roared. "Where is the courier?"

"We are not rabble. We come from the Estates," one of the men began, clumsily, with hostility. Karl Alexander threw himself upon him, seized the stammering, loutish man, shook him: "You have come to attack me, have you? Assassinate me? Heretics! Murderers!" He shouted and foamed at the mouth, so that the singer in the next room, who waited in nakedness, dived deep under

338

the blankets in apprehension and crossed herself. "But it is all up with you!" bellowed the Duke, giving freer rein to his fury. "I'll let you rot alive. You rabble! You traitors! Heretics! Curs! I'll fling you into my deepest dungeons along with your eleven fine brothers from the Sub-Committee!"

"That will not happen, Sir Duke," said one of the old men in a refined and courteous voice. "That will not happen at all." And he bowed several times. "What will happen, with your Highness's gracious permission, is that to-night nobody will be arrested in Stuttgart. And very few Bavarian and Würzburg troops will beset the town, and half of those who have already entered with the password '*Attempto*' are, with your Highness's gracious permission, Evangelical Brethren. And even though Commandant Röder is here, the Town Militia is none the less in readiness and will hold the town whatever happens."

Süss himself could not have intimated more roundly and precisely or in fewer words that the plot was absolutely exposed and betrayed than the small and haggard man, who continued to reveal more details very politely and with much foot-scraping and begging of permission. But he never got to the end and gist of his speech, for the Duke had heard only the first sentence when a terrible change took place in him. His hand, which had been clutching the thick-set and vulgar-looking delegate, gradually loosened its hold, his face suffused with purple, a curious, agonized, brutish rattle came from his chest, his mouth gasped helplessly, and all at once his massive bulk slid to the floor, convulsed and horribly distorted. The four citizens were terrified at this sight, lest they should be held responsible; the Castle was full of their enemies and they had been admitted by the mameluke unannounced, in a secret and suspicious manner by a back door; they feared that they might be mishandled or even summarily butchered, and they made speedily for the door and were glad to find their coach drawn up in the storm and rain waiting for them, and to be once more on the Stuttgart road, trembling with cold and excitement.

Karl Alexander meanwhile lay on the floor, alone with Süss and the brown slave. He had torn his clothes off his enormous and hairy chest. The naked girl in the next room crouched in dismay and listened to the wild and brutish rattle which issued from his mouth. With terrible difficulty he rolled his glazing eyes around, asking a question full of wild and boundless hatred. Süss stepped towards him and said: "Yes, Your Highness."

The Jew did not know if he had willed this, or indeed how he had willed the Duke to take the betrayal and ruin of the plot. Nor did he ask himself whether the Duke's fatigue after the Carnival or the aphrodisiac were partly the cause of the collapse, or whether he alone was deliberately responsible for it. As if driven by fate he had arranged everything just as it had happened; he had planned that the heated Duke should find at night these unlucky delegates instead of the expected herald of good fortune. He had known for certain that he would pierce his enemy to the heart, and lame his spirit, and crush it for life. If this external collapse were now to be added, it was none the less welcome, although he had not willed it.

With all his strength he heaved the heavy body into an armchair, giving a curt order to the brown slave: "It would be as well for you to go and fetch Father Kaspar." Otman departed, after a slight hesitation, leaving the Jew alone with the dying man.

A chilly shudder crept over the singer in the next room as she heard a low voice, vibrating almost to breaking point with wild emotion and glowing rage, addressing the now silent Duke. She could not make out the sense of the words, but the gruesome and hateful triumph in the hot and whispering voice paralysed her.

What the Jew was saying was this: "Duke! Brute and simpleton of a Duke! Stupid, blockheaded Karl Alexander! Now you would like to stop your ears, wouldn't you? You would like to clear out and hear no more? You would like to pray, and get absolution from your confessor, and have the oil of grace trickled over you? But I won't grant you that. I won't let you die till you have listened to me. Roll your eyes as you may, and rattle your lungs, you'll have to listen! I am speaking quite low, without raising my voice, but what I say is filling your ears and your shameless, violent heart. And you must keep quite still, and you dare not die yet, and you have to listen.

"Yes, my child died a different death. You were hallooing and yelling behind her, your stinking, accursed breath was on her neck; but she could smile and be light-hearted, and a thousand good angels received her in their arms. And you stood by the corpse with your bewildered and stupid butcher's face and because I didn't spit on you, you believed that all was well, and nothing altered. But, you see, Karl Alexander, you see, you stupid and dull-witted Duke, I didn't spring on your leering face then, I didn't do it quite so simply, because I wanted first to make you ready, to prepare you so that you should look like a decent human being, yes, even like a prince. What, do you kick against it? Do you snort? Yes, there you lie, a pathetic and absurd lump of flesh, utterly ridiculous to yourself and to others. For, you see, you wretched fool, all your grand ideas of puffing yourself up to be the Swabian Louis XIV, and your dreams of being a Cæsar, were suggested to you by me. You were never anything more than a petty, violent dukeling all your days, seated by pure chance on a throne, and I pulled the strings, and fattened you up till you were ready."

He stopped, and left the dying man alone while he meditated; then he began again in a changed and gentler tone. "Yes, I was drawn to you, and I could have been your friend. But whenever you were aware of such a feeling you thrust it from you, and argued it down, and accepted only the worst of me, and let that blossom and flourish. You great prince and hero, you German Louis XIV! You poor fool and simpleton!"

Outside in the corridor there were breathless, excited voices. Doctor Wendelin Breyer arrived, with Neuffer, the valet, and a little later, Father Kaspar, the confessor; it had not been so easy to find him, for he was sitting in the confectioner's with the insignificant and shrewd-looking Privy Councillor from Würzburg, who was comfortably drinking many cups of black coffee and without being affected by the general uneasiness was relishing the triumph of the previous night. Now they all came rushing in, and fussed helplessly and senselessly around the dying man, whose face was shockingly distorted, and put confused questions to Süss, who answered them with vague carelessness and soon slipped away unnoticed in the bustle.

341

In the next room the singer was putting on her clothes. That low, hot, triumphant voice, full of devouring hate, still rang in her ears and made her tremble; pale, shivering, and shaken with wide-eyed horror, she threw her clothes on anyhow and ran with averted head through the corridors, pursued by the uncanny voice, and drew a long breath of relief when she had the front door of the castle behind her, and felt the wind blowing.

Doctor Wendelin Breyer wanted to open one of the Duke's veins, but he did not get so far. The silent mameluke, who had returned with them, had advanced quietly to the man in the armchair; with gruesome coolness he regarded the clenched, cramped fists, the swollen black-and-blue face, the protruding tongue, the wildly staring and bulging eyes. Then in his gloomy and peculiarly hoarse voice, that most of them had never heard speak before, he said, so suddenly that everyone jumped: "He is dead." There was nothing left for Doctor Wendelin Breyer but to confirm this statement.

While the physician was still stammering out in his hollow and resonant voice vague remarks such as "sudden attack of *spasmus diaphragmatis,* choking catarrh, *stagnatio sanguinis plenaria,*" confusedly cudgelling his brains and summoning all his importance under the quiet and scornful eye of the brown slave, the whisper ran through the lobbies, flew through the ante-rooms, and was announced in the ball-room by the master of ceremonies: "The Duke is dead." The music broke off. Sheer paralysed horror everywhere, and pale distorted faces. Then bewildered chaos, a clearing of the floor, and a rush to the corners. Embarrassment and unwillingness to appear conscious was depicted on the faces of the guests, the Imperial, Bavarian and Würzburger lords and gentlemen. The officers stood about like great, stupid, dangerous beasts of prey suddenly caught in a trap. Such a confounded accident just at this moment might cost each of them not only his position and his possessions, but even his life. Even the little Privy Councillor Fichtel lost his composure; for decades he had been self-controlled both in private and in public; but now all at once his face became hard, pinched, and shrewish like a peasant's and he swore foully beneath his breath. Meanwhile Süss stood alone in a remote side-room. He bothered himself about nothing; the hubbub of the general excitement did not penetrate so far. The storm outside was gradually passing over. The Jew saw nothing, heard nothing, and heeded nothing: everything around him was blotted out. He was waiting. Now, in a moment, his child would appear; she would surround him like a pleasant air, and she would flow pleasantly into him, making him light and airy. He sat still, with a relaxed and almost foolish smile, waiting.

She did not come. Nothing came. With every passing minute he felt himself becoming colder, emptier and heavier. And suddenly he knew that she would never come. He saw the Duke, with his discoloured twisted face, his protruding tongue, and his bulging eyes. He felt nauseated. He shrank in terror. He could no longer comprehend how that could have satisfied and exalted him. In the name of God, what had that to do with his child? The child was white, comforting, as serene as the moon. And his dealings with the Duke, that vermilion sea, his passion and his wild outburst of savagery, aye, in what kind of brainsick seizure had he believed that that would bring him to his child? In anxious dejection he tried to reconstruct it, but could no longer understand himself. His duologue with the dying Karl Alexander had been a wild, palpitating flood and ebb, like intercourse with a woman, but not exaltation and release. And now he was dejected and sad, full of nausea, and further away from his child than ever.

He felt a cold raw breath on the back of his neck. He lifted his shoulders with a shiver of revulsion. A face looked over his shoulder. It was his own face.

He shook himself and stood up. The storm had begun again, and he shut the window more tightly. There was a voice in the wind; it was at his ear, in the room, a harsh and sorrowful voice, the voice of his uncle. It was not loud, but it completely filled the room, and filled the castle; the whole world was full of that voice. Then he knew for certain that he had been on the wrong road.

Curiously enough, he was not disappointed at this discovery, nor even annoyed. No, it was all right. He saw himself again treading in that silent and shadowy quadrille, with Rabbi Gabriel holding his right hand and the Duke his left. They crossed and balanced to each other and bowed. But to-day there was no sense of torment in the cloudy and colourless picture. For now the dancers loosened their hands and looked quietly and seriously at each other, without enmity; they nodded for the last time to each other, and then dispersed.

A boundless lassitude fell upon him. Never in his life had he been so exhausted by real physical weariness and weakness. He felt as if he were sitting in a warm bath, letting his life drain out drop by drop from an opened vein. Everything in him was melting, weakening, collapsing. It was a delicious, soothing, relaxing ache. Surrender, downfall, being carried away. Willing nothing, letting oneself for the first time be swept along, a blissful, will-less gliding and flowing along. As if his blood were flowing out, taking with it all his impulses and desires, he felt himself sinking into an ecstatic, painful, limitless state of stupor.

So he was discovered a little later by the old and shaky man who came to extinguish the lights and plunge the room into darkness. He started in terror when he recognized the pale and sunken figure, and dropped his extinguisher, crying: "Jesus! The Finance Director!" But the latter, raising himself wearily, told him to bring something to eat, anything at all, for he was faint with hunger. The old man, crossing himself in his embarrassment, hastened to bring what was required. Süss, eating ravenously with his fingers, told the old man to go on with his work. He stammered that it was not fitting, he could not leave the Finance Director in the darkness. But Süss interrupted him: "Put out your lights and don't bother about me." The old man confusedly went to work. The storm had set in with renewed strength and fury. Süss ate and swallowed. The old man set about his business, climbing his ladder and putting out the lights, looking furtively at the Finance Director. He kept on eating hastily, devouring the food with relish. Finally, with a remarkably happy laugh, he said: "Put not thy trust in princes! That's in the Bible, isn't it?" "I don't understand Your Excellency," stuttered the old man in fear. "Never mind it," said Süss, swallowing the last morsel; "light me on my way!" The room was left in darkness, and Süss followed the man's small lantern through gloomy suites of rooms into the main corridor of the castle.

Here in an adjoining room sat the leaders of the Catholic

344

Plot, Ministers and Generals. There were many Württembergers among them. The gentlemen from Würzburg and Bavaria and His Apostolic Majesty's Ambassador, had all scurried away with great promptitude in spite of storm and rain. There sat now the Swabian gentlemen, pale and perspiring, in high tension and bewilderment. They breathed more freely as Süss entered, looking to him in eager hope as their rescuer.

The Jew ran his brown eyes round the dejected circle gently, quietly, and almost with a smile. Then he said to the burly Major Röder, who was even more rigid and stupefied than the others: "You do not see quite clearly, Major, what is to be done in this unusual situation?" He came close up to the other, who was staring at him dully and uncomprehendingly, and said very pleasantly: "Arrest me; and then you are safe, whoever comes out on top." He said this quite casually and courteously, almost in a conversational tone.

The gentlemen gaped in amazement. But then their eyes gleamed with a hard, malicious glitter. It was not quite clear what the Jew was up to, but this much was certain, if he were to be seized and arrested there would be a conspicuous scapegoat to intercept the first outbreak of wrath and to be held responsible for the worst. For a long moment there was a death-like silence in the room. Everyone, almost in the same words and in the same order, had the same thoughts. And they all came to the same conclusion: Yes, arrest the Jew! That will be our salvation! The Jew must hang!

And so they achieved something after all. So there was no further need to sit in such a state of stupid, oppressive and shameful anxiety. So, confound it, they managed after all to keep their ends up in the fight; why had they given way to that stupid, disgraceful, cowardly fear which had produced such a sinking feeling? It was delightful to be able to shake off that wretched mood in such an excellent way. In a minute they would have overcome and forgotten the whole abominable, lamentable and miserable business.

And Major Röder was already on his feet. He seemed in his own eyes and in those of the others wholly a patriot, a Christian, and a soldier. Full of character, convinced of his own loyalty and honesty, he advanced imposingly towards Süss, and laid his shapeless, gauntleted hand on the other's slim and elegant shoulder. He opened his hard mouth importantly: "In the name of the Duchess and of the Constitution, I arrest you, Jew."

In a twinkling the oppressive silence had given way to exultant and bestial clamour. The Jew smiled, solitary, still, and very aloof; while the gentlemen by filthy abuse, pushing and trampling and insulting him, strove to keep the sight of this smile from piercing them to the marrow.

Book Five

THE OTHERS

Book Five

THE OTHERS

WHERE the Orient and the Occident meet, there lies the land of Canaan, infinitely small. And the land of the noon-day sun, the ancient land of Mithra, stretches out a tongue to touch their meeting-place. Where the roads from the west cut across the roads from the east, there lies the city of Jerusalem, the fortress of Zion. And the Jews, when they acknowledge the God of Israel, the One who is omnipotent, Jehovah, at sunrise and at sunset, stand with their feet together and their faces towards Jerusalem, towards Zion; those in the west turn to the east, and those in the Orient turn to the west, all at the same hour, all facing towards Jerusalem.

From the Occident there beats a wild continuous wave upon the land of Canaan: a thirst for life and personality, a will for action, for happiness, for power. To accumulate, to gather in knowledge, possessions and happiness, more happiness, more possessions, to live, to fight, to do. That is the message from the west. But in the south under the pointed pyramids there lie dead kings embalmed in gold and spices, refusing majestically to give their bodies to destruction; their images set in colossal alleys in the desert smile at death. And a wild continuous wave beats from the south upon the land of Canaan; a passionate cleaving to Being, a burning desire not to lose form and shape, not to lose the body, not to disintegrate. But from the east there comes a message of gentle wisdom: Sleep is better than waking, to be dead is better than to be alive. Non-resistance, surrender to annihilation, passivity, renunciation. And the mild continuous wave ebbs softly from the Orient towards Canaan.

Eternally these three waves flow over the tiny land and mingle

349

one with another; one clear and resounding of will and deed, one hot and glowing of majestic refusal to submit to death, one soft and dark of surrender and renunciation. The tiny land of Canaan lies still and attentive and lets the waves flow over it and into each other.

In that tiny land dwelt the folk of Israel, keen of eye and of ear. They gazed towards the east, hearkened towards the west, and scanned the horizon to the south. It is such a small nation, and it sits among colossi; Assyria, Babylon, Mithra, and Roman Syria. It must keep a sharp look-out if it is not to be crushed unawares or swallowed by the giants. And it does not want to be swallowed up, it wants to exist, it is a clever and brave little nation, and it has no intention of being crushed. The three waves keep on coming with constant uniformity. But the little nation stands fast. It is not stupid, it does not stand up against the impossible: it bends its head when a wave comes that is too high for it, and quietly lets itself be submerged over the very crown. But then it emerges again erect, and shakes itself, and is there again. It is stubborn, but not foolishly obstinate. It surrenders itself to all the waves, but not completely to any one of them. It takes to itself from the three currents what seems convenient and adapts it.

Its standing danger compels the little nation to ignore no movement of its gigantic neighbours, to be always prudent, to feel, to guess, to sift, to recognize. To sift, classify, and recognize the world becomes second nature to it. A great love grows up within it for the means of such knowledge, the Word. The laws of its religion excommunicate the unlettered, and a knowledge of the Scriptures is commanded by God. It harvests all that the three waves bring to it, and translates into its own self-created language the bright destructive doctrine of doing, the stubborn, ardent yearning for immortality, and the gentle ecstasy of refraining from action and will. And the little nation writes the two books which have most of all changed the face of the world, the great Book of Deeds, the Old Testament, and the great Book of Renunciation, the New Testament. But the stubborn desire for immortality remains the dominant note in all its living and writing.

The sons of the little nation go out into the world and live according to the doctrines of the West. Causation, struggle, accumulation. But in spite of all they are not quite at home in action, their place is on the bridge between action and renunciation. And they always turn back to gaze at Zion. Often in the fulfilment of victory, in the realization of defeat, in the very midst of their career, they come to a halt with a shudder of awe, hearing among a thousand brazen echoes a still, dying voice which says: "Will nothing, do nothing, renounce your ego."

And many a one follows the road to the very end; from the wild turmoil of doing, from power, happiness and possession, through a stubborn refusal to renounce, into the bliss of vacancy and absolution, into the ebb-tide of inaction and abnegation.

THROUGH a night of storm and clouds the couriers pounded towards Stuttgart. To the members of Parliament, to Remchingen, to the Duchess. They overtook the carriage with the deputation which had been sent to the Duke. The news of Karl Alexander's death reached the gates before it, and found its way hesitatingly through the dark and silent town, which was nevertheless at fever heat and full of whispers. The citizens ran out into the streets, sought their neighbors' houses. Was it true? The visitation of God, the visible finger of the Lord. Such an overwhelmingly great and unexpected deliverance! But was it really true? Was it not a trap? Timid lights were kindled in the houses. The rumour gained strength, the first half-suppressed shouts of joy were heard. Until at last it was certain, beyond all doubt, and from the Town Hall it was proclaimed that the Duke was dead. Then the long pent-up excitement broke loose. People embraced one another and prayed. The joy of deliverance shone on all faces. Illuminations, and a general holiday. The pig-eyed pastry cook Benz painted with the help of his bosom friends a picture on which, above a church with two towers, a winged devil was carrying off a man. Underneath it he printed in huge capitals the rhyme:

> See how into the devil's fold
> He goes who left his church for gold.

His sweaty hands trembling with joy, he set the picture in the window, illuminated with candles, and gloated when the people paused to look and to carry the rhyme through the town. Soon it was everywhere affirmed that the devil had carried away the Duke. Had you not heard how dreadfully blue and distorted the dead man's face was? Beelzebub had strangled the heretic Duke with his own talons.

Fluttered and disconcerted, Marie Auguste sat in her room. With her were the Chancellor Scheffer, General Remchingen, and her confessor, the Capucin, Father Florian. She sat in a charming negligée which had come by special express from Paris only that morning, and she could not help thinking what a shame it was that she had not had it a day sooner. For then she would have worn it on that last evening, and Karl Alexander would have seen it. Now he was dead of a horrible death, and never again would he see a negligée or a woman. She felt at least that it was to her credit that on this last night she had been complaisant to him. From beneath floated up the sound of the town's jubilation at the death of the Duke.

The bulky Remchingen, who in the middle of his grief and anxiety could not refrain from involuntary glances at Marie Auguste's bare arms, growled, inarticulate with helpless rage: "We must go on, go on! Accomplish the plan in spite of everything! We have the soldiers! I'll answer for the soldiers!" Even supposing one or two regiments were to mutiny, he would shoot them down. . . . They would take the oath to the Duchess. Semiramis. Elisabeth. Catherine. On with it! On with it! Quaking and anxious, the Chancellor deprecated all this. For God's sake, let there be no shedding of blood. The *coup d'état* had failed and was done with. Now they must just be careful and keep within the law. That would give them a handle. Father Florian urged the same arguments, but more positively and with less timorousness. The quick imagination of the Capucin was weaving a seductive chain. A clever diplomatist, confessor to a reigning Duchess in what was perhaps the most important state in the Empire, and the one with the brightest prospects, he dreamt of himself already as a German Richelieu or Mazarin, while he made mild and circumspect remarks. But while her pastel-coloured tiny head seemed to be listening attentively, Marie Auguste was very absent-minded; she was thinking of Karl Alexander, of her negligée, of the widow's

352

veil she would have to order—it might be made to look very piquant and modish; even the ugly Duchess of Angoulême had looked well in one: and after the gentlemen had made several definite proposals, she said suddenly in a small, important voice: *"Que faire, messieurs? Que faire?"*

The sub-committee of Parliament met before dawn; some of the other members of Parliament, too, could not be prevented from attending. How excited and important they were, how they boasted of their power! They behaved as if they had brought about the Duke's death themselves, as if their foresight and statesmanship had planned this simple solution of the crisis. Already their joy at their deliverance was dwarfed by their solid feelings of possession, power and revenge. Ha! Now they were on the top! Now they would pay off old scores against the Jew, the Catholics and all the others before whom they had cringed! Whatever Karl Alexander's will might be it was obvious that Duke Rudolf of Neuenstadt was the right Regent for the small heir. He could be trusted. He was a good Protestant and on their side. The very next day they would send for him. And that very day they would show the heretics and traitors and Yidds what was what. They did not dare to attack the military powers; but all Süss's civilian supporters who were in Stuttgart—not those in Ludwigsburg—were seized that night. It was a repetition of what had happened to the Countess's supporters after Eberhard Ludwig's death. The police and gendarmes went round arresting all the people who had fallen from favour, and dragged them scowling, cursing, railing, or wretchedly entreating and complaining, to the police headquarters, through crowds of gaping, jeering and delighted onlookers. Bühler, Mez and Hallwachs were all arrested, and so were Lamprechts and Knab, and even the Chancellor, Scheffer.

Remchingen looked on, grinding his teeth. Explicit orders from the Duchess forbade him to interfere. But let them only start to touch the army! Let them lay their stinking fingers on a single one of his officers! Then he would break loose, then he would strike out! But the emissaries of the Estates went out of their way to avoid encounters with the army.

Remarkably enough, there was only one man who was never spoken about in Stuttgart, or only referred to in whispers and without the mention of his name. And yet he was at the bottom of everybody's thoughts; he was the secret hope of the Duchess and the army, the secret fear of the citizens and the Parliament. What was Süss doing? Where would he range himself? Would he intervene? How would he defend himself, the slippery eel, the dexterous devil? He was in Ludwigsburg, and no one had a word from him, not a despatch, nothing. The first grey light of morning broke, a warm, rainy March morning. After the perplexities and fluctuations of the night people were exhausted, tired to death; they went home to bed. And still no news from the Jew. It was dissimulation, it was thoughtlessness, it was meanness. Into the first dreams of the Duchess's frantic partisans, of the triumphant Parliament, of those who were disgraced or in custody, there glided a dim hope or a dim fear which took the form of the question: "What was Süss doing?"

IN Ludwigsburg Doctor Wendelin Breyer was dictating a medical report. Together with his two colleagues Georg Burkhard Seeger and Ludwig Friedrich Bilfinger, he had conducted the postmortem.

All three had the same thought while they operated: "Aha! Now you are lying quiet and cannot kick me or break my bottles of medicine over my head!" But their faces preserved the seriousness and grave melancholy proper to men of science. And now Doctor Wendelin Breyer was dictating in his hollow voice and with large, sweeping gestures his detailed and conscientious *Iudicium medico-chirurgicum,* the report of the medical board. "From this *Viso reperto,*" he dictated, "it is sufficiently clear that His Princely Highness succumbed not to an apoplexy, nor to an inflammation, nor to a *gangræna,* nor to a hemorrhage, nor to a polypus, nor to anything of that kind, but to a catarrh which choked him so that he was suffocated. Without any doubt this rapid attack was facilitated partly by a *spasmus diaphragmatis*—a condition to which he was subject and which had been recently aggravated—acting upon a full and distended stomach which was pressing upon the midriff; partly, however, by the predisposition of his lungs *ad stagnationem sanguinis plenariam, ob atoniam et debilitatem connatam* (it is unfortunately proved by experience that most of the

354

Serene Dukes of the House of Württemberg succumb to chest complaints)."

On the day following Karl Alexander's death his will was opened in Stuttgart. In its original form it appointed the Duchess joint Regent with Duke Karl Rudolf of Neuenstadt. A later codicil witnessed by Privy Councillors Fichtel and Raab named the Archbishop of Würzburg as a third Regent, and a second clause signed by Karl Alexander shortly before his death endowed the Bishop with extra plenipotentiary powers.

A deputation from the Sub-Committee immediately set out for the quiet town of Neuenstadt to see the Duke Karl Rudolf and submissively to beg him to assume the Regency with all speed. Karl Rudolf was a sparing man well advanced in years. He had been a student at Tübingen, and in his youth had seen a great deal of the world; he had been in Switzerland, France, England and the Netherlands. He had then taken service under the Venetians and fought at Morea, distinguishing himself greatly in the siege of Negroponte. Then he had fought as a volunteer in Ireland, and in the War of the Spanish Succession had commanded twelve thousand Danish mercenaries and decided the issue of the bloody victory of Ramillies. Both Prince Eugene and Marlborough prized him highly, and he was renowned among the generals of Europe. But quite suddenly when, at the age of fifty, he inherited on the death of his brother the family estate of Württemberg-Neuenstadt, he gave up his military career and withdrew into his little town to live like a farmer—the strict and conscientious father of his little domain.

He had had no intercourse with Karl Alexander. That magnificent prince with his luxurious court and his shameless rascal of a Jew was an abomination to him. He was a strict and frugal man, and by this time over seventy. He loved his winding, flowery little town, and when Marie Auguste was mentioned, the heretic, the frivolous devotee of dress and ballet-dancing, he curled his hard lips in sour disgust. He was small, lean and a little bent; he spoke with military brevity; his attire and household were strictly regulated, clean and bare. He would say "Duty!" He would say "Authority!" He would say "Justice!" And in spite of his years he was a strenuous worker.

He listened in silence while the Stuttgart gentlemen unwound their circumstantial sentences, and even after they had repeated them he said nothing. He was getting old, he would have liked to pass his few remaining years in his little flowery town, he would have liked to inspect his fields and vineyards, an old farmer, and to see that his subjects treated their children and cattle properly. And now in his old age God had laid a heavy task upon him, to clean and purify before he died his forsaken country, to struggle against the Emperor and the Empire, to wrangle with the fat, sly Jesuit at Würzburg. It was God's command; he was a soldier and knew the importance of subordination; he submitted. He told the Stuttgarters that he would take over the administration, but on condition that he was the sole Regent; he would not co-operate with the Duchess, who was a Catholic from Regensburg, nor, certainly, with the Jesuit Bishop of Würzburg. He added that he would be in the Residence the very next day.

The Stuttgarters returned in high delight. This was the man they needed. He would make short work of Remchingen and of the Jew, too, of whom strangely enough one still heard nothing.

Remchingen immediately hit out savagely. He had always hated the dry Neuenstadter, and had often made fun of his stingy, bourgeois habits. He now took his stand on the codicil to the will, on the plenipotentiary powers of the Lord Bishop of Würzburg, on the troops under his command. He refused to swear allegiance to the Regent, or to take any orders from him, and forbade his subordinates to do so, pledging them to support Karl Alexander's will. To stir up the army against Karl Rudolf he announced that the new ruler had agreed with Parliament to reduce the army, and that wholesale dismissals were to be expected.

In such circumstances Karl Rudolf made his quiet and shabby entry into Stuttgart, took up his quarters in a side wing of the Castle, and waited upon the Duchess, who refused to see him. He did not trouble about that, and was at work next morning by six o'clock, as was his habit in spite of his seventy-one years. He began ruthlessly to set matters in order, in the capital first of all; untrustworthy officials were dismissed and their papers confiscated; many were arrested. Most of the leaders of the Catholic party had already fled.

Among the people there were loud and universal expressions of contempt for the dead Duke, who was not yet under the sod, and for the widowed Duchess, who sat fidgetting and fretting helplessly in her rooms. The Regent issued stern orders forbidding such expressions. His words were "Duty! Justice! Authority!"

In consequence of these orders Benz, the confectioner, among others, was put in gaol for three days in punishment for the poetic picture about the Duke and the devil which he had made. In gaol the pig-eyed man caught a severe influenza. When he came home he had to go to bed, and although he swallowed all sorts of boluses it was soon clear that he would not recover. His friends from the Blue Boar stood round his bed. He grinned wryly: "Under the last Duke but one a harlot ruled, under the last Duke, a Jew, and under this one, a fool." In dying he raged horribly, spitting out obscene curses. In the Blue Boar they said that the heretic Duke and his Jew had this good citizen's death as well to answer for.

Marie Auguste and Remchingen intrigued wildly and blindly against Karl Rudolf and the Parliament. It flattered her to be admired as a great woman. She had been long enough the first lady in Germany; now she was tempted to become the feminine counterpart of the young King of Prussia who had just ascended the throne. Aha, she would be the Catholic Roland to this great Protestant Oliver! Had she not the Emperor, the Electorate of Bavaria, her father, yes, even France, on her side? Would a clever, accomplished woman like her be incapable of dealing with such an old screw of a peasant, such a soured dunce and senile lout as Karl Rudolf—the impudent usurper? Together with Remchingen, her Capucin, Father Florian, and her librarian, Hophan, whom she took for a great politician, she span innumerable little childish intrigues and sulked if they did not succeed immediately. Thousands of despatches flew to Vienna, to Würzburg, and to her father at Brussels. To the court and the country she posed as the sorrowing widow; her small, pale, large-eyed face looked very charming in its pompous black. She sent to Brussels for her little son, the Duke, and she displayed the princely orphan, the child with the large starry eyes, to her affected people.

But Karl Rudolf, the old soldier, did not let himself be fooled.

357

He published a proclamation saying that he had no intention to reduce the army, and made Parliament corroborate this. Next day he appointed General von Gaisberg Commander in Chief of the troops, confined Remchingen, foaming with rage, to his house, and set guards before his doors. This was a bold step, it might mean bloodshed, war, armed opposition within and without; it might spell ruin or salvation. It endangered nothing. The troops and the country along with them submitted and did homage to the Regent.

The Emperor hesitated to recognize this powerful ruler. The Jesuits were urging him to uphold the validity of the last will appointing the Lord Bishop and the Duchess as co-Regents. The Lord Bishop himself sent his claims and protests to the Emperor in a letter written by his own hand. But after the suppression of Remchingen Karl Rudolf was firmly seated in power and could not be removed without a war, which no one wanted. The claims and protests were left hanging in the air.

The clever Würzburger of course had not expected anything else. He was working without inward conviction, simply to save his face. He listened to the advice of his diabolically sly and insignificant-looking Councillor, Fichtel. He agreed with him entirely. Nothing could be gained here by force. The Church had plenty of time, it took a long view of things. They had only to concentrate on the young Duke, and have him brought up strictly in the Catholic faith; the Bishop, of course, would not live to see this fruit ripen. For the rest, poor Karl Alexander! The good, steadfast, pleasant friend! *Requiescas in pace.* He would himself read masses for him. For the present the only thing to do was to withdraw gracefully from the Württemberg affair without being compromised.

Meanwhile the old Regent had quite won over the army by his soldierly character, and now he confined General Remchingen more closely, removing him to Asperg with his adjutant, Captain Gerhard.

Such treatment of her favourite and most important partisan drove Marie Auguste out of her haughty reserve towards the Duke Regent. She condescended to ask Karl Rudolf for an interview. The old man appeared without ceremony, and stood, shabby, rustic,

358

and bent, before the bejewelled and finely-perfumed lady, who had exploited all the resources of modern cosmetics. He was alone; she had with her her confessor, Father Florian, and her librarian, Franz Josef Hophan, the politician, a fashionably-clad, literary, soft and feline young man: after Remchingen's downfall he had become, next to the Capucin, the adviser most in her confidence. With cold wariness Karl Rudolf eyed this detestable trio which had grown like a weed in the good garden of Württemberg. On her side Marie Auguste surveyed with arrogance and a touch of amusement this shabby and penurious little soldier, who was certainly incapable of appreciating the subtleties of her mourning dress. Karl Rudolf listened in silence to her numerous complaints. His silence irritated her and she spoke more impetuously, in her confusion mingling childish and ridiculous with really important points; her two assistants had to disentangle her. Karl Rudolf listened with contemptuous distaste to her misuse of legal terms, which she usually brought in at the wrong time with an air of importance. The sacred ideals of the Constitution seemed to him to be profaned by her small, foolish, courtesan's mouth. His answer was curt, wary and rude; he took up adroitly all the nonsense she had talked and with hard contempt ignored the objections and corrections made by the Capucin and the fine librarian; he, the prince, would deal only with the princess. He scolded Marie Auguste; she had bad advisers, and it did not become her dignity to defend the wicked traitor Remchingen. He promised immediate redress on all the small points of etiquette which she had gravely and importantly brought up, and refused with all the greater firmness everything which was of real politicial importance. The monk and the librarian wrung their hands to see how triumphantly the Duchess pocketed these small concessions in return for sacrificing to the sly, uncivil usurper everything essential. With satisfaction and astonishment the Duke came to the conclusion that Marie Auguste was not the Scarlet Woman, but only a goose; and she in turn was satisfied and astonished to see that Karl Rudolf was not really a stiff-necked and obstinate usurper, but simply an ass. On this basis of mutual recognition they parted with a kind of supercilious and contemptuous good-will.

Later on, naturally, they had several small differences. But as the result of this one interview the Duke Regent was sufficiently aware what policy he ought to pursue. If he wanted to obtain a real concession from Marie Auguste he annoyed her in matters of etiquette, disputing one of her titles, perhaps, or sending her a subaltern instead of the usual staff officer to act as her guard, or tormenting her darling, the fine, fashionable librarian. When she protested, he demanded some political concession as the price of rectifying these delicate matters.

The preparations for Karl Alexander's burial provoked a serious quarrel. For two months Marie had been looking forward to making this the occasion to parade before the eyes of Europe as the most beautiful and accomplished widow in the Empire, as the great princess, surrounded by intrigue, on whom were set the hopes of Rome and of all the Catholic world. But the Regent forbade as too provocative the performance of Catholic rites at the funeral; the Catholic lords and princes then threatened to stay away, and Marie Auguste went sick and haggard with rage. The Emperor had to force Karl Rudolf to compliance by a personal letter. The obsequies were carried out with immense pomp. There were endless rows of mourning coaches, taper-bearers; and the princes, gentlemen and officials were all in black gala uniforms; there was a march past of troops which lasted for hours. There were bells, speeches, hymns, and volleys in honour of the dead. And there were thousands of admiring, passionate eyes fixed on the beautiful widowed Duchess. Her figure rose like a pliant and slender stalk above the sweeping black brocade of her skirt; her wrists and hands looked incredibly white and fine emerging from the black lace at her sleeves, and she wore no jewels save the cross and star of the Papal Order and a necklace of sixteen choice black pearls. Her widow's veil was so disposed that its black seemed to be dulled by the black splendour of her hair. Her small lizard-like head with the clear forehead the colour of fine old marble, looked delicate and desirable in spite of her air of remote majesty. And so Marie Auguste sunned herself in sorrow and elegance.

And after all it was an empty coffin for which the bells rang, the speeches were made, the hymns soared solemnly aloft, and the volleys of musketry crackled. In spite of the embalming skill of the doctors the dead Duke had decomposed so badly and become so noisome during his widow's quarrel with the Regent, that he had to be secretly buried in the new vault at Ludwigsburg long before his official obsequies were held.

THE diplomatists and officers who had been surprised at Ludwigsburg by Karl Alexander's death lay low for the present and waited. That they held Süss as a captive was at any rate a proof of their loyalty to the State. After a few days it became clear even to the thickheads that the Constitutional Party was to be victorious as a matter of course, and that it was all up with the military revolt and the Catholic plot. So they took their stand on simple fact. They had never thought of a military *coup d'état;* all the measures they had planned had of course been constitutional, and on the presupposition that they must be ratified by Parliament. There was but one apostle of crime and violence, the instigator of all that was vicious, the source of all trouble, the adviser of all evil, who had led the good Duke astray and perverted all his noble plans, a traitor, a rogue, a scoundrel, and only one,—the Jew. And the honour and loyalty of each one of them was shown by the fact that they had not let the Jew escape, but had arrested him immediately.

Now in reality Süss's capture had been a very easy matter, not exactly redounding to the glory of the gentlemen concerned. So the simple story of his arrest in Ludwigsburg had to be embellished a little and made noble and romantic. They set rumours circulating through Stuttgart which strengthened gradually into the certain knowledge that Süss had stolen forth from Ludwigsburg immediately after the Duke's death, had sneaked into his house in the capital and remained hidden for a time, and had finally made an attempt to flee the country with his jewels and incriminating papers. But the brave officers, led by the gallant Major Röder, an honest man and a good Protestant, who was loved and honoured by all, had in the nick of time discovered the scoundrel's presence and flight. The exact details were repeated. Süss had slipped through the vineyards, and was already a good way along the Kriegsberg road. But Major Röder had summoned his best riders —even their names were known, Guckenberger, Trifts, Weis, Mau, Meier—and so the six of them had pounded after Süss. They had overtaken the fugitive on the Kornwestheimer hill. The gallant Röder had thundered "Halt!" with his pistol cocked. All the Jew's impudence, his cries and threats, had been of no avail. The valiant horsemen had turned his carriage, and now they were going to bring him to Stuttgart over the gallows road through the Ludwigsburger gate.

A festive and noisy crowd awaited the carriage with the prisoner. Keen jests flew; there was happy excitement; all the street urchins were perched in trees or on the projections of the gate. In the Green Tree, a public house hard by the gate, young Langefass, a plump, high-spirited youth, very fair haired, with a red face and small blue eyes, sat with other comfortable burghers' sons. He treated his friends to Uhlbacher and noisily chaffed the girls; it was a merry party, as uproarious as last carnival. When amid hoots and yells the coach containing Süss at last passed through the gate escorted by Röder and his cavalry, several of the youths at Langefass's table rushed upon it, hauled out the prisoner, punched him, bumped him, thumped him, pushed and pulled him about. Meanwhile young Langefass pledged Major Röder, who accepted a glass and returned the compliment with a smirk, while the crowd were mishandling the Jew. In spite of everything Süss was not cowed and dispirited; he hit stoutly back and gave such a cuff to an urchin who had bitten him in the calf that he fell sprawling among the legs of the crowd; at the same time he returned vigorously the curses and abuse of those who were attacking him. It was not an outbreak of fanaticism, but a real juicy row. But although the crowd was really in a holiday mood, the Jew might have been beaten to death in the end out of pure enjoyment, had the Town Grenadiers not arrived and, with the help of the escort, rescued him. Exhausted and breathless he crouched in the carriage, torn and shaken, covered with dirt and blood. Young Langefass, who was a wag and in great favour with the ladies, playfully picked up the Jew's periwig, which had fallen in the scuffle, and paraded it on his stick through the town to everybody's delight. Thus, among cheers and hooting, Süss was conducted through the market-place and into the Chamber of Nobles.

Deprived of this victim, the rabble, led by young Langefass,

362

rounded up all the other Jews and diverted itself with them. They had especial sport with an old Jew who defended himself desperately while they plucked out his grey hair and beard, the process being accompanied by an entertaining speech from Langefass which met with great applause. A trembling young girl called Jentel Hirsch, who was by no means pretty, was stripped to the skin and searched for fleas amid screams of laughter. All the Jews in Stuttgart, from the old men to the infants, were captured by the busy mob in some such fashion and handed over to the Town Magistrate with an escort of street arabs flinging dirt and stones. Two Jews from Prague arrived by express coach in the middle of these occurrences, intending to arrange some banking business with the omnipotent Finance Director. They were not well informed about Swabian politics; they had in particular no idea of the connection between their banking business and the Catholic plot; they only knew that Süss was the most powerful Jew in Europe and that Jews in Württemberg enjoyed special protection. So they were all the more astonished when almost as soon as they left their coach they were pounced upon, shaken, beaten and thrust into prison—their first intimation of the miserable plight into which the powerful Finance Director had fallen. Several other Jews were killed in this persecution, among them three citizens of Frankfurt; and that free town on this account sent a strong protest to the Government of Württemberg. The Duke-Regent then said: "Duty! Authority! Justice!" and sent three of the culprits to gaol for two days.

A facile poet made a popular rhyme about Süss's capture. His couplets soon flew through Stuttgart and over the whole country: two lines in especial were quoted everywhere and stamped themselves forever on the memory of old and young:

"Then shouted Herr von Röder,
'Halt, or you're a deader!'"

Major Röder had become more popular than ever through the circumspection with which he had prevented the escape of the wily and godless Hebrew traitor, and wherever he showed himself with his hard mouth, low forehead, and snarling voice, he met with ovations from the enthusiastic citizens.

On the day when Süss was brought into Stuttgart the crowd attempted also to storm and plunder his palace in the Seegasse. The leader of this enterprise was Sophie Fischer, the daughter of the Transport Adviser, a former mistress of Süss. The beautiful, indolent, voluptuous creature had altered strangely. She screamed and burned, and wrought like a fury, her hair flying loose in thick, fair strands, and sweat trickling over her face. The houses of the other Jews were unprotected, and many a good piece of furniture and jewelry and even much hard cash was looted by the crowd on this occasion. But Süss's house was guarded by a strong military levy. Nicklas Pfäffle had seen to that in good time. There was also another man who had intervened powerfully and successfully to preserve the house, Dom Bartelemi Pancorbo. He appeared in the guise of a Government Commissary with police and soldiers, and confiscated the house and its contents. Guided by Nicklas Pfäffle, he shuffled slowly through the large, brilliant and very well-kept rooms, poking his lean purple face in every corner. He ignored contemptuously the noble tapestries, furniture, pictures and bric-a-brac. But the precious stones for which his heart and his fingers hungered were not there. Cautiously and suspiciously he cross-questioned Nicklas Pfäffle, and the pale plump man answered him with phlegmatic calm. The Portuguese began to threaten, but his cracked voice made no impression on the secretary's indifference. In the end they arrested Nicklas Pfäffle, examined him thoroughly, and went through all his correspondence. They found nothing, and the slow, silent, immovable fellow had to be released again.

Süss was at first confined in the fortress of Hohenneuffen and not badly treated. His tastes were consulted, and he fared well at his own expense; he was allowed to receive visitors and to send for whatever he wanted from his wardrobe and household stuff. He made only a moderate use of these privileges. He preferred solitude, and had plenty of it. At those times he walked up and down at his ease, pleased, almost smirking, humming to himself unmelodiously, wagging his head in sly delight like any old Jew in a gaberdine.

Aha, how good it was, how pleasant, to be at rest and a spec-

scented him! In the course of the long enquiry one or two of them had become well-disposed towards Süss, had developed a kind of liking for the man, who was certainly a rascal, but a most unusual and stimulating one, nimble of wit and keen of intellect. With almost tender mockery Süss observed how even the two young secretaries came, pushful and sly and stupid, to try their luck and their skill on him. The poor, half-witted creatures! Süss let them scramble over him like puppies, and then softly and indulgently put them down again.

All these were men of moderate gifts. Privy Councillor Johann Christoph Pflug, the motive power behind the Commission, was also moderately endowed by nature, but hatred of the Jews had sharpened his wits and made him keen-scented. If it had been the earlier Süss who was in the cell, he would have eaten his heart out at the innumerable petty humiliations contrived for him by that lean and bitter man. Herr von Pflug had to overcome a repugnance to the Jew's proximity which made him physically sick whenever he entered the cell. But he considered it his duty to keep on humiliating the depraved scoundrel, to destroy his self-respect and to keep turning the knife in the villain's wounds. His failure to succeed in this made him miserable, so that he was exhausted when he left the cell, but he always came back. Süss regarded him with contempt and commiseration. If the proud nobleman had learned that the spurned dog of a Jew was the son of Heydersdorff, Baron and Field Marshal, his whole world would have collapsed.

No advocate offered himself voluntarily to conduct Süss's defence. He was certain to be found guilty. A case of that kind would imperil one's reputation. So a representative for the defence had to be appointed by the Court. The Commissioners attached a high fee to this office, payable, of course, from the Finance Director's confiscated wealth, and entrusted it to a man from one of the leading Parliamentary families, a licensed advocate from the High Court of Justice called Michael Andreas Mögling. He had therefore to come to Stuttgart and take up the brief, for which he drew enormous fees. He was advised not to exert himself, since everybody knew that the defence was merely a matter of form. But Mögling, an honest, fair-haired fellow with a round,

367

rosy, friendly face, was an honourable man; he would not accept his fee for nothing and he took the case very seriously; he wrote hard and ran about until he sweated. The members of the Court smiled whenever they saw him, even the Jew himself smiled. The good man was sorely hampered in his work. Important documents were kept secret from him, and the reports of the individual hearings were denied him outright. Although practically no difficulties were raised when Süss had other visitors, the poor advocate was terribly bullied whenever he wanted to communicate with his client verbally or in writing. However, he was not to be daunted; he continued to do his duty honestly, assiduously, and without a spark of talent.

Süss was still in Hohenneuffen and well treated. Around him the members of the Commission fattened at his expense their bodies, souls, and purses. But he sat quiet and satisfied, in a strange kind of waking trance; he was as if wadded in cotton-wool, he could not be got at.

This rankled most of all in the lean and bitter Herr von Pflug. The enquiry was at a standstill, and they could get no further; the pariah of a Jew mocked at all of them. He asked Herr von Gaisberg to summon a full sitting to hear a new proposal. The ten members of the Commission assembled, and looked expectantly at Herr von Pflug. He stood up, lean, angular, eagle-nosed and thin-lipped, with dry, hard, greedy eyes, and said that hitherto they had enquired only into lese-majesty, high treason, and the coinage of false money; but the time had now come to investigate capital crimes committed by the Jew in another direction. According to the criminal code of the land carnal intercourse between a Jew and a Christian woman was punishable by death. Now everybody knew that the prisoner had deflowered Christian virgins and in the most disgusting fashion had exploited both high-born ladies and women of low degree. It was time to extend the scope of the enquiry to include these offences also.

The other gentlemen sat in uneasy silence. This was a delicate matter. If one rushed into it, where might it not end? Nosing into that kind of thing one might compromise all sorts of people. It would certainly be amusing to peer behind curtains and under sheets, and to insist on knowing from A to Z the when and where and how; and on a few of the gentlemen's faces there was already visible an expression of slightly embarrassed lasciviousness. But to display all this dirty linen to the Empire was a piece of hardihood not to be lightly undertaken. And who could tell how many families might be implicated, and who might be antagonized in the course of such an enquiry? It was a very delicate affair.

At last Johann Daniel Harpprecht, who was superior to considerations of that nature, stated that in his opinion the High Commission was not required to poke its nose into such filth. Of course it was deplorable that so many Christian girls and women had prostituted themselves to the Jew. But it was not for his carnal sins that the former Finance Director had been arraigned before a special court, and neither the Duke Regent nor the Cabinet nor the Parliament would have impeached him on that account alone. These offences had not imperilled the land or its sovereign. Besides, the criminal statute which made sexual intercourse between Jew and Christian a capital crime had not been enforced for two centuries, and had fallen into complete desuetude although not formally repealed. Further, they had to remember that this statute condemned not only the Jew to be burned to death but also the Christian women taken with him. They should therefore examine all the consequences of such a proceeding before committing themselves to it.

With cold fanaticism Privy Councillor Pflug retorted that he did not need to remind his wise and upright colleagues that they had been appointed to administer strict justice and not to pursue political ends. They were not required to be diplomatic, but only to be just, without any respect of persons.

The others meanwhile had been considering the pros and cons of the matter. They looked searchingly at each other, divining their neighbours' furtive thoughts and coming to joint secret understandings. If the enquiry were extended to include the sexual offences of the Jew, they would hold in the hollow of their hands the fate and reputation of countless women and countless families. Some names were already known, belonging to families which were great and widespread. In any case such an extension of the Commission's powers would mean an enormous accretion of prestige and influence for the individual Commissioners. They would hang

369

over the land like thunderclouds, and could blast or spare whom they pleased. And they would come into possession of innumerable secrets, which need not be used at the time, but which could be exploited later if they saw fit. They would be as powerful and mysterious as a Spanish Inquisition or the Secret Council of the Venetian Republic. That was an attractive, an exciting, an enticing prospect. What prim and eloquent expressions they would be able to assume! How many people would come fawning round them in anxious humility, on tenterhooks to know whether they were to be exposed or mercifully left alone! And how many piquant details they would secure, which could be retailed in confidence to a delighted friend or brother, wife or sweetheart, and which would later on provoke hilarious screams of laughter at some jovial drinking party! A slight smirk dawned on Privy Councillor Gaisberg's coarse and jolly face; the younger gentlemen relaxed their faces and twinkled with half-shut eyes. It was decided to adopt the measures recommended by Herr von Pflug.

Süss's first examination on this point occurred in a full sitting from which Professors Schöpf and Harpprecht had absented themselves. Süss had grown fatter and less erect; his shoulders sagged a little. His face seemed broader, his brown eyes were less arched, slower and milder. In his forehead one or two furrows were beginning to form between the eyebrows. His movements were gentler, he had a soft and elusive quietness about him.

When he was asked whether he had had carnal intercourse with Christian women his first reaction was a look of surprise. The law punishing intercourse of this kind with death had fallen into such desuetude that he never thought of it. He interpreted the question as one of scornful curiosity intended merely to humiliate him in some way, and as he did not know what the outcome might be he made no reply. Privy Councillor von Gaisberg insisted imperiously that he should inform the Court at once and without evasion what women he had slept with. The Jew looked at his judges attentively, summing them up one by one with his eye, and said simply, without mockery, that he was completely unable to see what that had to do with high treason and false coinage. Herr von Pflug retorted sharply that that was the judges' business, and that he was to drop his Jewish impudence.

370

Süss reflected for a moment, shaking his head. Then he recollected that statute in the Criminal Code which someone had once mentioned to him in jest, a statute which had not been taken seriously for centuries. What? Were they going to butcher him with that antique and rusty relic? Was he to die such a buffoon's death? All at once the old brilliant Süss re-appeared. He drew himself up, sending quick, roving glances over his judges, and answered them, slim and scornful: "That I have slept with Christian women I do not deny. If the gentlemen wish to condemn me to death on that score, let them do it. The whole Holy Roman Empire will laugh. But not at me." The indignant Commissioners let loose upon him a storm of hoots and screams of rage at his impudence, while Süss remained cold and immovable. He regarded his judges. He saw their hate, their lasciviousness, their cruelty, their inflated vanity. He divined the shameless cold-blooded extortionate game which they meant to play with the women. He saw their human masks riven off, he saw the naked ugliness beneath, the faces of wolves and swine. But before his concentrated fury could burst out, he had already relinquished it. He was overcome by pity for the wicked and wretched creatures in front of him. With the old, gentle, crafty smile upon his lips he said: "I will not give you the names. You must find out the ladies for yourselves."

The judges, even those who had been good-natured and hitherto benevolent to Süss, were bitterly indignant. They did not allow themselves to think that the Jew might be concealing the names out of consideration for the ladies. For it was impossible that they, the important gentlemen, should be less chivalrous than a Jew, or that the Jew should be nobler than a Württemberg Privy Councillor. No, it was sheer wickedness and contumacy that made the rascal refuse to divulge the names and share his sexual pleasures with those who had a legal right to the information. They had it all so well planned already, the sensation, the excitement, the why and the how, and now out of sheer malice he wanted to spoil it. But they would bring the scoundrel low, they would teach the pig of a Jew to have respect for a Swabian Court of Justice.

They removed him from the control of the friendly Command-

371

ant of Hohenneuffen, and confined him more straitly. He was taken under a strong guard to Asperg. Here the governor was Major Glaser, a pedantic man to whom discipline was the breath of life. Süss was thrust into a small damp hole. There was not much difference there between day and night; his clothes stank in the damp, mouldy air and rotted on his body. He had no bed, and the floor was bare, cold, bumpy and wet. He was put on bread and water, and fettered cross-wise to the wall for many hours. The rats ran disgustingly over his racked body, and he could not drive them away.

His chestnut-brown hair grew grey, his white, soft skin shrivelled and faded, and an ugly grey stubble covered his once smooth and chiselled cheeks. He let fly evil words at his warders, many curses and execrations, and he defended himself physically when they fettered him crosswise. But when he sat alone, famishing, his limbs strained in torture, coughing and freezing with cold, the warders who spied through the chink in the door often saw him shaking his head in strange satisfaction, and heard him speaking to himself, or humming to himself in a harsh voice. Many a time it seemed as if he were speaking to someone else; he nodded, waited for an answer, and replied again. But there was no one in the cell except the rats. The warders nudged each other, grinned and burst out laughing, supposing him to be deranged and insane.

But he was not at all insane. It was like this. He had hours so full of peace that he was beyond hunger and frost and the aching, tearing pains of his forcibly racked body. Then the rustling of the rats turned into a small and lovely voice, and he spoke and was spoken to and could well smile.

An obstinate struggle began between him and Major Glaser. The Major had been told that if only Süss would give a list of the women with whom he had slept he could be duly brought to judgment and crushed like an insect before everyone's eyes. So the Major cross-examined the Jew daily from nine till ten o'clock. Süss admitted having had women of both high and low degree. The Major said that was not sufficient, he must have names. Süss answered that as an officer he must understand that he would never give the names. The Major replied that what was proper for a Christian officer did not befit a stinking Jew, and treated his obstinacy with increasing sternness.

Süss was not at all trying to pose as a hero. He had fits of rage and depression after periods of smiling resignation. For instance, he was overcome with such disgust at his mouldering and evil-smelling clothes that he threw them away and walked about in his skin; the Commandant had the clothes forcibly put on him again. The Major reported to Herr von Pflug with pedantic exactness and bitter objectivity every movement of his prisoner. He stated that the Hebrew beast, since he could not obtain poison from Hofmann, a warder, had bitten off his own nails, supposing them to be poisonous, and had swallowed the pieces. They had all laughed thoroughly over his stupidity. Or else the Hebrew beast had not eaten a penny's worth for four days, and he had been afraid that he might lie down and die. But today he had eaten again, and so there was some hope of saving him alive for the gallows.

In his terrible weakness Süss once clamoured to know if his wealth were not enough for them, seeing that they were trying to kill him in such an abominable manner. Another time he said craftily that they could find no handle against him, and that it was all a stupid farce; he would bet fifty thousand gulden that he would soon be set free. Still another time, while his warders howled with laughter and slapped their thighs, he ordered, threatened and insisted that he should be released at once, for he had to go to Stuttgart to look after his household.

Then there were other weeks in which Süss was still and contented and spoke to the wet walls and the mouldy air in the solitude of his cell. He saw his father as plainly as in the flesh. He stood in the cell in his Capucin habit, his slim and elegant form stooped and relaxed, but with quiet and peaceful eyes. And he spoke with him and they were very friendly and went arm in arm together, the disgraced Marshal and the disgraced Minister, the begging friar and the tortured captive in his filthy rags, and they smiled to each other and walked comfortably up and down the close damp square of the cell, and the rats rustled about their feet.

373

The members of the Commission meanwhile continued their inquiries very slowly and without ceasing, and drew enormous salaries.

MARIE AUGUSTE, the Duchess Dowager, found political intrigues so interesting that they pushed even her toilette into the second place. Guided by Father Florian, her confessor, and by the librarian Franz Josef Hophan, she sat with delicate coquetry in her castle in Stuttgart or in her lovely dower-house at Teinach, hatching innumerable plots, complications and intrigues, and making life difficult for Karl Rudolf. The fashionable, young, feline, literary librarian thought out the plans at his desk, the tougher Father Florian, the Capucin monk, tried to put them into execution, and Marie Auguste interfered in everything with blind and amiable industry. The fine librarian was consumed with ecstatic and voluble admiration for the Duchess; he compared her in countless fashionable poems to everything beautiful in heaven and on earth. She subsided comfortably into his eloquent adoration; she even began gradually to adopt his vocabulary and his gestures.

But the matter-of-fact, soldierly, economical Duke-Regent was bothered by having to lose so much time in sweeping away their silly cobwebs. He decided once for all to get rid of this troublesome cabal-maker. The rumour suddenly arose all over the land that the Duchess Dowager was intending to carry out forcibly the plans of her happily deceased husband, and that she had already made preparations for having Catholic services in the Church of Teinach. The perfidy of the rumour lay in the fact that the Duchess had plotted a thousand other things, but that precisely in this there was not a word of truth. The Regent played a stroke of rude irony in making that the cause of her downfall. The people at any rate believed the rumour. Wild speeches were made and broadsides sent flying whenever she drove through the streets; her subjects shut their mouths and refused to salute her. After the police had interfered and arrested some of those who refused to salute her the streets were emptied whenever her coach appeared; people slipped into the houses or into the side streets to avoid greeting her. Marie Auguste could not bear that, and Father Florian and the fine librarian distributed large sums of money to

374

engage cheering people to stand on her route. But she noticed that they were hireling cheers, and was doubly depressed. Father Florian had to write to the Duke-Regent emphasizing indignantly Marie Auguste's spotless innocence in the Teinach affair, stigmatizing severely the shameless injustice of the popular uproar, and insisting haughtily that he should put a stop to it. Karl Rudolf did not reply. Foaming with rage Marie Auguste went to see him. He said that he could order her subjects not to behave improperly to the Duchess, but he could not compel them to greet her with delight and affection. He gave Her Highness the friendly advice to behave herself as he did, and then the people would salute her with proper respect without further orders and certainly without bribes.

After this humiliation the Duchess decided to leave ungrateful and stupid Swabia, to hold her court in Brussels, Regensburg and Vienna, and to wait obstinately, like a feminine Coriolanus, until she was recalled.

She took leave of Magdalen Sibylle. Magdalen Sibylle Rieger, wife of the Transport Adviser, sat with an air of serious domesticity beside the delicate, vivacious, quick-eye Duchess, who was younger and more capricious than usual because she was excited about her impending journey. Magdalen Sibylle was broad and imposing, she was with child, she carried a small Rieger. She had brought her friend a pedantic, wooden, correct hymn of farewell; Marie Auguste listened to it with fitting emotion and gratitude. But then, delighted to have done with the necessary serious business, she began to make fun of the doltish clod-hoppers of Swabians upon whom she would soon be turning her back, thank God! She made fun of the crooked, shabby, asinine Karl Rudolf, of Johann Jaakob Moser, the fiery comic orator, and of all the rude and uncouth populace. She regretted only one thing, that she had to leave her good, true, strong Remchingen in captivity in the Asperg. And oh! also her fine, amusing, gallant Jew. They were torturing him and fettering him cross-wise, and she, Marie Auguste, could do nothing for him. For—and she assumed her most important expression—that would make her unpopular, and for political reasons her dear librarian would never allow that. Apparently the Jew had murdered children and practised God

375

only knew what kinds of black magic. But he was a handsome and gallant man, and certainly the most amusing in this boring Stuttgart, and it was at any rate a shame that these coarse beasts should torture and disfigure him. *"Hélas, Hélas!"* she sighed, pursing her lips as her librarian was in the habit of doing.

For half a minute both women were silent. Both were thinking of Süss. Marie Auguste saw his warm, roving eyes, the insistent devotion of his bearing, his air, his insinuating, exciting, impertinent gallantry. Magdalen Sibylle sat quite still, her large, beautiful, womanly hands in her lap. She had met him in the wood at Hirsau as the Devil; then in Stuttgart he had not taken her, but had thrown her to the brute of a Duke; then he had spread that dream of power and intoxication before her eyes and taken her; and then he had turned strange and different and hard, and was polite to her. And now he sat in the Asperg and they were torturing him and disfiguring his limbs. But she was carrying a child, which would be a fine child, for it sprang from a fine man who was boundlessly devoted to her. It would grow big in the peaceful, comfortable rooms at Würtigheim, among fruit-trees and meadows full of sleek cattle. It would never sit in the Asperg, and it would certainly never meet the Devil. Perhaps it would make verses instead, brave and eloquent verses, which would move everybody and be a comfort to many. But it would certainly never meet the Devil.

Marie Auguste interrupted the brooding silence. With a crafty little smile she said that before she forgot it, she must give her parting gift to her dear Magdalen Sibylle, her friend and trusted comrade, a gift which she hoped was well-chosen and out of the common. *"Cara mia!"* she said, *"Cara mia Maddalena Sibilla!"* She whispered mysteriously that it was something for her hour of travail, and she came closer to the large woman, with a caress. It had helped her. That she had had such an easy time and had kept her figure young and unimpaired was entirely due to what she was now going to bestow as a gift upon her dear friend. She herself, even although she did not exactly intend to enter a nunnery, was scarcely likely to be in further need of it. With a sweet, naughty, titillating gesture she produced the amulet, the box belonging to the Jew who now sat twisted in fetters in a damp and stinking cell: the strip of parchment with its rectangular red Hebrew characters, the names of the Angels Senoi, Sansenoi, and Semangelof, and the disquieting crooked figures scattered over it, the primitive birds, squatting comically and threateningly.

She told with a giggle how she had got the box from Süss, and she repeated the lascivious little story about Lilith, the first wife of Adam, who had not given her the carnal satisfaction which she sought. Magdalen Sibylle put out her hand to take the amulet, let it drop again, and finally grasped it uncertainly and with a slight shudder.

Then Marie Auguste quitted Stuggart. She travelled with a large retinue, in her immediate train Father Florian and the soft librarian, who wore a fashionable travelling-suit. The enormous accumulations of her wardrobe had been already forwarded in an endless number of carriages. The street was thronged with onlookers. Now that the Duchess was going away, they were full of goodwill towards her and cracked good-humoured jokes. Her almoners and treasurers had been lavish of money, and the cheers were really hearty.

Johann Jaakob Moser was also in the street, accompanied by his wife. He was moved. "There she goes," he said. "She thinks she will not be able to resist temptation much longer, and so she rather flees from the country. Almighty God, how I thank Thee that Thou hast made me strong and self-controlled, and hast subdued my blood!" And he pressed his wife's hand warmly.

As her carriage was waiting for her the Duke-Regent, small, shabby and crooked, appeared punctually to bid her farewell. "I thought I would have to exorcise a devil," he was secretly congratulating himself, "and it's only a goose going cackling out of the house." But Marie Auguste thought with mocking superiority: "Like to like: asses and donkeys all." And her soft, pastel-tinted face under its spreading black hat nodded with amiable mockery at the old soldier, who shut the carriage door and saluted her with an unusually courteous smile.

In spite of all the tortures the Commission of Enquiry got nothing out of Süss but a general admission that he had slept with Christian women. So the footmen were brought up, and the chambermaids, and they were cross-examined on the smallest details. Some had peeped through keyholes, others had used their ears to good advantage. All that—the when, the where, the how long—was weighed, debated, digested, and incorporated among the documents. Sheets, chemises and chamberpots were brought into evidence and discussed in protocols. So they gradually procured a long list of women, high-born and lowly, married and unmarried. These were all cross-examined by the eager judges without the omission of the most minute detail. The findings were then drawn up in triplicate in black and white, to be committed as State papers to the archives.

The Court ordered the ladies Götz also to appear before it. Once more the young Privy Councillor Götz found himself in the utmost embarrassment. He had considered it desirable to send his mother and sister for a while to his country estate near Heilbronn. They could evade the ducal jurisdiction simply by going into the Free Town of Heilbronn; but then he too would have to resign his offices. Or they could present themselves before the Court; then it would become necessary for him to glare so threateningly at everyone who looked askance at him that the sneers would stick in their throats. That would be troublesome, for he would have to glare at many people, yes, almost at everybody. But he was a stout fellow, and he decided to do it.

So the ladies appeared before the judges on a radiant summer day. The men relished the piquancy of examining first a mother and then her daughter. It was difficult for them to disguise behind the grave indifference of their judicial masks their eagerness and lascivious delight in the situation. The delicate-hued loveliness of Elisabeth Salomea's fair face, with its hunted grey-blue eyes, was enhanced by the black simplicity of her dress as she stood there trembling and dismayed. It was a strange thing, but she, against her brother's express command, and although she usually wore no jewels, had on her finger the ring with the Eye of Paradise, and the eyes of the gentlemen were glued to it. She winced at the remorseless coolness of the filthy, inquisitive questions put to her by the judges, who felt themselves doubly justified by the sight of the priceless stone. Shivering in spite

378

of the brilliant sun of early summer, she was crushed by the brutal directness of these questions, many of which she did not understand at all. She cowered, and turned her quivering face aside to avoid their shameless glances, and stretched and twisted convulsively her small, bony fingers. Her answers were low, uttered in a half-strangled voice, many of them inaudible; their tenor could not be determined, and she had to repeat them; the deaf State Councillor Jäger shouted: "What? What?" and insisted on having many things repeated three times. In this manner the enquiry arrived at her affair with the Duke. Privy Councillor Pflug was the most severe in his examination; he wanted to construe it as lese-majesty that the Jew had forestalled the Duke. Young, fair and lovely as she was, she was impaled on an invisible stake and no one spared her; they all pressed her hard. First the lean, arrogant and sharp Herr von Pflug, who, full of hate and disgusted as if by a foul smell, kept on asking her if she had not been nauseated by the stench of the circumcised Jew; then the State Councillors Faber, Renz, Jäger, and Dann, those ambitious, industrious and middle-aged civil servants, who, diverted by this new and exciting turn of their duties, kept on asking for fresh particulars, paraphrasing them first with relish, as if they were rolling them on their tongues, and then stating them with blunt unambiguity; next the secretaries, Bardili the assessor and Gabler the actuary, who with sickening gallantry and in disagreeable intonations, such as good-natured men like them were wont to use in speaking to a harlot, tried to submit extenuating circumstances; and finally the President, Privy Councillor Gaisberg, who blustered in a hectoring voice that she need not play the weeping prude, she had done the thing and enjoyed it, and now she was not to pose there like a twelve-year-old virgin, but in the name of the three devils to open her mouth, loosen her tongue—she had been loose enough in other respects. With swooning limbs and throbbing temples she lay at last in a darkened room at home, half dead with shame and exhaustion; her brother stamped up and down declaiming with rage; his words tortured her although she did not comprehend them.

Although the Commissioners primmed up their faces myster-

379

iously and gave out that they were as silent as the grave, yet many details from these cross-examinations trickled through into the town and the country. Once more the house in the Seegasse, the gorgeous bed, the painting of Leda with the swan, filled everybody's thoughts. The names of the women became known, and their possessors could not creep sufficiently into obscurity; they were outlaws; people shouted filthy words after them in the streets, spat on them, and cut off their hair. Other particulars too became public. A wave of lust from Süss's long-past nights swept over the Duchy. Men told lewd stories in the public-houses and the waitresses could hardly defend themselves from their rough advances; the prostitutes did good business. The women and young girls tittered and were shocked; many became dry, envious and bitter; others breathed more softly with relaxed limbs and faces. An English collector offered to buy the Jew's famous bed at an enormous price.

Naturally young Michael Koppenhöfer heard of the disgrace of Elisabeth Salomea Götz. The altered times had drawn the young man back to Stuttgart. During his exile he had grown more manly; he had suffered for his convictions and was considered a martyr; and many young people looked to him as their ideal and guide. Perhaps one or two of his comrades knew that he was attached to Mademoiselle Götz, but they did not moderate on that account their strong expressions of contempt and scorn for the girl; they thought of branding her for all time with some vigorous emblem of their bitterness and their scorn. Nobody considered it possible that the affection of Michael Koppenhöfer, the steadfast, virtuous young democrat, could survive such an exposure. Michael Koppenhöfer, too, said nothing in her defence. But nothing in her despite either, as the others expected. He held his tongue. He was suffering. He was not disposed weakly to forgive her. But he saw her pure, bright face, her blond hair, and he suffered. He begged his uncle Harpprecht for the documents. For the latter a new day had dawned since the young man's return. His books, his law, democracy and the Fatherland, all he had lived for, came to life again and sat breathing beside him in the young man with the bold, brown cheeks and the deep, blue eyes. Since by this time the affair of Mademoiselle Götz was well known in the town, the old man looked with compunction at the boy's face; he knew that he was melancholy, and that his love for Elisabeth Salomea would not heal in a day. He saw the youth's face constrained to wear a look of indifference, and after some reflection gave him the documents. Michael began to read, but he could not continue; red anger flamed up in him against the Duke, the Jew, the judges, against all these men. It was more than clear from the protocol that Süss had not had to exert much force in overcoming the girl. But Michael wanted to see her as a victim, and he saw her as one. He saw her standing bright, gentle and lovely before the coarse, rough judges. He could not help it, it was probably sentimental, but his heart rose high when he thought of her; he could not tear her image out, and walk on with a firm and manly tread. He struggled terribly and evaded old Harpprecht's gentle and significant questions. He raked together all the bold free-thinking statements he had ever heard about the worthlessness of chastity, but they remained pure theory, which did not come to life for him; all his feelings fought against them. But he finally constrained himself. He determined to give up all practical politics and in spite of possible jeers at "the harlot's husband" to raise up and purify Elizabeth Salomea by marrying her, and to live as a quiet scholar, supported by her repentance and gratitude, secluded in the country with only his books and her.

Without telling old Harpprecht he took a journey to the Götz's estate near Heilbronn, whither the ladies had withdrawn after their trial. At first he was for a long time not admitted. Then he found Elisabeth Salomea in the middle of hasty and energetic preparations for departure. He did not manage to make his generous offer. The lady was surprisingly changed. She worked hastily among piles of toilet articles, bric-a-brac, books and underclothing, arranging, tying them up and packing them, and made frivolous conversation the while, bitter and scornful jests. She expressed shocking principles. That morality was altogether relative. That in Stuttgart a year ago it had been good form to be courtly and gallant, but that now the very opposite was demanded. In her opinion the Jew was the best man in Swabia and the only gentleman. For the rest, she was now going to leave the country, first for Dresden and Warsaw, and then for Naples and Paris. And so good-bye. She waved her hand to him with the Eye of Paradise blazing upon it in blinding radiance.

Michael Koppenhöfer returned with compressed lips, his whole life torn up by the roots. Later he heard that Elisabeth Salomea was leading the life of a great and successful adventuress in the Courts of Europe. In her train she had Otman, the dusky slave, as her confidential courier.

MASTER JAAKOB POLYKARP SCHOBER entered Süss's cell. It was dark and damp in the narrow square, the air was fusty and noisome. Süss squatted in a bent posture, he breathed with difficulty, he had grown fatter and flabby, his face was a waste of stubble.

The Master was shocked to the very marrow when after some hesitation he recognized in this wreck, his former great and powerful chief. He himself was in a bad way. He suffered from the consciousness of having brought to this condition the Finance Director who had saved the evangelical faith in the Duchy; it crushed the Master to the ground that he had sworn silence to the Jew; he wanted to speak out, to proclaim the innocence of this persecuted man, to set him free. Süss shook his head as he listened to his helpless and confused clamours, entreaties, and assurances, and said at last: "You are a good fellow, Master. There are not many such." And after a while with an enigmatical smile: "If you absolutely wish it, you can speak out now." The Master kissed his hand and went away happy.

He flew to the members of Parliament, to whom, by Süss's command, he had betrayed the Catholic project, and gave them explanations and assurances. They listened with astonishment and without comprehension. They thought he wanted an additional reward for his betrayal of the plot and for his share in exposing it. With a shade of reserve they promised to do what they could for him, and hinted at a government position. But as he persisted eagerly in asserting that it was with Süss's approval, nay, by his authority that he had revealed the heretic's plans, they grew impatient, and told him not to be silly; they saw in this an attempt at blackmail, some manœuvre or other of the Jew's. Privy Councillor Pflug especially scented some infamous plot of Süss's for his own defence, and arranged that the Master should be put in prison, since he would not stop trying to illuminate the judges with his fairy tales. And since the Jew himself said nothing in his defence to corroborate Schober's statements, they finally concluded that the Master was simply off his head, a harmless lunatic, driven insane by his pietism and religious enthusiasm, and they set him free after a sharp admonition. Exhausted by his horror at the blindness and entanglements of the world the Master went back to Hirsau and devoted himself to virtue, to his old cat, and to poetry.

Philip Heinrich Weissensee, too, soon followed him to Hirsau. Weissensee had had to resign his position as President of the Consistory. Perhaps the Weissensee of old times would have been able to stand fast, but now he was weary and at the end of his tether; he was not cast off, he rather dropped off. Magdalen Sibylle had become very deeply estranged from her father. But now in his downfall she was drawn to him, and tried to be reconciled; she found that he had been badly treated, and wrote verses to show that he had been superseded through no fault of his own, but through the chances of fate and the hatred of others. But the old Weissensee would have nothing to do with her; he hardened himself against her; her growing provincialism disgusted him and her pregnancy nauseated him. What had he to do with a grandchild born of her and Immanuel Rieger, that lean, insignificant, honest, pedantic, empty-faced man with a moustache? Besides, he was ashamed of his daughter's clumsy poetry. His own life had been made up of tact and a feeling for the great world, for distinction and the grand manner, and now he was affronted. Poor and threadbare he withdrew to Hirsau, and resumed his commentary on the Bible.

MEANWHILE the land flourished. It stretched itself, breathed deeply, no longer strangled by a constricting hand. Prices went down, sank below the level of Karl Alexander's first and good year of government. Six pounds of bread cost nine kreuzers, a pound of beef or pork five, a load of beechwood was ten gulden and a load of pinewood five. And even if the internal politics of the country looked a little threatening—"Duty!" said Karl Rudolf; "Justice! Authority!" and was not inclined to bate one jot or tittle of his sovereign rights in his dealing with Parliament— yet on the other hand Bilfinger, the clever, eloquent, circumspect Bilfinger, had been taken into the Cabinet, and the assurance of religious and municipal freedom together with the expansion of trade was quite enough to make everybody content. Old-fashioned pictures were fished out with Karl Rudolf at the head of troops in superannuated uniforms, fighting with Turks in baggy breeches and Saracens with curved scimitars; and many a cheer was raised whenever the small, shabby, crooked soldier appeared.

So with much wind and cloud a Spring had slipped by, a radiant early summer, a sultry and thundery mid-summer, and now a clear autumn was drawing to its close; the first frosts set in, and Süss was still pent between the close and dripping walls of his cell. He was now melancholy and dispirited. It was not difficult to endure torture, one might suppose it was also not difficult to die, but it became daily a heavier burden to breathe the foul air of the prison, to eat the vile bread of captivity. His back was bent, his limbs twisted, and his wrists and ankles scarred with fetters. There was air ouside, sun and wind, trees and fields, houses and clear voices; men were busy and important, children leaped, girls swung their skirts. Oh for one mouthful of free and windy air, for one walk of seven steps instead of the five and a half across the cell! He wrote letters. He wrote to the Duke-Regent. He was an old man and might listen to him. He wrote respectfully, objectively, and without servility. He pointed out briefly that according to the laws of the Duchy he was innocent. Even if he had here and there transgressed the code of the country he was protected by an absolution granted him by the late Duke Karl Alexander, according to which he could not be held responsible. Moreover he was prepared to make restitution of any losses sustained by anyone as the result of his actions. He had been already four and thirty weeks in prison, most of the time in fetters. He had become an old man in the fortress. He hoped therefore that the Duke Regent, at whose feet he threw himself, would be merciful to him.

In a tension such as he had not felt for a long time he waited for an answer. Morning came and evening and it was another day, and still another, and a week, and yet another week. At last, in the daily interview from nine to ten, after Major Glaser had triumphantly brandished before him another pair of women's names which the Commission had unearthed, he asked directly if no answer had come from the Duke Regent. The Major enquired with cold contempt if he seriously believed that they would molest the Duke with his Jewish impertinencies; his expectorations being those of an obstinate scoundrel and Jew had naturally been sent not to the Duke but only to his judges. In his daily report to Privy Councillor Pflug he stated that the Hebrew beast had shrunk into himself at this announcement.

But Süss had set in motion again all the wheels of his old persistence and ingenuity. He wanted air, he wanted to be in the light of day. Since the unfortunate attempts of Master Schober he had not been allowed to receive visitors, even his counsel for the defence, honest Mögling the licentiate, had not been admitted. But his old cunning reawoke in the sick and broken man. He asked in due form to be allowed to see a clergyman. They could not deny him that. He had the idea of using him as an intermediary between himself and the old Regent. His hopes, however, were quickly shattered; they sent him the Town Vicar Hoffmann, whom he rocognized as an old supporter of the Constitutional Party and an avowed enemy.

The Vicar naturally believed that it would be easy to convert Süss in his present plight, and began to speak to his conscience with a mixture of scorn and unction. The Jew shrugged his shoulders as he saw his last hope disappear with this unfortunate selection, and admitted simply and clearly that he had only asked for a clergyman in order by his mediation to achieve an interview with the Duke-Regent. The spiritual advisor snorted that that was not his office. Süss replied by thanking him drily for his visit.

But the Town Vicar came again. He was a zealous man; he had remarked the physical weakness of the Jew and he argued that a humbled body meant a humbled soul. Süss smiled when he saw him again. He listened to him quietly and with attention.

At the end of it, he shook his head and said: "To change his religion is a step for a free man, and ill befits a prisoner." But the Town Vicar did not acquiesce. He had made up his mind to convince this man, whose fame was widespread through the whole Empire, of the truth of the Augsburg Confession. He even brought an assistant with him, Prebendary Johann Konrad Rieger. Both the clergymen wrought hard; Johann Konrad Rieger displayed all his silken rhetoric and the Town Vicar seconded him strongly; a whole brotherhood of missionaries could not have assembled a greater number of arguments or more radical ones. But Süss, like an obdurate Jew, persisted in the error of his ways.

The other prisoners, Scheffer, Hallwachs, Bühler and Mez were treated with much more indulgence. They had family connections with several Parliamentarians, and their charges were leniently dealt with: the accusations were deflected, rewritten, and hushed up. The actions of these sworn State officials, their lese-majesty and high treason, were presented as mistakes of less and less importance; their prosecution became a mere matter of form. They were condemned to pay the costs of the law-suits, then released and banished from the country. Out of prudence they had sent abroad the most of the large sums of money which they had earned in Süss's service. They might as well not have done so, for even their possessions in the Duchy were not touched. They now removed themselves, together with other former colleagues of Süss, a mile and a half away to the Free Town of Esslingen, and lived in peace on their great wealth in that pleasant and friendly town, receiving daily visitors from Stuttgart, and following the case against Süss with benevolent interests as comfortable spectators; and there they waited for some change in the Government to summon them back, for the young Duke would not be a minor for ever, and Karl Rudolf was an old man.

Süss's wealth, or so much of it as could be seized in the Duchy, chief among this his palace, was confiscated for the present. The liquidation of the Finance Director's widely-spread and chaotic investments presented enormous difficulties. Dom Bartelemi Pancorbo was reluctantly compelled to call in Nicklas Pfäffle. The pale, stout fellow complied, but in his calm way he laid down conditions. He would allow no strange hand to meddle with the

386

things which had been his master's personal concern. As soon as
the Portuguese tried to interfere with these Nicklas Pfäffle became
at once refractory and tangled up the threads of the pending financial negotiations, putting up a passive resistance until Dom
Bartelemi had to take his dry fingers again out of those things
which the quiet secretary interdicted him.

In spite of good treatment the mare Assjadah pined at the
absence of her master's hand. Major Röder wanted to have her,
and the Portuguese agreed to that. But Nicklas Pfäffle prevented
him. The Major's offer was suddenly outbid; and before the
Major could counter it the noble animal was sold to the unknown
foreign bidder, and Herr von Röder, whose song "Halt, or you're
a deader!" was still in everybody's mouth, had to show himself
to the faithfully enthusiastic populace on his old chestnut. The
beautiful Daughter of the Morning then appeared as the property
of Mademoiselle Elisabeth Salomea Götz, and was attended to
by the dusky slave. Later, when she was sorely pressed for money,
the lady had to get rid of the mare. She sold her to a rich Moslem,
and the mare Assjadah vanished again into the Orient from which
she had come.

The parrot Akiba, too, who cried. *"Ma vie pour mon souverain!"* and "How did Your Highness condescend to sleep?" was
abstracted from the hands of the greedy victor by Nicklas Pfäffle.
He took the cage and the parrot himself to Isaac Landauer in
Frankfurt, who had procured a purchaser of whom he approved.
The great financier received the Secretary in the gloomy and
badly-ventilated private office of his ugly, crooked and tortuous
house in the Ghetto. He sat awkwardly and uncomfortably in
his greasy caftan before the pale, stout secretary, looked with dis-
like at the screaming bird, and said finally: "I said to him in
good time 'What does a Jew want with a parrot?'" He combed
his reddish faded goatee restlessly with his thin fingers, throwing
furtive, hasty, suspicious glances around him. Nicklas Pfäffle
said nothing. But after that they remained closetted for some
hours and spoke of many things, monosyllabic and indifferent
the one, quick, lamenting, threatening, complaining, emphatic and
urgent the other.

As a result of the conversation Isaac Landauer and Nicklas

387

Pfäffle made several journeys. From the beginning the Jews had tried to work on behalf of the disgraced Finance Director. Now these activities were organized. Among Ministers and influential men in the most widely separated European Courts there sat Jewish bankers talking about the Württemberg case. They did not attach importance to Süss himself, not even to the bad treatment he was subjected to; they rather emphasized the arbitrary and illegal way in which the case against him was being conducted, contrary to the laws of the Empire and of Germany, and of the Duchy itself. The sworn State officials were set at liberty and the private alien was prosecuted for treachery to the Constitution. A Ducal Edict existed which protected him by law from all indictments. This high and sacred document was ignored, and he was cited for lese-majesty. Was that justice? Could any one have guarantees of security in such a state? Could one negotiate with such a Government or enter into contracts with it? Süss had transgressed one single article of the code. He had slept with Christian women—oh, what a hardened criminal! On that account they had confiscated his property. Was that law? Was that justice? Could one give credit to such a State?

This went on at all the Courts. People fleered at the Württemberg ambassadors, and ridiculed the profitable morality of a State which exploited a private individual's hours of dalliance to cover the national deficit. It was also everywhere averred that the judges were only protracting the case in order to grow fat on their salaries. They were said to nose round every sexual act of the Jew until they had each earned his thousand dollars.

Johann Daniel Harpprecht called on the Duke-Regent to report the progress of the Commission. He was frank and direct. If that kind of thing continued Swabian justice would lose all its prestige. They had already made themselves sufficiently ridiculous. It was necessary for him to insist that he considered the Jew to be a poisonous insect. But that was no excuse for subjecting a man to such physical torture in a modern state of the Empire. They could at least summarize the arguments and proceed to a conclusive verdict. It was a scandal to have let the other much worse scoundrels out of the net. He could understand the political necessity of such mildness; but in that case they should not

388

expose themselves further by treating the Jew with unnecessary brutality. And in particular the whole affair about the women as conducted by the Commission was a sink of corruption in the country. The old lawyer spoke in strong terms until he was hot and red. If one were to insist on the bare letter of this obsolete law the women would have to be burned too. But nobody was thinking of doing that. What in the name of the three devils was the good of it? Every night a hundred thousand women in the Duchy slept with someone. In bed, sleeping with a woman, no Jew or heretic was endangering the safety of the State, or of the Constitution, or of religion. It would have been a good thing if the Jew had done nothing else night and day. Moreover he thought that the Jew, in refusing to divulge names, played a much nobler part than his zealous judges. And they should make an end of sticking their fingers and noses into such a filthy mess. The old Regent listened gloomily. Harpprecht was only giving clean and vigorous expression to what he had been vaguely feeling himself. Duty! Justice! And he gave instructions to quash the proceedings about the women. He caused a few of them to be flogged, and to draw the customary load of dung through the streets.

He gave orders that Süss was to be treated with humanity but not with indulgence. Major Glaser followed these instructions with pedantic exactitude. Not with indulgence. The Jew's cell measured only five and a half paces in each direction, he was fettered every second day, was allowed meat only on Sundays, and had to wear only the coarsest clothes. With humanity. He was given water to wash in from day to day, he had a wooden floor in his cell and a bench to sleep on.

The Regent's orders had their effect on the Commissioners. They too were beginning to feel uneasy at the growing volume of cleverly stirred-up disparagement from abroad, although they talked big enough. It was really not so very simple to find an unobjectionable ground for a formal conviction. There was no doubt that Harpprecht and Schöpf would not subscribe to one; but there were others, especially the younger members, who were also wavering, afraid of bringing themselves into ridicule. The honourable advocate Mögling blossomed out. He revised his notes

389

for the defence more relentlessly than ever, making his statements finer and smoother, so that he could comfortably say that he was earning his fees by the sweat of his brow.

Privy Councillor Pflug observed with bitterness and sorrow that Süss's condemnation and annihilation had been seriously endangered, if not made questionable, by Jewish intrigues. His arid fanaticism filled him with gnawing rage and gave him no rest. The prize had been too nearly within his grasp; if it were to evade him now he would not be able to survive it. Lean, bitter, obsessed by his desire and inaccessible to argument, he visited all the members of Parliament whom he knew to be the most avowed opponents of Süss. He conferred unweariedly with Dom Bartelemi Pancorbo. He spared neither money nor labour. Broadsides appeared against the Jew; the anger of the populace at the indulgence accorded to Mez, Bühler and Hallwachs was deflected in its full rancour against Süss. The rumour was started that Süss, too, was going to be released. Those judges who were suspected of any inclination. to mercy, even the highly respected Harpprecht, were harried on all sides and finally even annoyed in the public-houses. It came to riots and demonstrations. "The Jew must hang!" was the formula issued by Herr von Pflug and Dom Bartelemi. "The Jew must hang!" was thundered in Parliament and in the pulpits. "The Jew must hang!" roared the mob, while the street urchins sang it in a catchy popular rhythm and the peasants in the most isolated farms affirmed it with obtuse conviction.

Through this kind of pressure Herr von Pflug achieved the resignation of one or two Commissioners. They were replaced by personal enemies of Süss, whose votes were bound to fall on the right side. The erstwhile ministers, Forstner and Negendank, whom Süss had ruined; the cold and slippery devotee of ambition, Andreas Heinrich von Schütz, who had been hampered on all sides by Süss in Karl Alexander's time; yes, Herr von Pflug even managed to have young Privy Councillor von Götz co-opted, so that he might wreak his rage and revenge on the seducer of his mother and sister.

These were all now appointed as Süss's judges. They were consumed with hate rather than with a hunger for money; the populace pressed for a definite verdict, and they were quite ready to yield to that pressure. They speeded up the enquiry. The documents for the prosecution drawn up by State Councillor Philip Heinrich Jäger charged Süss with practically all the crimes which had been committed in Karl Alexander's reign, including many things which it was impossible for him to have known about. He was made responsible for the official acts of all the civil servants, from the members of the Cabinet down to the meanest clerk. The stout defence of the honest Mögling was hardly read. Blind with hate the judges ignored the plain facts, and barely mentioned in their summary the countless objections which were raised against their powers of jurisdiction and which ruled out the possibility of a legal conviction.

They found the Jew guilty of innumerable crimes; against the Duke in the first place; in the second place against his loyal Councillors and Ministers, and against the whole nation, whom he had denounced and brought into disfavour and under suspicion; thirdly and chiefly against Parliament and the Constitution— here many edicts of his were quoted, especially his ordinance about the chimney-sweeping; and fourthly against parishes and individual subjects. They found him guilty of lese-majesty, of breach of the peace, of false coinage, and of high treason.

On these grounds the special court appointed to enquire into his crimes condemned Josef Süss Oppenheimer, Jew and erstwhile Finance Director, to death by hanging. This mode of execution had been decided upon partly because it was the usual penalty for many of the crimes attributed to the accused; but partly as a compromise among the penalties of quartering usually reserved for lese-majesty, burning alive which was the ordained penalty for false coinage, and the more honourable penalty of execution on the block.

The gentlemen inflated their chests. They had clothed their verdict in a form which was fairly passable. Pedantic lawyers could pick holes in it; but they knew that the people and their sound instincts were on their side.

THE Darmstadt Financial Councillor and Cabinet Agent Baron Tauffenberger sat ill at ease and restless in his study crammed with papers. Opposite him sat his mother, Michaele Süss, helpless, lovely and foolish. For seven years, ever since he had renounced the name of Nathan Süss Oppenheimer and had been christened Baron Ludwig Philip Tauffenberger, she had not paid him a visit. The lovely old lady who filled her empty life with beauty-culture, correspondence, theatre-going, the patronage of young artists, travel and social life, had always anxiously avoided Darmstadt, the home of her elder son. She could have understood it if her younger son Josef had turned to his father's faith; yes, she might even have been glad of it, for she sought in the son with tender remorse the traits of the father. But that Nathan, the son of Isaschar Süsskind the cantor, had been converted to Christianity seemed to her a great sacrilege which would one day draw down a bitter vengeance. She viewed with distrust his good fortune and his career. That pious and noble Josef, who had saved Jecheskel Seligmann Freudenthal, and in spite of inducements and incredible temptations had remained a Jew, that he should now be so cruelly fallen while the sacrilegious renegade flourished wantonly, made her completely helpless and bewildered.

Michaele Süss had loved in her own way her husband, the cantor Isaschar. He had been a pleasant and obliging husband and a great singer and comedian, above all a mild, complaisant man who travelled a great deal and paid no attention to the malicious things which people told him about his wife, but was always tender to her and full of grateful admiration of her loveliness. She had loved many other men in her long, rich and gay life. But the months she had spent with the brilliant Georg Eberhardt Heydersdorff had been the crown of her days. When he was plunged into disgrace and misery it was the most genuine sorrow she had ever felt. She had then revived the father in the son, Josef; she had been breathless and weak with admiration as she watched his rise to fortune; she loved in her son all his youth and sweetness, his gaiety and brilliance, and she lived in a blissful ecstasy of unbounded faith in his genius, his star, his majesty. And now his father's reversal and downfall were repeated in him still more cruelly.

She had at first believed that her son's arrest was a trick, a disguise out of which he would emerge all the more brilliantly.

392

But now she had to recognize that it was in deadly earnest. The sentence was not yet pronounced on him, but all through the Empire the rumour was becoming more definite and threatening that the people of Württemberg were going to string up their former Finance Director within the next few weeks. The popular catch "The Jew must hang!" was being whistled not only on the Neckar but all down the Rhine. She could not get the abominable jingle out of her ears, and became more and more bewildered and helpless. She made clumsy attempts to help her son, and wrote foolish pleading letters to everybody. If only Rabbi Gabriel at least would send some news of himself! She wrote an urgent and helpless letter to him, but she did not know if it had reached him; for she had only guessed that he was in Holland, she did not know it for certain. She wrote to her married daughter in Vienna, and sent a whole series of letters in her rambling delicate handwriting to the Viennese Oppenheimers; then finally decided in her extremity to visit her eldest son, the renegade. There she now sat, her mouth half open with anxiety and expectation, and looked at him with scared and foolish eyes. "What are we to do?" she wailed.

Baron Tauffenberger shifted uneasily in his seat, fussed with his papers nervously and mechanically, and fidgeted. He was a rather stout man, almost too small, with a clear, well-cared-for skin and quick eyes which protruded too much; his bent fingers were thick, white and active, and in spite of his handsome and carefully-chosen clothes he was not elegant. His Christianity made him uneasy although he posed as a free-thinker. He liked to make fun of Jewish customs and Jewish habits, and associated with Professor Karl Anton of Helmstatt and Johann Friedrich Paulus, formerly Provost of Denkendorf, and now a preacher in Stuttgart, both converted Jews who were now fanatical apostles of Christian teaching. But he grudged it from the bottom of his soul to his younger brother that he had been able to rise so much higher than himself and yet remain a Jew. Besides, Josef had frankly and fully poured scorn and contempt on the renegade, and once when they met at the Palatinate Court had coldly turned his back upon him. If ever they crossed each other in business they went to law at once without any attempt at arbitration, and

393

the Christian was cut to the quick that his brother felt such disgust and loathing for him that even in important matters he would not condescend to meet him personally, but rather ran the risk of loss in employing agents. His brother's downfall and disgrace hit him hard, and exposed him to jeers and mockery; but all the same he could not suppress a slight feeling of triumph as his mother sat helpless before him begging his intervention for her more beloved and adored son. "There you are! There you are!" he said several times in his high, clear voice. "It is not possible to climb so high and remain a Jew. And it's not fitting either," he averred, gesticulating wildly, "it's not right; it is contrary to divine ordinance and human authority."

But Michaele ignored him. "What are we to do? What are we to do?" she wailed in a monotonous voice.

The stout man stood up and moved nervously about, shifting a bundle of papers from one side of his desk to the other. "There is only one way," he said at last. In answer to Michaele's eager and hopeful gaze he screwed up his courage and announced with a matter-of-fact air of indifference: "He must turn Christian."

Michaele reflected. Then she said dully: "He won't do it." And after a while: "Rabbi Gabriel won't permit it."

Her son echoed with scorn: "Won't permit it! He did not permit me either. If I had followed him I might now be in the same plight as Josef. Won't permit it! Won't permit it!" He worked himself up, railing in his clear voice and gesticulating with excitement. Then all at once he stood still, and said suddenly: "I don't know of any other way." His mother's dejection urged him to add: "I will gladly do what I can to save all that can be saved of his wealth. Although he has not deserved it of me. I will lay my hand on everything of his that can be rescued in Heidelberg, Frankfurt and Mannheim. Nor will I spare money to do what I can in Stuttgart with the Government, the judges and the prison officers. But if he does not turn Christian," he concluded with a shrug, "it won't be of much use." Michaele's feet were heavier when she went than when she came.

Meanwhile in Stuttgart Nicklas Pfäffle worked coolly and continuously for his master. Large sums of money flowed into the pockets of Government officials and clerks of justice. Since the

Duke-Regent had ordered a thorough investigation of Süss's possessions to decide what was clearly and legitimately his, and had forbidden that to be touched, the secretary had plenty of means at his command. Priceless vases, tapestries and jewels, were conveyed from Süss's house as remembrances to influential members of Parliament and Court and Government officials, who had no direct connection with the affair, but were all the more powerful as intermediaries.

But through the whole Jewish world the message ran with gathering strength: "He saved Reb Jecheskel Seligmann Freudenthal; he stretched out his hand and protected the Jews on the Neckar and the Rhine. Now Edom and all the unbelievers have gathered themselves together and fallen upon him. He was too great for them, he reflected too much glory upon the Jews. They have fallen upon him like Haman and are wishful to slay him. Help and rescue for Reb Josef Süss Oppenheimer, who was a good Jew and held his hand as a strong protection over all the Jews when he was in power!" There were prayers and fasts in all the synagogues, operations at all the Chancelleries and Cabinets; money was collected, much money, still more money, enormous sums of money, and all handed to Reb Isaac Landauer, court agent and good Jew, who was charged by the Rabbis and the communities to protect with all his strength and cunning and capacity the fallen Reb Josef Süss Oppenheimer, Israel's saviour in time of need. Isaac Landauer had a plan, not a particularly cunning plan, but a bold and direct one, to be followed if they should really dare to condemn Süss to death. For this plan he needed money in fabulous quantities. And fabulous quantities of money flowed into his coffers, yellow gold, bills of exchange, mortgages; small people gave small sums and great people gave greatly, from all countries and all communities, from the Jews of the whole world.

Johann Daniel Harpprecht sat at work in his library. The Duke-Regent had not confirmed the verdict of the Commission, but had ordered it to be kept secret for the present, and had sent it to Harpprecht, together with the enormous accumulation of relevant papers, for his decision.

The old man was grim with rage. This was the fourth winter since he had pronounced judgment in the case of Jecheskel Seligmann, and had been compelled to save the dog of a Jew against his will. The gnawing worms had now left off and crawled away; of those which had writhed to the top and grown fat, the Duke and the Jew, one was dead and the other lay helpless beneath his feet and he could crush it if he would. Aha! they had eaten well since that time. He, Harpprecht, had been a steadfast man, and now he was prematurely old because of them, and lands and woods and fields and human bodies and souls had been evilly consumed and destroyed because of them, and young Michael had been blighted and the gentle and lovely Elisabeth Salomea Götz had become a harlot because of them. And even though the brood of worms was driven out and had crawled away, it would return as always it had returned before, and the old building would collapse in ruin. And now there he sat and had to decide whether it was right to crush this gnawing and destructive worm.

Bilfinger appeared. He was now the real Regent of the country, a true and modest Regent who worked like a horse and achieved results. Work agreed with him, and the heavy full-blooded man looked ten years younger than Harpprecht, his contemporary.

"How does it stand, brother?" he enquired, glancing at the waste of papers. "Is it the same," he added, slowly and uneasily, "as it was that other time with the Jew Jecheskel?"

Outside there was a thick fall of soft snow. It was very still in the room. From the next room could be heard the step of young Michael Koppenhöfer. "Yes, brother," replied Harpprecht, "it is the same. Formally, according to the letter of the law, there is not sufficient proof."

Bilfinger picked up some of the papers, separated them, and shuffled them together again. "Is it not to be taken into consideration, brother," he said after a while, "that in the constitutional state of Württemberg he allowed himself so many departures from constitutional procedure that he must now submit with a good grace to being made the subject of a departure from judicial procedure?"

396

"That is to be taken into consideration," returned Harpprecht. "But not by me. By the Duke."

Meanwhile the prosecution of General Remchingen had also been carried through. This baron, Jesuit, and Austrian Commander was not so indulgently treated as the indigenous Hallwachs, Mez, Bühler, Lamprechts and Scheffer; he had no relations sitting in office; he had treated all civil servants as quill-drivers, and all who were not nobles, especially the members of Parliament, as mere *canaille,* proletariat, rabble; and he was well hated. Evidence against him was therefore keenly sought out, and sufficient had been accumulated to condemn him at least to lifelong imprisonment if not to death.

But it happened at this time that the agreement between Karl Rudolf and the Duchess Dowager about the Regency had been completed on very favourable terms for the Duke; it was now awaiting the Emperor's approval and confirmation together with the general plan of government for the time of the Regent's administration. It seemed highly inopportune at such a moment to irritate the Viennese Court by severely punishing a Catholic Austrian. So they decided to postpone his sentence, and he was set free on parole. As they had expected, Remchingen broke his parole immediately and fled the country to enter the Venetian service with General Schulenburg. He was condemned by default, against which he protested bitterly to the Emperor and the Empire in various appeals. For years afterwards he emitted a stream of filthy, bitter and poisonous abuse of Württemberg.

The populace was incensed at Remchingen's flight. All the hounds had now escaped scot-free, and sat a mile and a half away in Esslingen, laughing their belly-full, or, like Remchingen, had plunged the country into a mess of difficulties. There was only the Jew left. But he at least should pay the penalty. Once more Privy Councillors Pflug and Pancorbo were to the fore, stirring up and arranging demonstrations. More wildly, emphatically, threateningly and urgently the cry ran through the country: "The Jew must hang!"

This was the state of things when Harpprecht delivered the verdict to the Duke-Regent. The just and sincere man had not let himself be swayed by hatred of the Jew, nor by the clamouring people who bellowed for the Jew's death as if with one voice, nor by the favour or disfavour of Cabinet or Parliament. The Professor of Law gave as his decision: "The Councillors and Ministers, pledged to the Constitution and sworn into office, who signed the commands and ordinances to which objection is here taken, ought to be impeached and punished, but not the alien who took no oath and held no office. The former have committed capital crimes according to Roman and German law, but not the latter. With the exception of a single point, carnal intercourse with Christians—and the point for various reasons could not be seriously raised, nor has the Commission incorporated it in its findings." He concluded that the accused could not be sentenced to death on the basis of the existing laws of the Roman Empire and of the Duchy; what he had unlawfully acquired should be confiscated, and he should be banished from the country.

Small, shabby, and crooked sat the iron-grey, weather-beaten Duke, and listened attentively to this weighty, sincere, and objective exposition. "You think then," he said finally, "that the Commission has sentenced the Jew rather than the scoundrel?" "Yes," said Harpprecht. Outside someone whistled the popular catch: "The Jew must hang!" The old Regent shut his lips firmly. "I would I could follow your advice," he said at last, and with that dismissed the lawyer.

On the next day he signed the death warrant. "Better to hang the Jew unjustly," he said, "than to spare his life justly and have more trouble brewing in the land." He said also: "It is an unusual thing for a Jew to pay the penalty for Christian scoundrels."

THROUGH the bleak and gloomy corridors of the fortress of Hohenasperg and down its winding steps fluttered Michaele Süss, led by a surly corporal with an unwieldy bunch of keys. The pampered old lady's heart palpitated; there were so many walls and massive weapons, such concentrated and terrifying menace. The corporal walked ahead so quickly that she had difficulty in keeping up with him and was out of breath, but she did not dare to say anything. At last a sunken and hideous door grated open on creaking hinges. She looked panting into a bleak rectangle, and there on a bench sat an old man with bent back, flabby and unhealthily fat, with a dirty white neglected beard, humming to himself and dozing with an absent and foolish smile. She said timidly to the corporal: "This is not the right one, my good man; I want to see Josef Süss." The corporal replied crossly: "Well, that's the Jew, lady."

Profound and shuddering horror filled Michaele Süss as she looked at the prisoner, who turned his face slowly towards her with brown, blinking, and slightly inflamed eyes. The corporal locked the door outside with a ceremonious clashing of keys. That her son! That ugly neglected man, older than herself, her brilliant son! Oh, there was not a trace, not the slightest trace of Heydersdorff in him now; much rather, as she remarked with dread and curiosity, did he resemble Rabbi Gabriel, in spite of his beard. She looked at him timidly, filled with horror, feeling nothing of her former devouring and painful compassion, feeling only, as it vanished and left her empty, that this was a stranger, a dirty, neglected man for whom one had to be sorry, of course, for he was a prisoner and in trouble, and, besides, he was a Jew. But she had already closed and hardened her heart. She was embarrassed, like an elegant, strange lady standing before this unkempt man covered with filth.

When they spoke to each other she found that she could not be sincere. His words were gentle, full of an airy, superior, almost jesting tenderness, and he stroked her very white hands. She wept a little. But none of his words came home to her. She could only think: "This old man my son!" and felt herself hardening. She was genuinely glad when her time was up and the ill-tempered corporal came to take her away. As she went through the door she turned to look once more with timid dread at the old man who was her son. And when she quitted the fortress it was she who quickened her step.

Soon afterwards a mild, still, sorrowful man appeared in the cell bowing with great courtesy. He had long, white hands, sad and wandering eyes and a fleshy face, bluish with shaving. He spoke softly, in an eloquent and melancholy voice. It was Johann Friedrich Paulus the convert, once Provost of Denkendorf, now a preacher in Stuttgart. Hoffmann the Town Vicar had sent him.

The Town Vicar would have liked himself to win this contumacious man for the Church; but he saw that there was little hope for that, and he would rather have the work accomplished by another than not accomplished at all. The erstwhile Jew could perhaps feel his way more deeply and insinuatingly into the hardened soul to soften it.

Still and courteous the convert sat against the wall, and in spite of his bulk he was strangely shadowy. His sad almond eyes roamed round the bleak cell. He spoke softly in a conversational tone. "It's all only a mask and a garment," he said. "Your palace, this cell, your Judaism, my Christianity; masks and garments. The only thing is to feel the stream of God within. The only thing is to be a light within the light, a word behind the word. I have watched you rise, Finance Director; I have seen you in your glory high in the heavens. I am a friend and pupil of Rabbi Jonathan Eybeschütz, who is again a friend of your uncle Rabbi Gabriel. I often wanted to speak with you. Not because you perhaps despised me for my conversion to Christianity, and I wanted you to change your mind. When I see you now," he concluded, and his caressing voice was still softer and was almost quivering, "I can see very plainly that I have come for both our sakes, for my own sake no less than for yours."

"And yet you have come," said Süss, "to convert me to Christianity? You have been sent by the Town Vicar Hoffmann? Is it not so, reverend sir? Or shall I call you Rabbi Our Teacher?" he smiled. The still man by the wall said: "It is not difficult, and it is reasonable, to be obstinate and a martyr. Many despise me because I became a Christian. But it does not hurt me to be slandered. I do not wince, nor do I wash the slander off. For I did not do it for food and clothing and titles, but only for my idea, for my commandment. You have your commandment, your idea. Is it not perhaps honester to live out that commandment, to keep that light burning, even if one has to put on the garment of Christianity instead of the garment of Judaism? To live in such a cell"—he cast a soft and roving glance over the bleak walls—"is surely hard. But who tells your Excellency that everything hard is meritorious?"

400

"Reverend sir," said Süss, "you have a very amiable way of wrapping your religion's doctrine of salvation in a comfortable blanket. A soft bed, a warm room, venison and old Madeira are indisputable, accessible and pleasant realities; also what you say of being a light within the light and a word behind the word has a good and plausible ring about it. But you see, I have exchanged my palace in the Seegasse for this cell. Now, I have been called in question for everything, but no one has ever questioned that I am a good man of business. Obviously, then," and he smiled craftily, "I must have had my own good reasons for such an exchange. Tell the Town Vicar," he concluded, gaily and politely, "and tell yourself, that you have said and done all that a man could possibly do. It is my own concern, it is really only my own concern."

When he was alone again he hummed, smiled, and shook his head. He thought of Michaele. The dear and foolish woman. He felt light and weak, and pleasantly weary. Like an invalid comfortably convalescent in bed. So he sat on the bench and dozed. Then quite unexpectedly his child came to him, and spoke to him. She had become much younger and smaller, she was as small as a doll, and she sat strangely enough on his shoulder and pulled his beard tenderly and said: "Silly father! Silly father!" She stayed for about half an hour. She spoke too, but about all sorts of trifles; she spoke with the important gravity of a child about the tulips, about the meaning of a passage in the Song of Solomon, about the lining of her new skirt. When she went away Süss was breathing like a man asleep, his mouth half open; he was filled with happiness. So, he had called her and she did not come; he had summoned her with wild, hot, foolish deeds, kindling a glaring and monstrous human sacrifice for her, and she had not come. What a fool he had been! She was so tiny, such a tiny, gentle, contented creature. What could she have had to do with his great, blazing, screaming deeds and sacrifices? But now, when he was quite tranquil and already resigned never to see her again, now all at once she had come, and it was a great and satisfying gift. He walked up and down his cell, five and a half paces each way, and the cell was rich and overflowing, it was the whole world, and he stretched his arms out and laughed, a solitary, boyish, loud and happy laugh, so that the warden outside in the corridor started up and peered suspiciously into the cell.

MAJOR GLASER informed Süss that he must hold himself in readiness to go to Stuttgart early next morning. The Major knew that the Jew was going to Stuttgart to hear his sentence pronounced, but he had no orders to tell him so, and he did not think it necessary. Süss, still in the comfortable after-glow of Naemi's visit, believed that he was going back to his house into freedom. He did not consider it as even remotely possible that they would hang him in despite of the clear letter of the law. With a light heart and in gay good-humour he remarked that he was delighted to have such good weather for his journey, and asked the commandant, who was greatly addicted to snuff, if he might send him a box of tobacco for remembrance. The Major refused the offer with formality; but, hardly troubling to suppress a grin on his hard visage, granted permission for Süss to wear court dress for the journey. Before the warden, too, Süss indulged in light and playful remarks about his return to freedom, and presented the astonished man, who did not know what to do, with a cheque for a considerable sum as a tip.

When he lay down at night upon his bench he felt completely relieved and happy. He would go somewhere abroad, to some tiny and still retreat by a lake or by the sea and there dream out his life in modest peace. One or two books, or none at all. And then he would sink quietly and softly into silence, leaving nothing in the world but a loud and stupid echo of his life, unlike the original, with all its values changed beyond recognition, and presently even his name would lose its significance, and become merely a row of meaningless letters; and finally these too would die away, and there would be a great and holy silence, save for a ripple and a soft radiance in the upper world.

On the next morning, a clear white, sunny, frosty day, Süss left early, in an open carriage in spite of the cold. He crouched weak and happy in the bottom, with a warden beside him and another opposite. A strong armed guard, too, on each side and in front and behind. At first he tried to speak to his companions, but they had strict orders not to reply. That did not worry him.

He leaned back, and after so many gloomy months breathed, savoured, swallowed, saw and felt the pure, free, intoxicating air of heaven. A view unblocked by walls, how glorious! Trees with soft, lovely, pure snow upon them. Broad white fields, tender and open to the sky. A wide world, a fine, beautiful, undefiled, wide world! Air! Free and pleasant air! It was too much for him, he was unaccustomed to it after his imprisonment, and he leaned back weak, unmanned and exhausted; but he was blissfully happy. He had opened his red, gold-embroidered, taffeta coat with the tufted velvet lining, had even unfastened his green, gold-bordered shirt. His legs in their brown trousers trembled, and were very tired. His velvet hat and his periwig, which sat ill upon his unkempt hair, he had taken off, and as they drove fast he felt the draughts of air blow comfortably through his white hair.

But by the gate in Stuttgart there stood a dense mob, waiting. They screamed and yelled when the coach arrived, and flung mud and stones at it. They rushed upon the Jew, tore him out, pummelled him to and fro, and wrenched at his white beard. They lifted the children up: "Look at him! There he is, the scoundrel, the Judas, the murderer, the dog of a Jew!" Spat and stamped on him. Rent his fine red coat, and tramped his pleasant velvet hat in the mire. The topers from the Blue Boar said in rueful, sentimental remembrance: "Benz the confectioner, God rest his soul, should have lived to see this day." Only with difficulty did the escort succeed in extricating the Jew. He sat again in the carriage with heaving breast, his grey face gashed, trickles of blood and spittle running over his torn beard, the soldiers around him menacing the mob with their hands or their weapons.

The screams and yells penetrated into the large room where Magdalen Sibylle lay bearing Immanuel Rieger's child. The Transport Councillor would have liked her to be confined in the country at their lovely estate of Würtigheim; but since she wanted for some inexplicable reason to remain in the town, at all costs, he had to submit. She lay now in travail, while a garrulous and officious midwife waddled about busily, and the Transport Councillor walked dejectedly up and down, pale and sweating, ready for anything. Although she looked broad and well-fitted for child-

403

bearing, her confinement was not so easy as they had hoped. She lay screaming, straining and panting. The pains ceased for a moment, and she sank back, pale and clammy with sweat, palpitating and still shuddering. The howling of the mob burst in on the silence, and the words of the popular catch were clearly heard: "The Jew must hang!" The Transport Councillor rubbed his hands. "A good omen," he said, "that the child is being born under the star of justice!" But she cast a look full of hate upon the lean, insignificant man, and prayed inarticulately, without rhymes and graces, strong and insistent: "Lord God in heaven! Let it not be like him! Lord God in Heaven! Thou hast denied me much. Grant me this at least, grant that my child shall not be like its father!"

Süss meanwhile was conveyed to the Town Hall. The great chamber was packed with spectators, and the board of judges was solemnly assembled in black robes. The Jew saw the genially brutal, massive face of Gaisberg, the fine hook-nosed contemptuous face of Schütz, the hard, cruel and haggard face of Pflug; and even young Götz's face, which was usually dull, vacant and rosy, seemed to be alive with hate and triumphant revenge. Then he realized that he was destined not for freedom, but for death. And at that moment the President, Privy Councillor Gaisberg, began to read out the sentence with a strong Swabian accent in his droning, untutored voice. Süss heard in monotonous succession the words, corruption of the country, robbery and plunder, high treason, lese-majesty, capital crime; and the conclusion that he should be hanged by the neck until dead. He saw the thickly-packed throng in the over-heated room, all the great men, ministers, members of Parliament and generals, sweating, steaming, and full of noble emotions. He saw these small and loathsome creatures falling on the greater one who had laid himself down in voluntary defencelessness, biting and holding on firmly, swarming busily over each other so that each might sink his teeth madly into the expiring mass. The earlier Süss came suddenly to life again. He drew himself up and began to speak, the old and broken man, covered with the blood and dirt of maltreatment; he lifted his head and replied to his judges. Icily cool and objective, with cutting words he stripped the veneer of pathos from the verdict. His first sentences were listened to in silence. But then, red with rage at such impudence, the elegant gentlemen hurled themselves upon him exactly as the mob had done, howling and smiting him with the flat of their swords, and again the escort had difficulty in extricating the prisoner. While he was being led away Privy Councillor Pflug's hard and contemptuous voice rose behind him in the tumultuous room: "You said, Jew, that higher than the gallows we could not hang you.—We'll show you!"

RABBI GABRIEL OPPENHEIMER VAN STRAATEN and Rabbi Jonathan Eybeschütz travelled from Hamburg in a post-chaise. Throughout the long journey the two men hardly spoke. They looked at the trotting legs of the horses (which were often changed), brown, black and white; they looked at the fleeting landscape, flat plains, mountains, forests, rivers, vine-clad hills. But they looked only with their eyes, not with their minds. Milestone after milestone appeared and vanished. They saw nothing but the face which they were striving to reach before it should be extinguished.

Rabbi Gabriel sat with his usual surly and massive expression, his thick-set body clothed in prosperous but somewhat old-fashioned citizen garb. Rabbi Jonathan, in a silken caftan, his shrewd but not aged face beaming softly above his flowing milky beard, had plunged again after weeks of worldly pleasures into meditation, into knowledge, into God. The last phase and transformation of Süss attracted him with a gruesome fascination. Not because it was a spectacular downfall. Although they had exchanged no words on the subject, both he and Rabbi Gabriel knew and felt the strange amalgamation of free-will and compulsion in this ending. The mysterious bond of correspondence, the outflow from one to the other, had now drawn in Rabbi Jonathan; he rose and sank upon it. He lived in the other, one of his strangest roots would perish in the other. So the two men travelled to see Josef Süss die, their eyes fixed upon him, and like a heavy cloud the knowledge of their mutual bond brooded over them.

There were travellers too on other roads going to Stuttgart, towards Süss, for Süss's sake. With a great bodyguard there

405

came Isaac Simon Landauer, Court Agent; although he was wont to travel simply he had with him this time three Jewish cashiers and several stout and trustworthy fellows besides his hired guard of police. There came Jaakob Joshua Falk, the small and faded Rabbi of Frankfurt, and the bulky, excitable Rabbi of Fürth. These three men met in the neighbourhood of Stuttgart; they had an appointment with the Duke-Regent, and care had been taken to ensure that they were admitted to the town without molestation.

Karl Rudolf received them in the presence of Bilfinger and Pancorbo. The Rabbi of Fürth said: "Your Grace is renowned throughout the world for your uprightness. Is it just that the robbers are allowed to sit around in Esslingen and laugh and devour their booty, while the Jew, who is less guilty in the eyes of the law, has to pay the penalty for them? Your Grace is just to high and low, to Swabians and Austrians, to Catholics and Protestants. Be just also to your Jews." The Rabbi of Frankfurt said: "Reb Josef Süss Oppenheimer stood out among Jews, and he was born of an old, respected Jewish family. What he has done, people will say, was done by the whole of Jewry. If he is hanged, and the Christians, his colleagues, are left free, people will say that the Jews are to blame for everything, and there will be a new outburst of hate and persecution and malice against all Jews. Your Grace is a merciful prince and ruler. Your Grace knows that the Jew is no more and no less guilty than his Christian colleagues. There will be bitterness in the world, and new afflictions for the oppressed and down-trodden, if he is judged differently from the others. We entreat Your Grace with sorrowful and humble hearts to show mercy to him and to all Jews."

Isaac Landauer said: "What Reb Josef Süss Oppenheimer did has caused losses in money and property to this one and that and to the country of Württemberg. Monetary wrongs can be repaired by money. We have combined, all we Jews, and we have collected money, much money, an enormous sum of money. And so we have come and we beg Your Grace: let Reb Josef Süss Oppenheimer go free. We will make good what wrongs he may have done, we will make it good and more than good, so that the country of Württemberg can prosper and flourish. We offer you, if you let the Jew Josef Süss Oppenheimer go free, a voluntary recompense of five hundred thousand double ducats."

The Duke-Regent and the two ministers had listened to the Jews in silence. At the mention of Isaac Landauer's offer they started. The offer was a piece of impudence. But the sum offered was so enormous, so much bigger than the highest amount that had ever stood in the budget of the Duchy, that it was impossible to dismiss such an offer with simple words like shamelessness and arrogance. Five hundred thousand gold ducats! To attempt to buy off Josef Süss was a piece of impudence and stupidity. But to attempt to buy off Josef Süss with such an unheard-of sum was the bold project of a genius, which struck them dumb by its naïve grandeur. And Isaac Landauer had reckoned on that, he had based his plan on that. He had been convinced from the beginning that nothing could be achieved by stratagems, arguments, insistence on justice or entreaties for mercy. Perhaps such a blunt and naïve directness would achieve something. Gold could buy everything in the world; land and cattle, mountains, rivers and forests, Pope and Emperor, Cabinets and Parliaments. Why should it not purchase from these Swabian Goim their thirst for vengeance and their silly twaddle about justice? His stupid and crooked justice was dear to the Duke. Good, it would be dearly paid for. Five hundred thousand gold ducats. That would at need buy a small Duchy; it was a good price for a bit of so-called justice.

Before the gentlemen could recover from their surprise Isaac Landauer continued: "We will not pay in bills of exchange, nor in bonds. We are ready to pay down gold, shining gold. Gold ducats, full and unclipped." He slipped to the door and summoned his men with a shake of his head and a superior smile which challenged their astonishment. In dumb and tense bewilderment the Regent and his ministers gaped at the men who came in. They were carrying sacks, small and very heavy sacks, which they emptied at a sign from the unkempt man. Out poured a stream of gold, minted gold of all currencies, red gold, Spanish, African, Turkish, from every quarter of the world. It piled up, towered high, and never stopped; it grew man-high and as broad as a full-grown oak, a mountain of gold. Dumbly gazed the small, crooked

407

shabby Duke, and the bulky Bilfinger. Dom Bartelemi Pancorbo thrust his lean purple head out of his superannuated ruffle; his withered fingers crooked and stretched themselves, and could not resist the temptation to stroke the gold, the pleasant gold, to bathe in the endless river. Isaac Landauer stood beside it in his greasy caftan, his side-curls matted, in an awkward self-conscious posture, smiling disagreeably, one arm pressed close to his body with the palm of the hand flung outwards, while with the other he combed his reddish, greying, goat's-beard.

The offer of Isaac Landauer was refused. But the old men's words kept ringing in the Duke's ear. He was unjust! He was compelled to be unjust before he died. Not only to Süss, but to the rest of the Jews. Possessions left him cold; wealth did not move him. But these people clung to wealth. Gold, gold, was their life and their aspiration. And yet they had of their own free will levied and collected such an enormous sum to prevent him from being unjust. His duty was clear, he had first of all to be just to his Swabians, and therefore unjust to the Jews. But this mountain of gold oppressed him and chafed him raw.

In an urgent letter he begged Duke Karl Friedrich of Württemberg-Oels to pay him a visit. He wanted to resign the Regency to him. He had done his best to pull the land out of its terrible muddle, and he had succeeded. He had said: "Justice! Duty! Authority!" But it was not possible to administer a government on such principles in these times. He had had to look on passively while scoundrels worthy of death were set free, and now he would have to look on while the Jew was hanged unjustly. He was seventy-one and he was weary. He felt his physical and spiritual strength ebbing noticeably. It was a burden to him, he wrote to the Emperor and explained to the Privy Councillors, to administer adequately and to his own satisfaction the complicated details of a government as confused as it was important. The crooked, shabby, honourable soldier yearned for the country peace of his small, blossoming Neuenstadt, and for a quiet death.

AFTER the intractable insolence shown by Süss when his sentence was pronounced, he was fettered cross-wise in the Chamber of Nobles, where he was to be confined until execution, and kept without food all day in a bleak and completely bare room. He had quieted down immediately after his outburst before the judges, and with a smile and a shake of the head regarded the blood and dirt with which he was smeared. He squatted, cramped by his fetters, on the floor by the wall of the brilliant and empty room. Haman, the Minister of Ahasuerus, came to visit him; he had Herr von Pflug's hook-nose and hard, arrogant voice. Goliath came, and with Herr von Gaisberg's hand smote him bluntly, jovially and heavily on the shoulder, so that it hurt. Others came who were more friendly, speaking half in Swabian and half in Hebrew. Eliezer, the faithful Pfäffle, was there; and Abraham in the guise of Johann Daniel Harpprecht disputed with God about justice. And the men came who had appeared to Naemi; Isaiah the prophet grumbled and consoled him in the ill-tempered voice of his uncle; and by his rich hair Absalom hung in the branches; but the hair was white and the face under it was his own.

But a sudden yelping and baying and bellowing broke in upon him. Oh, that was Hoffmann again, the Town Vicar, extolling the blessings of the Augsburg Confession. Yes, the zealous saver of souls was once more on the spot; he believed the fruit was now ripe enough to pluck. But Süss was not at all disposed to argue with him. That coarse voice overwhelmed the softer ones around him. Quietly and without sarcasm he asked him to refrain; if he could only be left alone he would gladly leave ten thousand dollars in his will to the Evangelical Church for its attentions. The clergyman gave up all hope and departed in chagrin.

Another unexpected visitor appeared. A fine, elderly gentleman with a head like a greyhound's and expanded nostrils, inconspicuously and very elegantly clad. The Duchess Dowager's father, the old Prince Thurn and Taxis. This affair had given him no rest, had driven him hither from the Netherlands. It would not do, one could not allow Süss to die like that. A man whom his daughter had visited, and with whom he himself had shaken hands. A man whose services the Catholic Church had accepted, not officially, but yet in such a way that all the Courts were aware of it. No, no, that did not accord with his notions of courtesy, he had been too well brought up to suffer such a thing to happen. A man with whom one had gone so far was a gentleman. Tact, decorum and good manners required one not to allow such a man to come in contact with the gallows. The old Prince came himself to Stuttgart, incognito, as Baron Neuhoff. He had never been able to stand the Jew; he had never forgotten how Süss had killed his yellow coat with the yellow salon at Monbijou, and his wine-red suit with the wine-red livery of his footmen. It would be in bad taste to feel gratified now at the man's misfortunes, but, still, he did not need to be afraid that the Jew's surroundings would throw him out of focus this time.

He came with a sound plan. He would help Süss to escape as he had helped Remchingen. In the Jew's case that would not be so simple; but he was determined to spare neither effort nor money. Perhaps after all the uncongenial old boor and booby of a Regent would be glad to get rid of the Jew in such a way. At any rate, he would manage. He would lay down only one condition. It would not do to take so much trouble for a Jew. He would have to stop being a Jew. Yes, the Jew would have to become a convert, and situated as he was he would be unlikely to make any fuss about it. It would be a gain, a triumph, for the Catholic Church to receive into its bosom such a wily financier and shrewd politician, one who was besides much more of a cavalier than most of the so-called gentlemen of Swabia.

The elegant Prince, after crossing the threshold with a smile, relishing the surprise he was to bring, recoiled in horror. What was this? It was a crooked old Jew from the Ghetto crouching there. Was this the Finance Director? Was this the great Celadon? An uneasy feeling crept over him as if he himself were dirty. Süss saw his visitor's face. "Yes," he said, with an imperceptible smile; "yes, your Highness, it is I."

A bench, a stool and a table had now been put into the room. The Prince sat down carefully and ill at ease. He absolutely could not reconcile the man crouching before him with the elegant gentleman he remembered. Was the Jew trying to bluff the world again? Was it all a trick? He had the same unpleasant feeling as he had had in the yellow salon and on being confronted with the wine-red liveries. Had the Jew achieved the impossible and beaten him again in these circumstances, in this cell? Well, others might be imposed on, but not he. He had no mind to be limed by the Jew. He, a prince and a gentleman with his knowledge of the world and his scepticism, was not to be bluffed.

"There is no need to keep up pretences before me, your Excellency," he ventured smoothly and politely, as if he were in a drawing-room. "You cannot suppose that I believe in this mummery. It is a trick. Under the gallows you will suddenly whisk off your disfiguring beard and appear again as the clever, well-bred and accomplished cavalier of old days. It is a manœuvre," he asserted triumphantly. "Of course it is a manœuvre. But, my dear erstwhile Director of Finance, it is a comedy which may delude the gentlemen from Parliament, but it does not delude me. You cannot take me in."

Süss said nothing. "Apparently you still have a trump in your hand," ventured the Prince again, "which you mean to produce at the last moment. I imagine that you are playing the suffering saint now so as to have a more glorious resurrection. But be careful! They are in a dangerous mood here. Perhaps they will not give you the chance. Perhaps they will hang you—excuse my mentioning it—with all your trumps still in your hand."

Since Süss was still silent he became impatient. "Your Excellency! Man! Show some understanding! Speak, at least! I have come to help you. It can scarcely have been predicted for you that a ruling German prince would give himself so much trouble on your account. Listen to me! Say something!" Paralysed by the other's attitude he explained boldly his plan and its condition. When he had finished, Süss made no movement, nor did he open his mouth. The fine Prince felt himself more completely routed than ever. He had made this journey, and now the Jew sat there without even a pathetic refusal, simply saying nothing. The Prince felt suddenly old and weary, he could not endure the silence any longer, and he said with forced sarcasm: "You have forgotten your good manners in captivity. When anyone takes so much trouble about you, you might at least say 'Mille merci!'"

"Mille merci!" said Süss.

The Prince stood up. He felt it as a personal insult that this Jew would not let himself be rescued, but preferred to hang on

411

the gallows in broad daylight. "You are a large-sized fool, my dear fellow," he said, and his courteous voice became surprisingly sharp. "Your stoicism is completely out of date. One no longer dies to get a better showing in the school history books. Better a living dog than a dead lion, was very justly remarked by your King Solomon." He dusted his coat, and concluded, already at the door: "Have your beard shaved off, at least, and put on a good suit of clothes if you"—and he wrinkled up his nose—"*partout* insist on swinging. One may ask that much of a man whom one has received as a friend in one's circle. You have a numerous and prominent public. You have cut a good figure all your life. Don't undo your own reputation as a cavalier when you make your exit from this world-theatre."

And with that he went.

THE gallows on which Süss was to be hanged had been constructed a hundred and forty years previously. It was expensive, having cost three thousand South German gulden in those good old days of cheapness; it was altogether unusual, very different from the ordinary wooden gallows. It towered up for five and thirty feet. It was entirely made of iron, constructed from thirty-six hundredweight and eighteen pounds of iron procured by the alchemist Georg Honauer to make into gold for Duke Friedrich, a transaction in which the Duke was done out of two tons of gold. This gallows had been erected in honour of the same Georg Honauer, painted a pretty red ornamented with gold, and employed to hang him on.

Various alchemists accused of swindling Duke Friedrich had followed him in rapid succession. The first was an Italian called Petrus Montanus. A year afterwards it was Hans Heinrich Neuscheler from Zürich, known as the Blind Goldmaker. Still a year later came another Hans Heinrich, whose name was Von Müllenfels. His luck had lasted for a longer time; he had often made merry over his three colleagues swinging in the air; but now he swung as they did. Then for a long time the gallows was unused, until a smith from the county of Oettingen had the idea of taking it down and stealing it piecemeal. He had already pried off three shafts and made away by night with more than seven hundred-

412

weight of iron, when he was caught and hoisted on the instrument of his crime.

For more than a century since then the iron gallows had stood empty. Now Herr von Pflug, who had undertaken the arrangements for the execution, designed to make the Jew the sixth to suffer death on this extraordinary contrivance. From the beginning of the prosecution the lean, hard man had been waiting to prepare the banquet of his hate. Now he intended to celebrate it in such a way that Europe would never forget it.

He planned the execution with every refinement of opprobrium. The Jew's lewdness and carnal sins, the circumcised dog's violation of Christian German women, had unfortunately and sore against his will found no place in the charge-sheet. But for the execution he had a free hand. He would show up the Jew's lust and shameless depravity. He would not have him hanged simply on the gallows, no, he would hang him in a bird-cage, as a vulgar pun on Süss's dissolute nightly activities.

The Commission spent a lot of money on the solemn fulfilment of its verdict. Comfortable boxes for the ladies and gentlemen were erected on the place of execution, the Tunzenhofer Hill, also called the Gallows Hill, on the road to Prague. The soldiers who were to escort the delinquent and regulate the crowd rehearsed their parts. The iron gallows was thoroughly repaired, the tumbril was fitted with larger wheels, the malefactor's bell was given a new rope, and the hangmen put into new uniforms.

The greatest importance was attached to the proper execution of Herr von Pflug's witty idea. The Jew had jeered, saying that they could not hang him higher than the gallows. They would show him what they could do. They would simply hoist the iron bird-cage high up over the gallows.

The construction of the cage, all its complicated apparatus, was entrusted to the master-smiths Johann Christoph Faust and Veit Ludwig Rigler. The cage was detachable into two pieces; it was eight feet high and four feet wide; it had fourteen hoops round it and seventeen upright bars. Ingenious machinery enabled it to be swung easily above the gallows. Its construction was extraordinarily costly. In the end every smith in town had to ply his hammer on it. Two days before the execution the monstrous thing

413

was dragged up the steep Tunzenhofer Hill by six horses. The school-children of the Capital ran alongside. Wine and beer were on sale in hastily-erected booths, and hawkers offered broadsides with satiric verses and the Jew's picture. In the cold weather people thronged noisily to the place of execution, watched with interest the construction of the boxes, and admired the polish on the gallows and the ingenuity of the cage.

The bird-cage had an even greater success with the populace than Herr von Pflug had anticipated. An enormous grin ran through the town and over the whole country. Countless verses about birds were made, and sung by the children in the streets. Only, people refused to believe that Herr von Pflug had been the author of this excellent jest; they preferred to ascribe the ingenious idea of the bird-cage to their favourite, the widely popular Major von Röder. So that the verses about the birds were usually followed by the song containing the lines:

> "Then shouted Herr von Röder,
> 'Halt, or you're a deader!'"

RABBI GABRIEL and Rabbi Jonathan Eybeschütz sat in Süss's cell. The grand pass of the Netherland States had opened the prison gates without further ceremony to Mynheer Gabriel Oppenheimer van Straaten. Now the three men sat together and shared a meal. Rabbi Gabriel had brought in fruit, dates, figs and oranges, as well as pastry and strong wine of the South. Süss wore his scarlet-coloured coat with a skull-cap on his white hair, and his brow like those of the two Rabbis was cleft above the nose by three furrows making the letter Shin, the first letter in Shaddai, the name of God. He dipped figs into the wine. This was his last meal. Rabbi Gabriel divided an orange with his thick fingers. The three men sat and ate the fruits, silently and with great seriousness. But their thoughts flowed in a heavy tide from one to the other. Rabbi Gabriel and Süss were one, and for the first time Rabbi Gabriel felt his bond not as a compulsion and an evil fate, but as a privilege. The third man, however, Jonathan Eybeschütz, felt the same influence as they did, but was excluded from it; he stood on the shore and the wave did not carry him

414

away. He sat with them, he drank with them, like them he bore the mark of the Shin, like them he was an initiate and a seer; but the wave did not carry him away. Rabbi Gabriel carefully sprinkled the orange sections with sugar and shared them out. He poured out the black Southern wine. The cell was full of the unspoken word, full of thought, of vision, of God. But Rabbi Jonathan was consumed with bitterness and envy. He carried it off with a sardonic jest; it was easy to be exalted when one was going to be hanged. But this cold comfort was of no avail, and he, the rich and learned man, felt himself poor and envious, and half a traitor. And as he intoned in his turn the grace after meat, fine in his silken caftan and his flowing milky beard, reverend, wise, and highly honoured, he was a poor, troubled, lost man.

While upstairs the sentence was being once more pronounced on Süss and the staff broken over his head in the lobby of the Town Hall, the mild and faded Rabbi of Frankfurt, the burly and sanguine Rabbi of Fürth, and Isaac Landauer, excited and shivering, all waited for him. Large melting flakes of snow were falling and a pale sun fitfully pierced the murky clouds. Outside before the doorway there was a countless swarm of curious sightseers, Herr von Röder on his old chestnut at the head of a military escort, and around the gallows-cart, which towered bleakly on its high wheels, the hangman and his assistants in their crude colours.

At last Süss was led down the steps. The Jews had received permission to speak to him here for the last time. He bent his head, and the small Rabbi Jaakob Joshua Falk laid his mild and withered hands on it, and said: "The Lord bless thee and keep thee. The Lord let the light of His face shine upon thee, and be gracious unto thee. The Lord lift up His countenance upon thee, and give thee peace." "Amen. Selah," responded the other two.

The Jew was formally placed in the high gallows-cart and bound. In spite of the frost and the damp the whole market-place was thronged with people. All the windows of the Chamber of Nobles, the Town Hall, the chemist's shop and the Sun Inn were white with faces. Boys were clustered on the fountain and even on the wine merchant's crane and trestles. The people

415

stared in silence. Herr von Röder in his rasping voice gave his riders the word of command. The escort moved forward, first the Town Riders, then two drummers, and then a company of grenadiers on foot. One of the hangmen's assistants swung himself on to the tumbril horse and clicked his tongue, and the beast started. The little Rabbi Jaakob Joshua Falk repeated with blenched lips: "And give thee peace." The headstrong Rabbi of Fürth could not restrain himself and flung wild curses after the cart against Edom and Amalek, enemies and unbelievers. But Isaac Landauer broke into loud and uncontrolled howling like an animal. It was strange to see the great financier beating his head against the door-posts of the Town Hall and howling unrestrainedly. And now the malefactor's bell began to toll. Thin, sharp and resonant, it mingled with the howls of the Jew, piercing to the marrow as it rang through the wet and snowy air.

It echoed into Magdalen Sibylle's chamber. She had born the birth well, but she was still confined to bed. She looked at her child, a normal child, neither big nor small, neither beautiful nor ugly. She heard the sharp tinkle of the bell and she crumpled up nervously; she looked at the child which was hers and Immanuel Rieger's, and she did not love it.

The bell echoed into the Castle, too, where the old Regent was sitting with Bilfinger and Harpprecht. The three men were silent. At last Harpprecht said: "That tolling is not pleasant to my ear." Karl Rudolf said: "I had to do it. I am ashamed of myself, gentlemen."

Meanwhile Süss was conducted through the town towards the Gallows Hill. He sat on the tumbril uplifted like a heathen image, in his scarlet coat, and with the solitaire gleaming on his finger; the Duke Regent had forbidden him to be deprived of the ring. The streets were packed with people; snowflakes were falling; the procession's advance was strangely soundless, and strangely soundless was the mass of spectators. Once the delinquent was past, the thousands of onlookers fell in behind and around the escort on foot, on horseback and in carriages. In the pale and misty air, among the dirty melting snowflakes, everything moved twice as heavily and silently. Instead of taking the shortest way, they conducted the Jew slowly and formally by a circuitous route, for

416

many spectators had come from afar, the whole country wanted to look on—there were even some from beyond the frontiers—and everybody had to see the show. Süss was throned aloft on the cart, bound and rigid, with snow falling on his clothes and on his white beard.

Mögling the advocate stood by the wayside. He was troubled and oppressed, because his defence had been of no avail. He could certainly assure himself that he had done all he could, and, besides, the *vox populi* was loud and unanimous against the condemned man. But still it was bitter and depressing to know that the accused, who had been entrusted to him, was to be hanged without sufficient legal warrant. He felt shivery and uncomfortable. He caused one of the assistant hangmen to reach a beaker of wine up to Süss. Süss did not take it, he did not even say: "Thank you," but remained completely motionless; still, the advocate felt warmer and more relieved.

Schertlin's wife, the Waldensian, also stood waiting by the roadside. She saw Süss pinioned and remarkably still, as motionless as a holy image escorted in a procession through the town, with snow in his beard and on his coat. She alone of all the spectators had an inkling of the fact that this martyrdom was a voluntary one. She gazed greedily at the man, with scornful but despairing triumph, her small red lips half open, and her long eyes burning. A woman beside her muttered in broad Swabian: "He always wanted to be high up. Now he'll be high enough." *"Sale bête!"* said the Waldensian to the falling snowflakes.

At another turn of the road stood Johann Jaakob Moser, the publicist. When the procession came in sight he began to deliver a short, pithy and patriotic address. But his fiery words kindled nobody; the snow blotted them out and the people were unmoved, so that he closed his mouth again before he had finished. Shortly before the procession reached its end it passed Nicklas Pfäffle, the pale, phlegmatic secretary. As his master went by for the last time, he saluted him profoundly. Süss saw him, and nodded twice. When the cart was past Nicklas Pfäffle did not follow it to the end, but turned aside and sobbed.

Snow and clouds had cleared away by the time the procession reached the gallows. The vineyards were clear and frosty under the pale bright sky. The Jew looked up to the terraces and saw the little watch-tower,—the baths. He turned round and looked at Stuttgart, at the cathedral of Saint Leonard's, at the old Castle and at the new palace for which he had promised the money. On his left the high wooden gallows raised its bleak head. But it was insignificant beside the daring, ingenious, gigantic iron structure designed for him. A double ladder with innumerable rings and many supports soared into the air, and there was an involved network of wheels, pulleys and chains to hoist up the cage. The wide space was filled with people. They swarmed in eager expectation on every projection, on fence and tree. Those who were a long way off gazed through large round telescopes. The snow on Süss's coat was frozen and in the frosty brightness tiny crystals glittered on his cap and in his white beard.

On two grand-stands, each accommodating six hundred people, sat the ladies and gentlemen, the senior civil servants and officers, the foreign ambassadors, the members of the Commission and of Parliament. Privy Councillor von Pflug was well to the fore. He had been afraid up to the very last that the Hebrew beast would escape after all through some crafty Jewish trick. But now the hour had come, now the aim of his life had been achieved. Now, now this very minute, his hated enemy would swing aloft and be strangled. The Privy Councillor's hard eyes greedily spied out under the coat collar the Jew's neck, the place for the halter. It is glorious to look on at the death of an enemy, it is as balm to the eyes; pleasant and lovely is the sound of the death-drums, and the clang of the bell. Among the ladies were many who had known Süss intimately and yet escaped the inquisition for some reason or other. They now gazed at the man with whom they had been involved, alienated and shuddering. For he had passed as very young, and he had possessed a young man's strength, as they knew, and he could not be more than forty at the very most; but now he had white hair and looked like an old Rabbi. One should really feel ashamed of having been in bed with him. But it was remarkable that they did not feel ashamed. They gazed at this extraordinary man with eager fascination. In a minute he would be dead, in a minute he would be dumb for ever, and all danger would be over and they would be disentangled from him

418

by a forcible and gruesome deed. They sat waiting for that, eager and trembling, yearning for it, and shrinking from it in terror. Most of them would rather have lived all their lives in fear of discovery if he could have been kept alive.

Young Michael Koppenhöfer was also on the grand-stand. At last the millstone would be ground to powder which had for so long hung round the country's neck; at last the corrupter of the land would die a disgraceful death. But—this man had not been dismissed by Elisabeth Salomea, casually and hastily among bundles of books and underclothing, this man had taken her, without even having to exert himself particularly. The old and broken Jew, what was it he possessed? What was his secret? With bitter envy he stared at the man in the gallows-cart. But the young Privy Councillor Götz, sitting among the Commissioners, looked on with silent and gloomy satisfaction. Now his mother's and sister's disgrace would be wiped out. Let everybody dare to look askance at him after this! How he would blast them! How well he would know what to do!

Weissensee, old and worn, sat, elegant and feeble, on the tribune. Thou hast conquered, O Judæan! Thou hast conquered, O Judæan! Ah, the Jew had triumphed over him again. The Jew had tasted of every dish—had relished with his eyes, his sense and his brain all the daintiest pleasures of the world, had emptied to the dregs every cup of triumph and despair, had been filled with the tragic end of his child and then had prepared and accomplished a conspicuous, over-subtle, hellishly diabolical revenge; and now he died this death with the eyes of the whole world upon him, this romantic and apparently voluntary death, much more heroic than death on the field of battle. Surrounded by raucous hate and cherishing love, ambiguous and great. What would be left of himself, Weissensee? A couple of lamentable verses by his poor bourgeoise daughter. But the other was sure of immortality. What he was, his life, his observations, his thoughts and his death, would be of perpetual interest to later ages; his ideas, his life, his feelings and his death would be appreciatively re-enacted.

Süss was unbound from the gallows-cart. He stood blinking, his limbs numb. He saw the people in the boxes, the periwigs, the painted faces of the ladies. He saw the troops, who made a cordon round the gallows place. Aha, they had exerted themselves! There were at least five companies round the gallows alone. Of course Major von Röder was in command, and conspicuously at his post. Yes, it needed a lot of strategy to get him completely out of the world. Süss saw the tens of thousands of faces, curious women, with their mouths ready to bawl, men ready to smack their lips and growl with satisfaction, children's faces, chubby and large-eyed, destined to become as empty and malicious as the ugly visages of their parents. He saw the breath of the mob, rising in a white vapour, very solid in the clear frost, the ravening eyes, the stretched necks, which had formerly bowed before him so devotedly. He saw the bird-cage, the complicated and dishonourable devices for his execution. And while he was looking at all this something lowed and bleated in his ear. It was the Town Vicar Hoffmann who had insisted on waiting for him by the gallows and was now speaking to him once more of heaven and earth, forgiveness of sin, of God, faith and atonement. Süss gazed around him while he listened to the other, and then slowly looked the Town Vicar up and down, and turned away and spat. Eyes opened wide, and a low hiss of indignation arose from the crowd and as quickly died away.

Now the assistant hangmen in their gaudy new uniforms seized him and opened his coat. At the touch of their coarse, clumsy hands he recoiled with disgust, his numbness disappeared and he hit out desperately to defend himself. All necks were stretched still further. It was curious to see how the man in the white beard and the fine clothes, with the diamond blazing on his hand, fought and struggled with the assistants. The children laughed with glee and clapped their hands; on one of the stands a rouged lady began to scream shrilly and continuously, and had to be removed. The Jew's cap fell on the damp ground and was trodden into the slush. The hangmen seized him firmly, tore off his coat, pushed him into the cage and put the halter round his neck.

There he stood. He heard a little breeze, the breathing of the mob, the clattering hoofs of horses, the curses of the clergymen. Were these the last things he was to hear on earth? He thirsted to hear something else, he opened wide his heart and his ears, yearning to hear something else. But he heard nothing else, save his own breathing and the pulse of his own blood. The cage was already rocking and rising. And then, through the empty and cruel hubbub there soared another sound, the sound of loud and guttural voices crying: "One and Eternal is the God of Israel, Jehovah, Adonai, the Everlasting, the Infinite!" It is the Jews, the small Jaakob Joshua Falk, the burly Rabbi of Fürth, the shabby Isaac Landauer. They are standing wrapped in their praying-cloaks, they and seven others, making ten as is prescribed; they pay no heed to the crowd, which turns its eyes away from the gallows towards them; they sway their bodies wildly, and they stand crying, shrilling, wailing the prayer for the dying, clear over the broad square. "Hear, O Israel. One and Eternal is Jehovah Adonai!" The words mount from their lips as white vapour in the strong frost, up to the ears of the man in the cage, and the son of Marshal Heydersdorff opens his mouth and cries in answer: "One and Eternal is Jehovah Adonai."

Nimbly the gaudy hangmen swarm and clamber up the ladders. The cage rises, the halter tightens. Underneath, the Town Vicar execrates the dying man: "Depart into hell, accursed Jew and villain!" But the shrill Adonai of the Jews is in the air and in the ears of everyone. It is returned from the cage, until the voice is strangled by the halter.

Right in front of the stand, Privy Councillor Dom Bartelemi Pancorbo has stood up, and propping his lean bony hands on the railing he stretches his fleshless, purple head out of his enormous ruff. His eyes behind their wrinkled lids greedily follow the cage as it sways aloft, and in it the man with the fine scarlet coat on whose finger the solitaire blazes like a rainbow in the clear wintry air.

After the cordon of troops was removed the mob thronged to a closer view of the gallows, and one or two boys climbed half-way up the ladders; they examined the scaffolding and saw above on the bars of the cage black birds sitting in dense flocks.

The crowd wound slowly back to the town. The day was held as a holiday, there was good eating and drinking, carousing and dancing and brawling in the beer-houses. The young citizen Langefass had looted Süss's trodden cap out of the mire; he

421

was a jolly fellow and a famous wag; he cocked the cap on his head, and set it on the heads of girls and waiting-maids, who screamed in affright at the touch of the cap of the hanged Jew. But all the same the right holiday mood did not come. One did not quite know why but the day did not come up to expectations; it should have been freer and merrier. People sang: "The Jew must hang!" and they sang: "Then shouted Herr von Röder, Halt, or you're a deader.'" But they could not get the Adonai of the Jews out of their ears. The children played at hanging, and the game went like this: one child stood aloft and cried "Adonai," and the others stood below and cried and screamed and hallooed "Adonai."

DURING the night following the execution, at about three o'clock, a tall lean gentleman came up the Tunzenhofer Hill to the iron gallows. The road was a foul mixture of mud and melting snow, and the going was heavy. The lean gentleman, shivering with cold, was well wrapped up in a broad cloak of an ancient cut. He had two young fellows with him, the ne'er-do-well sons of respectable citizens, who were notorious in Stuttgart for being courageous enough to undertake any enterprise if they were only well paid. The two young lads promptly climbed up the ladder to the gallows. It was a difficult climb, for the rungs were frozen and slippery, and they swore beneath their breath as they climbed. Round them fluttered the birds who sat in dense flocks on the gallows both night and day. When they were at the top the young fellows stayed there for an unconscionably long time. The lean gentleman waiting below lifted his shoulders nervously, and shifted from one foot to the other, muttering to himself in a surly, suppressed voice. "Have you got it?" he demanded in a low tone, when at last they descended. "It is not there!" they stammered in confusion. "You have stolen it, you have stolen the stone!" raged the Portuguese in hoarse and carefully muffled tones. "I'll have you prosecuted; I'll have you broken on the wheel!" But the frightened young fellows assured him: "The Jew isn't there at all. It's another man who is hanging in the cage. The devil must have carried him off." Dom Bartelemi was incredulous for a long time, and finally caused the cage to be searched officially by

422

hussars during the night. Yes, the corpse had been stolen, and another put in its place.

Very early in the morning the cheated and raging man visited the Duke-Regent. That was the result of His Grace's mildness! Now the Jews had stolen the solitaire! The solitaire? Karl Rudolf thought of the heap of gold, and did not believe it. The corpse, well, they might have stolen that. He reflected, and his face cleared with a smile. They were really devils, these Jews. Simply abstracted a corpse from the gallows in broad daylight; soldiers and Christians could not have done it better. He did not grudge them the solitaire in return, and he refused to prosecute them. Blue and red, raging sullenly, and venting horrible curses in his sepulchral voice, the lean Portuguese had to withdraw.

Meanwhile the corpse, hastily wrapped in wool, had been hidden beneath bales of hardware and merchandise, and taken to Fürth on a cart. Jewish pedlars accompanied it, and relieved each other in relays at every town they passed. The solitaire was still on the dead man's finger, and no one of his escort feared that his successor would steal it.

In Fürth the corpse was washed, wrapped in a long white shroud, and coffined. The index, middle, and ring fingers were arranged in the form of Shin, the first letter in the Divine Name, Shaddai; a small heap of earth was laid under the head, black and crumbling earth, earth from Zion. The authorities were informed that an unknown Jew from Frankfurt, who had died by the roadside, was being buried. No other information was given even to the members of the Jewish community. But the whisper flew from mouth to mouth.

There lay the unknown man, his black-and-blue strangled face strangely framed in its dirty white beard; the staring eyes, brown and clouded, bulged out and could not be closed; but the three furrows of the letter Shin were deeply cleft in the forehead. Out of the simple white shroud flashed the solitaire, huge and bewildering. The ten most respected men in the community sat behind drawn curtains among great candles and kept watch.

Into the midst of them came a stranger, thick-set, with a beardless and massive face, troubled stony grey eyes, dressed in old Frankish style. He poured water behind him as he entered the death-chamber, and water at the dead man's head and feet. The others recognized the Cabbalist, and made way for him, whispering.

Rabbi Gabriel advanced to the corpse, and in his unpleasant voice rasped the benediction: "Praised be Thou, Jehovah, God, righteous Judge." With his thick fingers he carefully touched the dead man's eyelids, and the eyelids closed. Then he sat down on the floor and sank his head between his knees. The ten men had backed close up to the wall. Quite solitary in spite of their presence, a small and forlorn heap, Rabbi Gabriel crouched by the dead.

All the Jews in Fürth were at the cemetery when the unknown was buried. They lowered the coffin into the ground. The solitaire was on the dead man's finger, and under his head the small heap of earth from the land of Zion. In chorus they answered their leader. "Vain and deceitful and fleeting as wind is the world; but One and Eternal is the God of Israel, the Everlasting, the Infinite, Jehovah." Then they plucked up grass and cast it behind them. And they said: "We are like the grass that withers." And they said: "We remember that we are dust." Then they washed their hands in flowing holy-water and left the cemetery.

The End

death-chamber, and water at the dead man's head and feet. The others recognized the Cabbalist, and made way for him, whispering. Rabbi Gabriel advanced to the corpse, and in his unpleasant voice rasped the benediction: "Praised be Thou, Jehovah, God, righteous Judge." With his thick fingers he carefully touched the dead man's eyelids, and the eyelids closed. Then he sat down on the floor and sank his head between his knees. The ten men had backed close up to the wall. Quite solitary in spite of their presence, a small and forlorn heap, Rabbi Gabriel crouched by the dead.

All the Jews in Fürth were at the cemetery when the unknown was buried. They lowered the coffin into the ground. The solitaire was on the dead man's finger, and under his head the small heap of earth from the land of Zion. In chorus they answered their leader: "Vain and deceitful and fleeting as wind is the world; but One and Eternal is the God of Israel, the Everlasting, the Infinite, Jehovah." Then they plucked up grass and cast it behind them. And they said, "We are like the grass that withers." And they said, "We remember that we are dust." Then they washed their hands in flowing holy-water and left the cemetery.

The End